No One Laughs at a Dead Clown

A Razz McNeil Mystery

DC ERICKSON

This novel is a work of fiction. All of the characters, organizations, places, and events used in this novel are either works of the author's imagination or used fictitiously. Any resemblance to actual events or people, living or dead, is purely coincidental.

No One Laughs at a Dead Clown

A Razz McNeil Mystery

Published by Bionic Publishing
www.bionicpublishing.com

Second Edition

To my Family,
Given and Chosen

Special thanks to Lisa, John, Rick, Ted, Jim, Karen, Chuck, Myrna, Dave, Neva, Ana, and Dan.

No One Laughs at a Dead Clown

1

Call it courage or the carefree ignorance of youth, but in early November, 1977, Razz McNeil emblazoned his name into the annals of surfing folklore by being the first and only person to surf under the entire length of the San Margarita Pier. He would remain the only one to do so, because with successively longer, more sturdily built piers, it was now impossible. But that was what they had thought back then, too, before Razz proved them wrong.

December 11, 2004

It was a blustery, cold December day, two weeks before Christmas. In San Margarita, that meant the thermostat inched all the way down to fifty-five degrees Fahrenheit. Short-sleeved shirt weather for people in the Northeast and Midwest, but this was Southern California, so leather jackets were the norm today. Named after Saint Marge, patron saint of tequila drinks, an ugly saint who magically got better looking around two a.m., San Margarita is a coastal town renowned for its warm weather, beautiful beaches and even more beautiful women, the province of real estate speculators, lawyers, the homeless, and enough psychiatrists and shamans to take care of them all. You had to be very rich or very poor to live in San Margarita and people of each ilk were moving in daily, bursting the town's social services and social fabric. Only thirty years earlier, it was a sleepy beach community of twenty-five thousand mostly white, middle-class working people. Now at eighty thousand residents, San Margarita had become a suburb of Los Angeles that just happened to have expensive ocean frontage. It was no longer a close-knit community, something its long-time residents bemoaned daily.

The beaches were empty on this day, except for a few hardy, snow-bunny tourists thrilled to be anywhere but in the snow. That meant the Pier was almost empty, too. The Pier. A monstrosity that extended over a quarter-mile into the Pacific Ocean, the Pier had been built and rebuilt five times in its relatively short existence. Originated in 1946 as a Works project after the War, that first Pier collapsed in the Great Storm of 1952. After much political wrangling, it was rebuilt in 1955 only to be lost to a suspicious fire in 1960. The Pier's most recent incarnation, after its predecessor's partial collapse in the Northridge earthquake of 1994, was built to withstand Armageddon. Hundreds of huge, concrete pilings were anchored deep into the ocean floor.

Intended to be a tourist draw, this Pier included an amusement park with a Ferris wheel, roller coaster, and assorted other attractions that appealed primarily to small children and drunken teenagers. An array of tourist-trap shops selling expensive trinkets, restaurant-bars, and a carousel rounded out the Pier's attractions. Oh, and the police station. Because of an influx of gangbangers shortly after this latest pier was built, a police substation was opened to help create an illusion of safety.

Twelve people had died at the Pier in the last six years alone. Two succumbed in food poisoning incidents, which could have happened to anyone eating the PCB-poisoned fish caught in San Margarita Bay, three were killed in rival gang battles, and one fried when an electric-powered bumper car inexplicably short-circuited sending thousands of volts through its innocent driver. Three fishermen had drowned in separate incidents by reaching too far over the waist-high railing to haul in their catches and then toppling over thirty feet into treacherous waters below. Those railings had since been raised a foot, damaging the Pier's aesthetic, but much improving its safety. The remaining three deaths were classified as suicides. Three years earlier, a young couple, high on life and crystal meth, had leapt from the top of the world's largest solar-powered Ferris wheel trying to make perfect swan dives into the Pacific. Unfortunately, they only made it as far as the heavy wooden planking of the Pier and their necks broke on impact. And, last year, a mentally deranged transient jumped onto the tracks of an oncoming roller coaster car splattering himself on four unsuspecting tourists whose subsequent treatments continue to enrich psychiatrists back in their home state of Indiana.

People said it was The Curse. But Razz McNeil didn't believe in The Curse, or any curse, for that matter. Born and bred in San Margarita, Razz was a stereotypical, strawberry-blonde-haired surfer dude who, in his late thirties, finally realized he should settle down or, at least, try to make a living. People all around him were making tons of money in real estate, in the stock market, or in dealing drugs, but Razz had until then contented himself with the shapely surf off San Margarita's shore and the shapely blondes onshore.

Combining his love of the water and his love of women and fun, Razz went to work at the Surf's Up Saloon on the Pier. Starting as a busboy, he quickly worked his way up to doorman. He was, after all, a likable, intelligent, personable young man, just the sort a restaurant owner wanted greeting his patrons—especially the women. Razz liked being a doorman, because he got to meet every sexy thing, young and old, who walked in the Surf's Up door. He always remembered their names, mainly because he slept with many of them. That was one of the perks of the job. Because of his positive effect on business, despite several catfights between jealous paramours during his doorman tenure, management promoted him to bartender, figuring he would be safer behind a large, deep wooden bar.

Bartending helped Razz first appreciate the psychologically calming influence of having money in the bank. Pulling down three to four hundred dollars on busy summer nights, he quickly built a nest egg of several thousand dollars. Unfortunately, following the ouster of his boss who was caught snorting cocaine from a restaurant salt shaker, Razz was elevated to manager. Now in his mid-forties, he made less money than when he was a bartender and got less pussy than when he was a busboy. It was the worst of all worlds. The responsibility of being a manager seemed to crimp his sexual style. Perhaps, as manager, he was more threatening to the female clientele. Or, perhaps, it was because he was now married with two young children.

It was almost four in the afternoon when Razz found a parking spot for his 1967 dark moss green Mustang convertible, a happy remnant from his youth. Like always, he parked on a meter-free side street instead of paying the eight-dollar parking fee on the Pier. He hated paying for parking and enjoyed walking along the lower boardwalk at beach level before having to face customers at the Surf's Up.

"Hey, mister, can you spare a dime?"

Razz looked to see the recognizable faces of two men sitting at a concrete chess table, one of many permanently affixed to the landscape near this part of the boardwalk. They were two of a number of homeless men and women in various stages of chess playing, eating and sleeping.

"I always do," said Razz, approaching. He fished in his wallet for a five-dollar bill and placed it on the table amongst chess pieces and stale bread crusts that had been retrieved from a local sub shop dumpster.

The two men, one white and one black, considered him noncommittally. Their clothes were clean, but well-worn. Each man had seen better days.

"And make sure you don't spend it on alcohol," Razz continued.

"Says the man who runs a bar," said the black man.

"Hey, it's a bar-restaurant," Razz responded, and the three men cracked up laughing. "What's up, James?" He greeted the black man first and then tried helplessly to follow his elaborate handshake ritual until giving up and ending with a simple fist bump.

"Man, you so white. You're just like him," said James, pointing to his friend.

Smiling, Razz shook the friend's hand in the old, white businessman's style. "How you doing, Ryan?" In truth, Ryan looked pale and tired, but before he could speak, Razz said, "I haven't seen you guys in a while."

"Oh, you know, been busy. World cruise and what-not," said James.

"Yeah, me, too." Another laugh and then a pause that grew uncomfortably long. "Well, glad you're back. I've got to get to work." Razz tapped on their table, acknowledging them, and then continued down the boardwalk.

"Hey, thanks, man," James yelled after him.

Razz waved, but he didn't look back. As he thought about the two men, men he had seen hundreds of times in the past several years, his smile faded. Despite their friendly banter, he barely knew them. He had never seen either man without the other, but couldn't say if they were a couple or just good friends, partners in the full-time job of surviving the streets. His thought made him melancholy, but he cheered himself by vowing to invite them to the restaurant for a good meal the next time he saw them.

There were no bikini-clad beauties on this California-cold day, so there were no sight-seeing delays to Razz' stepping up the thirteen wooden steps onto the main pier. Most people got to the Pier, walking or driving, by way of a connecting street bridge from Ocean Boulevard, a street that, aptly, ran parallel to the Pacific Ocean along the elevated cliffs of San Margarita and offered a magnificent view of the Pier and amusement park below. Had Razz approached from Ocean Boulevard, he wouldn't have been surprised by the police tape which he now found blocking his path to the Surf's Up.

"What the hell?"

Looking up, he saw several police officers wearing heavy-duty gas masks shooing away a few remaining lily-white tourist-types. Police vehicles' lights flashed in warning. Razz saw a flurry of activity around the police substation halfway down the Pier, as officers outfitted in gas masks poured forth, moving out in all directions. The Ferris wheel in the distance was still, its usually insistent flashing lights ominously reposed. A siren blasted and Razz turned to see a HazMat truck screaming down the connecting bridge. Waved through the police barricade, the vehicle sped the length of the Pier, finally screeching to a stop in front of the Sol a Sol, a cheap, tacky Tex-Mex restaurant.

No wonder they need HazMat, he thought, *people have been eating Sol a Sol food.* Though Razz had rubbed his belly in more than a few gutters in his day, he still had some standards. The Sol a Sol was the worst restaurant in town, but because of its cheap prices and its prime location at the end of the Pier, it did some of the best business. *Someone ate a bean burrito, and then burped. Better call HazMat.*

"Get the hell out of here, Razz."

He turned to see Police Sergeant Gerard "Sharky" Sampson and burst out laughing at the sight of his ridiculous-looking gas mask. Too big for his small head, Sharky struggled to keep it in place with his right hand.

"You've got to leave. Now."

"Hey, Sharky, didn't you hear? Halloween's over."

"It's Gerard."

Razz nodded. "So what's the fuss, Sharky?"

Sergeant Sampson fumed, but quickly recovered, for he had come to expect such insolence from Razz. "There's a scare. The Pier's closed until further notice."

"A scare? I'm not scared," Razz scoffed. "What the hell are you talking about?"

Sharky looked like a man who desperately wanted to tell his secret. "You've just got to go."

Razz had known Sharky since they were kids. They'd been surfing buddies early on, and Sharky had watched from shore on the day of Razz' greatest triumph. He had never been sure that Sharky, in a losing bout with jealousy, had not secretly hoped he would fail and bite the dust, or, at least, take a large chunk out of a piling. He felt God sufficiently answered the question a few years after his feat when a confused five-foot tiger shark inexplicably attacked him and mangled his lower left leg. He knew it was mean to make fun of him, but Sharky had lost what little sense of humor he'd ever had the day of his attack, so Razz couldn't help himself sometimes.

"And take her with you," said Sharky, referring to a woman struggling to free herself from his grasp. She was Carlotta Gugliotta, the Surf's Up assistant manager. Razz had to hand it to him; Sharky was wiry strong, but he definitely had to work on his way with women.

Carlotta was a Mexican bombshell only somewhat past her prime who had once been married to an Italian Prince for three days before she sent him packing. She kept the name Gugliotta, because it was more rhythmical with Carlotta than her family name of Diaz. Because it was more fun and most apt, she was simply known as Lotta. And she was a lotta you-name-it—tits, ass, mouth. While Sharky hated his nickname and Razz lived comfortably with his, Lotta enjoyed hers to the fullest. Full-figured and dark-haired, she had enormous appetites. She might have been known as an enormous cock-tease, except that she did not tease. She and Razz had had their dalliances years back and were still tempted from time to time. But, in a concession to maturity and Razz' marriage, they realized that working together and sleeping together, even infrequently, could only come to a disastrous end.

"Get him the fuck off me, Razz. He wouldn't even let me lock up."

He wanted to laugh again, not used to Lotta asking anyone for anything. She usually just told people what she wanted and they happily obliged.

"Sharky, what the fuck, you're hurting the lady." Razz knew Lotta was no lady and that Sharky, even if he'd had a sledgehammer, couldn't hurt her.

Lotta pursed her lips in anger directed now at Razz. "Ooh, you men, you all the same." She ripped her arm violently from Sharky's grasp, and then folded both arms across her chest as if to punish the impudent men by covering her ample cleavage.

"Sharky, let us, at least, close up the bar."

"You can't cross the tape, Razz. This is serious."

"What's serious? Another bomb scare? Christ, the things that get people's rocks off these days."

Lotta couldn't help but flash Razz a desiring look when she heard the words "rocks off." She loved dirty talk, but she quickly veiled any sexual desire with the indignity of having been held against her will. Tie her up, handcuff her, even slap her around a bit, but do it only when she says so.

"It's anthrax."

Razz' mouth dropped open in shock. Lotta didn't know what anthrax was, so was unfazed. Razz took Sharky aside.

"Anthrax? What the fuck are you talking about?"

"There was a call about half-hour ago. Someone left a suitcase containing anthrax outside the Sol a Sol. It's hooked to a bomb set to go off in five minutes. So, will you please get the hell out of here?"

Anthrax. At least it couldn't have happened to a worse restaurant. After his initial fear, Razz now considered this a hoax less serious than the Pier's bi-monthly bomb scares. "So who do you think called it in, some terrorist in Pakistan?"

"What?"

"You think Osama's been calling from his spider-hole?" Razz waited for at least a smile, but no recognition of humor was forthcoming. "This is just some jerk-off copycatting these other scares."

Lotta perked up when she heard some magic words, but she still didn't understand the true gist of the conversation.

"Fucking anthrax. Are you shitting me? You know better, Sharky."

"Look, it doesn't matter what I know or what you think you know. You have to get out of here—now."

'You're starting to piss me off, you know."

"Yeah, well, that's what friends are for."

Razz couldn't remember the last time he'd considered Sharky a friend, but he suspected Sharky would have the same trouble with him. He didn't want to leave the restaurant open where hundreds of dollars were probably sitting amiably in the cash register available for a warm hand to wrap itself around them. Razz knew there were plenty of warm hands in the police department, but, before he could argue further, the HazMat siren gave off such an annoyingly loud, piercing sound that one would think Hell had found its way to the San Margarita Pier.

"Oh, fuck. They found something," said Sharky.

At first, Razz couldn't believe it, but when policemen scurried away from the Sol a Sol toward the connecting bridge, he decided that discretion would be better than stupidity. He grabbed Lotta and pulled her down the steps toward his car.

"What the fuck? You men, you all alike."

She fought against him, but appreciated his strength and good looks enough not to fight too hard. She even thought she might get lucky.

Lotta did get lucky that day. So did Razz, Sharky, and all of San Margarita, because there wasn't a bomb, only a timer that couldn't be defused before it triggered open the worn Samsonite to release its contents into the air. This time, its contents were harmless. The case contained twenty pounds of baby powder, not weaponized anthrax.

If it had been anthrax, killer spores would have wafted into onshore winds blowing across San Margarita toward the City of Angels itself, and that would have marked the end of this story and thousands or, perhaps, tens of thousands, of others.

2

In high school, when Razz was still known as Robbie, he had been obsessed with surfing. On one particularly wave-challenged day, as the annoyingly gentle waters lapped against his legs which dangled easily over each side of his board, he found himself staring at the wavelets rolling past some of the Pier's hundred-odd, pressure-treated wood pilings toward shore and thought, "What if I surfed into shore between the pilings under the Pier?"

The next morning, as his kids, Ronnie and Caitlin, bickered over the rightful ownership of a LeapFrog LeapPad, Razz sat on his back porch reading that morning's *Monitor*, the local newspaper. Fairside, where the McNeils lived, sat just to the east of San Margarita, but the two towns shared almost everything—schools, community facilities, newspapers. Everything, that is, but the wealth. Fairside was a nice, upstanding, but decidedly poor, relation to San Margarita.

The *Monitor*'s front page headline trumpeted, "Anthrax Scare at S.M. Pier!" *Just what we need, as if business isn't bad enough already,* he thought. Razz put down the paper in disgust and looked out over the top of his ficus trees, just able to glimpse the ocean, miles in the distance. He looked at his kids, who were now getting physically violent, and wondered if this was all there was and would ever be to his life.

"Honey, you've got a phone call." His wife, Sarah, poked her head out the back door.

"Who is it?"

"It's Paul. He wants to talk to you."

Paul. The current owner of the Surf's Up. Pier eccentric. The owner of a fifteen-year-old mutt named Miss Scruffy, a dog that could barely see, barely hear, and barely walk, but who went with him everywhere. On cold winter nights, when Miss Scruffy's arthritis would flare up, Paul would carry her to the Surf's Up for dinner and place the dog on top of his table where he could keep an eye on her. As Paul would munch on his half-pound charbroiled hamburger, so would Miss

Scruffy. Complaining patrons found the gastronomic situation intolerable, so Paul had grudgingly agreed to move his doggy tête-à-tête to a dark, private corner table. Razz still found it disgusting and humiliating. Here he was trying to run a respectable restaurant, trying to increase business, and the owner undercut his efforts because of a queer, obsessive love for a mangy mutt. Not that Paul didn't like women, he did. Given a choice, he just liked his dog better. Like many couples, they had even begun to look alike—unkempt hair, pooch belly, beady eyes. At least, they didn't dress alike. Paul wore a Hawaiian shirt, pair of shorts, and sandals every single day of the year no matter what the weather. Miss Scruffy went au naturel.

"I'll take it."

Excited to hear some good news, Razz waited for her to hand him the phone, but Sarah hadn't brought the portable with her. These kinds of minor events used to make him laugh, but now they just gnawed at him.

"Could you bring me the phone, please?" he asked, trying to maintain a semblance of politeness.

"Oh. Sure."

"Waaggh!" screamed Caitlin, holding her head where Ronnie had just whacked her with the LeapPad.

"Waaggh! Daddy, Daddy, Wonnie hit me," she cried as she ran toward her father.

Day after day, it was the same. One kid would hit the other kid who would then scream bloody murder. Later, they swapped roles and the other would get to release his or her blood-curdling cry.

"There, there, honey, I'm sure Ronnie didn't mean it." Razz knew Ronnie meant it with all his three-year-old heart, and, when six-year-old Caitlin retaliated, she would mean it, too.

"Here," Sarah said, handing Razz the phone. Then she noticed the growing welt on her daughter's forehead. "What happened?"

"Wonnie hit me with the WeapPad," Caitlin whimpered.

Sarah glared at him. "I thought you were watching them."

"Hey, Paul." Razz couldn't face his wife's accusatory stare. Whenever something bad happened to one of the kids, it always seemed to be his fault.

"Yeah. Uh-huh." His heart sank. "I'm sorry to hear that. Yeah, well, thanks for considering it. All right, see you later."

As Sarah cared for Caitlin's wound, Razz licked his own wound. Paul had scoffed at his offer to buy the Surf's Up, declaring the price ridiculously low. *Too low? The place is losing more money every day!* Sometimes he wasn't even sure why he wanted to buy it. Unlike the Sol a Sol, the Surf's Up had very little view of the water despite sitting only about thirty feet above it, so it didn't have the natural drawing card that landlocked tourists loved so much. Besides, the Surf's Up's expenses were higher than the Sol a Sol's because they served something other than re-fried beans and animal fat.

Now wasn't the time to argue with Paul or to wallow in self-pity. His daughter was screaming, his wife was angry because of his supposed parental negligence, and his young son was crawling toward a twenty-foot precipice at the edge of their house lot.

"Hey!" Razz sprang off the porch, deftly avoiding Caitlin and Sarah. "Hey, buddy!"

If little Ronnie understood his father's warning, he didn't let on, for he kept right on scooting toward Deep Valley. Though he was three and could walk and run as well as any three-year-old, Ronnie sometimes liked to pretend he was still a baby and go on all fours. Thank God he did, because it gave Razz enough time to dive and catch Ronnie's left ankle just before he did a belly flop down the embankment.

"Aaggh!" Sarah screamed, running toward her son.

"No! No! You can't play over here!" Razz yelled, cradling his pride and joy tightly to his chest.

Frightened and squished, Ronnie responded by wailing bloody murder.

"You can't play here. Understand?"

Of course, he didn't understand. He was three.

When Sarah reached them, she took the still-screaming Ronnie into her arms. "I told you we need a fence back here."

It was at times like these that Razz felt his most impotent, that he couldn't do anything right. Now all three members of his family were against him.

"Tell your father," he said as he walked toward the house.

Sarah entered the hallway, gently closing Caitlin's bedroom door behind her. She looked into Ronnie's room. He snored blissfully, his face scrunched into his pillow.

"They're finally down," she said suggestively as she sashayed toward Razz, sitting pensively in the living room.

"Huh?"

"The kids, they're asleep." She sat on the arm of his favorite leather chair and stroked his hair.

"I'm sorry about this morning, honey. I know it wasn't your fault. Forgive me?" she said before kissing his neck playfully.

"Hey, stop that," he said as she nibbled on his ear. "I've got to get to work."

"Not until four. We can play until three-thirty. That gives us forty-five minutes." She nuzzled closer to him, then unbuttoned one of his buttons before sliding her hand onto his warm, still-firm chest.

"Oh, baby, I'm not feeling very well."

"What's the matter? Are you getting sick? I'll make you some soup," rattling off each sentence so quickly they seemed as one.

Not being a psychologically deep thinker at heart, Razz didn't always know why he got into his funks, but he knew why today. "No, no, it's just something at work."

Though Sarah would have gladly listened to his complaints for hours if it would help him feel better, Razz kept business matters to himself figuring he would get more frustrated trying to make her understand.

"I know what you need," she cooed as she unzipped his pants.

"You don't have to—" was as far as he got before he began a moan that would last for the next several minutes until, finally, it turned into one long, climactic grunt.

Sarah wiped her lips, zipped his pants, and smiled. He smiled back and shook his head in disbelief at his good fortune now kneeling at his feet.

"Come here," he said softly. He encircled her with his arms and felt for the moment that the world was all right, after all. "I love you."

She loved it when he said that. "I love you, too."

"Daddy?"

Their eyes popped when they heard the tiny voice. Sarah flipped herself over and sat on the corner of the chair. Razz sat up, annoyed and amused at his harsh trip back to the realities of parenthood. Little Ronnie leaned against a doorjamb, innocently sucking his thumb.

Well, if he's going to be scarred for life, this is as good a reason as any. "Hey, buddy."

Ronnie ran over and threw himself happily into his father's chest, knocking him back into the chair, and then giggled with glee when Razz held his little man high above his head.

God, I'm a lucky man, Razz thought.

"Who's been skweaming?"

Rubbing her eyes, Caitlin appeared from around the corner. She stumbled sleepily over to her mother as her parents just laughed and laughed.

Razz' amusement wore off quickly. When he arrived at work fifteen minutes after four, Lotta was waiting outside, her car keys in hand.

"I've got to pick up my daughter, you know."

Lotta's daughter, Imelda, was twelve and a "special" child, the product of a forgotten ship that had done a little more than pass Lotta's one night. High-strung and emotionally volatile, Imelda didn't like it when her mother was late picking her up from Daybreak School, a school for emotionally and physically disadvantaged kids.

"I'm sorry. Something came up at home."

"I bet."

Razz caught her unmistakable sarcasm squarely in the face, but didn't have time to respond before she informed him that the restaurant's cash receipts were several hundred dollars short from the previous day's anthrax debacle.

"Shit! Why didn't you call me?"

"And interrupt your busy day?" she said, spewing more sarcasm his way. "What was the rush? What could you do?"

She had done him a favor by not telling him until now. He only would have stressed out about it.

"Does Paul know?"

She shook her head no.

Not only won't I be buying the restaurant, maybe I should worry about my job. Oh, well, I can always get a bartending job somewhere. At forty-five, he had hoped for better.

"Any ideas on who might have taken it?"

She looked down the Pier toward the police substation, implying what

Razz already suspected.

"I was the last one here when they kicked us out yesterday. I left the figures on your desk. Bye."

Razz couldn't help admiring Lotta's ass as she hurried off to her car, then he entered the Surf's Up Saloon.

It was quiet. Other than the two servers, Sharon and Tom, the bartender, Rick, a busboy, and the kitchen staff, the place was empty. *And Paul won't part with this?*

"I won't be in tomorrow. I'm starting at the Sol a Sol."

Razz turned expecting to see Sharon still holding the handle of the stake she had just driven into his heart. *The Sol a Sol!* Sharon was a cute piece of ass, a typical, struggling actress-type just off the bus from Oklahoma, but Razz knew she'd probably be a waitress the rest of her life unless she got lucky and married into money. He had seen too many like her to think anything different.

"Why would you go to The Sol a Sol? They just had an anthrax scare, for God's sakes. No one will be going there."

"Well, no one ever comes here. Besides, my friend, Charisse, said that people always come to the Sol a Sol, no matter what. She makes a hundred-and-fifty dollars in tips sometimes at lunch, a hundred on a bad day. Even in the winter. I made twelve today."

Razz couldn't begin to fight her logic. He nodded helplessly. "Good luck."

Though the Surf's Up was one of the first establishments people saw at the Pier, it was also one of the first they passed by. On arrival, tourists usually walked the Pier's length to check out the carousel, amusement park, arcade, and view of the Pacific before getting thirsty or hungry, or both, just about the time they'd hiked the quarter mile to the end, right at the Sol a Sol's door.

He and Paul had changed decor a year earlier to upscale beach, renaming the restaurant, Paul's Cafe, but customers greeted both changes, along with the new menu, with a yawn. Failing to garner a more affluent crowd, the Surf's Up returned to cater to passing tourists and locals who liked the casual hospitality and generous helpings. Bringing in bands on weekends and karaoke on Tuesday nights helped sales, but barely covered the additional expense. Yet Razz was convinced things would be different if he owned the place. *At least, I won't allow dogs on the tables or anywhere near my damn restaurant.*

He would keep the restaurant's current surf theme, of course. When Razz walked in the door around four o'clock every afternoon except Mondays, he felt an immediate peace, at least until confronted with the harsh realities of the business. Entering the Surf's Up always took him back to his youth, however briefly, and he longed for those simpler days. You see, the Surf's Up was a shrine to the early days of surfing. Twenty-seven different surfboards, each telling a chapter of California surfing history, lined the walls. And Razz was forever a part of that history. He had even lent three of his own boards to the restaurant for display—his Bing Lightweight, Quigg stock, and his Hap Jacobs. He had learned to surf on those boards over thirty years ago, so they held a special place in his heart, but he admired all of the boards at the Surf's Up—the Greg Noll stock, the Corky Carroll, the Harbour Cheater. Every one of them told a story and it was a story that began and ended with freedom—the freedom of being on the water, joking with pals, conquering, or being conquered by, watery nature, pitying the landlubbers in their cars frantically rushing to get to dead-end jobs on time. Razz never imagined that one day he'd be one of them.

"Jesus fucking Christ!" Paul said when Razz told him about the missing money.

That Paul, he sure has a way with words. Even Miss Scruffy seemed indignant in her subtle at-death's-door way.

"Who do you think took it? I bet it was Diego, that little bastard. I've never trusted that—"

"Paul!" Razz couldn't stand to hear his xenophobic insults, especially when directed at an innocent, hard-working busboy. If you weren't white and born within twenty miles of San Margarita, Paul thought there was something wrong with you. "It wasn't anyone from here. Lotta was the last one out."

"Then what about Lotta?"

Whatever Lotta was, Razz couldn't conceive of her being a thief. "No."

"You're protecting her. What are you, fucking her?"

Oh, how Razz wanted to punch him in his ugly, stupid dog face.

"I never trusted that fucking dago bitch. You're the one that promoted her to assistant manager, remember, so you're responsible. Four hundred dollars is a lot of money for this place, you know. Maybe I should just take it out of your salary," Paul said in a parting shot, just before he picked up his canine pride and joy from their candlelit table and stormed out.

Maybe you should just shut the fuck up, or sell me the God damn place and leave the misery to me. At least, get your insults straight! Lotta's a wetback, not a dago! Stupid asshole!

Although The Beach Boys' "Good Vibrations" wafted through the restaurant, the song didn't help Razz feel any. He knew Paul had a right to be angry. It was just business, after all. Paul's business. At least, he hadn't been fired—yet.

He blew out the table's candle. It looked like another slow, uneventful December weeknight. Three couples dined quietly and a few men propped themselves at the bar drinking beers. Each man watched the door more than ESPN, as if hoping Miss Bikini California would walk in, choose him, and change his life forever. *Everyone seems depressed right now.* Razz sure knew he was.

His depression turned to anger minutes later when Lotta staggered in, cackling loudly, followed by several of her Mexican gangbanger friends and their "dates." Razz knew they were gangbangers because Lotta's cousin, Luis Marcayda, leader of the Twentieth Street Boys, was the last person in the door.

Sharply-dressed in an expensive Italian suit, Luis, who preferred the Americanized spelling and pronunciation of Louis, as in Saint Louis, was a small, wiry sort who had power way beyond his physique. If he preferred Louis, not Luis, it was Louis. As the mostly white-bread customers turned to see the raucous off-white crowd at the front door, Razz could sense them deciding to eat and drink faster, no longer lingering over coffee or their Black Forest chocolate cake.

Lotta waved as she led her contingent to a large corner table near the front. Tom, the waiter, cheered up considerably at the prospect of getting a decent tip, but Razz didn't like the gang crowd on the Pier, and definitely didn't want them in the Surf's Up.

"Hey, everyone. Welcome to the Surf's Up," Razz said, trying hard to be polite.

"Hey, Razz," Lotta said before surprising him with an open-mouthed kiss. His arms involuntarily closed around her and she pressed her breasts into him. He could smell desire all over her and she could feel his desire growing behind his zipper. He pulled away.

"Hey, Lotta. I didn't think I'd see you again till tomorrow."

"Sometimes you get lucky," she said and giggled at her own cleverness. "You know my cousin, Louis."

"Of course."

Louis stood to shake hands, his strong grip silently insisting that Razz accept his unseen offering. Louis' dark eyes looked straight through him and when they released hands, Razz had tacitly accepted a one hundred dollar bill and their presence.

"Your best Champagne," said Louis and Tom's eyes lit up.

"Bring two bottles of the Dom 1996. One's on the house," Razz said and Tom scurried happily away.

"Join us, please."

"No, thank you. I have some work to do upstairs. I'll check in on you later, if that's all right."

"It's all right," said Lotta, smiling.

As Tom returned with the bottles of Dom Pérignon 1996 and three white couples headed toward the door, Razz wondered what Lotta had up her sleeve and couldn't help but think about what she had everywhere else.

Ensconced safely in his office, Razz struggled with a decision he knew was inevitable. He would have to let go one busboy and one server in order to decrease the restaurant's weekly deficit. Maybe he would also decrease Rick's hours, taking over some of the bartending tasks himself. Though Diego was a good worker, letting him go would make Paul happy. Razz would decide which server to let go tomorrow. With Sharon leaving anyway, at least he didn't have to fire two.

He had been upstairs for almost two hours listening to Lotta and her friends carry on. He'd busied himself with accounting and staffing issues, but he was mainly trying to avoid Louis and the whole situation downstairs.

"Razz?"

He turned to see Lotta, who grinned seductively as she approached. Razz edged his chair back, afraid to let her get too close. He wasn't noted for his willpower and she was particularly aggressive this evening.

"I'm sorry. I'm a little drunk," she said, giggling out the words as she flopped onto his lap.

"Wrong, Lotta, you're a lot drunk. Maybe you should go home."

"Mmm, maybe you should come with me," she whispered into his ear, bringing her breasts ominously close to his face.

"What's the hell's up?"

"You tell me," she said, reaching for his crotch.

Though Lotta always felt really, really right to him, something else didn't. She knew better than to bring Louis' crowd into the Surf's Up. And although she could flirt with the best of them, they had an unwritten agreement against fooling around. But as she fondled his manhood, he knew she was way past flirting.

He struggled up out of his chair and almost toppled her to the floor.

"What the fuck, Razz!"

That Lotta—love you to hate you in two seconds flat. It was just another reason for him to be nervous.

"Let's go see how your friends are doing."

She smiled slyly. "Louis likes you."

Why the fuck would Louis like me? What could he want from me? Please, God, let Louis shower me with benign neglect.

Razz had good reason to worry. Luis "Louis" Marcayda had risen to the top of the Twentieth Street Boys gang, partly by being its first active member to survive past thirty. Now, at thirty-seven, with a wife and two young children, he was a good front man. And, although he hadn't graduated from high school, he was smart enough not to rub his power in the faces of important people in town. The police and city government normally looked the other way when it came to Louis' activities. They knew they couldn't stop the Boys, for they had tried many times, but they felt that they could control Louis. And Louis could control the Boys.

The Boys were a notoriously vicious gang that had originated in Tijuana before arriving in Southern California in the mid-eighties in the form of Louis. Through violence and intimidation, they got a foothold in the poorest section of San Margarita. Through drug running and prostitution, they got rich. Louis plowed the money back into the area by buying most of it, making Louis and the Boys landlords. Through an intricate maze of corporations and friends, Louis now owned or controlled a good portion of the eastern end of San Margarita, from Seventeenth to Twenty-Third Streets and from Alameda Street to Sunrise Terrace. As long as they stayed there, away from the whiter, fancier parts of town, no one seemed to mind too much. Many people thought Louis and the Boys provided a great service for they had the best hookers and best drugs anywhere in the area. Importing the hottest chiquitas and purest cocaine from sources in Mexico and South America, the Boys' turf became party central on Friday and Saturday nights. Police cruisers would sit idly by as Mercedes, Beemers, even Rolls-Royces, carried their studio executives, entertainment lawyers, and money managers through Louis' territory to deposit their money and semen. Because of Louis' skills in forging alliances with nearby gangs and the Boys' history of strong-armed tactics, the Boys had little competition.

"Carlotta, Louis wants to go," said a Spanish-tinged voice from the stairwell.

"Let's go see your friends off."

"I'd rather see you off," Lotta responded, once again reaching for his crotch.

"Carlotta." The unseen voice, more insistent, finally convinced an unrepentant Lotta to drop what she was trying to do and go downstairs.

"I'll be right down," Razz said as he watched her go. *Christ, I'm weak. I should fire her right now.* He knew he wouldn't, because he liked the thrill. Besides, she was good at her job and good for business, particularly adept at attracting men to the restaurant.

Louis and his friends were readying to leave when Razz got downstairs. Tom discretely waved the nine hundred and forty three dollar food and bar bill the party had built up.

"I hope everything was satisfactory," Razz said in his best, most diplomatic, bar manager voice.

Louis turned and reached out his hand all in the same motion. When Razz took it, he felt he was already under Louis' spell, helplessly awaiting his command. And when he extricated his grip, seemingly an eternity later, there was another hundred dollar bill in his hand.

"Thank you for an enjoyable evening. You have a very nice place."

"Thanks, but it's not exactly mine."

"Perhaps it will be one day. We will speak again," said Louis with a certainty that chilled Razz.

After signing the receipt, Louis nodded and he and his cohorts walked out into the night, leaving Tom beaming and Razz trembling.

"He left me a two hundred dollar tip," Tom said gleefully.

Me, too. But Razz felt no glee about it at all.

When he got home that night, he felt dirty. Not from his dalliance with Lotta, but from his dalliance with Louis. He had closed the bar early, before midnight, just after Louis and his friends left, in part, because business was slow and, in part, because he badly wanted a shower to cleanse himself of his new association. For he suspected he was now inextricably associated with Louis. He just didn't know yet what that meant.

"We will speak again."

Louis' words echoed in his brain as he slipped down into his cold leather chair. As he replayed the night's events, he gradually gave in to his need for sleep. He would not get his badly needed shower that night, nor would he wake early to check the next morning's surf.

Razz McNeil's life was already changing more than he could possibly imagine.

3

In moments of inspiration, some men devote their lives to God while some devote themselves to curing heretofore incurable diseases, but Robbie/Razz had realized a different epiphany. He would surf under the San Margarita Pier.

December 23, 2004

As Gerard "Sharky" Sampson pulled on trousers over his disfigured left calf, a slender, dark-haired woman quickly pulled on fishnet stockings and a too-mini, leather mini-skirt, then headed for the door of Sharky's first floor apartment, taking with her a hundred dollar bill from his dresser.

"Next week, Rosie?" he asked, already knowing the answer.

She nodded silently, and then exited into the mid-day sun.

Sharky dragged himself up from his disheveled bed and grudgingly opened the shades, letting light into his cavernous existence. His eyes burned as they adjusted to the brightness reflecting off his empty white walls. He worked the night shift on Thursdays, so he liked waking up late, getting a fifteen minute lay from his favorite hooker, then walking down to Mae's, the local grease joint, for coffee and doughnuts. There he would schmooze some of his contacts from the street, getting whatever lowdown they were low enough to give him in exchange for breakfast or a few bucks.

Although there were few felonies of note in relatively tame San Margarita, Sharky had solved an infamous case a couple years earlier involving a mysterious daylight murder of a Swiss tourist. Working through one of his sources, he traced the murder to a member of one of the Twentieth Street Boys' rival gangs who was now sitting on death row. Congratulatory on the outside, his peers at the station secretly believed Sharky and the Boys set him up. For Sharky knew Louis and the Boys well. He rented one of their apartments and one of their hookers, both at reduced rates.

Fellow detectives griped about his "arrangement", but the then-new mayor, Jaime Hidalgo, was only too happy to pin a medal on his uniform in appreciation for catching the brazen daylight killer of San Margarita's Swiss guest.

"¿Qué pasa?" Sharky shouted from his patrol car to several Mexican thugs who were hanging out in front of the Boys' clubhouse, which doubled as a high-class brothel. Louis kept most of what went on in Boys' Town behind closed doors: behind a closed car door for men in a hurry, or behind a door of one of his bordellos, distinguished by not-so-original red lights, for those who could linger.

Behind the clubhouse doors, one could hear the best Latin music, drink the best Mexican tequila, and fuck the best Mexican whores, but only special guests could sample the drugs. Typical drug customers were waved down a secluded alleyway off Twentieth Street. There, they often waited in a five-car-deep line to make their purchase at a drive-through window in a process so efficient it would make McDonald's jealous, and then were sent on their way. Controlling men with their pants down around their ankles was easy. They got satisfied and left happily, back to their wives and girlfriends. Druggies could be difficult, and Louis tried hard to keep the neighborhood safe for his kids and his friends' kids. And for business.

It seemed like any other Thursday night as Sharky cruised through Boys' Town, which was named purely for its ownership, and then down Westerly Boulevard toward the beach. When his radio blasted a call around one a.m., he couldn't believe it. The cops were making a bust in Boys' Town.

Tires screeching and heart racing, Sharky pulled a U-turn.

When he arrived at the Boys' clubhouse, amidst the flashing lights of five other patrol cars, police were already dragging Louis away with several of his entourage. Officers hoarded scantily clad hookers into the back of a large police van as handcuffed johns attempted to shield their faces from any cameras that might be nearby.

"What the fuck, Chief?" Sharky stormed up to the Chief of Police, Phillip Wilson. "I'm right here in the neighborhood and you don't tell me what's going down?"

"Calm down."

"Fuck 'calm down.'"

The Chief waved for a couple officers to take Sharky away before he did something he'd regret.

"You're fucking with my credibility here!" Sharky didn't stop with his tirade, but fortunately, he was dragged out of the Chief's earshot.

"Shut up, asshole," warned Lieutenant Johnnie Johnson, a black man in his late forties who was the closest thing to whom Sharky could call a friend on the force. "It was my call, not the Chief's. I was trying to protect you. This thing just came down an hour ago and you were too close."

"Fuck that!"

"It's true. The mayor had to show what a big dick he has. That's all. These guys will make bail, the mayor will get some good press, and then it will be back to business as usual."

"And I'll still look like an asshole."

"If the shoe fits ..."

Sharky didn't laugh at Johnson's joke, but did try to calm down enough so he'd let him out of a vise-like headlock. Sharky felt picked on, and he raged at its injustice, just like when the bigger boys used to harass him in school. This time, however, he knew it could put him in real danger. Because he was the closest to the Boys, in proximity and relationship, Louis might have to make an example of him.

"So, Johnnie, were you worried I was going to warn him?"

"Should I have been?"

"Fuck you!"

Had Johnson not been a graduate of the same academy class and his one-time partner, Sharky might have been demoted on the spot.

He wasn't sure which potential hangman he cared for least, Louis or the police force. With Louis, it would likely be a clean shot. No pain, no struggle. But the police could kill you in oh-so-many ways. They could freeze you out as they had tonight and make you a pariah on the street. They could be slow to back you up in a critical situation. Or they could shoot you with a criminal's weapon and then pretend to mourn at your funeral. *Oh, fuck, I'm getting more paranoid than usual*, he thought. *It's just what Johnson said. Mayor's got a bug up his ass, that's all.*

Sharky's paranoia multiplied when he saw Louis glaring at him from the back seat of a police cruiser on his way to the city jail.

"God damn it," Razz said to himself, inadvertently loud enough to get Sarah's attention.

"What's that, honey?"

"Oh, just something in the paper."

He walked out into his back yard and couldn't help but stare at the new white picket fence that Sarah's father had his construction crew build the day after Ronnie's almost-plunge. "*Tell your father*" he remembered himself saying. And she did.

He again looked at the *Monitor*'s Friday headline, "Cops Sweep Boys' Town. Arrest Twenty-Three!" Louis' defiant scowl greeted him from the front page.

Razz looked down at his right palm where he had twice accepted money from Louis almost two weeks earlier. Drug money. Money from prostitution. He looked again at the white picket fence surrounding his backyard, a gift from his wife's wealthy father, and wondered which made him feel worse.

"Honey, we have to go," Sarah yelled through the screen door.

They arrived at Richard and Elizabeth Gold's seven thousand square foot faux-Roman mansion minutes late, around three-fifteen, and a valet greeted them in the drive. The home's physical structure was modest compared to many high-end homes in the area, but its three acres bordering the Pacific Ocean made the Gold estate one of the most desirable. Its location was the only thing Razz liked about it. If he owned the property, he would burn the pretentious old building to the ground, but he would surf every day off its lovely shores.

Greeted at the door by a snooty, middle-aged Englishman dressed in black-tie and tails, they entered the high-ceilinged foyer where an attractive French girl who looked a lot like a young Audrey Hepburn took their coats. Both looked straight from Central Casting.

He looked down at Caitlin, who was a picture of going-to-the-ball cuteness dressed in a green velvet dress, and Ronnie, who looked like a miniature businessman in his new navy-blue suit. They were the most beautiful kids in the world, but Razz liked them better in shorts and T-shirts. He himself opted for a sports jacket, refusing to own a suit, let alone wear one, while Sarah looked great in a ridiculously expensive Halston dress.

When they reached the parlor, Caitlin and Ronnie, despite their grown-up clothes, remembered they were still kids and tore off to look at their presents sitting under what looked to be a designer tree. When Ronnie skidded to a stop under the Douglas fir, Razz couldn't resist a laugh.

He's a chip off the old block.

"Come say hello to Grammie and Grampa Gold," said Sarah.

Richard and Elizabeth Gold sat stiffly on their seventeenth century Queen Anne sofa holding their afternoon cocktails.

"Hi, Grammie Gold! Hi, Grampie Gold! What do you have for us?" Caitlin and Ronnie yelled, almost in unison, as they ran over to hug their grandparents. With Ronnie's small arms unconditionally grasping her neck, Razz could see the Ice Queen beginning to melt before she quickly recovered her cool.

"There, there, calm down. We'll have presents in a little while," Mrs. Gold said, setting the two youngsters at attention before her. "Now, let me get a good look at you. Your shirt's not tucked, Ronald."

Her formality made Razz shiver.

"Come here, Caitlin. Let's fix that bow." She proceeded to untie and re-tie Caitlin's dress bow three times until she was sure it was perfect.

"How about a drink, Robert?"

Besides Mrs. Gold, Richard Gold was the only other person in the world that called Razz "Robert." It was just one more reason not to like him.

"Hi, honey. Merry Christmas," Gold said as he whisked past his daughter.

"Hi, Daddy."

"We're having glazed duck for dinner. I know how you like that, dear," Mrs. Gold said, greeting her daughter with air kisses near each cheek before proceeding to the bar for a refill.

"That sounds delicious. Thank you. Would it be all right if the kids went outside to play?"

Caitlin and Ronnie, still standing at attention, sneaked an excited, grateful look to their mother.

"That's a wonderful idea," Mrs. Gold said without turning.

Sarah nodded to her children and they ran helter-skelter through the parlor toward the back door. Razz marveled that Sarah was such a good mother given the circumstances of her upbringing, but then his drink came and his wonderment perished with the first taste of cognac.

The smoky wood flavor sent a shot of warmth coursing through his brain, pleasantly toasting his cranial cavity. This was the only part he liked about visiting the Golds. They had great liquor. From expensive bottles of wine to twenty-year-old Scotch, today he would drink the best.

Each person staked out their turf according to their roles. Mr. and Mrs. Gold held court on the Queen Anne's; Sarah sat in front of them in a large, high-backed Windsor chair with her feet barely touching the ground, their little girl awaiting their every command; and Razz sat to the side, the court jester, just off-kilter in a Frank Lloyd Wright. They soon realized they had little to discuss.

Razz tried first. "By the way, Richard, thanks again for the fence. It really ties the place together. Not to mention it keeps Ronnie from doing a nose dive into the drainage ditch."

"You're welcome," said Mr. Gold before again concentrating on his drink.

After a moment, Mrs. Gold gave it a shot. "I understand the New York City Opera is coming to town in March. We should all go."

Gold's grimace spoke volumes about what he thought about the opera.

"Oh, that sounds great," said Sarah, which elicited a similar opera-hating visage from Razz.

"Wonderful, I'll get tickets," said her mother, who appeared as proud of herself as if she'd just found the key to world peace.

Minutes seemed to pass, but Razz didn't mind. He amused himself by imagining himself sitting on his surfboard gently rocking in an easily rolling sea of cognac. The sweet nectar was already working to sweeten his dreams.

"Richard has some wonderful news. Tell them, honey," said Mrs. Gold, breaking the silence and Razz' reveries.

"No, they don't need to hear about that right now," Gold said, smiling, clearly wanting to tell his secret.

"Tell us, Daddy." Sarah knew that, if her father was the least bit excited, it must have something to do with business, for she had listened to him preach about cash flow, tax-loss carry-forwards, and the anti-competitive dangers of rent control for many years.

"It's nothing really, just another deal, but it's a pretty good one. I just purchased some property—seven acres overlooking the water. Actually, it's right near you, Robert."

Razz was no longer rocking listless and carefree on top of his board, but was now hanging on the edge of the Frank Lloyd Wright and on every coming word.

"I didn't know there was any property for sale near us," said Sarah, not understanding the magnitude of the knife that was soon to be stuck into her husband.

"No, dear, near the restaurant where Robert works," said Gold.

Where I work, not even where I manage. Razz braced himself for further disembowelment.

"Cost me thirty-five million and it's probably worth forty right now. Yeah, it's the last good buildable commercial property in San Margarita. The owner was defaulting on his—"

"I told you about that property," Razz interjected, no longer willing to spill himself listening to Gold crow about his business coup.

"What, Robert?"

"I told you about that damn property two months ago."

Sarah silently pleaded with Razz to avoid a confrontation.

"Ira Langer, my friend at San Margarita Savings, handled the loan. He told me about it. I've known him since high school."

"Well, Robert," said Gold, "I don't know how long you've known your friend, but Henry Banes, the bank president, called me about this specifically. He was going to have to build his loan loss reserve, which, as you may know, would negatively affect this quarter's earnings. I helped him out of a jam, because I could move fast. Besides, I have twenty people scouring for deals. I don't need a bartender telling me about real estate."

Razz barely held back his urge to crash the Wright chair through Gold's thick skull. "I told you about the plan. Build a luxury hotel with upscale shops and restaurants on the ground floor. You'd get the wealthy tourists staying at the hotel and the foot traffic from the street."

"Honey, let's go get the kids. It almost time to eat," said Sarah, but Razz didn't hear a word.

"You rotten prick."

Mrs. Gold scurried for another drink.

"I could have had it for thirty-two million. The bank would have had equity participation and so would I."

"Well, I got a hundred percent for thirty-five, and now the plans and permits are ready to go. Partners can be troublesome. Besides, what were you going to buy it with? Tip money?"

The swords were out and both women backed away from the battlefield.

"That's why I came to you. Three million in equity would have done it. I would have run it and we would have split the profits."

"Building and running a hotel is different than mixing drinks, Robert. Besides, I got it for no money down, just my personal guarantee. Thus, I'll get an infinite return. And I have managers. I'm sorry, Robert, but I don't recall talking with you about this. Maybe I wasn't paying attention, I don't know. You see, I deal with the heads of these lending institutions, not their loan officers. I go straight to the top. Henry and I play tennis together."

"That's right," Mrs. Gold chimed in, coming to her husband's defense. "His wife, Betty, is an old friend of mine. We play doubles sometimes."

Gold waved her off impatiently.

"Listen, Robert, I'm sorry if you somehow think you deserve part of the deal. If it makes you feel any better, you're probably going to get the property one day anyway. Just stay married to my little girl."

That was the tsunami that broke this surfer's board.

"Fuck you, you arrogant prick! You self-important bastard, keep your fucking property. I don't need it. I don't want another thing from you. And neither does Sarah."

As supportive as she was, Sarah couldn't exactly concur.

"And keep your shitty cognac!" Razz hurled his glass toward the fireplace, but missed wide right and cracked an expensive vase.

Mrs. Gold's heart seemed to crack with it. She hated incivilities and loved that vase.

Gold was pleased he had won another battle. He could afford to replace a vase many times over, but could never replace a damaged ego. His was still intact.

"Get the kids. I'll be in the car," said Razz.

Sarah obeyed, but not before apologizing profusely to her parents.

"Why aren't we going to open pwesents?" asked Caitlin as Sarah helped her with her jacket.

"Tomorrow we'll have presents," was all Sarah could say before dragging her confused daughter and screaming son outside.

On the silent drive home, Sarah wisely opted not to tell Razz about the shares of IBM stock, worth well over a hundred thousand dollars, that her father had given to each of their children as a Christmas present.

Sharky didn't have to worry about the pressures of having in-laws or celebrating the holidays. A holiday sometimes meant an extra sortie with a hooker, as his gift to himself, but was otherwise just another workday. He often worked a double-shift on Christmas, as he would today.

His was a different pressure. Only a little over twenty-four hours since Louis and his friends had met bail after spending a humiliating night in the city jail, Sharky's head was on a perpetual swivel, checking for danger at every step. He chose to make his rounds at the Pier, close to the substation. Despite his queasiness about being near the water, it was better than the queasiness from being anywhere near Louis and the Boys.

The Ferris wheel and roller coaster sat idle, rusting imperceptibly in the moist ocean air, on their one scheduled down day of the year. The arcade was silent, its bells, whistles, and masses of screaming teenagers only a memory until they all returned tomorrow. He noticed activity at the Sol a Sol and decided he should survey the Pier from the warmth and relative safety of the restaurant.

As he neared the front door, sounds of children's laughter grew louder. Though children were not his favorite people, he entered the restaurant anyway, only to be greeted by a squealing four-year-old Mexican girl chased by a screaming, young Mexican boy.

"Officer Sampson."

Sharky turned to see Ignacio Sol, the owner. Sol always seemed to be smiling, but today his bright, beaming face was enhanced by several cups of rum-spiked eggnog taken from a large bowl sitting on the bar.

"Sol," was all Sharky could get out before Sol had his arm around him.

"Merry Christmas, my friend."

Ignacio Sol considered everyone his friend today as he celebrated another year of good fortune. He had entered the United States illegally ten years earlier with only the clothes on his back, but through hard work and luck, he had acquired the lease on his restaurant. Once situated next to the Surf's Up, he had wrangled City Council permission to move the entire building to its current prime spot at the end of the newly rebuilt Pier. He renamed the place "Sol a Sol" in a tribute to his success, not because he liked the play on words. In Spanish, "sol" meant "sun," but for Ignacio Sol the restaurant's name meant "family", for it was, after all, a family business.

The warmth of Sol's rum-tinged smile warmed Sharky so that he couldn't help but smile himself. "Merry Christmas. Merry Christmas to you and to all of your family."

"Drinks on the house for my friend, Officer Sampson," directed Sol to his bartender, Miguel.

"Thank you, but I'm on duty," Sharky said, nodding respectfully to Mrs. Sol who now offered her hand to him in greeting.

"Oh, it's Christmas, Officer Sampson. Join us for a drink. What can go wrong on Christmas? There are no worries on Christmas," she said. Her enthusiasm and sincerity almost made him believe her.

"Thank you, Mrs. Sol, I'd better not. Just a coffee, thanks. Maybe a dessert."

"Miguel, give my friend anything he wants," said Sol.

Miguel, giddy with good spirit and good spirits, brought Sharky a coffee and flan, a deliciously rich Mexican dessert.

As he sat at the bar, watching the laughing, playing children and their proud parents, Sharky tried to hark back to Christmases of his youth. Back to his parents holding hands, to his half-sister happily playing with her new doll, to the comforting smell of baking turkey and apple pie, to him sitting in a huge pile of torn wrapping paper, oblivious to the world, playing joyously with a new toy fire truck, but he couldn't remember any such joy.

He had no memories of Christmas at all.

There was no valet at the McNeils' home. There was no snooty English doorman, and no one who looked like Audrey Hepburn. There was only Thomas McNeil, a ruddy-faced Irishman, and Sally McNeil, a San Margaritan born and bred. Both now in their late sixties, they had fallen in love and married forty-six years ago. Theirs was a love affair that had started the moment they set eyes on each other one night at O'Toole's Irish Pub and it continued to this day.

Tom McNeil was a good-hearted man who liked his whiskey, but, unlike many Irishmen, never got nasty, even when he drank too much. After particularly rough nights with friends, he would stagger home, plop down on the lawn outside Sally's window, and sing off-key Irish love songs to her. The fact that they lived in an apartment and that he woke everyone in the building didn't faze him for he knew he was the luckiest man in the world.

Sally McNeil was born to middle-class parents who passed away when Razz was still young. Hesitant to approve of Sally's union to what they considered an opportunistic young man just off the boat, Tom won them over by his good humor, gentleness, and respect for their daughter. They could see Sally was head-over-heels in love. She didn't mind that Tom worked in a machine shop or that he came home tired and filthy every night, for he always had a smile on his face when he looked at her. And that always brought a smile to hers.

Razz' parents greeted them at the door with broad grins and open arms.

"Merry Christmas!"

"Grammie! Grampa!"

Ronnie jumped into his grandfather's waiting arms and squealed with happiness when he flew like an airplane through the entryway.

"Hey, take it easy, Dad," said Razz.

"Aw, hush, you old worry-wart."

Razz always worried about his father overexerting himself, but when he saw his mother lifting his forty-five-pound daughter off the ground, he could only smile. His parents had already buried several of their friends, but they showed no signs of slowing down themselves.

"How's Caity bug, my lady bug?" said Tom, which made Caitlin giggle with delight.

Tom and Sally switched grandchildren and repeated their greeting rituals, although Caitlin flew at a lower altitude than had little Ronnie. After they had smothered them each with kisses, they sent them off to find their presents under the Christmas tree.

"You got any love left for us?" asked Razz.

"You betcha, laddie. How are you, son?" said Tom, bear hugging him.

"Hello, dear," said Sally, taking Sarah into her arms.

"Merry Christmas, Sally. You look wonderful."

Razz' mother blushed until Tom grabbed her from behind and gave her a squeeze.

"Isn't she the most beautiful woman in the world?" said Tom, and Sally giggled like a schoolgirl.

Razz' father spun his mother round and round, stopping only long enough to grab Sarah and spin her. Laughing, Razz didn't notice the tear of joy that crept from a corner of his eye.

"Are you all right, dear?" asked his mother.

"I'm great, Mom. Merry Christmas."

His arm around her shoulders, Razz entered his childhood home, a simple two-bedroom apartment filled to its rafters with love, fond memories, and the joyous screams of his two young children.

After finishing his flan and another cup of coffee, Sharky strolled through the Sol a Sol. He admired the Sol family photos from the forties and fifties hanging from the walls. There was a picture of Ignacio and his wife as children playing in the dusty streets of Guadalajara. When he looked at them now, smiling as broadly at each other as in the old, worn picture, Sharky knew they were a couple meant for each other.

"Heee!"

The laughing screech of the four-year-old girl, Ignacio's niece, Yasmin, jerked Sharky from his reverie. Grinning broadly, she stood on a stool gazing down into the restaurant's viewing glass, added a few years earlier to offer visitors a look at the tidal waters beneath the Pier. Essentially a novelty item for kids and undiscriminating tourists, the viewing glass held her in rapt attention.

"Heee! Look, Mommy, look," said little Yasmin. A couple of young boys jostled to be next in line as the noise grew and Yasmin's mother tried harder and harder to ignore them.

Sharky went outside to the back porch to be alone. He looked out over the water and couldn't help but wonder whether his tiger shark nemesis was still out there somewhere.

"Aaghh!"

That was no child's scream of joy.

"Aaghh! Help!" shouted Yasmin's mother. "Help!"

Ignacio Sol found Sharky already rushing in the back door. "Come quickly, come quickly," he said, and led him to the viewing glass.

Every child in the place now wailed in fear and confusion. Yasmin screamed as her mother whisked her away.

When Sharky looked through the glass to the water below, he understood why the children had laughed at first and the adults had immediately freaked out. Tied spread-eagle between four pilings beneath the Pier was a man, dressed in a clown suit, bobbing in the low tide's gentle surf, staring wide-eyed back at him. The clown's red and white face paint accentuated an already-grotesque grin and only partially obscured the fact that his face was decomposing into bluish-brown patches. *The kids must have believed it was all part of the act.*

But this clown was no laughing matter.

4

Day after day, at all hours, he would drift on his long board studying ocean currents. He intently watched how different wave types broke under the Pier. He studied wind conditions and their effects. Not usually the most interested student, he took an extension course in meteorology at the local community college. He ran hills, and performed endless push-ups, pull-ups and stomach crunches, readying his body. When his friends finally caught on to his plans, they thought he was even more crazy than usual.

December 29, 2004

The cool morning breeze caressed Razz' face as he reveled in his Christmas memories from days earlier. Sitting in a white wicker chair on his back porch, he wore the heather-green sweater his mother had knitted for him. The new lamb's wool and his mother's loving handiwork made him oblivious to the cold front that lingered over Southern California.

"I thought you'd be surfing," said Sarah, still in her nightgown, shivering at the open back door.

He smiled and shrugged; he was too content to explain. Sarah paused, and then closed the door against the cold, leaving Razz to his reveries.

Only moments later, when she brought him that morning's *Monitor*, his glow flickered. Richard Gold's beaming, ignorant, rich face greeted him from the front page, along with an announcement of his multi-million dollar purchase of the waterfront commercial land parcel.

I'll wipe that shitty grin from his face one day. Then he realized he didn't really care about Gold. No, what Razz wanted was to try on that same shit-eating grin, for it was the grin of a man who knew he was going to make a lot of money, not the grin of a man who knew he'd inherit it.

When he turned to the inside of the newspaper, his Christmas glow blew out for good. There, on page three, a photograph of a sickly-looking Sharky, stooped over next to the body of the dead clown, greeted him in black and white. Although, by now, he knew the details of the incident well, he didn't enjoy the reminder to add one more to the Pier's body count.

Sharky trembled as he extricated himself from his long-unwashed bed sheets and it wasn't due to cold or stench. The thermostat was always set at seventy-six degrees, his heater was blasting warm, dry air throughout his apartment, and he was used to the stench. He trembled because he couldn't stop thinking about the dead man, not because he'd had to cut the rotting, stinking corpse down from the pilings, but because of his memory of rocking helplessly in a tiny, tipsy skiff beneath the Pier where he had helped retrieve the body. He still felt as though he were rocking uncontrollably. Because he discovered the body, he'd had to venture into the water, despite his phobia. While a patrolman motored the small boat carefully between pilings, Sharky had clutched violently to its sides, trying to hold back a torrent of vomit that desperately wanted to release itself. Try as he might, the torrent eventually let loose when he was surprised by the rocking wake of a passing pleasure craft.

That day, after the police deposited the dead body into an emergency vehicle onshore, Sharky collapsed in the sand, unable to regain the use of his limbs for several minutes.

"Damn, you got it bad," Lieutenant Johnson had said.

He would have agreed, but he was shaking so much he couldn't control his face muscles enough to speak.

"This case is yours," Johnson had continued. "It will give you a chance to redeem yourself."

This time, had he been able, Sharky would have vehemently disagreed. With such an inauspicious beginning, the case didn't figure to bring him anything but more anguish.

Johnnie Johnson was in charge of the Pier substation and, therefore, was in charge of Sharky. Both were tough jobs. Although they had started at the academy together, Johnson had kept his nose clean and had risen to Lieutenant. Sharky, on the other hand, hung tenuously to his sergeant stripes due to repeated insubordination, suspected on-duty drinking, and an overall shitty attitude. After a recent infraction, he had been transferred to the substation only thirty feet above the Pacific Ocean, his worst nightmare. As further punishment, he was forced back onto a beat in his blues. The opportunity to be a detective again should have pleased him, but it didn't under these circumstances.

The police knew immediately who the dead man was. Everyone knew Wally. He had worked at the amusement park bringing smiles to little children's faces for years, ever since the new pier and park were built. Although he wasn't an official employee and he worked only for tip money, he had become a regular attraction at the park. A cross between Bozo and Ronald McDonald, Wally didn't have much of an act, but his good cheer, funny high voice, and lollipops made him a favorite with families. On good days, he could collect as much as three hundred dollars in cash, enough for him to afford an apartment at the Hempstead, a pricey complex that housed up-and-coming starlets, producers, and agents. Wally had even been cast in a few low-budget movies. But even that wasn't enough for someone to want him dead.

He'd been dead for four days when Sharky found him. Because of the holidays and slow tourist traffic, no one had thought it unusual that Wally hadn't been at the amusement park for a few days. Everyone who had noticed his absence figured he was spending time with family, although no one seemed to know him well enough to know whether he had any family.

Days later, Sharky had mostly recovered from his watery ordeal, although he did not again go into the surf. He knew that a concrete piling wouldn't yield incriminating fingerprints. There were no bits of clothing or blood and the rope used was generic enough to have come from any hardware store in America. Divers had found nothing, but Sharky knew that, had anything been inadvertently dropped into the water, it could have washed away to anywhere by now.

He also knew that Wally had been suffocated on land. He hadn't drowned. And because there were no bruises on his body, it was clear he hadn't put up much of a struggle. *But why had someone gone to so much trouble to tie an already-dead clown spread-eagle under the Sol a Sol?*

Interviews with Ignacio Sol yielded nothing. Sol had no enemies that he knew of, but it was curious to Sharky that the two recent Pier incidents, the anthrax scare and the discovery of Wally's body, had both taken place near the Sol a Sol. Each event could only be interpreted as being bad for business.

Sharky had dismissed it when Sol told him that his nephew, Julio, had offered to buy the restaurant only weeks before for a generous sum of money. Julio had worked his way up the restaurant food chain to become day manager and Sol considered him a trusted employee. But Sol had made it clear he wouldn't sell for any price, so Julio had not brought it up again. Sharky figured that Julio wouldn't have any reason to hurt the Sol a Sol's business, but did question how, on his modest salary, he could finance such a transaction. With no good explanation forthcoming, he decided he'd search for his clues elsewhere.

"Hey, Sharky," yelled Razz from across the room when he saw him enter the Surf's Up.

Sharky cringed, and then forced a half-hearted wave as Razz walked toward him.

"You're coming up in the world. I thought you only ate greasy Mexican food."

As a rule, Sharky did like greasy Mexican food, but he wasn't there for the food or ambiance.

"Bring over a couple menus, please," Razz said to Tom.

Razz seemed extra friendly today and it made Sharky suspicious.

"The Mako steak is especially good," said Razz before catching himself, "uh, but the burgers are always the best in town."

"Burger, burnt. And a Coke."

"Two burgers, medium-rare and well, and two Cokes," Razz said just as Tom got there with menus. A prompt about-face and Tom was off with their order.

"So, what's up, Jerry? You finally understand this is the only place on the Pier to eat?"

"I just wanted to ask you some questions about the recent Sol a Sol incident."

"Christ, you guys have already tortured me with questions. What the fuck would I know about a dead clown?"

Tom brought the Cokes and then disappeared, rightly sensing this meeting wasn't going to be a pleasant dining experience for anyone.

"Tell me about anthrax," said Sharky.

"What about it?"

"You weren't worried that day. You acted as if you knew it was a hoax."

"Any asshole, even you, had to know it was a hoax."

"Actually, I didn't know."

"Then you're more stupid than you look." Had he been guilty of something, Razz might have been more diplomatic, but having suffered through Sharky's insinuations before, he had very little cool left to lose.

"Where were you Christmas morning from two to four a.m.?"

"Fuck you."

"Where were you?"

"You know where I was. I was at home, sleeping with my wife. You guys already asked her."

"And she admitted that sometimes you slept in the living room before going surfing early in the morning. Hmm, surfing," he said, scratching his chin in his best Columbo impersonation. "Anyone tying Wally to those pilings would have to be pretty comfortable on the water, wouldn't he?"

"What are you trying to say, Sharky? You want me to break your fucking face now or after I shove your burger down your skinny, fucking pencil neck?"

Sharky trusted this Razz much more than the nice Razz. "I'm just wondering who would profit more from the Sol a Sol going under than you."

"Who? Anyone, except fucking stomach doctors. I don't own this place."

"But you've been trying to raise profits. You'll make more money if the restaurant does better, right?

"I don't know. Ask Paul."

"I already have."

"Listen, you stupid fuck—"

Tom set down their plates with a thud, and then hightailed back to the kitchen.

"—just because you're looking like an asshole and you don't have a clue about who killed Wally, don't come in here and harass me. Excuse me; I'm going to go find some better ambiance, maybe out by the trash cans. Your meal's on the house. Make sure you choke on it."

As Sharky watched Razz storm off, he knew Razz would have nothing to do with either an anthrax scare or murder. He just wasn't that kind of guy. But Razz was right, Sharky was starting to look like an asshole, and he had to do something about it. Quick.

Razz tore into his burger like it was Sharky's calf and he was a five-foot tiger shark. *That asshole! How the hell could he consider me a suspect?* After several bites of burger and various, vivid mutilation fantasies, he began to calm down. *I guess he's only doing his job. I just wish he'd do it somewhere else.*

He put his feet up on his ten-dollar Salvation Army desk and looked around his office. Situated above the restaurant, it was a sanctuary of sorts, but Good Housekeeping's Seal of Approval would not be forthcoming any time soon. Overwhelmed by boxes of Styrofoam cups, paper towels, and rolls of tissue paper, the office was a decorator's nightmare and a tinderbox. Only because of timely warnings from friends at the fire department had they ever passed a fire inspection.

The office was more cramped than usual, because New Year's Eve was two nights away. It was always the biggest, most profitable night of the year. Like many restaurants in town, they would exact an obscenely large cover charge from patrons in exchange for live entertainment, a few party favors, and a cheap midnight toast. With dinner and drinks, the Surf's Up would take in about eighty dollars per head compared to about twelve on normal nights. And the place would be packed. Over a hundred people had already reserved tickets and he expected a hundred or more walk-ins.

He didn't need Sharky or anyone else distracting him from last-minute preparations.

"Hey, there's Sherlock Holmes himself," said Robert Donati, a knuckle-dragging Neanderthal who happened to be a fellow sergeant, when Sharky entered the Pier substation. "Finding any clues at the doughnut shop?"

"How about from one of your 'girlfriends?'" mocked another detective.

"At least, I didn't get my stripes because of my daddy," said Sharky.

Donati forced a laugh, but didn't think it was at all funny. "But I'm only thirty-five, not fifty, and we all know you'll lose your stripes. It's just a matter of time."

Fists and teeth clenched, Sharky moved toward him.

"Sergeant Sampson," intoned Lieutenant Johnson, standing in his office doorway. "There's someone here to see you."

Sharky hesitated, and then turned away as the men burst into laughter. *I'll shut those fuckers up one day. And I'm only forty-four, you stupid pricks!* "Who the hell needs me?" he asked as he stormed into the office.

"Close the door," said Chief Wilson, seated behind Johnson's desk. Johnson stood at his side.

Still angry, Sharky closed the door harder than he'd intended, rattling the walls and the Chief's nerves.

"Hey! Cut the shit, Sergeant. If you can't take the pressure, get out of the steam cooker."

Steam this, you fucking moron. "Sure, Chief, sorry. What do you want?"

"The mayor would like to know the progress on our little murder investigation. I didn't have much to tell him, so why don't you enlighten me?"

"We've talked to everyone that was at the Pier that day, everyone who works at the Pier, everyone who's worked at the Pier in the last year, and everyone in the victim's apartment building. I've pretty much talked to everyone. No one knows anything, saw anything, or has any idea why anyone would want to kill poor, sweet Wally."

Missing Sharky's dripping sarcasm, the Chief responded the only way he knew how, with the obvious. "Well, someone's got to know something!"

"Yes, Chief, I'm working on it."

"Lieutenant Johnson went to bat for you on this one. You can walk a beat until your legs fall off, for all I care. So, I suggest you know something very soon!"

"Yes, Chief."

"Humph, so what do I tell the mayor?"

"Tell him ..." Sharky considered an anatomically impossible task for the mayor to try, but a look from Johnson convinced him to hold back stating it. "... Tell him I'm working on it."

Closing the door quietly behind him, Sharky wondered what had just happened. Normally, in a situation like that, he would tell the Chief to go fuck himself, and then tell the Chief to tell the same to the mayor, but today he felt too exhausted to bother. He wondered if he was coming down with something.

When Razz returned to the restaurant floor, after thrice counting out his inventory of sixty-two bottles of Freixenet Cordon Negro, he was surprised to find Lotta standing over the reservation book.

"I just added a reservation for twenty. It looks like Friday will be a big night." She sashayed out, looking back coyly.

The idea of more customers partially assuaged his annoyance with her until he looked at the reservation book. There, at the end of the list, Razz saw Louis Marcayda's name. He ran out only to see Lotta's Ford Explorer pulling away. As if to rub salt in his already-oozing open wound, she honked a friendly goodbye.

Lotta could have persuaded Louis and his friends to go elsewhere. She knew he didn't want them there. The Surf's Up would make a lot of money in two nights, but Razz couldn't help wondering—*what will be the cost?*

Going back inside, he decided he'd better check his inventory of Dom Pérignon 1996.

5

"That's suicide, dude."

"No one can do that, man."

"It's impossible, brah."

One friend would echo the next until Robbie couldn't listen anymore. He knew it could be done. He also knew, with one mistake, he could be one dead surf dude.

December 31, 2004

Louis Marcayda knotted his crimson Hermes tie, adjusted the lapel of his navy-blue Armani suit coat, and admired himself in the full-length mirror that covered one wall of his bedroom. Although standing only five-foot-six, Louis appeared much taller. Perhaps it was the aggrandizing effect of the mirror, but many would swear he was six-feet tall. Nice clothes and great power can add inches to a man.

Despite a taste for the finer things in life, Louis, his wife, Merice, and their children, Patrick and Melanie, lived modestly in a four-bedroom house on the outskirts of Boy's Town. Theirs was a typical, stucco California-suburban home on a house lot with barely enough lawn to require a mower. To the casual observer, it appeared that Louis lived like hundreds of thousands of other middle-class people in Los Angeles. He liked nothing better than to watch Patrick, now ten, play right field in his Little League games. Patrick wasn't particularly talented, but Louis had never gotten to play baseball growing up so he loved the fact that his son could. And he loved to go to seven-year-old Melanie's ballet dance recitals. She would never be a prima ballerina, but watching her spin happily round and round in her little pink leotard always made Louis smile.

"What do you think?"

He turned to see Merice standing in the bedroom doorway, her arms outstretched to show off her new, red-sequined, body-hugging, full-length gown.

Few women could wear the dress well enough that people wouldn't laugh, but no one would laugh at Merice. She was with Louis and she was a beauty. Hair in a bun with ringlets hanging provocatively from each side of her head and lightly bejeweled, she was striking. Backlighting from the hallway completed her spellbinding effect.

"It's beautiful. Take it off, baby," he said.

Merice laughed. "Not till later."

"You're the most beautiful woman in the world."

He had seen her twelve years earlier when she was walking home from high school. He had vowed that day to make her his wife. It took him a year of persuasion and expensive gifts to get permission from her parents to take her out. One year later, they were married and she was pregnant.

He brought her close and tried to kiss her.

"Come on, we'll be late," she said, giggling. She took his hand and led him down the hall.

He would have followed her anywhere.

Outside, everything was normal. A bulletproof Mercedes sat across the street. Behind its smoky windows, a well-armed security guard kept in constant radio contact with four other well-armed guards patrolling the Marcayda neighborhood, each in a bulletproof Mercedes. After his recent night in jail, Louis ordered an extra car stationed in the back alley for emergencies. He would trust only those closest to him. His cousin, Lotta, was one of those he trusted.

He and Lotta had grown up together, playing, along with several other young cousins, in the dirty streets of the poorest section of Tijuana, Mexico. Louis' father, Rudolpho, and Lotta's mother, Luz, were brother and sister, and when his father's naked dead body was found in a Tijuana sewer canal when Louis was six, Louis and his two sisters moved into a crumbling two-bedroom shack with Lotta's family.

Born only two months apart, he and Lotta became best friends. They attended school together, carried out pranks together, and often were expelled together. Although Louis was a small, shy kid, Lotta was well-developed early. She was beautiful and brazen enough for both of them. At thirteen, she would entice horny male tourists into alleyways where Louis, shaking with fear, laid in wait to surprise them. Armed only with a broom handle barely skinnier than he was, he would swing the stick with all his might, smacking the man on an Achilles tendon, and momentarily cripple him. That was as close as Louis would come to playing baseball. After grabbing the man's wallet, they'd run through Tijuana's back streets, ducking into one of their secret hiding spots to divvy up their financial home run. Through many similar triumphs, Louis lost his timidity and, through one of Lotta's many boyfriends, he was invited to join the Tijuana Boys.

Being a woman, Lotta couldn't technically join the gang, but she gained power in another way, working her way up the sexual hierarchy to date one of the most powerful men in the organization, Enrique Rios. A married man in his forties, Rios was smitten with the now sixteen-year-old Lotta. She used her power to help Louis who had by this time seen and done too much violence to turn back.

Because he was small, wiry, and fast, and knew all the shortcuts in town, he became one of the gang's best drug couriers. He could move drugs around Tijuana faster on foot than most could in a car or on a motorcycle. Later, he became supervisor for the Boys' in-town couriers, and then made some runs across the border himself. Barely one out of two runners made it safely to the U.S., which cost the Boys money, manpower, and a whole lot of drugs, so Louis determined to find a better way. He suggested they dig a tunnel under the border.

Though it wasn't the Chunnel in terms of an engineering feat, Louis supervised the building of a two hundred yard, four foot by four foot tunnel, ten feet underground, and he did much of the digging himself. They began by buying a run-down home near the border, using an elderly Mexican couple as a front. While several men worked around the property, painting exteriors and building a new roof, Louis and a few trusted men worked in the basement digging their way to America. More than once did DEA agents drop by without notice to check on the renovation's progress, but never did they suspect the kind of progress taking place in the basement.

Because of the effort and secrecy involved in building it, few people knew of the tunnel's existence, so Louis made the runs himself. Wearing protective gloves, kneepads, and a dust mask, he would crawl on all fours, dragging twenty to thirty pounds of pure heroin or cocaine over the dirt behind him. When his drug load increased to over fifty pounds, he fashioned himself a little wheelbarrow.

At twenty, Louis was moving up quickly in the Tijuana organization, but Lotta didn't like playing second fiddle to anyone, especially to her lover's wife. Divorcing a Catholic woman in Mexico was difficult enough, but divorcing the sister of a powerful priest would be suicide for Enrique. Lotta, the irresistible force, found herself up against an immovable object.

She pushed Enrique. And pushed some more. And when Enrique tired of being pushed back so tightly against the wall that he could barely breathe, he lashed out and cut Lotta loose. He gave word that no one in the gang could touch her for fear of reprisal. She was a pariah.

Louis was outraged, but he soon found that he was her only supporter and he wasn't as powerful as he'd thought. Lotta had burned far too many sexual bridges. Enrique quickly tired of Louis' threats and sent both he and Lotta packing.

Being ostracized from the Boys meant there was no turf in Tijuana that Louis could claim as his own, so, late one sunny afternoon, he visited the beautiful, newly-renovated border home, went down to the basement, and crawled into the two hundred yard long tunnel to make his way to America. And when a half moon rose in the October sky, he climbed out of the tunnel for the last time. But before he ran off, as a farewell gesture to the Tijuana Boys, he attached his worn gloves and kneepads to a dried tree limb and drove the limb into the ground at the tunnel's opening. The DEA couldn't miss it.

Although the Boys didn't appreciate his gesture or like losing their tunnel, with recent technological advances in radar avoidance, they had more efficient ways of smuggling drugs, so Louis wasn't hunted. And when he sent for Lotta two months later, they were more than glad to see her go.

It was different in America. Settling in East Los Angeles, Louis joined the Twenty-Niners, one of several small Mexican gangs in the area wrestling for power. He was no longer a gang golden boy and his physical skills in drug running weren't useful in the streets of LA, where everything was spread out and wide open. Besides, he was already wearing down. Running drugs was now a war of technology, logistics, and force. So he learned to kill. Being new in town and still looking like a high school kid, Louis could approach his victims unsuspected. He carried his gun in a backpack on a few hits, taking it out as if he were reaching for a school book, before he taught his victims their lesson for the day. Although rival gangs soon marked him for death, the Twenty-Niners protected him like gold.

Lotta's reputation preceded her arrival in California and she wiped her hands and thighs of the Tijuana Boys, the Twenty-Niners, and anyone remotely involved in gangs. She went to secretarial school, and then got a job as an executive's assistant. Just as her new life was taking shape, she was fired after refusing a sexual advance from her married boss. She felt it starting all over again. She could manage any one man, but a man in an organization, working under a higher power, was a different story. She needed to have some control. So she became a stripper.

That was how she got married. One night at her club, she met a tall, dark, handsome Italian prince named Vincent Gugliotta. Infatuated, inebriated, and much coked up, she suggested they fly to Vegas to celebrate their new friendship. After some rousing hotel sex and more cocaine, they decided to get married at a drive-through chapel. Back in LA three days later, when the thrill and the drugs had worn off, she told him to get lost.

Louis quickly got her out of the stripping business, because it was controlled by people who wanted to turn their dancers into junkies, hookers, or both. He didn't want her working in such a negative environment, so he helped her get a job in the restaurant business.

Lotta met Louis and Merice at the Surf's Up door. "Hi, sweetie." As tough as she was, she always softened when she saw her favorite cousin.

Louis hugged her. "Hey, baby."

Lotta turned to Merice. "You are one hot chiquita."

Merice liked Lotta, but wasn't totally comfortable with the closeness between her and Louis. "So are you. Happy New Year, Carlotta." They hugged.

Razz watched the proceedings from the far end of the restaurant. His belly churned as Lotta escorted her guests to the large corner table where their friends awaited.

"Hey, honey, want to dance?"

Razz turned to see his wife, lovely in a black Dior gown. She knew he didn't like to dance, but this time he surprised her. "Sure."

He took her in his arms, putting one hand just above her butt, and touched the skin of her open back. She felt good. They danced in a circle slowly, Razz bobbing from one foot to the other, almost on beat, much like an awkward eighth grader at his first junior high dance. Sarah didn't mind that Razz wasn't twinkle-toes, and when she felt his arousal next to her black satin, she cooed and pulled him closer.

His hard-on was an involuntary reflex, because Razz was only thinking of one thing. Try as he might, he couldn't help keeping an eye on Louis. But when

Lotta waved him over, he buried his head in his wife's hair and pretended not to notice. He wasn't ready to publicly acknowledge Louis' presence.

"Mmm, that's nice," Sarah said, as she nuzzled closer.

Capacity was one hundred and forty-three and there were at least two hundred mostly drunk people in the Surf's Up. Fire hazard be damned, Razz knew Paul would approve. Paul had stopped by earlier for dinner, but then had left to spend a quiet evening at home ushering in the New Year with Miss Scruffy.

It was now eleven-forty-five. Razz had avoided Louis all night, only once nodding an acknowledgement, despite repeated pleas from Lotta to go over and say hello. She told him that he was being rude and a bad host. He was and he intended to be, because he didn't want to encourage Louis. He was also scared.

The evening was coming off like clockwork. Everyone knew the routine, from Rick, the bartender, to Tom and the serving staff. But whenever Lotta approached him with some bit of business, he felt Sarah's gaze, or own his guilt, burn a hole through him.

"Are you going to toast with me at midnight? I want a big, wet, juicy kiss to bring in the New Year," Sarah said, already more than a little tipsy. His parents were staying home with the kids tonight, but Sarah didn't need a toast, she needed a cab.

He kissed her gently on the cheek, and then sat her in a chair. "I've got to go to work. I'll be back in a bit."

Her head bobbed in semi-acknowledgement.

He spoke to Rick at the bar, which began a flurry of activity. Razz, Lotta, and the staff toured the restaurant pouring cheap sparkling wine into thirsty plastic cups. Pouring with each hand, Razz was like a Freixenet ambassador, hurrying to get to everyone before midnight. He emptied his last bottle just as the New Year's countdown began. He looked up only to find he was where he had tried not to be all night—right next to Louis Marcayda's table.

"Ten, nine ..."

Lotta approached, smiling.

"... eight, seven ..."

Razz strained to see his wife far across the restaurant, as if seeking safe haven. "... six, five ..."

Louis stuck out his right hand.

"... four, three ..."

Razz looked over the top of the excited crowd. He saw Sarah leaning back, semi-comatose, in her chair. She would miss the New Year.

"... two, one ..."

Instinctively, Razz reached out. He and Louis shook hands as hands of clocks all around the West Coast struck midnight.

"... Happy New Year! Happy New Year!" Party favors flew into the air as kazoos sounded throughout the restaurant.

When Louis let go of Razz' hand, there were no dollar bills, but Razz could already feel strings attached. Having avoided Louis all night, he found himself surprised to be interested in finding out what those invisible strings might be.

"Happy New Year, Razz."

Lotta planted a big, wet, wonderful kiss on him and Razz' seed seemed to grow and grow. Whatever his fate would be, it was now sealed with a kiss.

Razz helped Sarah to a waiting taxi.

"I'm sorry, honey. Did I miss New Year's?"

"No, baby," he responded, helping her into the back seat.

"Did we kiss at midnight?"

He hesitated. "Of course, we did."

"I didn't mean to get so drunk. I don't know what happened."

"It's all right, honey. Are you going to be okay?"

It was only twelve-thirty, but the party was over for Sarah. She had sobered up just enough to feel ill, but Razz would be too busy cleaning up the party's aftermath to watch over her. He had already called his parents to warn them to have hot coffee and a cold shower ready.

"Uh-huh."

"See you when I get home." He kissed her, but she barely noticed.

As her cab moved away from the curb, Razz waved goodbye. He saw a limp, feeble wave in return, just before his wife's head sank helplessly into her seat to spend the cab ride in unconsciousness.

The remainder of the evening proceeded as New Year's Eve parties do at bars all across the country. There were hugs and kisses all around and more than a few business cards handed out. Although a couple of alcohol and testosterone-induced sword fights broke out, they were quickly subdued by a sober security staff. Fortunately, even at their most drunk and stupid, most men had enough sense not to draw swords against Louis or his friends.

When the band finished their last tune of the night, partygoers flowed outside to look for cabs already busy at hundreds of other celebrations in San Margarita. Finding little luck on the Pier, scores of drunks swayed their way up the connecting bridge toward Ocean Boulevard hoping to improve their chances of finding a sober ride home.

Had this been New York, the party would have just been starting, but this was California. Last call for alcohol was one-thirty and it came and went quietly as remaining customers sifted out. Louis and his friends were the last to leave. Razz had assiduously avoided them the rest of the evening, and as they rose to go, he ducked into the kitchen on some supposed business. From the safety of the fry griddle, he watched them exit out the back door to their waiting limousines.

The kitchen was spotless. His was a crack staff. Utensils hung on their designated hooks awaiting their next use. The grill was cleaner than those in most homes. The meat grinder sat in meticulously washed pieces on the counter, ready for reassembly the next day, when it would again create the freshest burgers this side of the Mississippi.

In the main room, the restaurant's worker ants sprang into action. Servers and bartenders counted their tips and prepared for business the next day. Tablecloths were pulled and replaced. Silverware was reset. The floor was mopped, the bar wiped down. Glasses were cleaned and alcohol restocked.

With the coast clear, Razz escaped upstairs to count the night's tally. He found that the Surf's Up had grossed sixteen thousand, four hundred and twenty-seven dollars. It was a very good night that would save an otherwise atrocious month.

Knock. Knock.

Razz turned toward the sound, and then reached into a desk drawer. The shiny black metal of a pistol's barrel extended from his shaking right hand. "Who is it?"

"It's me."

Lotta. That's just what I need, he thought. *Like I'm not already in enough trouble with Sarah.*

Relieved in one way, but nervous in another, he gently returned the pistol to its place and went to unlock the door. It swung open slowly and his heart raced when he saw Louis standing there. Lotta was right behind him.

"Hi" was all Razz could get out of his desert-dry mouth.

Louis entered his office like he owned it, like he entered every establishment. "I wanted to personally thank you for a wonderful evening. My wife and I enjoyed it very much."

"Y-you're welcome," Razz stuttered before regaining his composure. "I'm glad you and your friends could make it."

Razz was good, but Louis was better. Louis could read him like a book. He stood there, smiling, for what seemed to Razz an eternity, before speaking.

"I hope your wife will be okay."

Out of jealousy and protectiveness, he preferred that men not even notice his wife, but this was different. Louis was intentionally crossing a personal boundary.

"She'll be fine. Thank you. If you'll excuse me—"

"Lotta tells me you'd like to own this place."

Razz half-choked, somehow sensing that his response could alter the landscape of his life forever, but he wasn't sure in what way. He shrugged noncommittally.

"I'd like to help you buy it. You'd be in complete control. I'd be a silent partner only, but I could probably send a little business this way."

I bet he'd "send a little business this way".

"Lotta would be here to protect my interests, of course."

Smiling, baring her very sharp teeth, Lotta looked like a lioness inviting prey into her den for a pot-luck dinner.

"Why don't you just buy the place, kick me out, and have Lotta run it for you?"

"I considered that."

Razz felt like his heart stopped pumping. He didn't want to be involved with Louis in any way, but he didn't want to be pushed aside either. "I'll think about it," he said, amazing himself with his self-control.

Louis didn't blink. "I've been watching you. You know what you're doing. And you're hungry. You're the type of person I want to work with."

You mean the type of person you want to own. "I've already offered more than the place is worth. The owner doesn't want to sell."

Louis knew the details of Razz' offer and knew everything about Paul and the bar's history. He knew what the place grossed and what it lost to the dollar. And he didn't learn it all from Lotta, because even she didn't know what he knew. A man like Louis got more information from more sources than a man like Razz could imagine.

"You think about it."

He held out his hand and Razz reflexively rose from his chair to grasp it. A deal was cinched and Razz didn't even know it.

"I'll be in touch," Louis said, and then he and Lotta walked out.

If he just puts up the money and leaves me alone to run the place, maybe it could work. So what if a few gangbangers show up once in a while. They've got more class than many of the locals anyway and almost all of the tourists. Razz' mind whirled. Visions of grandeur, wealth, and ownership danced in his head.

"Anyone up there?" It was Rick.

Razz came crashing back to earth. "Yeah, it's me."

"I'm outta here. Everything's set for tomorrow. I'll lock up."

"Okay, thanks."

"Good night."

"Night."

Razz barely got the word above a whisper. He heard the back door close, as Rick left the Surf's Up. *I'm thinking of dancing with the Devil when I can't even dance.* He managed a weak, unsure laugh aimed directly at himself, before turning back to enjoy the large pile of money and credit card receipts that sat in front of him on his desk.

It was intoxicating.

6

A hundred large and very hard pilings were waiting to ensnare him and crush his brains out. If he misjudged a wave, he died. If he miscalculated the wind, he died. If he lost concentration, he died. And if he didn't die, he might wish he had, because he didn't want to suffer the humiliation of hundreds of "I told you so's" from an unforgiving surf crowd that would surely follow any defeat.

January 1, 2005

"Aaggh!" grunted Sharky, flapping his arms like a bird, except that he flapped them slowly and with fifteen pound weights in each hand. "Aaggh!" The pain was almost intolerable and he loved it.

Lateral raises, flies, and bench press. Skull-crushers, wrist curls and double crunches. Maybe twenty minutes on the recumbent bike. He'd work biceps, legs, and back tomorrow.

It was four a.m. on New Year's Day. Most Californians had long ago passed out, but Sharky was wired. He had welcomed in the New Year patrolling a relatively quiet Boys' Town. Although he'd stopped hiding from Louis, due to its futility, Sharky still sat lower in his seat when cruising through his territory. Unable to sleep after a nerve-racking shift, he was taking out his frustrations on his body and some innocent dumbbells.

"Aaggh! Shit!" he yelled as his dumbbells landed with a muffled thud on the rubber-matted floor. Screaming and dropping weights were not proper gym etiquette, but at this hour, there were few people to complain. Besides, Sharky didn't give a damn about etiquette. He felt his blood-pumped deltoid muscles and checked himself in the mirror, hoping for a miracle, but he was still only one hundred and fifty pounds, sopping wet.

Manny's Health Club never closed, open 365 days a year, 24 hours a day. It had been Manny's Delicatessen until one day thirty years ago when Manny's doctor told him he was overweight and should think about getting some regular exercise. So, he turned his deli into a health club. Because the deli was open 24/7, he decided those would be good hours for his new establishment. He didn't realize he was starting a trend for all-night gyms everywhere. Unfortunately, the exercise trend didn't reach Manny in time. He succumbed to a heart attack at the age of forty-two only days after his gym's opening, the victim of 260 pounds on a 5' 8" frame and way too many pastrami sandwiches.

Manny's was eclectic, to say the least, and was still run by Manny's now gray-haired widow, Laila. The floor plan hadn't changed since it was a deli except that they had added space from a bathhouse next door in an expansion several years ago. Instead of wide open spaces and endless walls of mirrors like most modern gyms, Manny's consisted of a multitude of surprising nooks and crannies, mostly tiny rooms filled with aging equipment, with little rhyme or reason to the layout.

At the most normal of business hours, Manny's attracted an odd assortment of characters in an odder assortment of moods and altered states. But four a.m. on New Year's Day was not the time for the mainstream. During daylight and early evening hours, when rich businessmen and lonely divorcees would shadow their ever-smiling personal trainers, searching for the Holy Grail of everlasting youth, it was a strange enough place. At this hour, it became surreal.

A guy and girl in their early twenties, reeking of marijuana and alcohol, dressed in punk street clothes, each with nose rings and spiked greenish-tinged hair, giggled through makeshift sets of shoulder shrugs. An overly-tanned bodybuilder, high on steroids, cursed at a mirror, as he psyched himself up for four hundred pound squats. Another man, in torn dirty sweats and ratty construction boots, held a heated discussion with two exactly similar dumbbells trying to determine which of the two he would honor with his use. Compared to these people, Sharky seemed downright normal.

He grunted his way through a third set of lateral raises, then immediately picked up a couple of twenty-fives for bent-arm chest flies. Lying on a flat bench, intent on his purpose, Sharky didn't notice three large, brown-skinned men walk in the front door. "Aaggh! Aaggh!"

His muscles burned and with little rest between sets, Sharky quickly finished three sets. Breathing heavily, his arms hanging numbly from his sides, he shuffled off to find a bench press.

Sounds of giggling and talking from his fellow gym denizens faded as Sharky maneuvered his way to a cubbyhole in the back. Lit only with one fluorescent bulb, the room probably hadn't changed much from its days as a private rendezvous spot for couples willing to spend ten dollars an hour for its use. A non-operational, tiled hot tub was covered over and used as a small stretching area.

Sharky added weights to a long bar readying for bench press. Thirty-fives on each side made seventy, plus the forty-five pounds of the bar made one hundred and fifteen. Twenty-five more on each side and it was up to one-sixty-five. He was near his maximum, but, because he felt hyped up, he decided to push it. A ten on each side made one-eighty-five, a lot of weight for a hundred and fifty pound man and ten more than he'd ever used before in sets. He massaged his chest, barely recovered from the chest flies, and then lay back on the bench. He grasped the bar and closed his eyes. His mind flashed uncontrollably to Wally, the smiling, dead clown strung up between Pier pilings. He saw the Sol a Sol in its every detail. He saw himself vomiting on the beach after cutting Wally free.

The images were unsettling and, as if to avoid more, he lifted the heavy bar from its cradle. His arms trembled under the weight and he was uncertain whether he could handle it. He lowered the bar, inches off his chest, and then strained to push it back to its starting position.

"One," he grunted before starting his next repetition.

"Two."

Sharky's voice echoed through the winding hallway as the three brown-skinned men approached his private cubby. They reached him just as he strained to finish his third repetition.

"Three—ugh!"

Suddenly, the barbell's one hundred and eighty-five pounds were resting squarely on Sharky's throat and a gym towel covered his face. One man on each side of the barbell held the weight firmly against his larynx, nearly crushing his windpipe.

"Aaggh," Sharky tried to scream, but he barely got it above a whisper. He flailed against the force of the weight, his arms and legs thrashing violently. Under the towel, his face went white from lack of oxygen and he gasped for the tiniest breaths of air.

"Tenga cuidado. Nadie se ríe de un payaso muerto."

Sharky's body relaxed, and his arms and legs went still. He knew struggling was useless.

Be careful. No one laughs at a dead clown. His English translation shot repeatedly through his brain.

On the verge of passing out, he barely noticed as the third man tied the towel tightly behind his head. He didn't see flashes of his life pass before his eyes, didn't see his soul rise above his body. But he did feel an enormous weight lift from his neck and land heavily on his chest. *Crack!* An excruciating pain shot through his torso as more than one rib gave way under the weight's pressure.

"Aaggh!"

At least he could breathe again, if only in sporadic gasps. And his breath was now the only one in the room. His supposed executioners hadn't been there to kill him, after all, but Sharky sort of wished they had. The pain was enormous, and now he didn't love it one tiny bit.

He rolled the barbell onto his stomach, then onto his legs, and his breathing began to normalize. The pain from the weight pressing deeply into his thighs was barely noticeable compared to the pain from his throat and cracked ribs.

Crash! Thud. The barbell rolled to a stop against the wall after Sharky had finally mustered the energy to push it off his legs. He reached for his throat to make sure it was still in one piece.

"Aaggh!"

A lightning bolt of pain shot through the left side of his chest as his pectoral muscles pulled his cracked seventh and eighth ribs away from their proper anatomical positions. Slowly lowering his left arm, he reached with his right hand to fumble with the towel still tied tightly around his head. After working the knot free, he struggled up to look in the mirror and saw the red indentation where the barbell had almost crushed his throat and his life. He knew he was lucky to be alive, but he sure didn't feel lucky.

By the time Razz had finished tallying the night's receipts, it was too late to bother going home. He expected great surf that morning and was determined to take advantage of it. Louis' late night visit had hyped him up so much he couldn't imagine sleeping anyway. Though he felt bad he wouldn't be home to check on Sarah, he was pretty sure that, in her alcohol-induced slumber, she wouldn't notice. He would make sure to get back in time to help nurse her hangover.

He walked outside. The normally frenetic Pier seemed as if it were resting, trying to recover from its own hangover due to the night's celebration. The only activity came from a lone sanitation worker hefting garbage pails of refuse into his truck and a swarm of seagulls hovering overhead waiting for leftovers. A few homeless men and women slept, huddled in makeshift, moveable box dwellings and filthy blankets. Though their presence was frowned upon at the Pier, the police substation was closed every day between two a.m. and sunrise, so they knew they could gather for a few hours of relative peace before being shooed away.

The Sol a Sol stood majestically at the end of the Pier. Drawn like a moth to a flame, Razz walked the Pier's length and admired for several minutes his rival and nemesis. It truly had a prime location. The view from its upper level was unparalleled in San Margarita, even by the high-rise hotels in town. Because of that view, Razz knew it would be impossible to ever really compete with the Sol a Sol, but last night's success gave him some hope that the Surf's Up could, at least, survive.

Even more encouraging were the five-foot swells he saw when he looked out over the water. For the next couple of hours, there would be no Louis, no Sol a Sol, no Surf's Up, and no hung over wife. There would be only him, a surfboard, and the ocean.

Sharky brought his 1992 Buick Skylark to a stop, its headlights trained on his apartment's front door. Everything looked normal. He turned off the car's ignition, then its lights. The sun was just beginning to appear, brightening the sky, but the neighborhood was not yet ready to awaken, still dormant on this first day of the year. He walked haltingly toward the door as if expecting a fatal ambush at every step. His ribs ached as he checked for trip wires, imagining he would be the victim of an assassin's bomb upon opening his door. He found nothing. He tried to peek through the front windows, but, as usual, he'd drawn his blinds before leaving for work the night before. He fumbled for his door key, started to insert it into the lock, and then decided he'd first better make one pass around the building.

His was a ground floor apartment in a small eight-unit building, two units stacked upon each other in a row of four. Each apartment had only one entrance with a window on either side in the front and two small, barred windows in the rear. Sharky definitely wanted to check the integrity of those bars.

He walked around the side of the building as the sun cast his shadow against the stucco wall. To an observer, it would appear he was being followed by some dark nemesis. Fortunately, an already-nervous Sharky didn't notice. He peeked around the back of the building, expecting the worst, but there was nothing. He took a few more halting steps to confirm that his rear windows were intact, their heavy metal bars still in place, and then he exhaled heavily.

"Aaggh!"

His injured ribs reminded him there were no sudden moves allowed, not even for breathing. He walked gingerly back to his door.

Inside, with the door locked and dead-bolted, Sharky carefully inspected the living room, bedroom, bathroom and kitchen. Everything looked to be as he'd left it. Relieved, he took a glass from the cupboard and filled it from the water faucet. As he raised the glass to his lips, his mind twisted again.

What if Louis lined my glasses with arsenic? What if the water supply is tainted? Sharky pondered these dark thoughts, and then quickly put the glass down.

He would eat and drink out from now on.

Razz struggled to lift the Harbour Cheater back to its exalted position over the front door of the Surf's Up. Although the restaurant's surfboard displays weren't intended for his private use, he sometimes borrowed a board rather than drive home for one of his and he always kept a wet suit in his car's trunk. His arms, exhausted from two hours of paddling, ached as he hurried to strap the board in place. It was almost eight-thirty. The Surf's Up would open for brunch at ten that day, so Lotta and a reduced day staff would be arriving any second. Normally closed on New Year's Day, Paul was squeezing the Surf's Up for revenue, figuring there would be enough Rose Bowl watchers and hair-of-the-dog drinkers to make it worthwhile.

The surfing had been great. Razz had gotten nine good runs in, falling only once when a wave broke earlier than expected, although more and more he chafed at fifteen-year-olds calling him "old man." Despite some body stiffness in the morning, he still felt young, but he also remembered when he was a teenage surf stud. At that time, anyone over twenty-two was considered ancient.

His musing was interrupted when Lotta's Explorer cruised past the front door on its way to the back parking lot. He almost stumbled off his perch, but after more straining, he finally got the Cheater safely in place. He hurried to lock the front door behind him. Lotta seemed to hesitate as she looked through the glass back door toward him and he quickly ducked away. He wasn't ready to face her or anyone remotely connected to Louis.

He ran toward where he'd parked his car, rounding the corner of the nearby carousel just as the Surf's Up front door opened and Lotta poked her head out. He was safe for a while longer.

When Razz arrived home, he was surprised to find his parents' car was gone. They had stayed overnight with the kids and he'd expected to see them before they left that morning. He now regretted his decision to surf, because his parents would be disappointed in him. They would have wanted him to be there for his wife, of course, not just to see them. And he knew he should have been. *It's New Year's Day, for God's sake, and I still chose surfing instead of taking care of my wife.* His guilt started to get the better of him, until he reminded himself that Sarah would understand. She always did. And he was home now to nurse her back to health, to make it up to her.

He opened the door and was again surprised. There were no screaming kids to be found.

"Caitlin. Ronnie," he half-whispered. He wondered if he'd missed something important and if everyone was all right. *Did someone have to go to the hospital? Sarah? Caitlin? Ronnie? Mom? Dad?* Starting to panic, he checked the answering machine, but there were no messages. He picked up the phone to call his parents, but just as he finished dialing, he noticed a note on the counter.

We've taken the kids to the park. Sarah's sleeping. Seems she's not feeling well. Hope you can make her feel better. We love you. Mom and Dad.

Razz smiled, greatly relieved. His parents were the best. Yes, he would try to make Sarah feel better. Although he hadn't slept in the last twenty-four hours, he would make a special breakfast for her. Eggs Benedict, fresh orange juice, and plenty of aspirin would help get her back on her feet. It was the least he could do.

Minutes later, when he opened the door to their bedroom, breakfast tray in hand, Sarah was snoring lightly. Her Dior gown lay in a heap at the foot of the bed. Her shoes, ten feet apart, led to the bathroom, undoubtedly her first stop on arriving home. He put the tray on a nightstand.

The side of Sarah's face lay smashed into the mattress, her mouth open, but she still looked beautiful. He knelt beside her.

She looked up at him, groggy and hung over, and smiled.

"Hi, beautiful," Razz said.

Smiling wider now, she grunted and dropped her head again to the mattress.

"I made you breakfast."

"Thanks. How was surfing?"

Most women would have lit angrily into their husbands for staying out all night, especially on New Year's Eve, but Sarah continually surprised him.

"It was great. Sorry, I wasn't here."

He went to kiss her cheek, wanting to let her sleep, but she met his lips with hers. She reached up and pulled him down on top of her. She knew what would make her feel better. He touched her soft, warm nakedness and she moaned in pleasure. Razz kicked off his flip-flops and worked his way under the bed sheets. Sarah tugged at his T-shirt and finally got it off with his assistance. She loved to feel him skin on skin, but that wasn't enough for her this morning. She reached for his surf baggies. They kissed passionately until Razz' lips fell to her neck, and then went to her right ear. More urgently now, she worked his shorts down to his ankles, and then Razz kicked them off the rest of the way. He kissed her breasts and was kissing his way down her abdomen when she stopped him. She brought him back up to her, grabbed his penis, and put it between her legs. Razz got the hint. He gently kissed her face and, when his mouth again met hers, he entered her. They moaned in unison.

Through an Advil-induced haze, Sharky had listened to neighboring apartment doors open and slam shut for hours. Whenever a car started, he felt the noise of the cranking engine grate through his bones like the sound of fingernails on a chalkboard. While the world awakened around him, he desperately wanted only to escape into sleep. He was exhausted, but, more importantly, if he was going to die, he didn't want to be conscious when it happened.

It was dark in his apartment, although, by that time, the sun outside was almost directly overhead. Just when he finally felt himself fading off, he heard a knock on his door. He sat up quickly and reached for his gun.

"Aaggh!"

His ribs pounded. There wasn't enough Advil in the world to protect him from this anguish. *Fuck this. I'll meet them head on, no closing my eyes.* Sharky wanted to live, but decided, if he did have to die, he'd make sure to take a bad guy or two with him.

Another knock. He moved very slowly toward the door.

"Jerry?"

He recognized the voice, accented and feminine. He'd forgotten he was going to start the New Year with a hooker day.

Outside, Rosie Rodriguez waited impatiently. Dressed in her usual fishnets and leather mini, she had places to go and people to do.

"What the fuck, Jerry, let me in," she said directly into the face of the cheap plywood door.

Sharky had already made his way to the window and was watching her through the blind. She was apparently alone, but he would take no chances. He pointed the gun at the door and reached for the handle. In one fluid, painful motion, he opened the door, pulled her inside, and covered her mouth with his left hand before she could scream.

Indignant, she bit him.

"Ow! Fuck! Aaggh!" First, his hand, then his ribs flashed pain signals.

"Put that toy away, Jerry," she said, pulling away from him.

Her toughness was disarming. He was more scared than she was. And he had the gun.

"Kinky stuff costs extra, you know. A gun will cost you two hundred."

Nursing his sore hand, Sharky kept the gun trained on her. "Who sent you?"

She looked at him, puzzled. "What?"

"Who sent you?"

"It's me, Rosie. Remember? We do this every week. Hello?" She took off her miniskirt. "Put your money on the table. Two hundred if you're going to play with the gun."

"Turn around."

"Hey, you know I don't do that shit. Get another girl for that stuff."

Sharky didn't want "that stuff," he just wanted to check her for anything that could be deemed hazardous to his health. He moved behind her and felt her up slowly, mainly because he couldn't do it any other way without causing himself extreme agony.

"Mmm, that's more like it, honey. Yeah, baby." She took off her blouse, revealing a purple Wonderbra that pinched her small breasts into impressiveness.

"What did Louis say?"

"Huh?"

"Louis. What did he say?"

"Louis-Fucking-Who?" she asked before realizing who he meant. "Louis? Why would Louis talk to me?"

"He didn't send you?"

"Honey, the only one who sends me anywhere is my dispatcher."

As if on cue, her cell phone vibrated in her pocketbook, startling him. In a case of runaway imagination, all he could think was that her phone was a remote controlled bomb, ready to explode upon being answered. She reached for it, but Sharky grabbed her wrist.

"Jerry, let me answer my fucking phone."

After a moment, he wisely decided she probably wouldn't be a kamikaze whore, so he let her go.

"Hola," she said into her Blackberry. Like good Boy Scouts, hookers always had to be prepared. "Uh-huh, okay. Yeah, I got it. Yeah, I got it already. Jesus." She clicked off the phone. "Come on, baby, I've only got twenty minutes. What do you want today? The usual or are we going to play with guns?"

When Razz awoke, he was alone in bed. The breakfast tray was gone, the Dior gown picked up from the floor, and Sarah's shoes from last night were now sitting in their proper place in the closet shoe rack. He wanted to roll over and return to his slumbers, but when he heard little Ronnie yelling outside his window, he knew he couldn't. If the kids were back, it had to be late. *Why didn't Sarah wake me?* In his laid back surfer dude way, he hated to have to rush, but he sprang out of bed, worried he would be late for work. He glanced at the alarm clock and saw it was only two o'clock. He had plenty of time.

Sarah was arranging a vase of flowers on the coffee table, her back to him, when Razz entered the living room. He snuck up on her and grabbed her around the waist.

"Oh!" she gasped. She turned and hugged him. "Hi, honey."

"Hey, baby. What are the kids doing back?"

"Your mom and dad had a couple things to do, so they brought them back early. It was nice of them to take them, though."

"Yeah, I'm just surprised, that's all. We usually have to fight to get our kids back."

"At least, it gave us some time together."

"Yeah." Razz smiled. "Hey, nice flowers. You shouldn't have."

"You weren't that good," she said, right back at him. "They were a gift. For me." She stuck out her tongue playfully.

"That was sweet of my parents."

"They're not from your parents. They're from the Marcaydas."

Razz heart skipped a beat and he hoped that Sarah wouldn't notice he was turning sheet-white. "The Marcaydas?"

"Yeah, the card said, 'we hope you're feeling better.' Did I meet them last night? Boy, I must have been drunk, because I don't recall meeting anyone named Marcayda."

Razz looked at the floral arrangement, a beautiful and, probably, well-intentioned gift, but it frightened him just the same.

"Yours is on the kitchen counter."

"Mine?"

"Yeah, it came with the flowers. It's heavy, so I didn't move it."

Razz imagined a UPS box of body parts from a collection of Louis' victims, arranged much like the begonias, tulips, and roses in Sarah's vase. He went to the kitchen and was relieved to see an innocuous-looking, cardboard box. He nudged it and the contents shifted ever so slightly. Razz could tell it was a case of some sort of alcohol. While Sarah admired her flowers in the next room, he carefully cut the packing tape that sealed the top, then slowly opened its corrugated flaps and looked inside.

For the briefest of moments, the box's contents made him smile, for there, staring back at him, were six bottles of Dom Pérignon 1996.

He reached for the card, lying on top of the bottles. It read, *Thank you for your wonderful hospitality. We look forward to seeing you and your wife again. Respectfully, Merice and Louis Marcayda.*

Whatever thought of smiling Razz had left him.

"Oh, just what we need," Sarah said when she saw the bottles. "That was nice, though. Who are these people anyway?"

"Just satisfied customers."

Sarah seemed satisfied, too. Had there been any further questions, they would have been interrupted by a screaming six-year-old named Caitlin.

"Mommy, Mommy, Wonnie's playing in the spwinkler."

Razz and Sarah hurried to the back door. When they reached the porch, they each burst into laughter. Ronnie was indeed playing in the sprinkler, getting absolutely soaked, and he loved every second of it. Toddling back and forth through the spray, slipping and skidding to a stop in the wet grass, he giggled gleefully.

"He's getting all wet," said Caitlin, concerned her parents weren't being strict enough with her younger brother.

"He's a chip off the old block. He loves the water," said Sarah.

"Yeah, I might have to get him a board soon."

Sarah arched her brows good-naturedly, but Caitlin was indignant with her parents' lax supervision.

"Daddy, Wonnie's doing bad."

But it felt good to little Ronnie. He was oblivious to the negotiations. He was still running, still falling, still skidding, and still squealing with laughter.

"He's just having fun, honey. He's all right."

Caitlin couldn't believe her ears. She wanted Ronnie to get yelled at and yelled at good, and she stormed off toward the door.

"Why don't we join him?"

That stopped her in her tiny tracks. She turned and looked at her father, still taken aback, but warming to the idea of getting wet and muddy and not getting in trouble for doing so. Her father was smiling and so was her mother. She looked at Ronnie, still giggling and oblivious.

"Okay."

She took her father's hand and ran down the lawn through the spray. Ronnie did a double-take, unsure he wanted to share his watery treasure, but, when he saw his father slip and fall on the grass, he joined his sister in laughing at him.

Pretending to be outraged, Razz chased his young children through the spray. Falling in mock clumsiness, he elicited gleeful squeals from his kids and even a few from his wife.

"Come on, Mommy," yelled Caitlin. "It's fwun."

"Yeah, come on, Mommy," said Razz, moving toward her.

Before she could make her escape into the house, he picked her up and carried her, kicking and screaming, to the sprinkler. Soon she was sopping wet and, amidst the watery festivities, she laughed almost as hard as the others.

Sharky sat up in bed, appalled with his life. Rosie stood near the bed, adjusting her fishnets, only slightly less appalled with hers. He gingerly reached for his wallet on the nightstand and took out a hundred dollar bill.

"I'm glad you finally put your gun away, sugar. I don't like guns," Rosie said as she took the hundred. "Hope you feel better." She kissed his forehead and went to the door.

"Tell Louis not to fuck with me."

She turned back. "Sure, I'll tell him, baby." She had no idea what he was talking about or any intention of speaking to Louis. "I'm the only one who'll "fuck" with you. Usual time Thursday?"

In spite of himself, he nodded. "Wait, how about Friday? Uh, give me an extra day to heal."

"Sure, hon," she said, checking her Blackberry before typing in the appointment. "I hope I wasn't too rough on you."

Sharky knew very well that Rosie would be his only comfort for the week. Despite his rib pain and disgust, he couldn't refuse. As she closed the door behind her and the room returned to its normal, dark, cave-like setting, Sharky, for the first time in too many years for him to remember, began to cry.

And cry. And cry.

7

Robbie, as he was known until that fateful day in November, did not tell his parents about his planned stunt. Although they indulged him at every turn, Tom and Sally McNeil wouldn't appreciate their only child risking his life and their only hope of getting to indulge grandchildren one day.

Monday, January 3, 2005

Had someone hit Razz in the stomach with a sledgehammer, he wouldn't have been in more pain. The room where he had grown up, where he had spent countless hours cutting out and hanging up pictures of his favorite surfers, where he had voraciously devoured scores of surf magazines, and where he had literally worn out phonograph records by listening over and over to the likes of The Beach Boys and Dick Dale, was empty. Only rectangular splotches of white, sheltered for years behind his pictures of Duke Kahanamoku, Hap Jacobs, and Mickey Munoz, broke up the drab dinginess of the long-neglected walls. Deep indentations in the dusty gray carpet created by bedposts unmoved for decades added testimony to the room's timelessness. His parents had kept the room exactly as it had been in Razz' youth, at least, until recently when they were so overrun by Sally McNeil's collection of knickknacks that they had grudgingly used part of the room for storage. Now everything was gone.

Razz didn't bother to try to blink back the tears that rolled freely down each cheek.

"I'm sorry, dear, we didn't have a choice. I've saved all your things for you though."

"W-why d-didn't you tell me?" he sputtered.

"We didn't want to worry you, dear. You have enough to think about. We'll be fine. We'll stay at Norma and Fred's for a few weeks till we can find a place we can afford."

"No, you'll stay with us."

"Honey, you don't have room. Norma and Fred have a guest house out back. We're putting our things in storage for now. Besides, Fred and your father have been best friends for years. He wants to help."

Well, so do I! You've given me everything! The words screamed through Razz' brain, but he didn't verbalize them. He knew his mother was right; she always was and always would be. He didn't have enough space at his home for his parents, the people who would and did do anything for him. He felt like he didn't have enough of anything for his family and it gnawed at him.

The dull humming of the moving van outside echoed in his brain. The McNeils were the first tenants to move, but soon everyone in the building would be displaced. The twenty-unit apartment building had been sold and was being vacated to make way for a condominium conversion. Each tenant would receive five thousand dollars and the use of a moving van for leaving the premises.

A lousy five thousand dollars apiece. Five thousand dollars for a home of over forty years. Five thousand dollars for a lifetime of memories.

Razz' eyes stung, and he hyperventilated like a frustrated child. "Wh-why didn't you talk to a lawyer? Th-they can't just, just kick you out."

"Oh, honey, we're too old to fight. If they want to make some money on their building, who are we to stop them? It's better if we just find another place."

He tried mightily to calm his breathing. "I wish you would have said something. I might have been able to help. Sarah's father is a real estate guy. He could have helped."

"Robbie," she said and Razz lost whatever emotional control he had left. She hugged him. "We'll be all right, dear."

She said it with such conviction that he almost believed her, but her eyes gave away her deep-seated sadness.

"Well, that's it."

Razz turned when he heard his father's voice.

"Everything's on the truck. Uh, your stuff's in the car, son."

His father stood before him, only slightly hunched over despite his nearly fifty years of hard labor at the machine shop. He had just loaded a moving van of the family's belongings practically by himself. His vitality was amazing.

Compared to the blubbering Razz, his parents seemed barely fazed by this life-changing event. They had known for weeks of their impending move, but they "didn't want to worry" him. They hadn't mentioned it during the happy hours they'd spent together at Christmas. Now Razz knew why they'd brought the kids home early on New Year's Day. They had needed to pack.

He marveled at them. They had been through so much together that he guessed they could face anything with the same astonishing equanimity. They still had each other, so any problems paled in comparison to that joy and their memories. Razz thought his myriad problems should pale similarly, but, today, that offered him no solace or equanimity.

"Come on, lad; help your old man unload this stuff. We've got storage over on Sixteenth Street."

With that, Razz wiped his eyes, hugged his mother and said "I love you," did the same to his father, and then walked shakily out of his childhood room for the last time.

Razz got up early the next day, Tuesday morning, not to go surfing, but because he'd been awake most of the night thinking about his parents. They had moved their precious belongings into storage along with most of his. Although he had room for his things at his home, he couldn't yet bear to have those memories staring at him full-time.

The first Tuesday of every month was inventory day at the Surf's Up. It was the one day of the month he paid for parking. He would arrive at eight a.m. along with his management staff and for two hours, he, Lotta, Rick, and Carlos, the head chef, would make sure the restaurant was only losing money and not supplies as well. Although Lotta was accustomed to coming in early, the rest hated inventory day. But it was part of the job.

"Seventeen, eighteen, nineteen, twenty," Razz said almost inaudibly, and then he checked his list for how many boxes of napkins there were supposed to be. Place mats, cartons of ketchup bottles, tablecloths, everything had to be counted. While Rick counted bottles of booze and Carlos counted frozen chicken breasts, Lotta confirmed their numbers. Because of the Surf's Up's lack of profits, Paul was convinced someone was stealing him blind, so he and Miss Scruffy usually joined in these monthly festivities, but they were nowhere to be seen today. *Thank God, as if taking inventory isn't unpleasant enough without having a smelly mutt hanging around.*

Everything added up, allowing for the usual shrinkage and waste. Rick mumbled something under his breath before he left, heading home to sleep some more before having to return for his regular shift that night. Lotta went downstairs to keep the clientele happy and the morning wait staff from rebelling. Carlos sent a five-pound slab of bacon down the dumbwaiter to the kitchen for the morning chef's use. Because of tight kitchen quarters, the large freezers were upstairs, so most of the food and supplies had to be transported via an ancient dumbwaiter system.

"My prep cook quit yesterday. I'm bringing in someone new. You want to meet him first?" said Carlos.

"Who is it?"

"Felipe Gomez. I worked with him at Hotel Americana. He knows his stuff."

"Just have him come in early to fill out a W-9." Razz had complete faith in Carlos' judgment. Carlos had worked at the Surf's Up for three years; he was the backbone of the kitchen staff. If this guy, Felipe, was good enough for him, he was good enough for Razz. Besides, he would be working directly for Carlos anyway.

"Okay, see you tonight," said Carlos as he walked downstairs.

Razz sat back in his chair. Moving his parents yesterday had been especially trying for him and inventory was never much fun. Now the worst seemed over, and with his parents somewhat comfortably ensconced at Fred and Norma's, he thought maybe he could enjoy, at least for a moment, the fact that it was a brand new year. *I just hope it's better than the last one.*

Razz hurried to the parking lot. He had just enough time to go home, catch a nap, play with his kids, and get back for his shift at four. He slid his key into the driver's door of his Mustang convertible, but something caught his eye, making him pause. He removed the key and walked cautiously toward a dark figure lurking in the alleyway between the Surf's Up and the adjacent carousel. Razz didn't like vagrants hanging around his place. But as he neared the man, half-hidden among the shadows, he realized it wasn't a vagrant at all.

"Hey, Sergeant."

Caught off guard, Sharky turned too quickly and grunted in pain.

"You okay? What's up, man? Looking for dangerous criminals here in the alley?" Razz soon realized it wasn't the time to joke around, because Sharky was a man on the edge.

Damned if he would willingly show it though. "Oh, hi, Razz," he said, doing his best imitation of cool. "I'm stuck on Pier duty today."

The fact was that Sharky had demanded Pier duty. After the police raid and his scare at the gym, he figured the further away from Boys' Town the better.

"You want some lunch? I'm heading home, but I'll have Lotta set you up."

Sharky looked at him dully. He had to hand it to Razz. Despite their differences, maybe he wasn't such a bad guy.

"No, thanks, I've got to get up to Ocean to patrol for a while. Thanks," he said before walking away.

"How about a ride? I'm going that way."

Sharky stopped abruptly. Although he was supposed to be on foot patrol today, he knew he'd feel safer riding in a car, surrounded by steel walls, than walking up the long, wide-open connecting bridge to Ocean Boulevard.

"Sure, thanks."

It was about a quarter of a mile, three minutes at most, to Ocean, but they were some of the most awkward three minutes Razz ever experienced. He could tell Sharky had way too much on his mind.

"Oh, hey, Happy New Year," Razz said, trying to lighten the mood.

Something told him it was the wrong thing to say, because Sharky reached over and opened his door on the moving Mustang. They were only halfway up the connecting bridge.

"I'll get out here."

"Whoa, I can't stop here. There are cars behind me. Are you on something, man? Hey, to each his own, but you should probably wait till after work. I mean, isn't that how you got in trouble in the first place? Relax; I'll drop you off at Ocean."

Sharky clicked shut his door and settled back in his seat, still wondering why Razz was being so nice to him. His imagination danced a paranoid jig as they neared Ocean Boulevard.

"What the fuck?" said Razz.

Off to his left, amidst a hundred or so onlookers, photographers, and reporters, stood Richard Gold and Mayor Hidalgo. Both men smiled broadly for the cameras. Next to them was Henry Banes, San Margarita Savings Bank's president. Gold and Hidalgo shared a shovel, readying to make a ceremonious dip into Razz' once-treasured, seven acres of virginal, ocean-view commercial heaven.

Razz stopped the car abruptly, no longer caring about traffic, and got out. The line of cars behind them furiously honked their disapproval.

Sharky's personal mind jig hesitated just long enough for his policeman instincts to take over. He waved a few vehicles around the Mustang, and then put on its hazard lights.

Hidalgo's voice became clearer as Razz approached.

"And with this symbolic first shovel full of earth, we begin the foundation for a better San Margarita. The new Gold Shore Hotel and Plaza, rising atop this gorgeous vista, will herald a new and better San Margarita, bringing jobs, attracting tourists, and increasing tax revenues to our fair city, and will do so in an environmentally-friendly and responsible manner. Everyone will be very proud to be associated with this wonderful new project."

Hidalgo, Banes and Gold raised each other's hand in victory and Razz almost vomited.

"Here are your keys."

Razz turned to see Sharky holding out his car keys. His car blinked innocently in the distance. He took the keys and turned back toward the gathering, but Gold and the mayor were already being hustled to a waiting car by several burly, black-clad bodyguards.

"Hey!"

Razz fought his way wildly through the crowd. Sharky chased after him, unsure of his intentions.

"Hey! Hey!" cried Razz.

The bodyguards turned as one toward the voice, prepared for anything. The mayor was hustled into the limo, but Gold hesitated, not quite recognizing his son-in-law. Two guards intercepted Razz, blocking his path. He attempted to move around them, but his efforts yielded nothing, other than to piss them off.

"Hey, Richard!"

The two men put him into an agonizing arm lock and carried him away from the limo, before pile driving him into the ground.

"Aaggh!"

They were about to beat him into the next county, but two things stopped them. Sharky pulled his gun, training it on the right temple of the bigger of the very big men, and Richard Gold worked his way over to them, finally recognizing Razz' voice. This was not the photo opportunity anyone had in mind, but the cameras were definitely popping.

"Let him go. Now," said Sharky.

"It's all right. Leave him alone. I know him," said Gold.

The guards backed off. Sharky hid his gun and beat a hasty retreat from the cameras and microphones being shoved toward him. Razz raised his face from the dirt and spit out some gravel and blades of grass.

"Robert, what the hell do you think you're doing?"

Razz looked up at his mega-wealthy father-in-law, nattily dressed, perfectly manicured, and wondered the same thing himself. He rose cautiously, not wanting to incite another near-riot.

"I wanted to ask you something."

"Robert, we've already talked about this prop—"

"No, it's not that."

Gold took him aside, waving off the bodyguards, while Sharky attempted to avoid the crowd.

"What is it, Robert? I'm in a bit of a hurry."

"My parents got kicked out of their home of forty years. I was wondering if there was anything that anybody could do."

Gold actually looked concerned and it surprised Razz. "I'm sorry to hear that," he said. "What building?"

"515 Enterra."

"Hmm, the condo conversion," replied Gold, understanding the situation immediately only by knowing the address. "Have they moved out yet?"

"Yesterday."

"Did they sign papers?"

"Uh-huh."

"So, they got their five thousand."

Razz didn't know how he knew so much, but he understood why he could never compete with guys like Gold. The playing field was tilted forty-five degrees in their favor. Razz would continually be running uphill, upwind, while they coasted. He nodded.

"I'm sorry, there's nothing I can do if they're already out of the building and they've signed an agreement. They might have been able to fight it or to hold out for more money, but now that they're out, that's it," said Gold, confirming what Razz knew, but didn't want to admit.

"Would you have any apartments available, like a two-bedroom, maybe around a thousand bucks?"

Whatever concern Gold may have had left him. Now they were talking about money. Besides, he didn't peddle in lowbrow, thousand dollar two-bedroom apartments.

"Call my leasing manager. Maybe she can help you out," he said, blowing Razz off. He moved toward the waiting limo.

"I'm asking for your help. I'm sorry about Christmas, about how I acted. Real estate is your business; I understand that. I was kidding myself thinking I could help you or compete with you, but I need your help now, for my parents.

"Robert, all my apartment buildings are owned by partnerships. I'm just the managing partner. Besides, one-bedrooms start around two thousand dollars; two-bedrooms run thirty-two hundred and more. I can't self-deal, rent for under market, even to family. I'd get sued for fraud. Now, if you want to make up the difference, I could probably find a nice place for them. There are a couple openings at the Hempstead."

Razz didn't have the heart to tell him he could barely subsidize a thousand-dollar apartment. His parents had rented their long-time residence for only five-fifty a month and couldn't afford much more. Now, with the dissolution of the town's rent-control laws, whenever a tenant moved from an apartment, the rent to a new tenant could be immediately raised to market price. He couldn't afford to help his parents with two- or three-thousand dollars a month, but he also couldn't bear to see them have to leave San Margarita.

"Robert, uh, I'm keeping the mayor waiting."

Indeed, the mayor was gesticulating from the rear seat of the limousine, trying to get Gold's attention, his face contorted in some sort of inexplicable anguish. Whatever his distress, it was enough for Gold. He hurried to the limo, climbed in beside the mayor, and they were off in a flash. The two hulking security men followed them in a second car, leaving Sharky and Razz to dodge cameras and reporters' questions.

"What was your conflict with Mr. Gold?" one reporter asked Razz.

"Is it police policy to draw a gun amidst a crowd of people? What if it had gone off by accident?" another asked of Sharky.

Had he been alone with the reporter, Sharky would have bloodied him then and there, but, with cameras still flashing, he resisted the urge. He walked away, but the reporter followed, badgering him.

"Is that police procedure, Officer Sampson? Is that what you call detective work? I thought you were famous for solving murders, and they've got you walking a beat now?"

Sharky turned back to the man, but Razz grabbed him before he could do anything he'd regret and dragged him toward the car. When they got there, the hazard lights were still flashing and there was a present on the windshield. It was a parking ticket for sixty-eight bucks.

They closed their car doors and the outside world seemed to dissolve away. The reporters and photographers dispersed, already moving on to their next story.

"Sorry to hear about your parents."

"Thanks. You heard."

"Bits and pieces. Gold must be in a real hurry to re-rent Wally's apartment."

"Huh?"

"Wally, the clown guy, he lived at the Hempstead."

Razz looked at him disbelievingly. "Man, that guy will do anything for money. That's just where I'd want my parents, in an apartment where a guy just got murdered."

"What did you say?"

"I don't know. What do you mean?"

"Why did you say Wally was murdered in his apartment?"

"Oh, Jesus, you told me he was dead before he was strapped up under the Pier. Don't even think of accusing me again, or I swear …"

Sharky wasn't listening. "Come on. It's right up here."

Razz wasn't sure what was "right up here", but he started the car and pulled out onto Ocean Boulevard anyway.

"Ocean and Arondale," said Sharky.

That Razz forgot to turn off his flashing hazard lights was somehow appropriate, because he was convinced his life was becoming more and more hazardous every moment.

8

Almost eleven months after his epiphany, one early morning before class during his senior year of high school, Robbie paddled out into San Margarita Bay. There wasn't a cloud in the boring, light-blue sky, and the temperature was already about sixty-five degrees when the sun peaked over the horizon. The water was only sixty degrees, but he was used to it. He'd made sure to wear his lightweight shorty today, so he would have his highest maneuverability.

As the Hempstead's janitor walked down the long hallway, his full key chain jangled fitfully. His hand trembled as he slid his master key into the door of apartment 703. The man had good reason to be nervous, because Sharky had just threatened to send his ass back to Guatemala for a green card violation, if he didn't let him into Wally's old apartment.

"Por favor, señor, no diga. Por favor, no diga," the man pleaded.

No, Sharky wouldn't tell, but he didn't bother to reassure him. The door swung open and he walked through.

"Fuck!"

He dragged Razz in behind him, leaving the janitor alone in the hall to ponder his upcoming living situation and a potential call from the INS.

"What's up? What's wrong?"

"Someone painted the fucking walls and replaced the carpet. They weren't supposed to do that shit for another week."

Indeed, the apartment looked brand new. Everything had been replaced: carpet, cupboards, light fixtures, dishwasher, stove, and refrigerator.

"I guess they are in a hurry to re-rent," said Razz. His explanation didn't make either of them feel the least bit better.

Although the police had already checked Wally's apartment for evidence several times, something in particular had bothered Sharky. They'd discovered no clues, no strange fingerprints. In fact, they'd found very few of Wally's own fingerprints. Sharky had wanted to check the place again, but he would find nothing of use now.

"Yeah, the place looks whitewashed clean," said Razz, more clairvoyant than he could imagine.

Sharky stared at him.

"What now?"

"Whitewashed clean," Sharky repeated. "That's it."

"Okay. What's it?"

"That's why there were no fingerprints, they'd been wiped clean. Someone had been here that didn't want us to know he, or she, was here."

"Makes sense. So what? I doubt any murderer would want to leave prints."

"But they wouldn't wipe everything down unless they thought they might have touched something before. So, the killer was someone who'd been here before, probably someone who knew Wally well. Now we just have to find out who. I bet Wally was killed right here."

Razz was already squeamish about being in a dead man's apartment, but the thought of someone being killed right where he stood churned his stomach like a washing machine. No, his parents would not live in this apartment even if Gold gave it to them.

"Yeah, okay, maybe, but 'we' don't have to find out anything; you have to find out. I'm just glad you're finally convinced it wasn't me. See you."

He headed for the door, but Sharky wasn't about to play nursemaid. He'd already made his way to the master bedroom.

Razz stopped. He wanted desperately to go to his car, drive off, and leave Sharky, Wally, the Hempstead, Gold, and everything else behind, but something made him turn back. He sighed, and then followed Sharky into the bedroom.

Sharky was on the balcony when he arrived. The view was spectacular, looking over all of San Margarita Bay. Razz could even see the flashing lights of the Pier's Ferris wheel. He'd forgotten about work in all the excitement, but was relieved to see the wall clock read only two-thirty. Unfortunately, he would not have time to go home.

"Not bad for an amusement park clown," he marveled.

"Huh?"

"At a buck a lollipop, this had to be a lot of lollipops," Razz said, only half-jokingly. "How the hell could Wally afford this?"

"It was only eleven-hundred bucks."

"What?"

It was a gorgeous two-bedroom apartment with an amazing ocean view. Richard Gold had just told him that his two-bedrooms rented for thirty-two hundred dollars and more. This one had to be more, probably much more.

"Get the fuck out of here. It had to cost four- or five-thousand a month."

"Wally had been here for seven years. It was still under rent control."

"What a lucky stiff, to have a place like this for a rent like that," said Razz, not noticing that, right now, Wally was definitely a stiff, but couldn't be considered particularly lucky.

"Yeah, well, the rich get richer," said Sharky. "I'm sure Gold can get that four- or five-grand now."

Razz hoped Sharky hadn't noticed the glimmer of recognition in his eye.

Gold would indeed get richer with the apartment out from under the burden of rent control laws. *No, dude, get a grip, even he doesn't want money that bad.*

"Don't even think what you're thinking," said Sharky, reading Razz' thoughts like a newspaper headline through Saran Wrap, because he'd had those same thoughts himself. "There are two other apartments that rent for less than this one. The rest are around market."

Razz couldn't believe that Richard Gold, the father of his wife, could be involved in murder, even for money. He was relieved that Sharky didn't seem to believe it either.

"Come on, I've seen this place too many times," said Sharky.

With that, they left Wally's apartment, somewhat more enlightened than when they'd arrived. Though wiser, Razz felt himself being sucked deeper and deeper into events outside his control, and he couldn't wait to get back to the relative safety of the Surf's Up.

"This way." Razz pointed to the elevators, the way they'd come in, but Sharky kept walking down the hall the other way. *Just get on the elevator and be done with it. Get on the elevator!*

When Sharky reached the end of the hallway about twenty feet away, he held open a door that led to the back stairs and waited.

Razz hesitated, shook his head in disbelief at what he was about to do, and then followed him.

"What the fuck are you looking for?" asked Razz as they stepped outside into the back alleyway. "Can I go back to work now?"

"Sure, thanks for your help." Sharky called his bluff and Razz again folded.

"Oh, what the hell, I've still got some time. You might need me to keep your ass out of trouble."

"Fucked by the government!"

Razz jumped when he heard the squeaky, grating voice and jumped again when he saw who'd made it. A tattered, sunburned, little old homeless man with no teeth smiled at him.

Sharky ignored them both and went to work.

"Fucked by the government!"

"Yeah, yeah, fucked by the government. Tough break," said Sharky as he walked down the alley, studying it for clues.

Razz didn't know what Sharky was searching for and was scared to death of what it might be, but was waiting on the edge of his seat to find out. He just didn't want to wait with this nut job.

"Fucked by the government!"

Razz couldn't help but feel for the guy. He'd obviously had some bad breaks in life, but Razz just wished he'd go away and experience his psychoses elsewhere.

"Fucked by the government!"

"Shut Up!" yelled Sharky, running back toward the man. "I'm the government here. If you don't want to get fucked by the government again, you'll shut the fuck up!"

The man quieted, seeming to understand.

Sharky looked up at the opposite building, a four-story warehouse building slated for demolition that had no windows on the alley side. No one there could have seen anything.

"Fucked, fucked, fucked every day. Hee-hee-hee."

Sharky's short fuse was lit. He walked toward the man, raising his right fist, ready to strike, but the man just giggled, a big, toothless grin on his face.

"Hee-hee. Fucked every day, fucked him every day."

Sharky was sure he was taunting him and wouldn't stand for it any longer. Not when he had the power. He was no longer a helpless kid confronted by violent, alcoholic parents. He wasn't floating on a surfboard circled by a vicious tiger shark. He wasn't hiding from Louis Marcayda. No, he had the power now and was ready to show this mutant how he'd use it.

"Hee-hee-hee."

Razz caught his arm just as Sharky started his down stroke toward the man's head. The man never flinched.

"He doesn't know what he's saying, man."

Sharky breathed heavily, trying to regain his composure.

"Fucked, fucked, fucked. Every day."

Razz held his eye and his fist until he knew it was safe to let them both go. Sharky nodded.

"Sorry. No wonder he's got no teeth," he said, trying to make light of his own dark and troubling behavior.

"Let's get out of here," said Razz and they walked down the alley toward the street.

"Fucked by the government. Yep, he sure was, every single day. Hee-hee-hee."

Razz and Sharky disappeared around a corner, but the homeless man continued to mutter.

"Fucked, fucked. Hee-hee-hee."

The strange little man shuffled away, looking around him as if searching for something. Deciding he'd found the magic spot, he stopped, dropped his pants to his ankles, and squatted, his grimy, bare ass inches from the ground.

"Fucked by the government."

He grunted as he relieved himself onto the pavement, in a strange ritual of civil protest. "That's what the government's done for me."

Surveying his work, he let out a satisfied giggle as a large shadow spread over him from behind. He turned his head, smiling. "¿Qué pasa, amigos?"

A silvery metal pipe about one inch in diameter flashed into view and crashed into the man's skull. He collapsed to the pavement with a thud. Blood gushed from his wound and began mixing with his feces, as pairs of footsteps scampered away in syncopated rhythm and disappeared up the alley into silence.

9

Fellow surfers ignored him, because for months he'd sat alone near the Pier watching waves break. They didn't expect this day to be any different from the last couple of hundred. But it was different. This was the day that Robbie/Razz would ride a wave underneath the Pier all the way to the beach. And live to tell about it.

"Did someone kick you out of the house?" asked Lotta when Razz walked into the Surf's Up early.

"Hey," was his only acknowledgment. He kept walking toward the office stairs.

"Wait, I want you to meet Felipe, our new prep cook."

On cue, a small, twenty-something Mexican man exited the kitchen, wiping his hands on a bloody kitchen apron.

Razz shuddered, because the man reminded him of Louis. "W-welcome aboard."

"Bienvenido," said Lotta, clarifying Razz' nautical greeting.

Felipe smiled and nodded happily. "Gracias, gracias."

He offered Razz his hand. It was cold and clammy, like death, but then Razz realized he'd just finished grinding hamburger meat. Of course, his hand felt like death.

Razz escaped upstairs and found Carlos standing in front of the dumbwaiter. "What are you doing here?"

Carlos turned, surprised. He was holding a tray of ground meat. "Uh, I came back early to help Felipe get settled. Did you meet him?"

"Yeah."

Carlos nodded and took the meat to the cooler. Razz went into his office and closed the door.

He put his feet up on his desk, his mind racing. Maybe work wouldn't be the respite he'd hoped for, but he couldn't wait for that night's customers to arrive to find out.

When Razz went downstairs an hour later, there were only nine people in the place, and seven of them were employees. A few stragglers came in, looked at the Surf's Up decor and glanced at a menu, then left. *Christ, we even have restaurant looky-loos in LA. We've got a good menu and good prices. We have a great Surf 'n Turf for only $14.95, for God's sakes.*

He went outside, menus in hand, to entice potential customers. He felt better once he'd convinced two cute twenty-one-year-old coeds to stop in for dinner, though he knew he'd likely end up comping their meals. But it was a small success, and he thought maybe the two would tell their cute twenty-one-year-old girlfriends about the Surf's Up. Razz felt like he was having a mid-life crisis.

But whatever crisis he was having was nothing compared to the crisis Paul must have been suffering. When he saw Paul walking down the connecting bridge, Razz knew something was seriously wrong. First, he never approached from that direction, always arriving from the back of the restaurant, which was the most direct route from his home. Second, he wasn't carrying Miss Scruffy.

Paul walked into the restaurant without a word, not even a discouraging one, and that sealed it. Miss Scruffy must have finally bit The Big One.

He went directly to his table, and by the time Razz got there, he was crying uncontrollably, face down, into the tablecloth.

"What is it, Paul?" As often as Razz had in the past wished Paul would keel over and die, he felt bad now that it looked like he might.

Paul shook his head, unable to speak.

"Are you all right? Is your family okay?" Razz asked, knowing that he wouldn't have cried this hard about losing any human family member.

Paul whimpered and struggled to raise his head from the table. Tears streaked his face. "Miss Scruffy, she's gone."

Razz held back a self-satisfied chuckle, knowing he would never again have a dog on one of his restaurant's tables. "I'm sorry. How'd she die?" he asked, knowing full well that Miss Scruffy had died from being two-thousand years old.

Paul looked at him in horror. "She's not dead, she can't be. She's just lost. She was gone when I got back this afternoon."

Razz knew animals often disappeared just before dying. If Miss Scruffy wasn't near death, then no animal was or ever would be.

"I must have left the door open, but I never do that. I don't understand." And with that, he let out an agonized wail.

"I'm sure she'll turn up. I mean, she can barely walk, so how far can she get" That didn't make him feel better, because he still thought of Miss Scruffy like a first love, fresh and vivacious.

"Uh, what can I get you, the usual?" continued Razz, unsure of what else to say.

Sonja, a petite, blonde-haired waitress, attended to Paul, and Razz went back outside to corral more guests. There was just enough nip in the air to make it a slow night on the Pier, making his task all the more difficult.

"Hey, how you doing? You folks interested in dinner? We've got a full menu, with some great seafood, and a kids menu, too," Razz said eagerly to a young couple.

Had they not been dragging their two children, tearing them away from the amusement park, he might have had more luck. The wife smiled politely before almost ripping her son's right arm from its socket.

Foot traffic was negligible. The Ferris wheel's lights did their usual hectic dance, but its seats turned round and round slowly, practically empty. The arcade was quieter than usual. Even the Sol a Sol seemed slow. A few hardy fishermen braved the cool breeze, but it didn't appear they were having any more luck trolling than was Razz.

Suddenly, blood-curdling screams emanated from inside the restaurant. He ran in to find the coeds locked in a fearful embrace. A hulking, middle-aged man, beer in hand, backed fearfully against the bar, as if under attack from an unfriendly alien. Sonja and Chad, the two servers, looked shocked, and they'd seen almost everything from working in the restaurant business.

"Aaggh! Aaggh! Aaggh!" screamed Paul, pushing his plate away as if it were his kryptonite.

The coeds ran out and Razz didn't expect them back soon. Even the beer-swilling, gut-bellied man at the bar decided to vacate the premises and his half-full glass.

When he arrived at Paul's table, Razz saw what had prompted the lamentations. From Paul's lips came a trickle of blood. A dollop of bloody, barely-cooked, half-chewed hamburger meat sat on the table near him. Paul stared at his burger in horror. Its top bun was off, revealing its contents. There, where a red, ripe, juicy tomato slice should sit, was a furry ear—a dog's ear. Yes, that ear had been Miss Scruffy's.

Apparently, it did not taste good.

Paul didn't feel any better a half-hour later when the police discovered the remainder of Miss Scruffy's half-frozen carcass in the upstairs freezer. Razz didn't feel great either. The good news was that he would no longer have to deal with a dog eating on top of a restaurant table. The bad news was that he had been summarily fired, along with Lotta, Carlos, and almost everyone else.

There was one person who wasn't actually fired, at least, not to his face, but that was only because he couldn't be found. Felipe had been seen scurrying out the back door about the time Paul was receiving his canine surprise. He wisely had chosen not to come back.

Razz came out of the kitchen holding two paper bags and saw Chad hightailing it for the exit. "Chad."

He stopped, grudgingly. "I got to go while I can, man. They've been harassing the shit out of me."

"Yeah, I know. Sorry about that. Where are you parked?"

"Over on Delphi. Why?"

"It looks like I might be here awhile. Uh, could you deliver these dinners to a couple guys for me? I don't think tonight's guests will be coming back for them. They'll probably be sitting at the chessboards, a black guy and a white guy."

"I know who they are."

"Would you mind?"

"No, no, it's on my way."

"Thanks, man. Hey, if I don't see you for awhile, best of luck."

"You, too. This whole thing's crazy, isn't it?

It's crazy all right, Razz thought, as he watched Chad make his escape. *There seems to be a whole lot of crazy in my life lately.*

"McNeil, you're up!"

When Sergeant Robert Donati questioned Razz about the events of that evening, he answered with the truth.

"Yes, I met Felipe, but only briefly. Carlos recommended him, but Carlos couldn't have had anything to do with it."

"No, there's no reason why any of the staff would want to hurt Paul or the restaurant."

"Yes, there was plenty of opportunity for someone like Felipe to sneak a dead dog onto the premises. Even though it was his first day, it was still his job to stock the kitchen and freezer."

"Yes, we had a delivery that afternoon from the butcher shop. Felipe might have snuck in a package containing Miss Scruffy then."

Then Donati asked him, "What about the butcher?"

"Abe Belknap? He's eighty years old. He's lived in San Margarita all his life."

"Well?"

"He couldn't have been involved. Besides, he loves dogs. He's got five or six of them, I think. It must have been Felipe."

At the other end of the restaurant, Paul was alternately livid and semi-comatose and was determined that someone fry for what had happened. After all, Miss Scruffy had.

Donati continued to badger Razz. "Could Carlos have been involved?"

"No, he'd been at the Surf's Up too long."

"How about Ms. Gugliotta?"

"Lotta? She wouldn't have anything to do with it. She wouldn't want to get fired any more than me or Carlos."

"What about you?"

"Fuck you."

Razz learned that was an inappropriate response, when his carotid artery was closed down by Donati's strong grip. Donati was five-foot-ten, a solid block of muscle except for between his ears where he was just a solid block. He was a goon, but Razz hadn't thought he would resort to violence. Razz had grown accustomed to ragging on Sharky without repercussion. This time, the repercussion almost led to a concussion when his head was thrust against the wall.

"Let me ask you again. What about you?"

He was dying to reiterate his previous answer, feeling it had been most concise, but not wanting to actually die, he responded in a mature, head-throbbing way.

"No, sir, I don't know anything about it. I'm sorry."

"That's better."

Razz wanted to file a police brutality complaint, but Donati had chosen a secluded spot behind a couple of areca palms for his interrogation and there were no witnesses to back him up. So, he decided against it. Right now, he just wanted to get the hell out of there—preferably alive.

The Surf's Up was shut down for the night, but it was no longer Razz' concern. He pondered what he might do for his next job. He was forty-five and had few marketable skills. True, he could mix a drink and run a restaurant, but, after news of tonight's events spread, he wouldn't get hired to pour coffee at Burger King. Perhaps he could become a salesman of some sort. That wouldn't require any particular skill, he figured. But he couldn't see himself schmoozing little old, gray-haired ladies in order to sell overpriced life insurance. He knew he was washed up.

As he prepared to go home, the bump on his head felt better, but the inside of his head was burning up. How could he face Sarah, his kids, or his parents? His parents! He couldn't begin to help them with an apartment now. He felt like a walking disaster, but, at least, he was still walking.

Although he'd vouched for Carlos, Razz didn't understand how he could have brought Felipe in to grind up a poor, defenseless mangy mutt. An image of Carlos standing at the dumbwaiter, tray of fresh Miss Scruffyburger in hand, shot into his head. *He said he'd come in early to help Felipe, so he must have been in on it! And Lotta had been in the restaurant when Felipe was grinding up Miss Scruffy. Wouldn't she have noticed something? She had to be in on it, too!* Then Razz realized he hadn't noticed anything unusual when he'd met Felipe, *so why would Lotta? And why would Carlos know the hamburger he was holding was actually dog meat?* Though there was an unusual amount of unusual coincidences, it was possible that Felipe did do it all on his own. *But what did he have against Paul?*

Only moments after condemning his once most trusted allies, Razz again gave them the benefit of the doubt. At least, he did until he saw them walking together up the connecting ramp, a hundred yards ahead. He would swear they were laughing.

He was tempted to chase after them, but was too tired and too frightened by what he might learn, so he ignored the urge. Instead, like any good coward, he went to his car, turned on the ignition, and sped from the scene. It had not been a good day and he wanted to distance himself from it as quickly as possible.

The next morning, Razz was greeted by two disconcerting front page headlines in the *Monitor*. He had told Sarah about the Miss Scruffy incident and she'd been totally supportive, morally and financially. Neither he nor his family would be out on the streets due to his firing.

When she read the headline "Mayor and Local Developer Accosted at Groundbreaking!" and saw the picture of Razz being forcefully carried away by the two security thugs, her father figuring prominently in the background, she wasn't as forgiving.

"Weren't you going to tell me? What were you doing there anyway? Jeez, Razz, why won't you stop pestering my father about real estate?"

He'd never seen her so angry. He couldn't blame her, given his Christmas Eve showstopper, but the fact was he'd forgotten all about yesterday's incident with her father. He'd been sidetracked by what had happened later at the Surf's Up.

"You know Daddy doesn't like to be shown up like that. God, he already helps us so much, Razz." She was even starting to raise her voice.

"I'm sorry, I didn't mean for it to happen. I didn't even know he was going to be there. When I was on my way home after inventory, I saw him, so I thought I'd ask him for some help for my parents."

That calmed her down, because she was concerned about Sally and Tom, too.

"The big goons got carried away. I just wanted to ask his advice."

"What did he say?"

"Because they've already moved out, he said there was nothing anyone could do. I asked him if he had any apartments available, but he didn't have anything close to affordable. I couldn't help them now anyway."

"I can help them."

Razz looked at her, surprised, but he didn't know why he should be. She sat there, concerned, innocent, and generous to a fault. As always, she was there when he needed her, no questions asked.

He took her hands and kissed them gratefully. "Thank you, but I'll manage something."

She nodded, understanding his need to help his parents on his own terms.

Razz didn't want anything more from Sarah than she'd already given, but he wasn't at all confident of his ability to manage anything at this point. After all, he'd just managed his way out of the only career he'd known.

Sharky didn't like being pictured on the *Monitor*'s front page either. Fortunately, the cameras hadn't captured him sticking his gun in the side of the bodyguard's head, but he knew he'd still have plenty to answer for.

Although he had written all of it up in his daily report, he'd downplayed the whole incident, hoping it would be overlooked. Now, there was no chance of that. But it wasn't his major concern of the day; he was still fixated on Wally's apartment. He'd dismissed Wally's low rent in front of Razz, but it had bothered him from the beginning.

Maybe it's just coincidental, but the coincidences seem to keep adding up. There were no other fingerprints and few of Wally's. Murderers try to cover their tracks, sure, but don't take the time to wipe a place clean. Besides, a premeditated murderer would wear gloves.

That's what bothered Sharky the most. Someone had tried way too hard to hide something that wouldn't normally need hiding. Now, with the apartment freshly painted and carpeted, and with new appliances installed, the scene appeared clue-proof.

When he arrived at the Hempstead early that morning, he was officially off-duty. It wasn't like him to work and not get paid for it, but he was starting to take Wally's murder personally. By not being able to solve it, he looked like a chump.

"May I help you? Are you looking for an apartment?" asked a blonde-haired, well-kept and well-siliconized woman who looked to be in her mid-forties. In the land of Botox and tummy tucks, it was impossible to know for sure. Her name tag read, "Terri"

Sharky was surprised he didn't recognize her, but was more surprised she didn't recognize him. He had been there often in the past week.

"Uh, yes, a two-bedroom," he said, deciding to milk his anonymity for all it was worth. "Are you new here?"

"Me? No, I've been here a few months, but I just got back from vacation last night. Why? Have you been here before? Have you spoken to someone else?"

"No, no, I was just wondering," he responded, wondering how best to play his hand.

"What's your name?"

"Jerry, Jerry Sam ... Simpson, Jerry Simpson."

"Nice to meet you, Jerry Simpson. I'm Terri Howard. How'd you hear about us?"

"Oh, I was just walking by. I'm thinking of moving down this way." He wouldn't tell her any more than needed.

She felt exactly the same way. "Okay, well, I've got a great two-bedroom that just opened up. You want to look at it?"

If she could avoid it, she wouldn't mention the fact that the apartment had become available because the former tenant had just died, possibly while inside. It probably wouldn't be good for business.

"Sure," said Sharky, AKA Jerry Simpson.

They continued their verbal dance, neither giving away much information, as they made their way down the hall to apartment 703.

"So where'd you say you were from?"

"I didn't," Sharky said flatly, then he smiled, trying to turn on the charm, such as it was. "Just east of here, actually. I want to get closer to the water. How much did you say the apartment was?"

"I didn't," she said, smiling.

He wasn't sure, but he almost thought she was flirting with him. That pleasant thought was interrupted when the Guatemalan janitor walked around the corner. Fortunately, the man didn't want to continue their discussion from yesterday any more than Sharky, so he turned and hurried back from where he'd come.

"Here it is," said the woman as she swung open Wally's apartment door. Apparently, she hadn't noticed the janitor's arrival and quick departure, but she did notice that Sharky appeared shaken. "What is it?"

He ignored her. "What a beautiful place," he said as he breezed past.

The apartment was just as he and Razz had left it, but he felt there had to be something important still there. Some bit of information they had all missed. He went straight to the master bedroom's balcony.

"You went right to the best spot. It's a beautiful view, isn't it?"

He decided he'd have to be more careful to not give himself away. He tried to read her, but inadvertently paused at her ample cleavage. "Yes, it must cost a lot."

She'd shown far too many apartments to far too many lecherous men to be fazed by innuendo or a longing gaze. "We're only asking forty-one hundred. It's a great deal. We could probably get forty-five hundred for it right now, but we'd rather rent it to the right person."

Forty-one hundred. Three thousand more than Wally had paid. Thirty-six thousand extra dollars a year in the landlord's pocket. Sharky knew it wasn't enough for Gold to commit murder, though. That was pocket change for him.

He looked down toward the Pier. Because it was the last vacation day before school started again, a decent-sized crowd had already gathered at the amusement park. He was fascinated that Wally could have kept track of the Pier's visitors and his potential clientele right from his apartment.

"Forty-one? Wow, that's pretty steep. How does anyone afford to live here?"

"Most everyone who lives here is wealthy ... or is taken care of by someone who is."

He wondered again if she might be coming on to him, she was so friendly, but he was too busy to find out. He walked back inside.

The master bedroom was empty aside from a hanging wall clock. It read, *ten-fifteen*. His watch read the same.

"Would you like to see the rest?"

When he turned to her, he would have sworn she'd unbuttoned another blouse button. Her cleavage displayed itself even more impressively than before.

"I've seen it," he said, flustered. "I mean, this is what I came to see, the view. It's still too much for me."

"Too bad, I'm sure it would have been nice to have you as a neighbor."

"You live here?"

"Apartment 310. Stop by sometime. It doesn't have the view this apartment does, but I think you'd like it just the same."

Sharky knew he'd love whatever view she cared to show him, but apartment 310 was one of the thousand-dollar apartments and he wondered how she got it.

"You must make a lot of money doing this job."

"No, not really, I just have connections," she said. "Well, have you seen everything you want to see?"

He thought for a second, before responding in a stroke of genius. "Would you mind if I saw your apartment? I'd like to see how it compares."

Terry's eyes lit up. "Sure." She closed the door to apartment 703 and led her prospect to the elevator.

By the time they'd reached her apartment, Sharky was no longer concentrating on Wally, the clown. He was thinking of his own little funny man. And when she pulled off her suit jacket, revealing more of her siliconized perfection, he was letting his Wally do all the thinking for him.

She draped her jacket over the back of a chair and went to the kitchen. "Do you want anything to drink?"

Even had he been on duty, he wouldn't have had a problem. "Sure, whatever you're having."

Get her drunk; that will make things easier. She sure seems interested.

Terri brought back two tall glasses of a brownish liquid. "Cheers," she said as she put her glass to her lovely lipsticked lips.

Sharky smiled, raised his glass, tasted the liquid and almost gagged.

"Don't you like it? It's herbal iced tea. I'm sorry. Do you take it with sugar?"

"Yes, a little, um, a lot of sugar, please."

He watched her walk back into the kitchen. *Maybe I won't get lucky, after all.* With Rosie, he didn't have to worry about whether he was going to get laid as long as he had his money up. It was more difficult out here in the real world.

He went into the living room. It looked expensively furnished, filled with what appeared to be antiques, but he couldn't be sure. Antiques and decorating weren't his specialties.

"I hope that's better," Terri said, offering his glass.

She sat down in a single chair, giving him no obvious opening. He sat on the couch, desperately hoping she would join him.

"Great place," he said.

"Thanks."

A disconcertingly long pause convinced him the party was over before it started.

"Do you want to see the bedroom?"

Sharky played it cool, aside from an involuntary grin that spread over his face. "Sure."

She took his hand and led him through the hallway. He could feel the warmth of her hand and he hoped she couldn't feel the sweat of his. The bedroom was dark, the curtains closed, but he could see a four-poster bed which dominated the room.

Oh, let there be handcuffs, he thought. *I'll eat all my vegetables from now on. I'll help little old ladies cross the street. I'll do anything!*

She flipped on a harshly-bright overhead light. "Most of the two-bedrooms in the back rent for three thousand dollars or more, so you see what a good deal 703 is. It's a higher floor and you can't beat that view. I don't even have a view here. You should really think about renting it."

She is just trying to rent a damn apartment, after all.

Then she unbuttoned her top shirt button. "I'm a little hot. Hope you don't mind." She continued to unbutton.

No, Sharky didn't mind. When she starting removing her blouse, he was so dumbstruck he couldn't move.

"Could you help me with this?" she asked, after getting her hand caught in her sleeve.

"Y-yeah, I can help."

He went over and unbuttoned her sleeve, but before he could help her further, she pushed him down onto the bed. She straddled him, her breasts hanging perilously close to his face. She thrust his hand down into her panties and moaned.

Sharky thought about being late for work, about his car's parking meter running out, about a whole host of insignificant matters, but wisely didn't let his thoughts distract him for long. He was undercover.

She smelled good. She was definitely well-kept, whatever her real age was. They tossed and turned and moaned and groaned. They groped at each other's clothing, finally dragging off any last remnants of modesty. Terri gasped when she saw Sharky's grotesque scar, but when she went down to kiss it tenderly, they each quickly forgave the other's personal scars.

It was noon. Sharky lay contentedly in the dark under the covers of the four-poster while the sound of running water emanated from the bathroom. He would be late for work, but he didn't care. He had just been well laid and it hadn't cost him a cent. It renewed his faith in the world.

"I've got to get back to the office. You want to take a shower?" Terry asked as she poked her head out of the bathroom.

"No, I'm fine."

"Okay, honey."

Sharky wondered if a person could fall in love this fast, but Terri seemed like everything he ever wanted in a woman—big breasts, great body, and really horny. His musing was interrupted when she turned on the overhead light.

"Ah," he said, shielding his eyes.

"Sorry, baby, but I've got to go, so you have to, too. I hope you'll think about renting that apartment though. I think you'd like it here."

He smiled at the thought of living so near her, despite the painfully brilliant light now piercing his skull. He scratched his head and rolled out from under the covers, as Terri put on her under garments. He sat on the side of the bed, his eyes adjusting to the brightness, and watched her. Not quite believing his good fortune, he laughed.

"What is it?"

He grinned broadly.

"Okay, okay, hurry up. I've got to get back to the office." She kissed him sweetly on the forehead, then went back into the bathroom and closed the door.

Sharky dragged himself off the bed and reached for his pants. He glanced at a collection of pictures sitting on her night stand. One caught his eye and his good humor instantly left him. He slid into his clothes like a man who knew how to make a quick getaway.

"Think about that apartment, baby. It's a great deal," said a voice from the bathroom that he no longer recognized. She sounded more and more like the Devil every moment.

Sharky didn't say goodbye. He left no warm, lingering kisses, no heartfelt thank you's, and no phone number. He just wanted to get out of that building as fast as he could. His life was becoming far too complicated and dangerous.

When he started his car and screeched away from the curb, he wasn't thinking about Terri's beautiful body, her apartment, or about the great sex he'd just had. He could only think of one thing—the picture on her night stand. That picture meant he would now have to worry about two powerful people. Louis

Marcayda was bad enough, but this other man was wealthier, maybe more powerful in his way, so Sharky felt more trapped than ever.

The man in the picture was Richard Gold.

10

There was a perfect offshore breeze, just like the weather lady predicted. That breeze would help kick up five- to six-foot swells, but he knew the wind could act differently buffeted between the pilings beneath the Pier.

"You're late, Sergeant."

Sharky recognized Chief Wilson's voice coming from Johnson's office. *Why the hell is he here again?* He ignored him, but could only until Wilson yelled louder.

"Get in here!"

Okay, that makes three dangerous men against me. I'm getting it from all sides now. And I don't like what I'm getting.

"Be right there, Chief."

He ambled into the office like a man who'd just gotten laid, but when Wilson slammed the door behind him, he couldn't help but jump a little. He could usually handle Wilson, because he didn't generally give a damn about anything, but the Chief seemed more overwrought than usual today—and more powerful. Perhaps, the sight of Richard Gold's mug on Terri's bed stand had made his legs and his will go limp. Or maybe it was just the great sex. Either way, he'd lost his edge and he knew he was in trouble. And Johnson was nowhere in sight to help him.

"What the hell is this?"

Sharky looked at that day's *Monitor* which Chief Wilson held toward him.

"The newspaper?"

Whoosh! Sharky ducked when a manila file folder flew past his head. Papers from the file floated to the ground around him.

That was pretty dumb. Now you'll have to pick—

He couldn't even finish his thought before Wilson had his throat grasped tightly in his right hand. Sharky wondered if he'd have to worry about Louis Marcayda or Richard Gold, after all.

"Go, Chief!"

"Yeah, Chief. Bust him up good!"

Several cops jockeyed for position in the hallway, not wanting to miss a moment of the action.

"Get the fuck out of here! Go!" The Chief rustled across the strewn papers toward his troops.

Sharky didn't notice the uniforms and plainclothes scatter; he was too busy trying to catch his breath.

Wilson was quickly back at his throat. "You shape the fuck up or get the fuck out. Don't ever embarrass me like that again. You understand?"

Sharky intended to say "yes," but a tiny squeak was all he could muster. It seemed to be enough though, because Wilson let go of his neck.

"Don't ... you ... want to hear what happened?"

"I know what happened. Your friend accosted Richard Gold, so the security people did their job, then you had to come along and make the whole police force look like a bunch of idiot cowboys by drawing your weapon in public. HOW DID I DO?"

Sharky felt like his brain was going to explode, uncertain whether it was from Wilson hollering directly into his ear or from the injustice of the tongue-lashing. He'd done what he had to do to keep Razz from being beaten, but it didn't matter now. He wisely chose not to further the fight in this kangaroo court.

"I'm sorry."

His apology only slightly mollified the chief, but now, at least, Wilson was occupied picking up papers, not cutting off the blood to Sharky's brain.

"Get someone in here to clean this up!" Wilson yelled toward the desk sergeant, before going behind the desk. His face seemed to be returning to a semi-normal shade of pink from its earlier deep purple.

"Fine, you're sorry. Big deal. Listen, I don't care what you do; just stay the hell out of my way. And stay the hell out of the papers! If you so much as—"

Bzzzz! Sharky had never been so happy to hear the buzz of a cell phone in his life.

Wilson answered the phone, but didn't get to say a word. Someone was screaming at him. After the yelling finally ceased, he clicked off, deflated.

"You're off the Wally Bumpers case. The Mayor's changed his mind about you. He's disgusted by your behavior and doesn't want you around. You're suspended with pay for two weeks."

The Mayor? What's his fucking problem? He was safe in his fucking limo the whole time! At least, I didn't stick the gun in his head. He was about to rage at the injustice, the absurdity, the—

"With pay?"

Wilson looked at him incredulously. "Yes, with pay. Now, get the fuck out of here!"

Sharky wondered what he might do for the next two weeks. He thought about taking a trip; he had never really traveled. He considered asking Terri to go with him, but remembered he hadn't even said goodbye to her in his panic. And she was still somehow connected to Richard Gold. *Oh, well, maybe Rosie would like to go somewhere. No, she'd cost me too much if she charged by the hour.*

He stepped past a kneeling clerk who was organizing the scattered papers. If he hurried, he could get home just in time for *Days of Our Lives.*

Razz watched helplessly as another moving van left the front yard of his childhood home. He'd watched them come and go for hours. He'd watched families, most of them he didn't know, load their belongings and lives into some anonymous, impersonal van, trusting it to deliver them to a better place. He suspected they knew deep-down, despite their five-thousand dollar payoffs, that they would not be moving toward better lives or anywhere near the lap of luxury. They would be lucky to find new apartments half as nice for twice as much.

He had started out that morning to go surfing with his new Wegener wood board, but his childhood memories tugged harder at him than did the four-foot swells and offshore winds. So, there he'd been, sitting in his car at 515 Enterra Street, barely moving, watching for the past two-hundred and thirty-seven minutes. No longer having a job, Razz had little idea what else to do with himself.

He'd watched little children crying, distraught over the prospect of moving into the unknown. He'd watched husbands and wives hugging, bucking each other up for the next new chapter in their lives. He'd watched moving men, stoic and workmanlike, come and go like ants, hauling their bounty, intentionally oblivious to the personal dramas around them.

Finally, Razz started his car, let out a deep, profound sigh, and drove out of the yard for what he thought would be the last time. He was unsure exactly how he felt, but suspected it was a mélange of how the children, the parents, and the moving men he'd just witnessed must have felt. He wanted to cry, he wanted to be strong, and he wanted to deny the whole thing, all at the same time.

He surveyed the friendly small town of his youth as he passed through, except that now it was an impersonal mid-sized city. As if a cloak of denial were lifted, he saw just how much it had changed and how it continued to change right before his eyes.

There, before him, at the site of Richard Gold's proposed Gold Shore Hotel and Plaza, an excavator chugged away. Also known as an earth mover, an excavator was a huge piece of machinery that heralds the beginning of physical development for a commercial property. And there it was, working impressively. Its shiny, strong body made huge, insatiable bites into the earth to create a massive hole where the foundation would lay, and then deposited its gravelly booty into the beds of waiting twenty-ton dump trucks. Razz had to hand it to Gold. He was an earth mover, too. People just couldn't move and shake in this town like he could.

A beat-up Chevy pickup's horn blasted behind him and jerked him from his somber reverie. He shifted the Mustang back into gear, made an illegal U-turn, and headed, resignedly, toward home. He had seen enough.

Sarah greeted him at the door. "How was surfing?" she asked, way too cheerfully for his mood.

"I didn't go."

"Oh, no waves?"

Razz looked at her blankly. She was so good, so kind, and he just felt so bad and so worthless. But he didn't have to say anything.

She took him in her arms. "It's okay. Your folks will be fine, dear. And so will we."

Her confidence almost made him believe her. But he didn't feel like he would be okay ever again. His boyhood, his livelihood, and, because of the rapid development of the Gold Shore Hotel, his manhood had all been taken from him within the course of the last forty-eight hours. He regained some hope when he saw little Ronnie screaming around the corner from his bedroom, followed closely by Caitlin.

"Hi, Dad."

"Hi, Daddy. Have you been swurfing?" Caitlin still loved her w's.

He smiled and, for a moment, left his wallowing pool of self-pity behind. There, before him, was his youth, in the shape of his two beautiful, innocent children. He hadn't lost that at all. Then his wife kissed him, reminding him of his manhood. He'd worry about a livelihood later.

"Come on, who wants to play kickball?" Razz asked in what seemed to be a stroke of genius at the time.

"I do! I do!" His two kids yelled as one.

The three of them hustled to the door. Razz turned back toward Sarah. "You want to play, honey?"

"You kids go ahead. I've got things to do in here. Have fun."

And the kids did have fun, running, kicking and tossing the ball at each other. They had so much fun that, when Sarah looked a half-hour later, it was hard to tell which of her kids was having the most—Caitlin, Ronnie, or Razz.

A half-hour later, it was obvious who wasn't having fun when Razz limped into the house, his concerned kids in tow.

"Daddy hurt himswelf," said Caitlin as her mother appeared from the kitchen.

He had indeed hurt himself, straining his left hamstring muscle rounding a makeshift third base in their makeshift kickball contest.

"Daddy's funny," added little Ronnie, still too young to understand his father's physical plight.

"Oh, baby, are you all right?" asked Sarah as she helped Razz to his chair.

"Aaggh! Careful." He slowly lowered himself onto the leather.

Ronnie giggled. "Daddy's funny."

"Yes, your daddy's funny," added Sarah.

"Is Daddy alwight?" Caitlin laid her head on her father's shoulder. She was just like her mother, supportive and kind, at least, when she wasn't trying to rip little Ronnie's head off.

"I'll be all right, honey. Thank you." He kissed her, and then winced when he felt a knife slice through his inner thigh.

"Okay, you kids go play. I'll take care of your father. We've got to find you some kids your own age to play with. All of you," Sarah said pointing her sarcasm good-naturedly in Razz' direction.

He wasn't sure he appreciated it, but when he looked up, her broad smile melted any possible resentment.

"I'll get you some ice."

He felt his groin where his hamstring had partially given way. It was hot and starting to throb. "Hey, honey, hurry up, it's really starting to hurt."

After a moment, she walked back in with a full ice bag. "Here, this will help." She gently laid the bag under his left leg and between his thighs.

"Mmm, that's better."

Holding the ice with one hand, Sarah worked her other hand toward his crotch.

"Mmm, that's better still," he said, smiling contentedly.

Now she had both hands full. One held the ice bag, soothing Razz' sore, aching leg muscle, while the other hand soothed another sore, aching muscle.

"The kids," he warned, and then he moved her hand away from his crotch.

She looked at him quizzically, which finally convinced him of what he'd already known deep-down—he was getting old. If pulling a hamstring muscle while playing an easy game of kickball hadn't convinced him, turning down his wife's sexual advances certainly did. His body had betrayed him earlier, now it was his mind. He was thinking more about his parental responsibilities than about sex.

Sarah didn't have time to argue, because the phone rang. "Take this," she said, leaving ice bag responsibility to him.

He felt guilty that he'd turned her down. He also felt stupid. Then he remembered the other day when Ronnie had surprised them while they were in a similarly compromising position. *Whew, I'm just having a bad week. Losing my job, now hurting my leg, these things shall pass. I'll be back on my feet in no time and I'll find another job somewhere.* Not believing any of it, Razz felt like crawling towards the edge of his property just like little Ronnie had days earlier and hurling himself over the embankment which, fortunately, Ronnie had not.

"It's for you." She did not look happy. "It's Carlotta."

Skeptical, he took the phone. "What the hell could she want?"

She must have assumed the question was rhetorical, because she didn't respond. She also didn't want to think about it.

"Hello," said Razz into the receiver.

Sarah busied herself tidying up, secretly anxious to hear why Carlotta would call her husband at home when there was no longer any restaurant business to discuss.

Razz listened, nodding every so often. Then he clicked off the phone without saying good-bye. He looked puzzled. "I got my old job back."

She stopped cleaning.

"It looks like I'll be managing the Sol a Sol, too."

It was a toss-up who was more confused.

With the soaps and *Oprah* over for the day, Sharky sat alone in the dark of his apartment, not sure what to do with himself.

After a moment, he limped over to his living room window and opened the dusty drapes. His windows were filthy, but he didn't notice. All he saw was a buxom, blonde bombshell by the name of Terri, arms folded across her chest, leaning against the hood of her green 1998 Pontiac Grand Am. She didn't look pleased.

"So, I called the police station and told them some schmuck had just stiffed me," said Terri as she stormed into the apartment.

Sharky suspected she hadn't meant that as a pleasant double-entendre.

"I asked him, 'How can I find out where a Jerry Simpson lives?' The guy must have thought I said Sampson, 'cause he started laughing. 'That Sharky,' he said, 'what's he done now?' You know Jerry, if you're going incognito, you really should change more than one letter in your last name."

He knew he had nowhere to run, but he wasn't going down without a fight. "Yeah, okay, so how did you find me? I know they didn't give you my address."

She picked up a phone book from the filthy carpet. "You're in the book, moron!"

He winced. He didn't like to be called names, though it certainly fit in this case.

"I'm sorry. I didn't mean that, I'm just angry. I mean, you just left, Jerry. How do you think that made me feel?"

The waters were way too deep for him now. Feelings were a whirlpool into an abyss that he assiduously avoided, but she seemed so disappointed in him that he couldn't help but feel he was swirling downward, almost drowning already. He highly preferred Rosie's paid nonchalance. Feelings only messed up an otherwise good time.

"What do you want?" he asked, unable to face her.

"What do I want? How about another fuck?"

He got excited by the mention of one of his favorite past times until he realized she was being facetious.

She was excited, too, but not the way he wanted. Her carotid arteries popped from her neck and her forehead burned with blood and humiliation. "What are you so afraid of? Christ! We just made love, for God's sake. I didn't ask you to marry me. And you ran out without saying good-bye, a kiss, or even an acknowledgement."

"I, uh, I had to get back to the station."

"Bullshit."

Now Sharky's face reddened as he tried to come up with a good excuse for running out on her.

"Well?"

He felt like he would explode. *Feelings! Feelings! Feelings! Just leave me the fuck alone. You got laid, now I'm getting screwed, so let's just let it go.* He desperately wanted to scream, but no words came out.

"You hurt me."

There it was; she'd said it. The knife was so deep in him now that he felt like he couldn't breathe, each lung punctured by her words. He was on life support, barely alive, his glassy eyes looking for help, but he knew none would be forthcoming. He was on his own in dangerous, uncharted waters.

So, he fought back the only way he knew how. "Well, how the hell do you know Richard Gold?" he roared, setting her back a notch. "I saw his picture on your night stand!"

She hesitated, trying to fathom him. "Is that it? It's about Richard? Baby, he was my lover."

"Yeah, well, no shit."

"He's not my lover anymore. I mean, that ended a couple of weeks ago. I broke it off before Christmas; that's why I went away. I just couldn't stand being in that apartment. It looks like I'll be leaving San Margarita for good soon."

"Huh?"

Sharky had gone from Mach five to zero in about twenty seconds. His eyes almost popped from the emotional g-force.

"I was hired at the Hempstead back in October. Richard came in one day, I mean, I didn't even know who he was, and we kind of hit it off. We flirted a little and one thing led to another, so we started dating, if you could call it that. You know, we'd spend evenings together in the apartment. Once in a great while, we'd go out to some really dark restaurant. That should have been a clue, 'cause I didn't know he was married at first, I swear. But then, I didn't exactly ask him either. See, I'd just moved here from Arizona and I didn't know anyone, so I was happy he took an interest in me. Then he offered to put me up in his apartment. He was so generous—"

"Huh?" He was moving again at normal speed, curiosity and paranoia propelling him, his eyes back squarely in their sockets. "What do you mean?"

"Well, he lent me some money for my bills."

"No, I mean about the apartment."

"What about it?"

"You said he put you up in 'his' apartment."

"Yeah. So?"

"The one at the Hempstead? The one you're in now?"

"The one I'm in for three more days. Yeah, that's Richard's apartment."

Sharky's brain wheels spun and he raced to his desk, which was strewn with papers and case files. Despite the seeming chaos, he knew exactly where to look. He tore through one particular file, searching, and grabbed a sheet of paper. He looked down a list of names and then thrust the page at Terri.

"The apartment you're in is leased to an Emma Northrup. It's not Richard Gold's."

She looked confused. The piece of paper indeed listed Emma Northrup as the lessee of apartment 310.

"Well, he told me it was his. What difference does it make?"

He grabbed her around the waist, and then swung her round happily.

"Jerry, what are you doing?" Nervous at first, she soon got caught up in his excitement. "I just don't understand you," she said, before breaking into laughter with him.

He kissed her. She kissed him back. Then they kissed each other, locked in a passionate, needy embrace. Sharky was definitely excited now and the heat in his apartment felt way past its normal seventy-six degrees. He inched the two of them over to the window, still embraced and kissing hungrily, then he pulled the drapes closed.

He wasn't sure what excited him most. Was it that he was about to make love to a beautiful woman? Was it because this would make twice in one day? Was it that way down in the deep, dark recesses of his heart he was beginning to care for her? Or was it that he might have found a clue that could help him solve the Wally Bumpers murder. Uncertain as he was about almost everything else, he knew one thing—Richard Gold was guilty. He just wasn't sure of how much.

For Gold to rent an apartment under market value from a partnership he controlled was fraud, self-dealing, and very illegal. Apartment 310 rented for about one-thousand dollars a month, way under market price. *But who's Emma Northrup? And why does Gold control an apartment leased in her name? Did he do something to her to get the apartment?* It all made Sharky wonder to what lengths, or depths, Gold would go for money.

Razz limped toward the Surf's Up, dragging his almost useless left leg. He turned back carefully to see Caitlin and Ronnie waving from the rear seat of his wife's Range Rover as Sarah drove away. He waved, and then cringed in pain. Although he had drugged himself heavily with Tylenol, his leg still hurt like hell, but he wasn't about to miss this meeting.

The restaurant was closed to customers, but when he entered, he could see it was more full than usual at this time of the afternoon. Lotta, Carlos, and Rick sat together at the bar, talking and laughing, acting as if nothing had happened, despite the recent distasteful experience of Miss Scruffy becoming a dog burger. Razz figured they were just happy to have their jobs back. The servers, Tom, Sonja, and Chad, sat at one table, while several Mexican men and women he recognized as staff from the Sol a Sol were at an adjacent table.

"What happened to you?"

Razz turned too quickly toward the voice. "Huh? Ow!" Pain exploded through his injured leg. He crumpled over, trying to protect himself from another inadvertent move. As the pain subsided, he looked up to the voice's source.

Louis stood above him, impeccable in a blue pin-striped business suit and way overdressed for a California beach town. He appeared overpowering and seven-feet tall from Razz' angle, but he still looked concerned. His bodyguards, three wiry Mexicans barely bigger than him, held their distance only yards away, keeping watch.

"Razz, I'm so glad you made it."

Before Razz could give warning, Lotta hugged him, squeezing her soft, perfect breasts into him.

"Aaggh!"

She pulled away. "Sorry, what's wrong?" She'd never gotten that response from a man before.

He backed carefully away from all animate objects. He didn't want to be near anything that could move, bump into him, grab him, or surprise him. He sat down in a chair, his back to the wall, his left leg out of harm's way under a table. "I hurt myself playing kickball with my kids."

Louis roared in good-natured laughter. "Ha-ha. Oh, it's great having kids, isn't it? How old are yours?" he asked, though he already knew the answer.

Razz didn't share his enthusiasm at the moment, but, after a moment, had to chuckle himself. "My daughter, Caitlin, is six. Ronnie's three."

"A boy and a girl just like me. I hope they all become good friends one day."

He wasn't sure he shared his enthusiasm on that point either, but he wouldn't have time to discuss it.

"Welcome to the new Surf's Up. Today, I finalized the purchase of this restaurant as well as the Sol a Sol. It's unfortunate these businesses have had some bad public relations of late, but I'm sure nothing like that will happen again."

As Louis spoke, Razz watched his every move, his every gesture. He seemed so sure of himself. Razz wished he could be half as confident. When he said he was sure "nothing like that will happen again," Razz believed it with every fiber left in his being. *But why? How could Louis possibly guard against an anthrax hoax, an extra-rare dog burger, or a stale clown?* Was it his delivery and composure that made Razz believe him? Perhaps it was the implied power of his business suit. Razz couldn't put his finger on it, but then it came to him in a flash and he felt like he'd put his finger on a red-hot stove. *Louis controlled those events. He made them happen, so, of course, he can prevent them from happening again. What other explanation could there be?*

"And I look forward to working with each of you in making these the best and most profitable restaurants in San Margarita."

Louis' words seemed disconnected from his mouth, just disembodied sound floating in air, until Razz noticed the room was spinning. It was he who was disconnected. Too many Tylenols and a whirl of realization had left him dizzy. He rose unsteadily from his chair.

"I'd like to introduce you to the manager of the Surf's Up ..."

Razz made his way to the bar to get some water.

"... as well as the new manager of the Sol a Sol—Mr. Razz McNeil."

In what should have been a triumph, a culmination of many dreams and much hard work, a moment for him to relish for years to come, Razz hadn't noticed his introduction. He was groveling behind the bar, searching for a clean water glass, certain he was going to die of thirst.

And, if not of thirst, then of something worse.

11

He also knew, from geometry class, that only a wave approaching the end of the Pier within ten degrees of head-on would allow him to ride beneath the Pier its full three hundred foot length. And he'd have to cut back at least twice. And he knew he'd have to do it all while the sun was still low in the sky, so the pilings wouldn't be in shadows and possibly surprise him right in the face.

Razz' head pounded, throbbing almost as much as his leg. He'd taken several aspirin, in addition to his previous Tylenols, but listening to Louis' grand plans for the last hour had overpowered any analgesic effect. The other workers had gone home, but Louis, Lotta, and Razz continued their meeting in Razz' upstairs office. Technically, it could be considered Louis' office until Razz decided he wanted it back. Louis wanted Razz to work for him and, despite his massive headache, leg ache, and general trepidation, something kept Razz in his seat, super-glued by his ass. He wanted to get all the facts before he decided for or against any unholy alliance. Ashamed he was listening to a man who may have dubiously engineered a takeover of two establishments whose owners had been ferociously determined not to sell, he suspected his headache was trying to warn him there might be lots of pain ahead if he chose unwisely, but he couldn't help himself. He had always wanted to manage both restaurants. He thought they belonged together and that there were potential synergies that common ownership and management could realize. Louis apparently agreed and stated many of the same beliefs that he'd held. Both restaurants, closed today, were set to re-open tomorrow. Razz could manage them both if he wanted to, assisted by Lotta, but he wasn't sure he liked the smell of the whole thing.

"And, of course, you'll own twenty percent."

Razz' jaw dropped, his headache subsided, and a smile unintentionally crept across his face. "Huh?"

"You'll own twenty percent. Didn't I say that before?" Louis asked, not-so-innocently.

Razz' thoughts did joyous cartwheels until they crashed into an immovable object and crumbled to stillness. "I don't have any money for equity."

"You don't need money. I'm asking you to be my partner. I'll take the financial risk and you'll run the business the best way you know how. You'll earn your equity."

It all seemed too good to be true, and he hesitated, knowing it probably was, because of his doubts about Louis' deal-making techniques.

"What's wrong? You're worried about something."

He knew he'd have to check his emotions, because Louis seemed to know them as soon as he did. "How did you get both restaurants?"

"I paid too much money for them."

He wished he could read him like Louis read him, but Louis was poker-faced. "Excuse me, but, with all due respect, there have been some strange events lately involving the Sol a Sol and Surf's Up," said Razz, choosing his words carefully, not wanting to tug too hard on Superman's cape.

"To what 'strange events' are you referring?" said the five-foot-six, off-colored Superman.

Razz struggled to find the right words.

"I've been negotiating with each owner separately for about ten months," said Louis, as if to put him out of his misery. "Because of the recent incidents to which you so cautiously referred, I thought they might be more inclined to accept my previous offers. They weren't. So, finally, I just had to pay them too much money. Everyone has a price and both places are worth more to me than to anyone else. As you may or may not know, I own some real estate in the eastern part of town. I've wanted to own near the water, but have had problems getting people to sell to me. These two restaurants, if successful, will help me establish credibility with the people who run this town. You see, I have bigger plans than just the restaurant business."

Razz tried to read his eyes, but they were the most sincere, bottomless black pits he'd ever seen. He felt as if he might fall into them and never find his way out. He even began to believe him.

"Listen, Razz, I know you've wanted to buy this place for some time. The main reason you couldn't was that I'd already offered twice as much. I bought it for three times what you offered."

Three times! Maybe you aren't as smart as I thought you were!

"As I said, it's worth more to me than to anyone else. I'm trying to buy respect. That can be expensive."

Razz felt like he no longer had to say a word. Louis knew what he was thinking anyway, but he still had one nagging concern. "So, you didn't have anything to do with sabotaging either restaurant?"

Louis stared at him ominously. Lotta looked worried. Razz closed his eyes as if resigned to being struck down. Then Louis laughed. And Lotta laughed.

"I told you he was paranoid," said Lotta, laughing so hard now that her eyes watered.

"That you did, cousin, that you did," said Louis between guffaws. "He'll be the perfect manager."

Razz wasn't sure he appreciated the humor at his expense, but, under the circumstances, he felt quite relieved it was only laughter cutting through him.

Sharky was floating he was so happy. He couldn't remember the last time he'd held a beautiful woman he hadn't paid for tightly in his arms. Even better, she wasn't struggling to get free.

Terri purred softly, shifting closer to him. Her bottle blonde hair brushed against his cheek bone. It smelled of coconut.

It was apt, because he was already nuts about her. He couldn't help smiling.

"I saw that," she said.

"Sorry, I won't be happy again. I promise." Sharky wondered where he'd found a sense of humor. Love and sex can do wonders for a man.

"I'm happy, too. We'll be very happy here."

Sharky started choking and jumped out of bed. "Excuse me, I need some water."

He went to the bathroom, closed the door, and stared into the mirror. He would swear he was sweating, but it wasn't visible. He turned on the tap and doused his face repeatedly with cool water.

"Are you okay, Jerry?"

Her voice again sounded like the Devil's, just like when he'd seen Richard Gold's picture on her night stand.

"Yeah, fine."

His words were a whisper, barely audible through his parched throat. He poured himself a glass of water and drank it without a breath. Then he did it again. When he finished the second glass, he'd begun to calm down.

Come on, she only wants to move in. What's the big deal?

Then it came to him. She had to be out of Richard Gold's apartment in three days, so she needed a place to stay! Now, he was pissed and he stormed out of the bathroom, ready for battle. Entering his bedroom, his bastion of dysfunctional maleness, he saw something that cut him short, making his anger wilt like a certain appendage of a sexually-satisfied man.

Terri was straightening up his room. The bed was already made. The floor was now navigable, his dirty clothes piled in a corner of the closet.

"I didn't mean to invite myself and I didn't mean to scare you. I have enough money; I can get a place on my own. I just thought ... I thought maybe we could ..."

Sharky's freeze-dried heart melted all over again. "I'm sorry. You caught me off guard, that's all."

She nodded, sniffling. "Do you want me to go?"

He felt like he was being cut in half and it was more painful than any shark attack. "No," he said. "Don't go. I don't want you to go."

"Are you sure?"

Sharky moved toward her, his legs barely under his command. Awkward and uncertain, he reached for her and hugged her tightly. "I'm sure. Please, don't go. Ever."

It was ten o'clock in the evening and Razz knew he wouldn't be home for hours. He'd already called Sarah, the excitement in his voice giving away the news before he could even tell her. He'd accepted the offer, convinced Louis was a businessman, not a saboteur, and that recent events at the Pier had been random coincidences.

The pain from his head had subsided and he ignored the pain in his leg. In fact, he felt great. He'd been given complete freedom in determining how best to run both restaurants. He'd gotten a substantial raise and an equity earn-out. And he'd gotten a cell phone. Louis explicitly told him to call him day or night if he needed anything. Never a fan of technology, Razz accepted it when he realized it meant he would finally be involved in a professionally-run operation.

He'd spent the past few hours planning his attack. He would move the Surf's Up's supplies into a large storage closet at the Sol a Sol, retrieving them only as needed. He'd convert extra space at the Sol a Sol into more dining area, raising potential revenues, and still keep two offices upstairs, one for him and one for Louis and Lotta. He'd consolidate buying and accounting functions between the restaurants, saving money. He would tweak the menus for each place, adding a few higher-end dishes at the Sol a Sol and reducing menu choices at the Surf's Up. Each restaurant would cater to different clienteles, but, together, they would capture most of the food business on the Pier.

Although he'd been to the Sol a Sol many times while inspecting the enemy, he wanted to double-check the square footage, the layout of the kitchen, and the decor. He'd always thought extra splashes of color would make the Sol a Sol more festive and enhance its ability to attract younger, fun-loving patrons who adored the margarita drinks that sold for only three dollars and fifty cents. He already planned to raise the price to four-twenty-five and the prospect of enhanced revenues and his new ability to make executive decisions brought a smile to his face.

He shoved his new phone into his pocket, grabbed a sweatshirt that he kept stored in his desk for emergencies, and walked outside. The damp night air hung heavily, but it was refreshing. He filled his lungs and it smelled good, because it smelled of freedom—freedom from Paul and Miss Scruffy. The Pier was quiet, because of the closure of the two restaurants. The Ferris wheel whirled round, but only three people, sitting separately, far apart, took the lonely ride. There was no one at all on the bumper car ride, its attendant anxiously waiting for his watch to read eleven, so he could close shop and go home. Even the police substation seemed quiet. Only a couple ratty-looking old men on a bench, passing a brown-bagged bottle between them, interrupted the solitude, every now and then laughing at inside jokes told by voices only they could hear.

Razz stopped twenty yards from the Sol a Sol to take in all its glory. It stood two stories tall with outdoor decks on three sides. It was much bigger than the Surf's Up and almost every seat was a good one. Continuing to the front door, he slid his new Sol a Sol key into the lock and turned it. He reveled in its satisfying click.

Inside, the wooden floor creaked wearily under his weight. He turned on the overhead lights to survey the guts of his new kingdom. Beautiful, it wasn't. The place had seemed brighter before, but then he remembered that he'd usually been there during the day. Tonight was one of the darkest nights of the year, overcast with a waning crescent moon offering just a sliver of light. He decided he would beef up the interior lighting, making the restaurant more inviting to nighttime visitors, and add strategically-placed floodlights to each outdoor deck. What he lost in intimacy, he knew he would gain in customer awareness and security. He wanted his new castle to shine as a bastion of safety, good food, cheap drinks and welcome.

He walked through the main dining area. It was clean, but it could be cleaner. He toured the kitchen next. He could tell the flow wasn't right, that the delivery of food needed to be more efficient, but he'd confer with Carlos tomorrow to start straightening out that mess. The decks were what they were, large, spacious, and solid, offering good views of the water. Other than needing new paint and the floodlights, they were great assets. He smiled when he walked into the ample storage closet knowing there would be more than enough room for the additional supplies from the Surf's Up. The bathrooms were small, but serviceable.

Razz had inspected almost everything, but there was one area he'd consciously avoided. He took a deep breath to gather his courage, then cautiously approached the viewing glass as if expecting Wally's ghost to rise up through the glass to wreak havoc on his person. Sharky's repeated inquisitions had etched the scene garishly into his brain. He'd also had a nightmare recently about a strange looking glass that served as a portal into a weird world filled with rabbits, dancing teacups and a grown-up clown in a little girl's dress. He decided he'd let Sarah read *Alice in Wonderland* to the kids from now on.

He sideways glanced into the viewing glass expecting the worst, but all he saw was blackness. After all of his mental preparation, he'd forgotten to turn on the lights under the Pier. Now he had to psyche himself up once more. He went behind the bar and flipped a switch. A beam of light shot through the viewing glass and splashed against the white-painted ceiling and walls, casting Razz' shadow against the bottle-laden bar. He jumped when he saw his doppelganger projected against several bottles of Jose Cuervo 1800.

That's what I call being scared of your own shadow. At least, I'm emblazoned against a great alcohol.

Creeping back toward the viewing glass, the light beam illuminated his face like he was in a bad horror movie. When he finally peeked through the glass, he was intrigued by what he saw. There were no dead bodies, no mawkish, hog-tied clowns. There was nothing frightening at all, unless you were a surfer like Razz.

Under the Pier, adrift in the tides and ricocheting between pilings, was an abandoned surfboard. It looked to be a relatively new Rip Curl, but it had a major problem. A huge chunk had been taken out of its side as if something very large had gotten very hungry for a fiberglass and Styrofoam sandwich. He couldn't help but think of Sharky's surfing incident many years ago and how lucky he'd been to escape with only a leg bite, but Razz feared the owner of this board could have fared much worse.

"Put your hands where I can see them!"

Razz' heart shot into his throat and his hands shot into the air.

Two plainclothes San Margarita cops trained their revolvers on him from the shadows near the door.

"I work here. I just—" Razz blubbered before cutting himself short.

The first cop stepped forward into the room. It was Robert Donati, the rogue who had choked him only days earlier. He smiled, as if relishing an opportunity to inflict more harm.

"Razz? Is that you?" said the second cop, still partially hidden in the shadows.

Johnnie Johnson stepped into the light. Razz was never so happy to see someone he barely knew, having met him through Sharky a few times. He believed Johnson to be a good cop. His feeling toward Donati wasn't nearly so warm and fuzzy.

"Put your gun down. I know him," Johnson said. He pushed Donati's gun to the side. "I said I know him."

Donati didn't look pleased, his powered usurped, but he grudgingly put his gun away.

"What are you doing here, Razz? Stealing recipes?" Johnson asked.

Why is every cop in Los Angeles gun-happy, an aspiring comedian, or both? Razz knew he could have wound up as another not-so-funny statistic if Johnson hadn't been there and recognized him, if he'd just been unlucky, or if Robert Donati had his way.

"I was inspecting the place. I manage it now," he stammered, not used to life-threatening situations.

"We heard there was a change of owners. Didn't know you were the new manager though. I expected someone ... well, someone else." Johnson couldn't quite explain. Being a black man and a victim of discrimination in the past, it was hard for him to admit to his own subconscious racial profiling.

Razz understood. Johnson had been expecting a Mexican. "My partners thought I was the best person for the job," he said, not sure why he felt the need to explain.

"Sure, sorry. We saw the light, you know, so we thought we'd check it out. I just didn't expect to see you."

Razz might have wondered why Johnson was so surprised to see him, so surprised he was the new manager, but he knew why and he questioned himself for it, too. Johnson couldn't believe he would be in business with Louis Marcayda.

"Until today, I would have been as surprised as you, but I am the new manager. And I'm part-owner," Razz said. "Thanks for looking out for the place, but I think we'll be fine."

Johnson nodded, understanding. He looked at Donati who was still smiling smugly. "Come on," he said, moving to the door. "Hey, good luck, Razz. Be careful."

"Yeah, be careful," added Donati. "You never know what bad things can happen at the Pier. I mean, we do what we can, but it can still be a dangerous place, especially, late at night. We wouldn't want anyone to get hurt."

"Let's go, Donati."

"Tell your new 'partner' not to get any funny ideas now that we've let him into our part of town," warned Donati.

Johnson fidgeted, nervous and angry. He wondered whose part of town it was exactly and whether he should consider himself lucky to be allowed in it as well.

"He'd better remember who runs this area," Donati continued. "It was nice of him to make that big donation to the Police Activities League though. Those new uniforms will look great next spring, but it doesn't buy him anything from me." With a parting sneer right out of a bad acting class, he was gone.

Razz had gotten the message. He had a new, very powerful partner who had some very powerful enemies. He felt right in the middle of an irresistible force and an immovable object. He just wasn't sure which was which.

Johnson shrugged, as if acknowledging that, despite running the substation, he knew he wasn't the power in this town, before going out to join his cohort.

Razz watched the two policemen walk back toward the substation. Walking side by side, they seemed miles apart in every way. It made him think of his dubious partnership with Louis. *We each have two kids. We each want them to have better lives. We're each in the restaurant business.* But, try as he might to find further kinship, Razz knew he and Louis were miles apart as well.

"He'd better remember who runs this area," Donati had said. Razz was certain that Louis knew exactly who ran the area and was equally certain that Donati, the poor chump, didn't have a clue.

12

In this part of the bay, the shore ran northwest to southeast, which meant that the rising sun would illuminate the waters under the Pier until approximately eight in the morning, just about the time his first-period class bell would ring. But he didn't have to wait that long.

Richard Gold looked down twenty-seven stories from the penthouse of Gold Tower, the tallest commercial building in San Margarita, one of many buildings he controlled through various partnerships. He surveyed work on his newest project, the bane of his son-in-law's existence, the Gold Shore Hotel and Resort. Excavators and dump trucks looked like toys from this height, but he could tell his toys were moving and were many, so he anticipated the building's completion by fall. Gold knew his creation would add to his already mythic stature as the foremost developer in San Margarita, as well as add to his formidable wealth. And it was good.

From his office, he could see almost everything that happened near the waterfront. He could see the Pier, Ocean Boulevard, even the Hempstead. He could monitor his construction company's progress and that of his competitors on rival projects. He should have been a man at peace, content with his impressive accomplishments, but he wasn't.

He glanced at a financial report offered to him by his assistant, an attractive, but harried-looking, brunette named Wendy. His brow furrowed and lips tightened before he exploded.

"What the hell is this shit!" He flung the report back in her direction and stormed into the hallway. "Where the hell is Masterson? That son of a bitch!"

Secretaries, project managers, and bean counters shook in their pumps and penny loafers, as Gold stormed down the hallway, followed closely by Wendy.

"Mr. Gold. Mr. Gold."

She tried to slow him down, but it was like a Schnauzer stepping in front of a speeding Amtrak. If she weren't careful, she'd be unrecognizable road kill.

"Masterson!"

Gold was out for blood. Something in the report had clearly pissed him off. He rounded a corner and disappeared into an office, still screaming.

"Masterson! You motherfucker!" rang out from the inside of the office. Then all was quiet.

After a moment, Gold poked his head out of the office. "Where the fuck is Masterson?"

"That's what I was trying—"

"Don't try, do. Didn't you see fucking Star Wars?"

Wendy wasn't sure what he meant, which angered him further.

"Where the fuck is he?"

"Uh, that's what I—"

"Just tell me!"

"He quit! He quit! He quit! And so do I!" She looked like she'd said a naughty word in front of a Catholic priest. Then she warmed to the concept, a tiny, relieved smile crossing her lips. "Yeah, I quit. I quit! I quit! I quit!" she sang out gleefully, dancing back to her desk.

The others in the office watched, unsure whether to cheer her on or alert the loony bin.

Gold took the bait. "You can't quit, you're fired! And so is Masterson!"

"Okay, then you owe us severance, unemployment benefits and health insurance." Wendy sure knew how to hurt a guy.

Gold did a quick calculation and decided what any financially astute businessman would decide—he reneged. "You heard her, she quit. She quit, she's not fired. Masterson quit, too."

Wendy laughed. "Whatever."

Smiles spread across the lips of several onlookers, but they were quickly wiped away.

"All of you get back to work!"

The workers hesitated. This was their moment of truth. Would they be brave and back up their working-class brethren? Would they form a solidified front to gain better pay and more respect, or would they crumble?

"I said to get the fuck back to work! Or does someone else want to quit, too?" As Wendy hummed a makeshift, but heartfelt, version of Three Dog Night's "Joy to the World," a project manager named Everett thought about his ten-year-old daughter who needed braces. Foregoing his opportunity to do something heroic, to do something that was right and good, he instead turned and went back to his desk.

Gold smiled. "Anyone?"

An accountant named Phyllis thought about the Caribbean vacation she'd always wanted, sunbathing half nude on a gloriously pristine beach surrounded by brown-skinned cabana boys with deliciously strong bodies offering deliciously strong drinks. She too turned tail and slunk back to her work pit, spineless.

One by one, the others followed, gutless and guilty, but Wendy didn't care. She'd moved on to humming "Sympathy with the Devil," giggling her way through it fairly certain that Gold didn't have a clue to whom or what she was referring. She proudly gathered her belongings, a picture of her husband and two adolescent boys, a coffee cup, and her purse, then walked calmly out to the elevator.

Gold eyed her as she went, suspicious she might be taking one of his company's coffee cups, petty to the bitter end.

When the elevator car arrived, she turned back to him, smiling. "Good luck, Mr. Gold."

He couldn't be sure if she'd just wished him a classy farewell or had warned him that he would, indeed, soon need a whole lot of good luck. "What are you all looking at?"

But no one was looking at anything. They were all back at their desks, working hard, under his spell and that of the almighty dollar. They were his kind of people.

Gold slammed his office door shut. He sunk into his cushy Eames executive chair, clunked his Edward Green Oxfords onto his huge mahogany desk like a studio mogul, and pondered his dilemma. He needed a new executive assistant as well as a project manager for the Gold Shore Hotel and Resort.

A ringing phone outside his office interrupted his mental machinations.

"Wendy! Christ, will you get that?

The phone continued to ring.

"Fuck!"

Gold went to yell at Wendy until he remembered she was no longer there. He kept going, because he knew he'd find someone to scream at and he'd feel better once he did. He threw open the door.

"Will someone get that fucking—"

"Mr. Gold, sir, it's Mr. Banes from San Margarita Savings Bank. He wants to discuss the Gold Shore project."

Gold did a triple-take when he saw a beautiful brunette who looked to be in her mid-twenties, holding the phone. She was wearing a mid-thigh blue skirt and a white, form-fitting silk blouse. And it was a lovely form indeed.

"Who are you?"

"Natalie Wesson. I started here last week. I work for Mr. Jacobs in accounts receivable."

He looked at this perfect young creature with her perfect long legs and knew exactly what he had to do. And, like any man committed to success, he didn't hesitate. "No, you're working for me now. And expect to work late tonight."

Despite her seemingly tender years, she understood him perfectly. "It will be my pleasure, sir."

"And it will be my pleasure, too, I'm sure."

They stared at each other, Gold undressing her to nakedness, imagining all the pleasure he could have with her exquisite body, while she undressed him to his bulging wallet, imagining all the pleasure she could have with his exquisite money. They would be a perfect match.

"Mr. Gold? Do you want to take the call?"

"Huh? Oh, the call, sure. Put it through to my office, Miss Wesson. Thank you."

His smile widened as did his appetite. He went into his office, but found it exceedingly difficult to concentrate. Outside, Natalie Wesson was moving her belongings to Wendy's former desk. Gold watched her walk, sit, stand, and bend over, and he couldn't focus on what Henry Banes was saying. He was fairly sure it had something to do with cost overruns, loan covenants, and the like, but he had his mind on other matters.

Razz rolled over in bed, cracked open a crusty eyelid and peeked at the clock. It was nine-thirty. His eyes shot wide open and he jumped out of bed. He had wanted to go in early on his first official day as an employee and potential part-owner of Cardinal Restaurants, Inc., but hadn't gotten home until 3 a.m. after his disconcerting run-in with the police, so he would be late. He had been promised equity in Cardinal Restaurants, Louis' holding company for the Surf's Up and Sol a Sol, if all went well. He was determined that it would.

Although he'd gone over opening day details with Lotta, and each staff member knew exactly what had to be done, he had wanted to make a good impression with Louis. He knew he had to step up his effort, and that there would be no mediocrity allowed, because there were no longer mediocre owners or mangy mutts to use for excuses. It was up to him to excel now.

As a hot shower soothed his tired body, his tired mind raced over restaurant details. He would consolidate purchasing functions and reduce the number of suppliers to simplify administrative duties. With two restaurants, he could negotiate better pricing. If a supplier didn't like it, tough noogies; he'd find another. He would change the Sol a Sol's drab tablecloths to more colorful ones, an inexpensive, but effective, way to brighten up the place. He'd give the task of selecting tablecloths to Lotta, but he'd keep final approval. He couldn't wait to try out his ideas, to prove his value to Louis and start earning his equity.

The shower curtain flew open.

"Ahh!" Razz backed against the shower wall as if Mrs. Bates was about to skewer him in some gruesome Hitchcockian scene.

"Oh, sorry," Sarah said. "Did you have to get up this morning?"

He looked at his sweet, simple wife and wanted to strangle her. "Yes, I said 'wake me at eight.' Christ, it's the first day and I'm going to be late."

"Sorry, but you woke me from a deep sleep. I thought it might have been a dream."

Razz knew he should apologize, and that he was capable of setting an alarm clock, but he had no intention of doing so. He felt she'd jeopardized his first opportunity to impress his new boss.

"Why are you going in so early?"

He didn't want to explain. He just wanted her to understand, to think through the possibilities herself. "I just need to go in, that's all. There's a lot of work to be done."

"Oh. Sure." She wanted to question him further, assuming correctly that there were already competent employees busy doing whatever work needed to be done, but she decided against it. "Well, have a good day. I'll be back before the kids get home."

"Where are you going?"

"Daddy needs some help at the office. A couple people left this morning unexpectedly."

"You're not going to work for your father."

"He needs my help."

"Yeah, sure. He can hire someone else. You're staying home with the kids."

"It will only be three mornings a week, while Ronnie's with the tutor. Caitlin will be in school anyway."

"It doesn't matter. We don't need the money. With this new job, we'll be doing fine."

"It's not about the money, he asked me to help."

Sarah was loyal and always had been, but now she had divided loyalties, to Razz, to her father, and to herself.

"Last time, he didn't even pay you."

Her silence told him volumes.

"He isn't going to pay you, is he? That cheap bastard."

"I don't know. I don't care, but don't talk like that about my father. He already does so much for us."

"He puts some money in a trust fund for you that he controls and you think it's because he's generous. He did that because he couldn't stand the thought of paying more taxes to the government. It wasn't for you, it was for him. It was the lesser of the evils."

She was steaming more than the shower now, but he was too self-involved to notice. He hated how Richard Gold controlled his daughter, but he hated more how she didn't seem to care. To him, Sarah seemed to see the world through rose-colored glasses.

"Go fuck yourself, Razz."

Shocked, he waited for an apology, but she stood strong, stone-faced.

"What did you say?"

"You heard me. You know I don't like vulgar language, but, at times like this, nothing else seems appropriate. Whether you like it or not, Razz, he's my father. And just as you'd do anything for your father, without question, I'll do the same for mine. Just as I hope that Ronnie and Caitlin will do for you one day, no matter how insensitive or stupid you've become."

He thought about screaming at the top of his lungs to beat down his wife's emotional logic. He thought of telling her again how greedy Gold was, how he, Razz, should have had part of the Gold Shore deal. Or of telling her how Gold was rumored to have mistresses all over town. Or about how people considered many of his business dealings to lie on the shadier side of the commercial street. But he didn't tell her anything of the sort, because, despite his limited self, he knew she was right.

"I'm sorry."

In most cases, an apology would have been enough to appease her, but not this time. She didn't hear him. She was already strapped into her Range Rover, speeding out of the driveway to go help her father.

Razz was late for work and his wife hated him. It was only ten o'clock and already it was a bad day. Cruising too fast down Palm View Boulevard, he tried to admire the stately, Canary Island date palms that dotted each side of the street, but he wasn't in the mood. The radio blared Ozzy Osbourne's "Old LA Tonight" until he couldn't take it any longer and he switched to a New Age station offering mellow, bubble gum jazz. He hoped the caressing sounds of Kenny G's saxophone would calm him, but he soon turned the radio back to Ozzy. He figured it was better to be miserable and alive than content and brain dead.

Whatever else he might do in his life, and he felt it wasn't much thus far, he knew his family would always be his greatest accomplishment. Along with his parents, Sarah had always been his biggest supporter. So what if Richard Gold was a rotten, selfish son-of-a-bitch, he was still her father. And, as much as Razz hated to admit it, he did personally benefit from Gold's affluence. And that continued to gnaw at him.

He was determined to make it up to her. He had to. He would change his ways and make sure she knew how much he appreciated her, that she and the kids came first, that—*smack!*

Razz looked back to see something unrecognizable slide off his trunk. When he did, the tires hit the soft, gravelly shoulder, and his car lurched completely off the pavement. He saw a gigantic palm tree ahead, fast approaching. His mind flashed back to his triumphant day surfing under the Pier when every piling seemed to have his name written on it. He didn't like his chances now any better than he had then.

He yanked the wheel to the left and his car went into a skid, careening closer to oblivion. If he hit the tree at this speed, he knew all the King's horses and all the King's men wouldn't be able to put him together again. The tires on the left side strained to grasp the earth as the right side dug in. He turned back to the right to try to straighten out the car. Fellow drivers whizzed past, concerned looks on their faces. He could see them in such detail, as if seated next to them, and every astonished wrinkle made a statement. The statement was that he was going to die.

Across the street, a yapping French Poodle with a bad haircut caught his eye. Its owner, a silver-haired, little old lady with her own bad haircut, held on tightly to her prized possession, which was struggling to free itself. And Razz was still hurtling towards the massive, unforgiving tree.

Straining to keep his eyes open, but dying not to watch, he turned the wheel carefully to the left and the car shifted slightly. He tapped the brakes gently. It was going to be close. One more tiny turn of the wheel and his car slid by unscathed.

He tapped the brakes several more times and the Mustang finally rolled to a stop. He looked at his fellow motorists passing by, but he could no longer make out their faces. They were safely ensconced, incognito, behind smoked glass. He looked for the yapping poodle, but could no longer see or hear it. He wondered if he'd imagined the whole incident until he looked back at the majestic, fifty-year-old date palm and realized his memory was intact and that he was extremely lucky to still have one.

Razz got out of his car, his legs shaking, and walked back toward the scene of the almost-crime. The tree no longer seemed as daunting as when he was approaching it at fifty miles an hour. Looking at it now, he almost wondered what the fuss had been about.

A thrashing in the bushes alerted him that, whatever he'd hit, it was still alive. He raced over and quickly regretted it, because he wished he'd never seen his victim at all. It was only a garden variety pigeon, the kind you often see searching for food in the street and you're never sure whether they'll be smart enough to move out of your car's way. This one clearly wasn't. The sight of it, haphazardly flapping one limp wing, its broken neck skewing its head to one side, a glazed look in its eyes, was enough to turn Razz' stomach. The pigeon moved itself around in the dirt in a jagged circle, trying to fly, unaware that its flying days were officially over.

Razz crawled into the bushes and let loose his breakfast, a raisin bagel and a glass of orange juice. The orange-green-black mixture burned as it convulsed out of his body. He wasn't squeamish at heart, but this bird was so badly hurt, so helpless, that Razz couldn't hold back. He felt responsible. He imagined Sarah, near death, flailing helplessly like this broken pigeon. Then he imagined Caitlin in the same situation. Then he imagined Ronnie. His breath quickened out of control, until he couldn't take it any longer.

He searched frantically for something that would end his horrible imagining, for something he could use to quiet this bird, and give them both some peace. Feeling around amongst the bushes, he touched a stone roughly the size of his fist. He took it and, barely looking at the pain-wracked pigeon, smashed the stone against the bird's skull.

He sat back and felt the pounding in his chest. He wondered if this was what a heart attack felt like. He looked again at the pigeon. The stone covered the pigeon's head and he was glad. He couldn't have withstood the bird's accusatory glare.

After a moment, Razz lifted himself to his feet. He thought about burying the victim, to give it a funeral of sorts, but he didn't. Instead, he turned, brushed himself off, and walked to his car. He would leave the dead pigeon for the roadside sanitation crews to clean up. He couldn't bear to look at that bird again.

Sarah couldn't forgive Razz this time. She could forgive his late nights, his flirtations in the name of business, even his selfishness, but she was sick of him trying to control her. She was sick of him putting down her father, because, when he did, she always felt he was putting her down, too. She was sick of Razz taking her for granted. She wondered if she might not be just plain sick of him.

She had studied accounting in college, partly due to her father's expectations and partly due to her own. She wanted to be ready, because she fully expected that she would run his empire one day, not figuring that Gold wouldn't retire till his dying breath. Or that she would become unexpectedly expectant. She hadn't exactly been disappointed when she found out she was pregnant from her dalliances with Razz. She'd always wanted a child. It was just that she felt she'd lost stature in her father's eyes, especially, when Caitlin turned out to be a girl. Redeemed somewhat after Ronnie's birth three years later, she still wanted to prove she was capable of running the business, of being the son her father had always wanted.

"Do you have those figures yet?"

She looked up and saw her dad standing in the doorway of Masterson's old office, his nose buried in a set of financial statements from another of his many projects.

"We've got to make those cash flows work. I'll be damned if I'm going to lose any of this deal," he continued, his nose still buried.

"But you always said that taking on partners, using their money, was how you diversified risk, Daddy."

He looked at her blankly, and then exploded. "If I need a God damn lecture, I'll get Masterson back!" He stormed off.

Sarah had seen him scream at helpless employees all through her childhood. She first worked for him when she was ten, filing papers and fetching coffee, just so she could be near him. She'd worked for him on weekends during high school and each summer during college, learning all she could about real estate. He had seemed so brilliant and powerful. To this day, although he was older, grayer and a tad shorter, he still seemed to her to tower over everyone and everything except the impressive buildings he created.

Although she had told Razz about many of her experiences, her husband never understood how much she knew. Richard Gold trusted her more than any of his employees, though that still didn't mean he completely trusted her.

"Sarah, I'm sorry."

She looked up and couldn't help smiling.

Gold walked into her office and hugged her. "I'm sorry, honey. I'm under a lot of stress right now. I hope you'll understand. I really appreciate your help."

With that, all was forgiven. "I understand, Daddy. I know you didn't mean it."

"That's my girl."

They continued to hug as Natalie Wesson walked around the corner, her face buried in some papers just like Gold's had been. She was a quick study.

"Mr. Gold, I wanted you to see this—oh, I'm sorry."

Wesson was taken aback by the sight of Gold hugging another woman. She already had designs on him and wondered if her task might be tougher than she first thought.

"Natalie, this is my daughter, Sarah. Sarah, this is Natalie Wesson, my new assistant."

Sarah checked her out. Wesson's short skirt and half-opened blouse seemed a far cry from professional wear and made her conservative suit seem downright dowdy. The two women approached each other cautiously, each protective, wary and suspicious. Sarah broke the ice, thrusting out her hand.

"Hi, Natalie. It's nice to meet you."

"You, too."

They shook firmly, like two men trying to impress each other with their strength, and looked directly into the other's eyes, trying to read her opponent's exact purpose and the extent of her threat.

"How long have you worked here?" asked Sarah.

"A week. I started working for Richard today."

Sarah released her grip. This woman had called her father "Richard" and, although Gold squirmed at the familiarity, he hadn't corrected her. Sarah already didn't like her.

"Delivery for Sarah McNeil," said a man, partially obscured behind a beautiful arrangement of red roses.

"Oh, for me? They're beautiful." Sarah beamed from ear to ear, and tried to remember how angry she was at her husband. She signed for the flowers and reached for the note, oblivious now to Gold and his assistant.

Dearest Sarah, the note started and her heart fluttered. *Thank you so much for your help. You'll always be my favorite girl. Love, Dad.*

"Thank you, Daddy." She kissed him on the cheek, then turned away to hide her face, flushed with humiliation and anger.

Natalie watched with a knowing smirk, correctly surmising what had happened to Sarah's expectations.

"I just wanted you to know how much I appreciate you. You're always here when I need you. I can always count on you," Gold said.

Sarah turned back and hugged him. "Yes, you can, Daddy."

He loved his daughter's attention, but it embarrassed him in front of his assistant, so he pulled away. "Well, I guess we can get back to work. See if you can get me those papers this morning."

"I will. And I'll have a full analysis by Wednesday."

Gold and Natalie Wesson excused themselves and Sarah went back to her desk to lick her wounds. She had expected the roses to be from Razz, an apology for being such an oaf this morning. When they weren't, even the nice gesture from her father felt like a letdown. She found it difficult to concentrate on the mundane financial details of the Gold Shore Hotel project and decided to get a cup of coffee to clear her mind. She went to her door and then stopped short.

Across the floor, a huge bouquet of orchids and expensive, exotic flowers sat in a vase on Natalie Wesson's desk. Wesson had her arms wrapped tightly around Gold's neck in what appeared to be an intimately unprofessional manner. She kissed his cheek and rubbed against him.

Their hug seemed too close for a polite thank you and was far too close for Sarah's comfort.

Razz wheeled past a languid parking attendant and flashed his parking pass. Yes, he now had parking privileges on the Pier and didn't have to pay a cent for them. At least, he didn't pay directly, because the fee came out of the expense budget for the restaurants.

It was ten-forty-five and the breakfast shift was almost over, so he wasn't expecting much business. A few half full tables and he'd be happy. He knew the Surf's Up was more of a lunch and dinner spot anyway. Most of the morning people at the Pier were fishermen and street people, not exactly a big spending clientele on which to build a restaurant's success.

When he got out of his car, he heard an unfamiliar buzz. He was surprised to see four tables on the outside back patio occupied. Two people were at each table. A young, nice looking couple appeared as if they had just come off an Iowa farm. There was a middle-aged, middle-class Hispanic couple. An older white couple seemed to have said everything they had to say to each other years ago. There were two attractive, well-dressed young women and Razz would have sworn they winked at him as he passed. The buzz grew louder and louder and he finally recognized its source. It was the buzz of people talking. He gazed through the glass back door and a stunned look came over his face. The Surf's Up was packed.

Razz opened the door and relished the wave of noise that washed over him. He waded through a veritable flotilla of customers.

"What are you doing here?"

He turned to see Lotta. Her hair was out of place, but everything else was exactly where it should be.

"I thought I'd see how things were going this morning."

"Great, we can use your help. It's busier than we're used to," she said in a masterstroke of understatement. "Table four needs a refill of decaf and table seven wanted to compliment the manager on our excellent service. Why don't you talk to them?"

"Yes, ma'am," he said good-naturedly.

"Got to go. By the way, congratulations."

"Congratulations to you."

Razz watched the hustle and bustle of the new Surf's Up. Servers and busboys hinted at exhaustion as they sped from one table to the next, but their exhaustion was largely hidden behind their pleasure in making more in tips than they'd ever made on a morning shift before. Physically, the Surf's Up looked the same as two days earlier, but this version was definitely new and improved. It was profitable.

He briefly daydreamed about jumping into mounds of dollar bills, before joining the fray. First, it was on to table four with a pot of decaf where three young professional women were finishing what seemed to be a business meeting. Friendly like they were already regulars, he hoped they would be. Then it was on to table seven where a fifty-something woman gushed about her cute young waiter. She said she was looking forward to coming back and she'd be certain to tell all her garden club friends about it.

Razz thanked her and excused himself. He thought these patrons must be offspring from Stepford; they were all so happy and perfect. He didn't know why he felt so nervous, but he didn't have time to dwell on it, because he had to set up table eleven for the next group of waiting customers.

13

He saw the wave coming only fifteen minutes after entering the water. Six-twenty-two a.m., November 5th, 1977. He had already let several almost perfect waves pass, but when he saw this wave two hundred feet away, his heart raced. This was The One. Two hundred feet is a long distance from which to judge a wave that hadn't formed yet, let alone THE WAVE, but Robbie/Razz knew from experience that it would be the one to turn him into a surfing legend or turn him into fish chum.

January 7, 2005

It was an unusual, late Friday morning, because Sharky had already been up for several hours. Terri had awakened him to go shopping and he'd just spent two thousand, forty-seven dollars and thirty-five cents buying curtains, bedspreads, a new chair, a vacuum cleaner, an entertainment center, a stereo to put in it, and sundry other useful items that he'd never gotten around to owning before. He was pleasantly shocked that he enjoyed seeing them all in his apartment.

"Maybe we could paint next weekend."

He looked at her busy scrubbing the kitchen counter, much of which was now white for the first time since shortly after he'd moved in. He wore a contented smile that hadn't left him even while he was spending seven hundred and twenty-three dollars for an overpriced La-Z-Boy recliner that she'd talked him into buying. She said he deserved it. For the first time in his life, he started to believe it.

"Sure." Anything she wanted.

Although he had worried at first that she was using him, that she just needed a place to stay now she could no longer live at Richard Gold's fancy Hempstead apartment, he was soon convinced of her sincerity, because she had thrown herself so wholeheartedly into making the apartment nicer. Terri had spent almost eighteen hundred dollars of her own money on a number of exotic-looking plants, a forty inch plasma TV, a DVD player, and a dining set for the kitchen. It no longer looked liked his apartment; it looked like a real home—their home.

"I'll get some swatches, so we can choose colors."

Sharky had never considered there could be any apartment color other than dingy white. He'd been surrounded by it for so long, it seemed natural, but natural was not the word to describe anything regarding his life.

"That sounds great," he said. Almost everything she said sounded great to him. Used to hearing his own sour thoughts rattling around his skull, he enjoyed her higher-pitched, happier sounds.

He grabbed her around the waist. "What do you say we go get some lunch? I'm hungry. The apartment can wait."

She threw her arms around him, pressing close, and he began to think that food should wait, too.

"I'm only half done with this counter and I want to finish. I can make you something though."

"No, no, I'll go get something. Is Mae's okay?"

Terri rolled her eyes, smiling. "Pastrami on rye with a green salad, no dressing, please," she said, resigned to the fact she wouldn't be dining at Spago any time soon. "Come back soon and maybe there'll be a surprise for you."

Sharky giggled like a school girl. He loved her surprises.

It was a beautiful January day, sixty-eight degrees and sunny when Sharky walked out his door—perfect Southern California weather. It was the type of winter weather that most people from northern states can't fathom until they see it for themselves. Then, when they do, they often stay. It sure beat shoveling snow.

It was only two blocks to Mae's and, because their service was so fast, Sharky hadn't bothered to call in his order. He knew he'd be home within fifteen minutes anyway.

He admired his neighborhood as if seeing it for the first time. Well-kept homes, apartment buildings and small businesses dotted the street. *This is all so quaint*, he thought. He smiled as he wondered the last time he'd thought of the word "'quaint."

An attractive woman walking a dog across the street made him wonder if Terri liked dogs. *Maybe I'll get her a puppy*. Never mind that his lease restricted pets and he generally hated animals, he was thinking about how he could make her happy, because she made him so happy. But when the dog relieved himself in a stranger's yard, prompting its master to bring out a plastic baggy to clean up after him, Sharky decided they'd stick with the house plants for now.

From the outside, Mae's looked packed as usual. Trust fund couples reading newspapers and chatting on cell phones, unemployed, single men hung over from grand revelries, and hungry, hard-working street walkers just off shift waited for tables in a line that stretched into the parking lot. It was worth the wait, because the food was cheap, coffee refills were free, and advice was plentiful. Ask a question on any topic and there were always a number of eccentric know-it-alls to enlighten you. Sharky had held court at the counter many times himself.

"Hey, Officer Sampson."

He recognized Mae's voice instantly. Mae was a fifty-six year old spinster married faithfully to her restaurant. Although officially still owned by her father, now eighty-three and holding tenuously to life in a nearby nursing home, Mae's was named after her when she was an infant and it had been her home ever since.

She'd washed dishes, cleaned tables and served coffee before she was ten, and had taken customer orders while standing on an apple box so she could be seen behind the counter. She handled the fry grill when she was thirteen and customers still swore the French fries tasted best when cooked by her. Never mind that every cook used the same grease and all any of them did was dump in freshly-cut potatoes and turn a switch. Eschewing an opportunity to go to college when she was eighteen, she decided to stay in San Margarita and make her namesake her life's work. Plump, jovial, and ruddy-faced, she looked like she'd been fried herself by splattering grease and hot steam, but many said it was because of the peach schnapps she not-so-secretly nipped on throughout the day.

"Hi, Mae. How's it shaking?" said Sharky.

Mae shook herself back and forth in an odd, arrhythmic dance, her breasts and large jowls hanging on for dear life. "You tell me!" She roared in laughter.

Sharky and the other customers couldn't help but laugh with her. That Mae. She wasn't the classiest broad in town, but she was the most down-to-earth. She was dirt-level.

"Pastrami on rye, green salad, no dressing."

"Green salad? Still got company, huh?" Mae smiled at him like a proud mother and Sharky turned red-faced.

"Uh, yeah."

"Good for you, sweetie. She seems like a special girl."

He smiled proudly and nodded in affirmation.

"And did you want something, too, sugar?"

"Oh, yeah, burger, fries, large coffee ... and throw in a couple of honey-glazed donuts, to go."

"That's more like it."

As customers in line moved forward, a successful-looking, young power couple, each partner talking into their cell phone, entered.

"Turn those frigging things off!" Mae would have used stronger language had there not been kids in the place.

The man and woman looked up at a handwritten sign above Mae that read, *Cell phones and smoking not allowed. Smoke and you will be asked to leave. Talk on a cell phone and the cell phone will be shoved up your ass, then your ass will be kicked out.*

Had it been the Four Seasons Hotel or a trendy new restaurant, they would have been so insulted they'd have stormed out, never to return. But not here.

"Sorry, Mae. Sorry, we forgot." They skulked to their table.

By the look on Mae's face, you'd think the couple had shit on her floor. You see, Mae was an old-fashioned girl and she didn't see the need for a cell phone, PDA or computer, because everyone she'd need to talk to would walk in her door within a few days anyway. Everything could wait a few days.

She brought Sharky's bag of goodies, still eyeing the cell phone couple. "Here, sugar. You take care of that woman."

"Thanks, Mae. See you soon." He took the brown bag, already spotted with grease from the French fries inside, and headed for the door.

"Hey, baby, are you feeding that girl now? You must be in love. You're really starting to spoil her," said an attractive, but worn, street hooker with jet-black hair who had just entered with two of her cohorts.

Sharky thought he vaguely recognized her. Perhaps, he'd been with her a few times before he'd met Rosie, but he couldn't be sure. He kept walking.

"I tried to warn her. Do a man every week and he's bound to fall in love sooner or later. Yeah, Rosie's got herself a live one."

He stopped dead in his tracks. He turned back, his heart pounding, and looked up at a wall clock. It was seven minutes past twelve. His breath left him in a furious, uncontrollable gasp. He dropped the bag and, as the food splattered onto the floor, he sped out the door.

"Terri! Terri!" Sharky wailed in a plea that rivaled Brando's as Stanley Kowalski begging for his Stella. He crashed through the door, expecting to see Terri in a jealous rage hovering over a dead Rosie with a long, sharp, bloody knife. He could handle that, but he prayed it wouldn't be the other way around.

He ran into the kitchen. A container of Bon Ami and a sponge sat on the counter, reminders of a task half-done. Terri hadn't finished the job like she'd planned; something or someone had distracted her. He ran into the bathroom and drew back the shower curtain, expecting the worst, but there was nothing but the new bath caddy and scented soaps that Terri had bought that morning. He sprinted back outside to look for her car, but the Grand Am was gone. Terri was gone.

Razz felt a bit gone, too. It was already afternoon when he woke, but he was still exhausted. He'd worked until four in the morning, restocking both restaurants' seriously depleted kitchens and bars, as well as counting and recounting cash and receipts. It had been a huge financial day for the Surf's Up and Sol a Sol, but it had taken an energy toll on all of the employees. He'd considered going in early again, but decided he'd let Lotta handle things until his regular shift at four o'clock. Besides, he wanted to see his kids and, deep down in the dark recesses of his male psyche, he remembered that he had an apology to make.

"Sarah?"

He'd crossed the line yesterday, insulting her by insulting her father. He'd meant to call her, to beg her forgiveness, to win her over by making her laugh somehow, but he'd gotten so busy at work that he'd forgotten until it was already after eleven at night. Waking a woman from a deep sleep in order to apologize didn't seem like the best strategy, so he'd waited until today.

"Sarah!" There was still no answer. "Ronnie! Caitlin!"

Wearing only his boxers, his hair tousled, he snuck into the hall and peeked around the corner into the living room. "Sarah?"

Only the sounds of Santa Ana winds beating against the living room's picture window responded. He went into the kitchen to look for a note proclaiming his family's whereabouts. There was nothing written on the chalk board. He searched the counters and the refrigerator door for a Post-it, but there was nothing.

He opened the refrigerator and grabbed a container of orange juice. About to pour himself a glass, he remembered his unpleasant experience from yesterday, barfing up burning, acidic liquid along the side of the roadway. He decided he'd drink water instead. He turned on the tap and looked out his kitchen window to the front yard. Sarah's Land Rover was gone.

Two burnt slices of toast and a glass of water later, Razz didn't feel any better, but he was ready to start his day. As he put his dirty glass in the sink, the phone rang.

He picked up the receiver. "Hello."

"Hello, dear."

"Hi, mom."

"Where have you been? We thought you fell off the earth. We miss you."

Even if his wife was going to kill him, his mother still loved him. But her unconditional love just proved how wrong he'd been to denigrate Sarah's father. He would never forgive her if she said nasty things about his mother or father. Of course, it would be impossible to do so honestly, because, unlike Richard Gold, his parents were salts-of-the-earth. But that was beside the point.

"It's been a crazy week, mom. Sorry," he said as he wandered into the living room.

"That's all right, dear. I know you're busy."

"How's dad?"

"He's good. His back's been acting up, what with this cold weather."

Razz looked outside and knew it had to be around seventy and knew his father's back was acting up from too many years of hard labor at the metal shop.

"You know him, though. He wouldn't complain if he got hit by a Mack truck."

"Yeah, I know him. When's he going to retire anyway?"

"What, so he can stay home and bother me all day?"

He laughed. He knew his mother would love to have his father home to pamper and fawn over all day, but also knew his dad would crumple and die if he were to stop working. Tom McNeil wasn't the type to take up golf.

"How's the new place?"

"Wonderful. It's so much easier to care for and we've got plenty of space now that we put everything in storage. I don't know why we kept all that stuff around anyway. This is a lovely, little place."

Razz had seen the "lovely, little place" when he'd moved them in, all four hundred and twenty-five square feet of it. And its size surpassed its loveliness. Needing paint, new carpet and drapes, their friends' guest house wasn't very welcoming, but he knew if anyone could make it a home, his mother could.

"How's your new job?"

Her question caught him off-guard. "Job? Oh, good, great. Jeez, I forgot to tell you, didn't I? I'm sorry, I got so caught up in things ... Who told you?"

"Sarah called this morning. Are you two all right?

Although her previous question had surprised him, this one scared the bejesus out of him. "Sure, we're fine. Why?"

"Don't play dumb with me. She didn't sound very happy."

Razz felt like he might as well just rent a billboard to broadcast his innermost secrets. "We had a little fight yesterday."

"I see. Well, you'd better take care of that girl. She's the best thing that ever happened to you."

"I know, Mom. I will. I'm going to apologize as soon as I see her. I did something really stupid yesterday."

He waited for her to ask what he'd done, to console him, or, at least, to praise him for his acknowledgement of fault. She did none of the above, which led him to think he was probably deeper in his wife's doghouse than he'd imagined.

"Uh, what did she call you for anyway?"

"She wanted to see if I could take the kids."

"Oh. For when?"

"They've been here since school. They're playing outside right now."

"The kids are there? Where's Sarah?"

"She said she was going shopping."

He breathed a sigh of relief, but, when he remembered she liked to show off the kids when she shopped, the sigh caught in his throat. "Oh. Uh, did she say where?"

The door behind him opened and he whirled to see Sarah. Her make-up was battered from crying.

"I saw a lawyer."

"Is someone there, dear?" asked his mother.

"I'll have to call you back, Mom," he mumbled, then hung up the phone without waiting for a response.

He knelt before his wife and took her reluctant hand. "I'm sorry, I'm sorry, I'm sorry. I'll never insult your father or your family again. I'm nothing without you, baby. Please forgive me."

Sarah looked deep into his most sincere eyes and choked back a sob. "I filed for a legal separation."

She ran into the bedroom, leaving Razz prostrate, like Lear in the wilderness, distraught and disbelieving, his kingdom crumbled around him.

Of all the men in the whole wide world, Sharky was the one who probably best understood the depths of what Razz was feeling. Had he remembered to call Rosie to cancel his weekly appointment, he'd be basking in the glow of his new-found love, not sitting on the toilet in the dark, crying.

The new bath caddy lay in the tub, mangled, crushed under Sharky's weight during a fit of rage. In the kitchen, Terri's container of Bon Ami lay open on the linoleum floor, having spilled its contents shortly after it gouged a jagged hole in a plaster wall due to his seventy mile an hour fastball. Vestiges of his tirade were everywhere. A dresser drawer flung open in the bedroom left Terri's underclothes lying strewn upon the carpet. A new kitchen chair lay tipped onto its side in the living room where it had been hurled, just missing the overhead light. His home now looked like a disaster area, a sort of dysfunctional shrine to his emotional state.

He flushed the toilet absentmindedly, though he hadn't used it for anything but sitting. He picked up the bath caddy and tossed it into a tiny trash can. In its new, crumpled state, it fit with room to spare. He pulled the shower curtain closed and trudged into the living room. He picked up the kitchen chair and returned it to the dining table, where it sat unsteadily, its back left leg no longer symmetrical with its brethren. He dumped the remains of the Bon Ami in the garbage and looked at his half-white counter. He doubted he would ever finish the job. He leaned his elbows on the counter and rubbed his forehead. He felt an enormous headache coming on.

He closed the living room drapes, retreating into his pre-Terri, cave-like existence. It felt oddly normal, but it didn't feel good. He turned on the new television and the screen glowed and a laugh track played, but it only made his headache worse. He sat down in his La-Z-Boy recliner that didn't seem as comfortable as it had at the store. He flipped through stations until his head screamed. He clicked off the television just before sending the remote control on a fast flight into the bathroom unexpectedly shattering the mirror.

Had Sharky any tears left, he would have cried again then and there. *How could everything go so right, so wrong, so right, and then so wrong again so damn quickly?* The thought of being alone in his apartment for the next two weeks, waiting for his suspension to end, was almost overwhelming. He couldn't imagine spending the rest of his life alone now, although one short week ago it was not unhappily considered a given.

He decided there was only one thing to do—sleep. He would get blind drunk later to help him get through a lonely Friday night, but, for now, the black, soundless, thoughtless void of sleep would do. He dragged himself into the bedroom and flopped onto his nicely-made bed. He knew this would probably be the last time it would look so nice.

He drew the bedspread around him, still fully clothed, and curled into a fetal position. His eyelids fluttered as he began to nod off, his emotional exhaustion overpowering his mental ramblings. As he faded toward sleep, he thought he heard a female's voice and his eyes shot open. He waited for more, listening intently, but the voice was gone. He wasn't sure if it had just been wishful thinking, but it disturbed him so much that he lay wide awake for many minutes, torn between the certainty of miserable thoughts and the possibility of more miserable dreams.

It was three o'clock on the worst afternoon of his life, but the monotonous clicking of the clock's second hand helped him focus and gradually he relaxed. Whatever horrible dreams might come, he decided he'd take them over his horrid thought-filled reality any day.

His head sank heavily onto his pillow, and his breathing deepened. He snored softly.

Sharky trembled when his apartment's front door quietly opened, letting in a cool late afternoon breeze, but he did not wake. He continued to sleep as the living room carpet dulled the pit-pat of approaching footsteps. But when someone opened the bedroom door, causing the slightest of squeaks from a rusty hinge, all hell broke loose. He awoke and, in one graceful, elongated move, the kind that Hollywood directors spend years dreaming up, he opened his night stand drawer, retrieved a revolver, cocked it, spun onto the floor, and pointed the gun directly at the intruder's forehead.

"Freeze!"

"Aaggh!" two distinctly feminine voices screamed.

Sharky was stunned into silence, not because he was surprised by female burglars screaming, but because they weren't burglars at all. No, this confrontation was more unusual and, in a way, more unsettling. In front of him, Terri held a Ross shopping bag brimming with bargains. Behind her stood Rosie, also carrying a full Ross bag.

"Jerry, it's me."

He lowered the gun, but was too confused to put it away. "What, uh, what are you doing here?"

"I live here, silly. Remember?" Terri laughed and then spread out her new clothes on the bed. "Look what we got."

Sharky watched, dumbfounded, while she arranged her clothes.

"See this outfit. Rosie found this for me."

He looked at Rosie who hadn't moved since she entered the room. "What are you doing here?"

Terri answered for her. "You invited her. You owe her a hundred dollars, by the way. You forgot to tell her you wouldn't need her services anymore. I mean, you don't plan on needing her services, do you?"

He wondered if this was a trick. Surely, however he answered, he would shoot himself in the foot. "Uh, I hope not. I mean, no offense, Rosie, but, uh, no, I guess not," was the best he could muster.

"You guess not?" asked Terri.

"No, I mean, uh, are you two friends?"

Whether it was because of his naively innocent question or the sight of his stupefied state, the women couldn't hold back any longer and burst into laughter.

"There, there, let mama tell you all about it."

He recoiled when Terri reached for him, afraid she might have a knife ready to transfer into his back. Instead, she kissed him.

When their lips parted, he was still confused, but he sure felt better. "Aren't you mad?"

"I admit I wasn't pleased when Rosie came to the door looking for you. I wanted to belt her, but I mostly wanted to belt you. Then I realized I should thank her. If it weren't for her, you probably wouldn't be such a wonderful lover."

An involuntary grin came over his face as he proudly considered his sexual prowess. "I'm a wonderful lover?"

Terri grabbed his crotch. "Yes, baby, but if you've got any other women out there, you won't be much longer."

"No, no, that's it, just her," he said, carefully extricating his nut sack.

"Good, now give Rosie her hundred dollars and tell her you'll no longer be requiring her services."

Sharky thought for a second, caught by an inescapable tendency to be cheap, then jumped for his wallet. He took out five twenties, then two more for a tip, and gave them to his now-former hooker. "Thank you, Rosie, but I'll no longer be requiring your services. I, uh, I'm in love with the greatest woman in the world."

Rosie took the money and smiled, first at him, then at Terri. She gave him a kiss on the cheek, and then did the same to her.

"Take care of this woman, Jerry. They don't make them like her anymore." With that, she left the room, the apartment, and Terri and Sharky's lives.

He watched the door close, the oddest of triangles now back to a comfortable pairing, and felt an enormous weight lift from his shoulders. "Thank you."

Terri welcomed him into her arms. "And thank you."

"For what?"

She looked him straight in the eye, and then handed him a credit card. It was his. "You just spent five hundred dollars on clothes and foot massages for Rosie and me. We thought it was the least you could do."

He quickly came to the same conclusion. It was the least he could do, because she had taught him a valuable lesson—don't forget to cancel your hooker appointments when you've already met the love of your life.

He laughed at the absurdity of his day. He had gone from the heights of love to the depths of despair and back again all in a matter of hours. Terri joined him laughing, and then they tumbled onto the bed to laugh and screw and laugh and screw for hours.

As was his weekly habit, Sharky had his sexual romp, only this time it had cost him far more than a hundred dollars, and it was well worth the price.

It was worth any price.

14

The sun was perfect, rising slowly. The wind was just right. He looked one more time toward the underbelly of the Pier. It was waiting for him. To his left, ten or twelve surfers whooped it up catching waves to ride easily into shore. On top of the Pier, two early morning fishermen readied to cast their lines into the water. Robbie's heart leapt into his throat. He had forgotten about the fishermen!

January 11, 2005

It was decided—Razz would move out of the home he had shared with his wife for the past six and a half years. He had pleaded, apologized, begged, and cajoled, but Sarah was unexpectedly solid in her decision to kick him out. He'd had no idea how far he had let their relationship slide. Her gentleness and good humor, not to mention the afternoon sexual delights, had lulled him into a false sense of security. He thought the sexual frolics were due to her love for him and her desire to please him, but it turned out they happened largely because she was horny. She told him he needed to grow up and, try as he might, he couldn't begin to come up with an argument for that one.

Sarah told him there wasn't another man, but he knew that only meant there wasn't one yet. Although most men would shy away from a nearly forty year old woman with two young children, the potential burden of those children was mitigated by the fact she could support many men several times over with her huge trust fund dowry. He knew he would have to act fast to keep his place in her life.

"I'm here to look at the apartment for rent," Razz said to a beer-bellied, overly-hairy creature when the man cracked open his apartment door. "You are the manager, aren't you?"

He thought the guy looked more like a skid row reject, rather than a manager of a forty-five unit apartment building located in a nice part of Fairside.

"It's been rented," the guy growled and he started to close the door.

Razz thrust his hand out, stopping the door's progress. "Well, you must have others."

The man-beast stared him up and down through the foot-wide crack in the door. "Not for you," he said and slammed the door shut so hard the windows rattled.

After scouring the *Monitor*'s real estate section for rental possibilities, making over thirty phone calls, and visiting seven buildings that day, Razz was exhausted. Although Sarah had let him stay the last two nights, relegated to a small room normally used as an office, she had given him an ultimatum—be out by today, Tuesday, or the police would escort him out. They had spoken to their kids who had cried copiously, but Caitlin and Ronnie still didn't fully understand the ramifications of their parents' split.

In his apartment search, he received various excuses why managers couldn't rent to him: the apartment was rented, they didn't allow kids, or his credit wasn't good enough. He had put himself on wait lists at three different buildings, but number twenty-seven was his highest position on any list. It might be five years before he'd be allowed the privilege of renting an overpriced five hundred square foot studio, and then only if his credit passed muster.

When Razz approached the Surf's Up back door at three minutes after four, he was convinced he was a failure. He was sure if he looked up "failure" in the dictionary, the definition, "Razz McNeil," would stare back at him. He rubbed a painful crook in his neck, the result of sleeping his six-foot frame on a five-foot couch, and entered the Surf's Up.

He was crestfallen to see only three occupied tables. Perhaps their busy first few days were flukes, as he had feared. Then he noticed his workers looked like they'd been churned through a blender at high speed.

"What happened to you?" he asked Chad who shuffled past, tousled and smiling vacantly.

"Four four-tops, three three-tops, and seven two-tops," he explained, slumping against a wall. Two seconds later, he was up again, miraculously rejuvenated, and delivering Coke refills to table five.

Razz saw a restaurant askew. Chairs hadn't yet been pushed back under tables that hadn't yet been bussed. Several salt shakers were low and pieces of dirty silverware lay randomly on the floor. On a normal day, Razz would be furious, because there could be no excuses for such sloppiness. But he knew he must have arrived during the calm after an apparent gale force lunch storm. Besides, he was way too tired to bitch about much of anything.

Chad had serviced fourteen tables during the lunch shift—four with four customers, three with three customers, and seven with two customers each. That meant thirty-nine paying customers for just one server. With Sonja also working the lunch shift, and Lotta available to handle any overflow, he figured they must have served seventy or, possibly, eighty meals in the five-hour shift. Either number would be a record for his tenure.

"Thank God, you're here."

Razz turned to see Lotta stagger from the kitchen.

"You'll need asparagus, provolone and chicken breasts right away. The lunch special sold out." She poured herself a Chardonnay, and then collapsed onto a stool in front of the bar.

"What's going on? Is this the same restaurant?"

"Louis knows a lot of people. Get used to it."

He wondered if many of their new customers weren't enticed by some sort of frequent hooker points program, like air miles for heavy credit card users, set up at Louis' other establishments, but this amount of business couldn't be explained even by that type of dubious cross-promotion.

He pulled up a stool and sat down. While Lotta nursed her Chardonnay, he nursed his sore neck and sore ego.

"What's with you? I thought you'd be thrilled."

"Oh, I am."

"What's the matter?"

"Nothing."

Although he appreciated her concern, he didn't feel his current problems were any of her business. Besides, he didn't want to be tempted to cry on her shoulder. Her comfort would feel far too comforting.

As Chad and Sonja toiled to restore order behind them, Lotta and Razz sat silently at the bar, like two old warriors who'd seen it all and were too tired to talk about any of it.

Finally, he asked, "Hey, you don't know of any apartments for rent here in town, do you?"

She looked up, surprised and interested that he might need a place to stay, but the gleam in her eye told him that he could be in danger.

"For my parents."

That piece of information doused her fire. "Oh. No, sorry."

He nodded. "Thanks, anyway."

She dragged herself up from her stool, like a proud prizefighter after fifteen tough rounds. "Well, see you tomorrow."

"Have a good night." Razz forced himself not to look as she sashayed toward the parking lot. He didn't feel he deserved such vicarious pleasure.

Lotta exited out the back door just as Tom and the Surf's Up new server, Petra, entered through the front. *One potential problem gone and another arrived to take her place.* Although Petra had claimed varied restaurant experience on her employment application, Razz knew from her performance she was green, so he'd have to watch her carefully. At least, she was cute and young, so watching her wouldn't be too painful. And she was married, so she wasn't a threat like Lotta could be. Despite flirtations outside his own marriage, he tried never to flirt with married women. Besides, Petra's husband, Vlad, a young, Russian-born thug and Mafia wannabe, would probably come in and watch from the bar all night to make sure no one disrespected her, just as he had on Sunday.

Tom breezed past on his way to the kitchen. "Someone's at the back, wants to see you."

Great, probably a damn process server, Razz thought. *I'll get another place already!* But when he got to the back door, James, his homeless acquaintance, was waiting for him. Razz wasn't thrilled about the coincidence with his current situation.

"Hey, man, how you… where's Ryan?"

"That's why I'm here. Ryan died last night… of cancer."

"I'm sorry. Is there anything I can do? You need some money?"

"No, no, I'm fine. Thanks."

Razz didn't know what to say to comfort this man he'd spoken to score of times, but whom he hardly knew, so he went with the old restaurant stand-by. "Are you hungry? Can I get you something?"

"No, please. I just wanted thank you. The food you sent by the other night was really nice. Ryan and I joked it was like his Last Supper." James smiled, but it came across more like a grimace, the best a man in his emotional state could muster. "Anyway, he was grateful. And so was I."

Razz put away his wallet, ashamed he couldn't offer something more than money or food. "I'm sorry," was the best he could do.

James held out his hand and Razz took it. "I'll be leaving tomorrow."

"Where are you going?"

"Back home to upstate New York. Going to see my family; it's been a while. Ryan loved it out here. I love the snow."

Razz didn't know why, but he wanted to know something personal about these men, as if death weren't personal enough.

"So, you and Ryan, you were …"

"Friends? Yeah, we were best friends." James had shared as much as he'd wanted. Under different circumstances, the three of them might have become friends, but that was all behind them now. "You were one of the good guys," he said, before he turned and walked away.

"Take care of yourself!"

James didn't look back; he simply raised his hand in acknowledgment. Then he mingled into the crowd and disappeared around the corner of the carousel.

Razz didn't feel like one of the good guys, but he didn't have long to think about James, Ryan, Petra, Vlad, Lotta, or how exhausted he felt, because two groups of four, all young professionals, arrived for an early dinner. It was time to go to work.

Richard Gold was working, too. He was working hard figuring out how he could get into Natalie Wesson's pants or, depending on the day, her skirt. Moreover, he'd been thinking about it since the moment he'd met her.

She had brushed aside his aggressive advances last week, when they'd worked together late in his office, but she did so in a way that enticed him further. Even after she extricated herself and left for home, he couldn't stop thinking about her. Her perfectly round breasts, her long, brown hair that smelled of jasmine, her longer, tanned legs that looked of perfection, and the gravity-defying ass that tied the whole package together. The previous night, he'd thought about her so hard that, in his excitement, he had to sexually relieve himself with his surprised, but happily willing, wife.

He couldn't help but watch her through the office door that he'd conveniently propped open. Natalie dressed less provocatively today, as if to tease him, wearing slacks with a blazer over a white satin top. She moved fluidly, like a dancer, even when answering the phone or typing a letter. She understood figures almost as well as Gold and had her own figure that men would kill, or die, for. She seemed like the perfect specimen, but he saw her as more than a temporary plaything, as Terri had been. He could almost see her as his business partner, except that he had definite, old-fashioned ideas about where women belonged.

Indeed, he hungered to have her in the kitchen, the bedroom, and any other place. He couldn't recall when he'd felt this alive or this scared. His major concern wasn't that he was married, that had never stopped him before, but that he wouldn't be able to convince Natalie Wesson to forgo her choice of any handsome young buck in Los Angeles for a wealthy, but sagging and somewhat sexually dysfunctional, sixty-five year old. He decided to call his doctor and stock up on Viagra, just in case.

"Call for you on two, it's your daughter."

Getting no response, Wesson came to his door. "Richard, your daughter's on line two. Can you take it?"

"Oh, sure, thanks."

"Will I be working late tonight?"

Tiny beads of sweat formed on his brow, his nerves betraying him. Not even during multimillion dollar business negotiations had he ever felt this nervous. "Uh, yes, Miss Wesson, I believe I will require your services tonight." He blushed, not meaning it to come out quite that way, but he did require her services desperately.

She noticed his embarrassment, as well as the lump in his pants, but she didn't flinch.

"Maybe, we'll talk about a raise for you," he continued. *A raise?*

Had he not been so flustered or had he said what he wanted straight out, he might have impressed her with his candor. Instead, he looked like a doddering, helplessly horny, old man.

She was cool, though. She didn't laugh or make him feel foolish. "All right."

Her self-control made Gold want her even more. He was so entranced he never did answer his daughter's phone call.

Sarah couldn't wait any longer, so she hung up. She had her hands full with two screaming, depressed kids who kept asking where their father was.

"Kids, we discussed this yesterday. Daddy and I are just taking some time away from each other. It's going to be the three of us for a little while, but you'll see him real soon, I promise."

Caitlin and Ronnie weren't mollified. Caitlin had claimed a stomach ache that morning that kept her from school, but Sarah figured her daughter's pain was more than physical and didn't press the issue. Squirming at the kitchen table, picking at their food, the kids alternately pouted and wailed. When Ronnie became too exhausted to cry any further, Caitlin would pick up where he left off. And vice versa. It was starting to drive Sarah mad.

It was okay her daughter wouldn't eat her French fries and her son wouldn't drink his milk, but she had important work to do. She was trying to make sense of some figures from the Gold Shore project, but screaming kids weren't helping her concentration.

Her kids couldn't have cared less. They didn't understand the ramifications of their parents' split and that's what scared them most—the pitch-black darkness of the unknown. The worst fear wasn't the bogeyman, the ominous, imagined creature of the night. Losing a father was far scarier, because every kid knew fathers would protect them against the bogeyman and against all sorts of other dangers. As loving and protective as Sarah was, Caitlin and Ronnie wanted their dad.

"No!" Caitlin screamed when Ronnie grabbed one of her fries. "That's mine!"

When Ronnie reached for another one, she made her point stronger by jamming the prongs of her fork into his tiny hand.

"Aaggh! Aaggh!" he wailed. "Mommy! Mommy!"

"Caitlin!"

"They're my fwies, Mommy, my fwies!"

"Aaggh! Aaggh!" By this time, droplets of blood appeared on Ronnie's hand to freak them out even more.

"Aaggh! Aaggh!" they each screamed.

"Be quiet! I want you to both be quiet!" Sarah's yelling only raised the volume from her kids.

Caitlin jabbed at her plate to make it perfectly clear that interlopers would pay with blood.

"Stop that, Caitlin," pleaded Sarah. She pulled Ronnie's chair away from the table, so he was out of the line of fire.

"My fwies! My fwies!"

Sarah's floodgate finally burst. "Yes, they're your fries, so just shut the hell up!"

For the shortest of moments, a mouse creeping across the floor would have sounded like a Boeing 747; it was so quiet in that room. Caitlin looked at her mommy quizzically. Ronnie looked down at his hand. The blood had started to fascinate, not scare, him.

"I'm sorry." Although Sarah was profoundly sorry for yelling, apologizing showed her kids her weak spot. So they took full advantage of it and began bawling again.

A father, in his more gruff and unforgiving way, would have yelled and threatened until his kids had shut up, gone to their respective rooms, and relative peace had been restored in the household. Never mind the psychological trauma he'd inflict for his children to cope with in later years, he would get his point across far better than the prongs of any dinner fork could by deeply grinding that point in until they submitted.

As Caitlin and Ronnie yelled, cried and screamed, Sarah wondered if she'd made a terrible mistake. Not by yelling at her children. Not even by apologizing to them. No, she wondered if she might have made a mistake in sending Razz away.

Mistakes were not allowed in Richard Gold's book. If an employee made a mistake, honest or not, he or she was sent packing. That's why Gold's frustration was growing exponentially—he kept making mistakes in his pursuit of Natalie Wesson. He kept putting his foot in his mouth and he found that it held a sour taste. As she bent over his desk, reviewing with him a cash flow statement from one of his many projects, an opening in her blouse offered the slightest view of her right breast. The breast overflowed from her white lace bra and seemed to mesmerize him.

"This is from the breast per—" He caught himself, but was now sucking hard on his other foot. "I mean, this is the best performing project we have."

He wasn't used to being the pursuer, even of such a prime catch as this. He was Richard Gold, multi-multi-millionaire developer, a man who knew almost everyone of importance in Los Angeles. Everyone took his phone calls, from Mayor Hidalgo to bank presidents to Police Chief Wilson. Everyone wanted him on their side. Despite her flirtations, Natalie Wesson seemed to be playing by a different set of rules.

"Should we continue this over dinner?" she asked. "I'm getting hungry."

"Yes, yes, we should." He hoped a change of venue would help him. He knew it couldn't hurt.

When they got outside, a clear, balmy night greeted them. Gleeful cries from young roller coaster riders on the Pier some distance away lifted Gold's spirits. The lights of the Ferris wheel danced lightheartedly and he wondered the last time he'd thought about the Pier in anything other than a purely financial sense.

"Let's go down there," she suggested.

Ah, youth. "Sure," he said, before reconsidering. "No, I mean, I've got a better place. The food at Primo's is the best in town. And you deserve the best."

He knew he'd feel safer in his regular booth, set back in a dark, private corner of Primo's Ristorante, than he would at the well-lit, public Pier. "It's right around the corner."

She didn't argue, didn't fight him, but she didn't give in either. She allowed him to lead her to Primo's, walking through the gentle breeze down Ocean Boulevard, but she was still very much in control.

Primo Marucci met them at the door. The owner and proprietor of this old-fashioned Italian eatery, he was used to seeing Richard Gold at this hour, in for a quick night cap or a more lingering late dinner. And he was used to seeing him with women other than his wife.

"Good evening, Mr. Gold. It's so good to see you. How are you this evening?" Primo had been in the restaurant business for over forty years. He'd done so by knowing what to say and what not to say to his clientele. If a man came in with a woman he'd not seen before, he would wait for an introduction. Tonight, there was none forthcoming. he could tell from Gold's nervous fidgeting that this was serious.

"This way, please." He whisked them through the dimly-lit restaurant.

Gold felt better when he'd sat down at his table, his back resting comfortably against the worn, red vinyl next to the wall. In the darkness, looking out from his corner booth, he could just make out the faces of men he'd seen here many times before, but he knew they couldn't see him. As if to mask his presence further and to enhance his partner's, he moved the table's single candle toward Wesson. Her exquisite face glowed like a figure from a Rembrandt painting or an old-time movie star basking in her key light.

He knew he was being silly, but he felt like he was falling in love. He had gone beyond lust and just wanted this young woman in his presence. He shook his head as if to bring himself back to reality.

"What's wrong, Richard?"

"Nothing, nothing at all."

"So, about those numbers on the Lone Ridge Project—"

"Let's just eat and enjoy ourselves. No numbers tonight, okay?"

"Whatever you say, Richard." She touched his hand and a tiny quiver, which felt to him like an earthquake, went down the length of his spine, through his legs, then back up to his heart where it seemed to explode and expand within him. He'd never felt happier.

The wonderful, warm fuzzy feeling didn't last for long, because it turned to pure ecstasy when Natalie Wesson put her hand on his crotch, then slowly and sensuously unzipped his fly all the while staring deeply into his glazed-over eyes. She worked her hand into his trousers and, as Gold's eyes fell back into their sockets, she went down on him.

Appetizers would have to wait.

Although they'd fought her tooth and nail before succumbing, Sarah finally got her kids down, too. Nestled in their respective beds, the lights out, she felt like she could breathe for the first time all day. It was ten o'clock and she had to finish her work for tomorrow. She was preparing a cash flow statement for the Gold Shore Resort and Hotel project. Masterson had left the figures and they weren't pretty. Despite Gold's crowing about controlling the project with just his personal guarantee, Sarah saw in the numbers something that was definitely not worth crowing about. Notwithstanding the forty million dollar construction loan from the bank, Gold was going to run short on cash. Due to high interest payments and excessive overtime wages, the project was already well over budget. At the current cash burn rate, he wouldn't be able to finish the Gold Shore without a partner or without a major renegotiation of his loan terms.

She went over the numbers again and again, but couldn't make them work under any reasonable assumptions. If they could open the hotel two months early and start bringing in cash or if they could somehow cut the construction budget and save five million dollars, they could possibly squeak by. But, given the Gold Shore was already behind an impossibly ambitious schedule and was over budget, Sarah didn't have high hopes for either possibility.

Nevertheless, she felt good, because she knew her father would have many options in refinancing such a high-profile and potentially highly-lucrative project. She hadn't done this sort of rigorous analysis for years, since shortly after she'd met Razz, and was pleased she could still do it well. She had given up her real estate career to take care of her kids and her husband, but had missed the intellectual stimulation it offered. Razz never suspected the depth of her financial knowledge, because she'd kept that part of her life to herself. Whenever he would dream up some real estate scheme, she'd keep quiet, especially when she knew it was a pie in the sky idea. She loved him, but he didn't know real estate and men like her father would chew him up and spit him out if he tried to compete with them. And she knew it could cost her much of her trust fund's cash flow while he learned from his mistakes. She wasn't willing to risk that for any man.

As she faded off to sleep, numbers danced in her head and loan covenants pervaded her dreams. An involuntary smile crept over her face and she began to snore. Despite the tumult from her kids, her husband and her father, it had been a good night. She would sleep very soundly.

It had been a good night at the Surf's Up, too, with over one hundred meals served in addition to a big bar tab. Razz was sure they'd grossed over four thousand dollars. After only six days, Paul and Miss Scruffy were becoming a distant memory.

Despite his worries about Petra's skills, she was getting the hang of her job. She'd kept most of her orders straight and hadn't dropped anything on the customers. Her husband again sat at the bar, sipping draft beer all night, watching her every move. Fortunately, at the end of the night, he paid his nine-dollar bar tab for the three beers and left without incident. Rick was about to say something to him about the American custom of tipping, but, with one look from Razz, he decided to let it drop.

Tom was his usual proficient and professional, if, sometimes, petulant self. He'd handled over forty meals for the night and, although he felt he'd gotten stiffed by a few customers, he still made over two hundred dollars. Despite being a prima donna at times, money had a way of calming him down. He was absolutely meditative by the end of the night.

Chad had stayed to work a double shift and, although he'd sleepwalked through much of it, due to exhaustion, his presence had helped cut Petra's load. It also added to his afternoon booty, so he would bring home over three hundred dollars for the day in tips. It had been a long time since any server had pulled that kind of money out of the Surf's Up.

As the last customer exited, a tired contentment permeated the restaurant. Chad dragged himself through the place, realigning tables and chairs. Tom contentedly counted his tips at the bar while Rick washed it down around him. Petra reset the tables with napkins and silverware as Vlad smoked cigarette after cigarette, patiently awaiting her, outside.

Only Razz seemed on edge. He had a pressing problem on his hands—he didn't have a place to sleep. He couldn't go back to Sarah's and his parents no longer had room for him. His buddy, Ira Langer, would have let him sleep on his couch, but it was too late to ask him now. He would have to sleep in his office.

In one's twenties, sleeping on a floor after a hard night at a bar wasn't a problem. Often, it gave bragging rights, an opportunity to embellish an otherwise mundane work story, to one who needed that sort of thing. In one's thirties, sleeping in an office could still be considered a badge of honor for working hard and late. But, in one's forties, you were supposed to be beyond all that. You shouldn't need bragging rights and were supposed to have assistants to do all the late night dirty work. For Razz, sleeping in his office would be far more embarrassing than honorable, and it would be a pain in the neck—literally. He was still hurting from the night before and couldn't imagine what aches he might have tomorrow, but, at forty-five, he knew he would have plenty of them.

And he still had to get up early to try and find a place to live.

15

Looking back at his wave, still forming, but approaching rapidly, only a hundred feet behind him, he felt like shouting, "Don't throw your hooks in the water! I don't want to be caught like some scaly sea bass!"

January 12, 2005

It was eight a.m. and Sharky was back at work at the Pier substation, his suspension ended unexpectedly a week early. Lieutenant Johnson had called the night before to tell him what he thought would be taken as good news, but Sharky was mad. He and Terri had been having the best of times: waking up late, going for easy walks around the neighborhood, dining at Mae's and, once in a while, finer establishments, and making love whenever they chose.

He was confused by the affection and loving attention, but he was easing into it. Had he been able to afford not to go back to work, he would have told Johnson in no uncertain terms what to do with his job and the police force. But Terri didn't have a new job yet and, considering they'd just spent much of his hard-earned savings to fix up the apartment, the prudent course was to suck it up and return to the force.

Going back to work was bad enough, but when he saw Chief Wilson with Lieutenant Johnson waiting for him in Johnson's office, he knew something was very wrong in the world. And when he was told he was back on the Wally Bumpers case, he felt a size eleven boot drop-kicked into his stomach. Sharky had stopped thinking about Wally, about finding him under the Pier, about sloshing around in a tiny watercraft while retrieving his dead, bloated body, and about his apartment at the Hempstead. He was satisfied with the outcome of his investigation—he had met Terri and nothing else mattered. His attitude was to let sleeping clowns lie.

"I want this murderer. No one gets away with murder in San Margarita! No one!" Veins in Wilson's neck bulged.

Sharky found the Chief's ferociousness laughable, but he fought back a smile with help from a cautionary look from Johnson.

"Do you understand? Everyone here depends on us and I'm depending on you! You're the best I've got."

Sharky waited for a punch line.

But Wilson appeared dead serious.

I'm the best you've got? He wondered if the Chief had finally gotten that brain implant he'd suggested five years ago. "Sure, Chief. Thank you."

"Now, one more thing," said Wilson, much quieter now. "This is all strictly confidential. You'll be working undercover and on your own. Officially, as far as anyone on the force is concerned, and that includes me, Sergeant Donati will have the Bumpers case. You can't tell anyone anything. If you do, I'll disavow all knowledge of this conversation and make your life a living hell. I'll make you wish you'd never heard my name. Do you understand?"

Sharky no longer felt like laughing and already wished he'd never heard Wilson's name. He wished he'd never received a call last night or agreed to come back to work this morning. "Chief, look, if you don't want me around, just fire me. I won't sue the department or anything. I've fucked up plenty of times; I know you have cause. Just don't set me up for a fall, man, please. I mean, I haven't been that bad, have I?"

Wilson didn't know what to say for a moment. "Uh, you don't seem to understand, Sergeant, I need your help. This is a big assignment. You'll be working directly for me: no written reports, no clocking in, no uniform, no nothing. Just find the murderer. Do whatever you have to do."

This is getting too weird. The Chief actually seems to be begging. "But what do you need me for?"

"I told you, you're the best I've got."

He waited for more.

"Okay, Donati's a moron, we all know it. If his daddy hadn't been councilman, he'd still be writing speeding tickets. I want someone to watch his ass, because he couldn't solve a fucking jigsaw puzzle."

"Then why not put me back in charge and send Donati out to catch jaywalkers?"

"Because he would beat them all up." After a moment, Wilson smiled at his exaggeration.

Sharky got a strange feeling he had entered another dimension. Something had changed drastically since he'd been gone.

"The mayor's still got a hair across his ass about you."

There it is. The mayor hates me for upstaging him at the Gold Shore groundbreaking.

He was on the mayor's shit list. In a way, that knowledge made him more comfortable; he was used to people hating him, but the whole thing still didn't make sense. As if he suffered from some weird strain of Tourette's, he couldn't help but ask, "Since when do you go against the mayor?"

Johnson looked nervous, but Wilson simply said, "Things are changing around here. Leave it at that."

Sharky looked at the Chief. His veins weren't popping, steam wasn't rising from his ears, nor was his head spinning around.

"Just do your job, Sergeant. Solve Wally Bumpers' murder and you'll be a hero and well rewarded. Trust me. Now give me your keys, gun, and badge."

Sharky would have scoffed at the words "trust me" had Wilson not looked so sincere. "Uh, okay. But how am I going to do all this without my stuff?"

"I'm sure you'll think of something. Now, you're undercover and no one knows a thing. You'll work out of your house, use your own car. Here's my private line," Wilson said, handing him a card with his cell phone number. "Call me with your progress or if you need help, twenty-four hours a day. Who do you trust most in the department?"

He nodded toward the Lieutenant. "Him."

"Okay. In a pinch, either Johnson or I will be there for you. In the meantime, only the three of us know what's up. Now, I have to fire you."

"Huh?"

"No one can know you're on the case. The mayor doesn't even want you on the force, but I need you. So, here goes."

Sharky didn't understand at first, but caught on when the Chief threw another full file folder, and papers floated throughout the room. *He's really keeping that clerk busy.*

"Now, get the fuck out of here and stay out! If I never see your rotten face again, it will be too soon!"

Cops gathered for the spectacle, but Sharky didn't move.

"Get out of here. Be pissed off," Wilson whispered, motioning to the door. Then he shoved the desk chair into the wall. "You fucking prick, how dare you insult me! I was going to give you another chance, but you will never work on this force again!"

Sharky heard cheering outside and finally got the message. This was a stage play and Chief Wilson was its director, so he decided to take full advantage of his audition. "Yeah, well, fuck you and the horse you rode in on!"

"You son of a bitch, after everything we've done for you. You're nothing without this force! Nothing! Now get out of here, you fucking prick!"

Sharky shot up from his seat, enjoying his role now, and strode proudly down the hallway.

"Go, Chief!"

"Get out of here, loser."

"Go back where you belong, Bozo."

Donati and several cops mocked him, pointing and making faces. Johnson watched them, not amused by their behavior.

Exiting, Sharky slammed the vestibule door so hard the glass cracked.

"Everyone get back to work! Someone fix that glass! And send that fucker the bill!" Wilson closed the office door, took a breath, and then looked at Johnson. "You sure he's clean?"

Johnson hesitated, and then nodded yes. "He's an asshole, but he's clean."

"He'd better be, for both your sakes."

By the time Sharky reached the parking lot, he was relieved to be free from punching a clock, patrolling, and from wearing his blues, but something else overrode his sense of freedom. He had to solve an impossible case alone. Wilson said he or Johnson would be there for support, but could he really trust they would? As far as his fellow cops knew, Sharky was long gone. They wouldn't cross the street to piss on him if he were burning. If Donati caught him snooping on his turf, he'd do as he pleased—charge him with obstruction of justice, or maybe just shoot him.

None of it made any sense. Chief Wilson was a spit and polish guy who played by the book. As much as Sharky believed he was the best guy on the force for this dubious job, it was unlike Wilson to go outside police protocol.

Although the whole situation reeked, for now, he planned to go home and bask in Terri's glow, have lunch, maybe have sex, and worry about solving Wally's crime later—perhaps, much later.

The crash of a fry pan alerted Razz to the new day. It was still dark, but only because there were no windows in his office. He recognized Lotta's voice downstairs barking orders to the day staff. He arose quickly from his makeshift bed, made of empty shipping boxes with a toilet roll for a pillow, and tried to sneak downstairs before anyone found out he was there.

"Christ, Razz, you look awful," Lotta said, quickly climbing the stairs.

That made perfect sense, because he felt awful. The crook in his neck from yesterday had invaded his whole body. "Hi, Lotta."

"Did you work late or something?"

"Uh, yeah, I fell asleep."

She flipped on the office light and saw the boxes gathered on the floor. "Oh, your wife kicked you out."

"Actually, we're separating," he said, though he was uncertain why he offered specifics.

"You can stay at my place for a few days."

The temptation was great, but he fought it off. "Thanks, but I'll be fine. I'm sure I'll find an apartment today."

"So, that's why you were asking about apartments yesterday."

"No, well, my parents do need a place. They got kicked out of their home of forty years two weeks ago. I just happened to get kicked out, too."

She seemed concerned. "I'll see what I can do, you know, if I hear of anything."

He nodded, relieved their discussion was over, and then headed for the stairs. He stopped after two steps, and decided the least he could do was clean up the empty boxes before he left.

When Razz made it outside, although the marine layer had not yet burned off, it looked like it would be another lovely day in San Margarita.

"You look like shit."

Startled, he turned and saw Sharky leaning against his former patrol car. "Thanks, same to you. What's up?"

"Nothing, I just got fired."

"You don't seem too upset."

"Shit happens."

Yes, it certainly does. I'm feeling quite shit upon these days, Razz thought. "Well, have a good one," he said, then he went to a newspaper dispenser and bought that morning's *Monitor*.

"Are you having problems at home?"

Even Sharky can see through me like a just-washed window!

"I know it's none of my business, I was just concerned."

He did look concerned, like a friend who wanted to comfort another after a devastating loss. Razz couldn't handle the incongruence, so he began reading the paper. "Look at this, it's our friend."

Mayor Jaime Hidalgo's beaming face dominated page one, along with a story about his plans to announce his re-election bid this morning outside City Hall. Sharky stared at the picture, not so carefree now. "I'll need a ride."

"Sorry, I've got things to do."

Sharky didn't care if he did and jumped into Razz' Mustang. "Come on. We can just make it."

Razz considered the possibility that Sharky had finally lost his marbles. He'd been unusually nice earlier and now he wanted to go back into the belly of the beast. After the debacle of a week ago, Razz wondered why he'd push his luck with the Mayor, but got into his car and drove up the connecting bridge toward City Hall.

"Take me home first," said Sharky.

Too tired to fight, Razz did as he was told. When they arrived, he suggested Sharky take his own car, but Sharky would have none of it.

"No, we'll go together. Wait here."

Minutes later, Razz got the inkling there was more to his presence than Sharky's desire for company. No longer in police blues, Sharky was dressed in old, ratty clothes, sneakers, and a baseball cap. He looked like a bum.

"Okay, let's go," he said.

Now, Razz was captivated. Sharky had something up his sleeve, and he wanted to find out just what it was.

The press conference was held in front of San Margarita's City Hall. A large crowd had gathered and camera crews from all the local stations were in place, cameras rolling, as reporters jockeyed for position.

Mayor Jaime Hidalgo was already speaking when the guys arrived a few minutes late. Behind him stood prominent business and civic leaders of all shapes, sizes, colors, and economic levels in an impressive show of support.

"... but there's more to be done. I believe we can build on the successes of my first term and continue to make San Margarita a better place for all of its citizens."

A large group of Latinos, whites, and blacks, many holding placards that read, *Hidalgo - I will work for you!,* cheered loudly.

A small group of Mexican men held signs denouncing Hidalgo. *Anyone but Hidalgo!, One term only!,* and *We need a new mayor!.*

Razz thought it odd that these men were parading against him, because Hidalgo was Mexican through and through. He'd been born forty-seven years ago to itinerant farm worker parents, both multi-generational Mexicans. Hidalgo had run as a political outsider four years earlier, having made his reputation as a criminal defense attorney primarily by defending the lower-class, many of them Mexican-Americans, those who could least afford his services. Because the Latino make-up of San Margarita had grown to almost thirty percent and, because the previous white mayor had been mired in a financial scandal and, at seventy, was well past his prime, Hidalgo had squeaked through to win the mayor's race, gathering almost ninety percent of the Latino vote. Latino supporters had marched in the streets reveling in Hidalgo's victory which they justifiably felt was also their own.

Wealthy whites in San Margarita had not been as happy, because they didn't feel their interests would be protected. After all, what did they care about raising the city's minimum wage to ten dollars an hour? That had been one of Hidalgo's main campaign promises and it didn't endear him to them. White businessmen didn't live on minimum wage, they paid it. They'd said it would drive businesses away from San Margarita and that they would all go broke and have to leave town, but nothing of the sort happened. As usual, the rich got richer as the town prospered, but, surprisingly, the poor actually did become a little less poor. It had been a win-win situation for everyone. A poll in that morning's *Monitor* had given Hidalgo a seventy-five percent approval rating from a cross-section of potential voters. Another poll stated that, had the mayor's race been run that day, Hidalgo would garner eighty percent of the vote. Never mind that no one yet dared run against him.

"We must all join together for our common good. We have proven we can all prosper if we work together and help one another."

Jaime Hidalgo was smooth and polished. He was a successful, first-generation Mexican-American, handsome, well-dressed, and well-educated at UCLA, with a law degree from Berkeley. His attractive wife of fifteen years and three boys, twelve, ten, and seven, stood beside him in a picture of family perfectness. Thinking about his own fractured family, it made Razz jealous.

He saw Sharky rummage through a garbage can and started to doubt his sanity. Then he saw Chief Wilson and several of his men in the back of the crowd and figured he was just trying to avoid them. *Act like a street bum and no one notices you.*

"Down with Hidalgo!" the Mexican men cried as cameras caught their remonstrations.

The mayor spoke louder to combat the distraction. "I want to lead this community to even greater successes than those we've already experienced. In my first four years in office, we passed the new living wage ordinance and stricter zoning laws, and we created cleaner streets and beaches. Now, there are those who would break us apart, those who would try and injure our community. Ignore them, because together we'll continue to do better and become stronger. I promise to work hard for all of you to help make your lives better. I will work for you!"

Hidalgo raised his arms in a sign of victory and cheering from his supporters clashed with cries of outrage from the group of Mexican men.

Hidalgo's handlers rushed him to the safety of City Hall just as a skirmish broke out which might have grown much worse had Chief Wilson and his men not moved in immediately to restore the peace. Camera crews caught it all and reporters soon thrust microphones at Wilson asking for his views on the conflict.

It would all make for an interesting six o'clock newscast.

16

He had enough to think about without having to dodge fishing lines. But when he again looked behind him and saw his wave only yards away, he started paddling furiously toward shore.

Richard Gold had expected to be at Mayor Hidalgo's re-election announcement. He had planned on it since attending a private meeting with him, two weeks before the Gold Shore Hotel and Resort groundbreaking, when they decided Gold would become the Mayor's Campaign Finance Chairman and the man in charge of raising the funds necessary to run a winning campaign. In exchange, he would have Hidalgo's full and immediate support for the Gold Shore project.

But, right now, Gold was seriously sleep deprived. Natalie Wesson had fucked him practically all night long at his Hempstead apartment. He was a man that had been rode hard and put away wet.

He thought he was having a heart attack at one point and briefly reconsidered the wisdom in trying to keep up with a young sex vixen. But she continued to play him just right—stroke his ego and his body, build him up slowly, then faster and faster, finally, to climax. He was on a roller-coaster of ecstasy, a slow, steady climb leading to one greater, more exhilarating thrill ride after another. He hadn't known he was so virile, but she'd done it to him again and again. He hadn't even needed his Viagra.

"Sorry about your meeting, honey. I hope it wasn't too important," she said, turning on the shower.

Gold watched as she soaped behind the conveniently see-through shower curtain he'd chosen especially for occasions such as these. She washed her breasts first, then her crotch, then the crack of her ass. She lingered at each stop, lathering sensuously.

"You know perfectly well I was supposed to meet with the mayor this morning."

He tried hard to sound like he was scolding her, but his smile gave him away. He watched, mesmerized, as she rinsed her hair and suds fell down around her beautiful body. He was trying to brush his teeth, but he couldn't concentrate on anything but her. The phone rang, but he wasn't about to answer it.

"Do you want me to get that?" she asked as she stepped out, still dripping, from the shower. "I mean, I am your assistant."

"No, no, I think you've done quite enough for me this morning. Thank you," he mumbled with his mouth full of toothpaste. He spit into the sink and rinsed.

My wife and I haven't shared a bathroom in twenty years. What have I done to deserve all this?

Wesson kissed him and every thought in his head, but one, was forgotten. She pulled back, smiling, and said, "Let's go to work."

It was eleven o'clock when Richard Gold and Natalie Wesson got to the office, well past his usual seven-thirty arrival time and an hour and a half after he was scheduled to be at the mayor's news conference. Dan Manley, the Mayor's irate assistant, had called several times as had Elizabeth Gold, Gold's irate wife. Only Sarah Gold McNeil, his supportive daughter, had been worried about his health and welfare. But that changed when she saw the two lovers cavort through the office.

"I have to talk to you," Sarah said when she entered his office. "Alone."

"Anything you have to say to me can be said in front of Natalie."

Gold's coolly confident voice sent shivers down her spine.

Wesson smiled, her teeth bared.

It's true! My father and this girl! Sarah struggled to cover her disgust. "I have those Gold Shore numbers for you."

"Thank you. You can leave them on my desk."

She waited for something more, a morsel of remorse or apology, but there was nothing.

"Close the door behind you, please."

With those words, a sharp knife sliced through Sarah, splitting her in half, creating a huge chasm in her heart. Richard Gold had chosen sides and he hadn't chosen hers.

Sharky was beginning to enjoy his new role as homeless man about town. He could move at will, unfettered, just another of the nameless and faceless wearing dirty clothes. He could go into alleys, peek into windows, or simply hang around and listen, and no one bothered him. And, like an over-zealous Method actor, he was going deep into his new persona. He'd rolled himself in dirt and was even starting to mumble to himself.

But Sharky wasn't loony tunes, didn't have a split personality, wasn't broke or homeless; he was just undercover. Only minutes before, he'd seen Richard Gold's black Mercedes 600CL pass by and he knew Gold wasn't coming from his home or office, because they lay in entirely different directions. He'd seen two dark figures, almost hidden behind smoky glass, one figure leaning in close to the driver. They didn't look like business associates and it made him suspicious, so he was on his way to the Hempstead.

Razz sat outside a Starbucks at Ocean Boulevard and Emerald Street, sipping a morning coffee and searching the *Monitor*'s classified ads. He wasn't having much luck; there were only three suitable apartment listings in his price range and the coffee sucked. He couldn't figure out why there were seemingly hundreds of Starbucks in town, perched on almost every busy street corner, but there were no affordable apartments. He wondered if the idle rich of San Margarita did anything other than drink bad coffee, eat overpriced scones, and scheme to keep the poor people out of their town.

He pressed his sore back into the aluminum chair slats and heard a pop. *One vertebra back in place. Only about twenty-nine more to go.* He moved his head from side to side, stretching his neck muscles. Another pop. *Twenty-eight more.* He knew he had to find an apartment soon. He couldn't sleep on boxes and toilet paper again.

As he flipped the page and looked out over Ocean Boulevard and the Pacific Ocean beyond, something caught his eye. It was Sharky. Razz watched, fascinated by his transformation. At first, he wasn't even sure it was him, but the slight limp gave him away. He tried to focus on the classifieds, but when he saw Sharky go into a garbage can to pull out a soda can, he was hooked.

He resisted the urge to catch up and enquire what he was doing, because the show was too entertaining, better than anything he'd seen on television in years. He leaned against a signpost, as if casually waiting for a bus, and kept one eye on Sharky. He saw him look back, checking the street, and dust himself off in front of the Hempstead. Razz averted his eyes for a moment and, when he looked again, Sharky was already inside.

There's a glutton for punishment. Let him play his game; I've got to find a place to live.

Try as he might, Razz couldn't resist the temptation to find out what in the hell Sharky thought he was doing. After a few minutes, he followed him into the Hempstead.

Sharky had already reached apartment 310, Richard Gold's apartment by way of the mysterious Emma Northrup, by the time Razz entered the building.

"Was anyone here today?" he demanded of the frightened Guatemalan janitor who he'd found vacuuming the hallway two floors above.

When the man first saw Sharky, he ran, expecting to be put on the next boat out of the United States. But Sharky tackled him and reassured him he could stay—if he helped him.

"¿Estaba alguien en este apartamento esta mañana?" Sharky asked in the best Spanish he could muster.

"Señor, por favor, prometo que conseguiré mi visa."

"I don't give a shit if you're getting a Knighthood from the Queen."

The man looked confused.

Sharky attempted to translate. "No doy una mierda si usted obtiene … ah, una Caballería de la Reina."

Now, the guy was totally confused. *What does the Queen have to do with anything? And why does she have a cavalry?*

"¿Dígame, quien estaba aquí?" Sharky shoved a police badge, a duplicate he'd had created during one of his previous suspensions, hard into the man's nose, and things seemed to crystallize for him.

"Ah, sí, señor, un hombre y una mujer estaban aquí."

"That's better. ¿Quién era ellos?"

The man hesitated, uncertain which was the greater of two evils: piss off a cop who could send you to another country, or piss off the man who ultimately pays your wages. "Mr. Gold, he owns this apartment, sir. They tell me he owns the building, too. I don't know the lady."

"You speak English."

"Yes, sir."

"Well, why the fuck didn't you say so?"

"You didn't ask me, sir."

Sharky resisted the urge to belt the man all the way back to Guatemala and asked, "What did this woman look like?"

As the man described Natalie Wesson in detail, in English, Sharky took notes on a small pad of paper, for he was a prepared little homeless man. As he scribbled, a picture came into view. She looked to him like a hooker.

He figured he'd find nothing here; Gold had been with a call girl. Sharky, of all people, understood the need for a man to get his sexual relief. The fact that this woman was beautiful and young just meant that Gold could afford the best.

Why would he give a call girl a ride? Whoever she is, she was really close to him in his car. That rules out his wife. Maybe he's got another mistress.

He became angry when he thought of Terri sleeping with Gold, but calmed when he realized she never would again. Call her a mistress, call girl, or hooker, Richard Gold could afford to get laid whenever he wanted and there was no reason to think anything unusual about it. "Let me in."

"No, sir, I can't, I—"

Sharky thrust the badge at his face and the man quickly opened the door to apartment 310.

Razz looked up and smiled self-consciously at Susan Berne, the Hempstead's leasing manager, then returned to filling out his rental application. Given his dubious appearance, she was certain he couldn't afford one of their apartments, so she was certain he was wasting her time.

"And what do you do for work, Mr. McNeil?"

"Oh, I manage two restaurants. Down on the Pier."

She became friendlier when the vision of dollar signs danced in her head. "Oh, well, we have two apartments available right now."

"Great."

He paused when he came to the question of his yearly earnings. He thought for a second, and then did what anyone would do in such a situation; he lied. He wrote down one hundred thousand dollars per year.

Berne surveyed his application and was disappointed. "Is this earnings figure correct?"

"Well, it's a ball park figure."

"I was hoping for a bigger ballpark."

Razz didn't appreciate the joke, but he played along. "So was I."

He wondered how Sharky had gotten past her eagle eyes, because she'd caught him as soon as he'd entered. Cornered and desperately needing an apartment, he'd agreed to fill out an application. "Have you worked here long?" he asked, making small talk.

"About ten years, off and on."

"Off and on?"

"I took some time off recently. Will your children be staying with you?"

"I hope so."

"Then you'll need a two-bedroom. You know you'll have to sign a year's lease?"

"Sure."

"Well, we prefer our tenants' rental payments to be less than thirty-five per cent of their annual earnings. Your payments would be well over forty-five, almost fifty per cent, of your income. That's with the least expensive two-bedroom we have available. We'll call you if something becomes available—something cheaper, that is."

"Miss Berne, I really don't think you—"

At that moment, Sharky turned the corner and surprised them. He froze.

Berne moved first. "Get the hell out of here! You bums should go find a box somewhere!"

Sharky made the next move and ran out, not because of Berne, but because Razz' presence made him nervous.

Then it was Razz' turn. "I'll be in touch," he said just before racing out after Sharky.

With that, Susan Berne sat back on her fat ass to wait for the next yahoo who wanted to rent an apartment and couldn't afford it.

Sarah was beside herself. It had been two hours since her father snubbed her and he hadn't spoken to her since. He and Natalie Wesson had been holed up in his office the entire time and Sarah had heard about all she could stand of Wesson's cloying giggle.

She'd busied herself by studying the financial statements from two other of Gold's commercial projects, a strip mall in Las Vegas and an office building in downtown Los Angeles, but he had asked her advice only on the Gold Shore. And now he was ignoring it. She had been up until two in the morning finalizing her numbers, listing the likely refinancing options available to him, and specifying her recommendations. And now it felt like a waste of time and effort. All in all, she'd rather be home with her screaming kids.

"Sarah, could you come in here, please?"

She jumped when she heard her father's voice. When she entered his office, she saw him sitting behind his desk with Wesson sitting to his side. They looked like King and Queen upon their thrones, rather than a boss and his subordinate. Sarah already didn't like how this was shaping up.

"Sarah, we've been looking at your numbers," he began.

"We?" Sarah wanted to scream. *Why is your assistant looking at my analysis and why do you care what she thinks?*

"We think you're being dramatic with your recommendations."

There was that word again. *"We". "'We" is father and daughter. "We" is husband and wife. "We" isn't boss and slutty assistant who's been working for you for only a week!*

"I told you what I think. There's a problem and, to finish the project, you'll need to refinance or take on a partner."

Gold considered his unpleasant options, but Wesson beat him to the punch.

"Maybe you're rusty. Richard tells me you haven't done this type of work in a while."

"And where have you done your analytical work? Grade school?"

Wesson seemed unmoved, but Richard Gold couldn't picture a good outcome in a fight between his lover and his daughter.

"Actually, I have an MBA from New York University."

"Really? Well, it's interesting to see what they're teaching at business school these days—how to fuck your way up the corporate ladder."

There was a long moment of awkward silence.

Sarah had surprised even herself, but she wasn't about to back down. Neither was Wesson. Gold was busy picking his jaw up off the ground.

"Well, I guess we'll see who's right, won't we?" said Wesson. "I don't think Richard will have any cash flow problems with the Gold Shore. We'll speed up construction and bring in cash earlier than projected. The construction and acquisition loans are current and will continue to be."

She stated it as fact and that made Gold feel better. He wanted to believe everything she told him.

"Well, if you'd been able to understand my analysis, you'd know that I included that as a possibility. Unfortunately, it's a remote possibility. It's highly unlikely we'll be able to speed up construction enough and still maintain the necessary quality for a project like this. Without that quality, we won't be able to command the necessary rents and room rates required to service the accumulated debt. Construction is behind schedule and falling further behind as we speak. I've discussed this with the construction supervisor, and he agrees. We'll end up behind schedule, probably by several months, not ahead of schedule. If we wait to refinance, we won't have the same options available. Refinance now or, down the road, our competitors will smell blood and they'll try to take the whole project away."

"We won't let them."

Natalie Wesson said it with such certainty and conviction that Sarah briefly wondered if she might be right. It was possible she was being overly conservative with her projections. *Maybe this Wesson girl really does know her stuff. Or, just as likely, she doesn't know her ass from an HP-12C.* But, one thing Sarah knew for sure, the project, as is, wasn't worth the risk to her father's net worth.

Normally, Gold would question his employees' reasoning till they were bloody and begging for mercy, but this woman had cowed him in only a few days.

Sarah thought he must be pussy-whipped, but the thought sickened her so much, she opted to chalk it up to a bad day.

Finally, Gold spoke. “Thank you for your analysis, Sarah.”

He spoke with such gravity that she already knew his decision.

“I know you’ve thought about this issue very deeply. I’m grateful. I’ve always trusted your analysis.”

Here it comes.

“But, in this case, why don’t we just wait a while and see what happens with construction? I’ll go down there personally and see if I can speed things up. See what they can do for the man who signs their checks, you know?”

Just say it, for God’s sake.

“Uh, so, for now, I think I’d like to go with Natalie ... uh, Miss Wesson’s analysis.”

Wesson couldn’t resist a satisfied smile.

Sarah desperately wanted to knock the smugness off her rival’s face. “Fine, I’ll be in my office.”

She spent the rest of the day behind closed doors, waiting for an explanation and apology. She reviewed her analysis several more times and knew she was right. Her father was personally guaranteeing huge loans for the Gold Shore project and refusing to take on partners to spread his risk—all because of a twenty-something year old assistant.

Richard Gold never did explain or apologize.

17

He caught the wave perfectly just as it was gaining strength, strong enough to carry him with it, but still conserving enough energy to last the duration of its once-in-a-lifetime mission. This would have to be a wave with enough stamina and consistency to carry him the length of the Pier without fading early or surprising him dangerously.

Razz never found Sharky again that day, nor did he find a place to live. All three apartments listed in the *Monitor* had already been rented. In fact, they'd been rented before the newspaper had come out. Such was the nature of San Margarita real estate—multiple bids for lackluster homes in up-and-coming, but never-quite-there, neighborhoods and large, under-the-table payments to secure leases to lousy, bug-infested studio apartments.

It was almost four o'clock and Razz had to go to work. He would spend some time tonight at the Sol a Sol, because Julio, Ignacio Sol's nephew, needed a couple hours off. Julio hadn't been able to buy the Sol a Sol, but had made a big leap to night manager when Louis took over. He was good at his job, which made for fewer worries for Razz.

The Sol a Sol had done its usual solid business during the first six days of the Louis the First era. Most of the new business had gone to the Surf's Up, but Razz had no worries about the Sol a Sol. With summer coming and as people adjusted to the new prices, he was sure the place would take off.

The Surf's Up was busy. Loud, happy people, including several who were already drunk, took some of the sting from the day's failures. Razz worried it was all unsustainable, that it wouldn't last, that he'd be out on his ear in a week, until he caught himself. *When did I become so pessimistic? Christ, just enjoy it. I've earned it.*

He felt better after his instant self-analysis, but, deep down, he knew there was more causing his angst. His biggest worry was that he hadn't seen his children in two days.

Sharky hadn't found anything incriminating in Richard Gold's apartment other than cum stains on the bed sheets. He looked through the dresser drawers, through the bathroom garbage, anywhere that might yield a clue as to Gold's companion, but the woman hadn't left a trace, not a lipstick case or jar of face cream, not even a used tissue. He'd also looked for anything he could use against Richard Gold. After all, Wally Bumpers' murder may have happened right there at the Hempstead. He dismissed any financial motive, despite the quadrupling of Wally's apartment rent, but still felt compelled to keep Gold on his list of possible suspects. Right now, he didn't have anyone else on it.

"Hey, baby, where were—" Terri stopped after she entered their apartment, grocery bags in hand. "What happened to you?"

Sharky had been home for an hour, but he'd gotten so wrapped up in his mental machinations that he'd forgotten to change out of his filthy clothes. "Uh, I was working around the yard."

"Yeah? Since when do you do yard work?"

He gave in instantly. "I'm working on a case. The murder case I told you about last night."

She waited.

"I'm undercover."

She considered him, rattling his nerves, before asking, "Can I help in any way?"

"Huh?"

"Is there anything I can do to help you?"

"You believe me?"

"Of course, I believe you. Aren't you telling me the truth?"

"Yes, of course ... but it seems like an unlikely story, you know. I'm not sure I believe it myself."

Terri put down the groceries and went over to sit on his lap. "You won't ever have a reason to lie to me, so I'll always believe you."

She was right. He wouldn't and couldn't lie to her.

"Now, get out of those dirty, old clothes and do some undercover work for me," she said as she unbuttoned her blouse.

Sharky grinned. This type of undercover work was more to his liking.

They were short-handed at the Surf's Up. Petra had called in sick, but Razz, in his most suspicious manager's way, doubted her veracity. Actually, her husband had called for her, so he had an even better reason to doubt it. Anyone who drank cheap draft beers all night and didn't leave a good-sized tip was suspect in his book.

Lotta had come in to help during the six to eight p.m. dinner rush. After that, there would be mostly drinks to serve, so it would be easier. If a customer felt they were waiting too long for drink service, they could go to the bar and order. But at nine o'clock, Razz still had to cover for Julio at the Sol a Sol.

It was only six-thirty. Tom was working six tables, Chad had five, and Lotta handled a party of thirteen rough-looking construction workers on the back porch. Razz caught any overflow.

He looked out from behind the bar and liked what he saw. Things were running smoothly. Even the boys out back were under control, likely caught under Lotta's spell. He forgot that the police station next door might have held some calming influence as well.

The phone rang behind him until Rick stopped mid-pour to answer it. "Hey, Razz, it's for you."

"Sorry," Razz said as he picked up the line. "Hello. Yes, I'm Razz McNeil."

He listened, then grabbed a piece of paper and scribbled down information. "Yes, that sounds perfect. Great, I'll see you tomorrow. Yes, thanks. Thank you."

He started to hang up, and then remembered something. "Hey, how did you hear about me? Hello?"

The caller was gone, but Razz didn't care. He'd just learned from a real estate broker about two apartments for rent—a one-bedroom for his parents and a two-bedroom for him. They sounded perfect.

Showered, shaved, and well laid, Sharky sat at the kitchen table contentedly drinking a Budweiser. He had suggested they go out for dinner, but Terri knew what that meant. She'd had as much of Mae's greasy food as she could stand, so she was making him a healthier version of chicken fajitas instead.

"Ow!" She sucked the top of her hand.

"What happened?"

"The oil splattered. Nothing serious."

Sharky got an ice cube from the freezer and caressed her hand with it.

"Thanks, honey. That feels better."

"That's what I'm here for, baby. To make you feel better. We can still go to Mae's, you know."

She rolled her eyes and he had his answer. He knew he'd have to do better than Mae's soon, but he was a creature of habit. He'd been going there for so many years, sometimes three times a day, it had become like a second home. But watching Terri, at the stove, in the kitchen, or anywhere in the apartment, made him realize there was no place like their home.

"Can I help?" he asked as she carried the steaming fajita mix to the table.

"No, you just relax. Would you like another beer?"

"Yeah, thanks." He sat back in his chair and watched her as she reached into the refrigerator. He chuckled.

"What is it?"

"I don't know. I was watching your ass and I just laughed."

"Thanks a lot."

"No, I mean ... well, I guess I'm just happy."

She brought him the Bud and twisted off the top. "I'm happy, too." She kissed him. "Now, let's eat. I'm starved."

Had he been Dr. Frankenstein and able to invent her, he could not have done it better. The fajitas tasted great. Though not as greasy as he liked, he could get used to them. He downed one and reached to fill another tortilla.

"Easy, Turbo. Let your stomach catch up," she said, gently scolding him.

The phone rang and she rose to answer it.

"Don't bother with it, babe," he mumbled, a piece of green pepper falling from his mouth.

"But it might be about a job." She picked up the phone and was disappointed. "It's for you."

"Tell them to call back."

"We're eating. Can you call back in twenty minutes?" she asked the caller.

"No! Tell him to pick the fuck up!" yelled a raspy voice through the receiver.

She moved the phone from her ear.

"It's about Wally," the voice said, softer now.

Disgusted, she handed him the phone. "He insisted you pick up. He was very rude."

Sharky was going to tell this unknown caller that yelling at his woman was not acceptable behavior and, if he ever did it again, he would reach through the phone line and pull the asshole through it, and then beat the shit out of him.

"He said it was about some Wally guy."

Suddenly, he was no longer angry. He wasn't relaxed, happy, or hungry anymore. He was just scared. "Hello," he said into the receiver.

"You were warm today," said an unrecognizable male voice, "but you were in the wrong apartment. Keep looking. You'll see everything very clearly from there, even the time."

"What? What do you—"

Click. "Hello! Hello!" Sharky realized his homeless disguise might not make him so invisible, after all.

Who could have seen me at the Hempstead besides Razz and the janitor? The leasing agent thought I was a street bum. The janitor wouldn't dare say anything. Could Razz be playing a joke? Or does he know something? He must have followed me there. After a moment's reflection, even with his natural paranoia humming along at full speed, he had to dismiss the possibility of Razz being the caller. He figured Razz wasn't that funny or stupid.

The message was clear—there were clues at the Hempstead. *If Richard Gold's was the wrong apartment, did that mean Wally's was the right one? What would there be to find now since they'd painted and re-carpeted? Or was there another apartment that would give clues to Wally's murder? And who the hell was this caller?* It had sounded like a man's voice, but had also sounded unnatural, as though distorted by something like a heavy cloth or some sort of mask.

"What is it, honey? Who's Wally?"

He ignored her and ran to his caller ID box in the bedroom. It read, *310-555-4376*. He dialed *69 and waited.

"Hello. Hello. Who are you?" he asked when someone answered.

"Hello-dee-do-dee-do-dee," someone said through the phone. The voice sounded bright and cheerful, too cheerful.

"What did you mean by 'the wrong apartment'? What did you mean?"

"Hello-dee-do-dee-do-dee," again was the happy reply.

"Give me that, Donnie. We've got to get you home," said a woman's voice from the background.

"Noooo!" Donnie no longer sounded so happy.

The receiver clanged against something metallic. The two people were arguing, but Sharky couldn't make out the details. Then the arguing faded and all he could hear was an indistinct buzz of activity and some music. It sounded like music from a carousel.

"What's going on?" Terri didn't like bothersome crank callers, but this call had gone far past bothersome.

"Hello! Hello!" Sharky yelled. "Hello!"

"Hello?" said an uncertain-sounding voice from the other end.

"Did you just call me?"

"Why would I call you, homey? I don't know who the fuck you are."

Sharky thought the new voice sounded Hispanic and male. He heard laughter through the phone, then another burst that sounded some distance away. "Where are you?"

"I'm at the fucking Pier, what's it to you?"

"Did you see anyone on this phone? Before you, who was on the phone?"

The man didn't answer, but Sharky could hear him breathing.

"Do you see anyone there?" he asked again, more urgently.

Slowly and calmly, the man said, "Yeah, I see about a thousand motherfuckers here right now. I don't know who the fuck you are, homeboy, but why don't you come down here and suck my dick?"

Raucous laughter, much louder now, blasted Sharky through the receiver. It only lasted a moment, though, until the receiver was smashed onto its cradle and the line went dead.

"Hello!" He slowly hung up.

"Who was it? What's happening?" asked Terri.

"No one, nothing, it's nothing to worry about. Just a crank call. Let's finish our dinner."

As they sat back down to their fajitas, Terri calmed slightly, but Sharky knew his caller was anything but a crank. He'd been very clear. "Keep looking," he'd said, just not in Richard Gold's apartment. Sharky would have to go back into Wally Bumpers' apartment.

But how will I get in without Donati finding out? And how would this guy know there's something to find there anyway? More importantly, what could it be?

18

He looked at the two Hispanic fishermen high above him, and then deftly avoided their fishing lines. They looked down at the crazy gringo, not understanding what he was doing until he disappeared from their view under the Pier.

"¿Qué diablos está haciendo? ¿Está loco?" yelled one, so disconcerted he fumbled his fishing rod into the ocean and to a watery grave.

Early the next morning, Louis Marcayda sat at his breakfast table looking over the gross receipt numbers from his two restaurants and he was pleased. If they continued to perform this well, he knew he would get his investment back quickly. And the busy summer months hadn't even arrived yet.

The numbers didn't surprise him. He had bought the restaurants only after careful consideration. He'd planned to get the word out to friends, associates, people that worked for him and those that wanted to, that patronizing the Surf's Up and Sol a Sol would be looked upon favorably. Louis did know many, many people in the San Margarita area and had long tentacles that reached into places and pocketbooks that people like Razz couldn't imagine. His plan was working perfectly thus far.

He picked up that morning's *Monitor* and his self-satisfied smile grew larger when he looked at the front page. The newspaper's cover story told all about Mayor Hidalgo's re-election announcement the day before. It spoke glowingly about the Mayor, his speech and his poll ratings. However, in this case, a picture was worth more than a thousand glowing words. Despite the relatively small group of protesters yesterday, an eighth page picture of Police Chief Wilson, hands outspread, holding back the quarreling parties made yesterday's announcement appear like a debacle for Mayor Hidalgo. It was, once again, just part of Louis' plan.

Yes, Louis had sent a small cadre of his men to upset Mayor Hidalgo's love fest. It wasn't only because Hidalgo had embarrassed him by insisting the police raid his operations weeks ago; he had also let him down. He had chosen a side and it wasn't Louis'. He had chosen Richard Gold's.

Gold was establishment. Gold was old San Margarita. Gold was also rich and it was critical that politicians have rich friends, but he was rich in a way that was acceptable to most voters and to Hidalgo's sensibilities. You see, Jaime Hidalgo had visions of the governor's mansion and no longer wanted to be associated with Louis Marcayda.

When he was struggling in his first run for Mayor, behind in the polls by more than twenty per cent, Hidalgo did something that ambitious men sometimes do out of desperation, he went against his better judgment. He asked Louis Marcayda for his support.

Hidalgo knew what Louis was, what he did for a living, how he'd gained his power, but Hidalgo also knew he needed him. Louis offered him financial support, but also offered hordes of free workers. These "volunteers" went house to house and made thousands of phone calls to drum up support and rally the Latino and ethnic vote. It was only because of Louis Marcayda that Jaime Hidalgo had been elected.

Now, Mayor Hidalgo wanted nothing to do with him. He couldn't bring Louis' empire down, but he did try to marginalize him. He made him look bad by raiding his brothels and bringing him unflattering headlines. He had embarrassed Louis in his fellow Latinos' eyes. Now Louis had done the same to him.

As he finished his coffee, Louis wondered what Hidalgo's next move would be. He was certain he could outwit and outmaneuver him and almost anyone else, because he didn't have to play by anyone else's rules. He made his own.

"Hi, Daddy."

"Hey, Pop."

Melanie and Patrick raced around the corner, still in their pajamas, and jumped into his lap.

"Good morning, good morning." He couldn't help but chuckle. *I'm ready for almost anything, but my kids still surprise me every morning.*

Merice, groggy from sleep, entered and gave him a kiss. "Good morning, honey."

"Hey, baby. How's my beautiful woman?"

She smiled, knowing she was not yet beautiful, but also knowing she would be soon. One cup of coffee and a dash of make-up and she'd again be a knockout.

"Come on, kids; time to get ready for school," she said and they shot off down the hallway.

Merice poured herself a cup of coffee, his kids argued over who would use a bathroom first, and Chief Wilson's face stared back at him from the front page of the *Monitor*. It was just another day in the very good life of Louis Marcayda—business deals, behind-the-scenes machinations, and his loving family. He was certainly a man of contrasts.

Razz McNeil was a man of contrasts, too. From yesterday's disappointments to this morning's hopefulness, he'd done an emotional one-eighty. And he had gotten a good night's sleep for the first time in days.

Last night at work had gone smoothly, first at the Surf's Up, then at the Sol a Sol. Business was great and showed no signs of slowing down. He had covered for Julio at the Sol a Sol, and Lotta had stayed to cover for him at the Surf's Up. He knew he owed her one for her help, but he owed her more for letting him sleep on her couch. Luckily, by the time they got back from work, they were both too exhausted to even flirt, so he'd slept with a clear conscience. Her living room's foldout couch felt like bedding at the St. Regis, so much better than folded up boxes on an office floor.

"Hey." Lotta entered from her bedroom, dressed in a skimpy nightgown.

"Hey," he said and then looked away. *Easy, big fella. Down, boy.* He looked back, but she'd already gone into the bathroom. *Whew, I can't stay here too long.*

"Help yourself to breakfast," she hollered from behind the closed door.

"Thanks, I'll get something later. I just need a quick shower."

"Come on in."

He hesitated, and then moved cautiously toward the bathroom. He heard water running. "Are you decent?"

No response.

"Can I come in?" he asked louder.

"Come in," came Lotta's muffled reply.

It sounded like she was brushing her teeth. *That's harmless. The coast is clear.* He opened the door and gasped when he saw her. She was naked and very much waiting for him.

"I'm more than decent, Razz."

He couldn't move, except for one muscle twitching below his waistline. But when she nestled up against him, he put his arms around her. He couldn't resist her and they went together to the floor.

Razz had a glorious morning, despite serious pangs of guilt. He and Lotta had sex on the bathroom rug and then again in the shower, erotic, illicit, sensuous sex. She had even made him breakfast.

He watched Imelda as she concentrated on eating her oatmeal, then he glanced at the kitchen clock. If he escaped now, he wouldn't need to rush to his appointment. "Thanks for everything, Lotta."

"No, thank you."

He blushed and then walked toward the door, before turning back. "Uh, could I talk to you?"

Imelda didn't look up, as her mother joined him.

"Listen, I'm sorry I let that happen this morning. I mean, it was incredible and all—"

"Yes, it was."

"But I'm still married. And what would Louis think if his two managers were screwing around?"

"He wants me to be happy."

She's not making this easy. "I love my wife and kids very much."

"Okay."

He waited, but that was all she said, as if it explained everything. "So, you're cool?"

"Of course I am, Razz."

Relief spread through his brain as if he'd taken a ten-milligram Valium. "Great, great, I'll see you at work. Just like nothing happened."

"Sure, see you later."

She was so composed it made him wonder if she cared. *Maybe I'm no good sexually.* Marriage, after all, could do that to a man. You can get lazy in many ways when you're married; sex was just one of the most important ways. *No wonder Sarah left me. I didn't please her.*

"By the way, you were great," she said and his ego expanded at light speed.

"Thanks," he gushed. "So were you."

"Good luck with your apartment."She sounded so supportive, just like Sarah used to sound. It made him feel good until he remembered he hadn't told her anything about his appointment.

"Huh? How did you know?"

"Who do you think set it up for you?"

She looked innocent, but he was already in too deep with her and didn't want to be at her mercy. "How did you set it up so quickly? How did this guy find the apartments? I've been searching everywhere."

"Let's just say, I know a few people."

I bet you do, he thought.

"The guy owed me a favor. That's all."

Razz knew she could hold their sexual liaison over him. Now he'd be beholden to her for an apartment as well, but he needed the place badly. "Thank you, Lotta. I owe you one."

"You're welcome, but you gave me two this morning." Her smile grew until she broke into laughter.

Razz laughed, too. *Maybe it will be okay. Maybe we can still work together. We are grown-ups, after all.* He needed to believe he was, but he didn't have the time for further reflection. He had to get to his appointment and Imelda was screaming, unhappy now with her oatmeal.

Lotta kissed him on his cheek. "See you later," she said before going to rescue her daughter.

He walked outside and felt the spot where her lips had touched him. It had been a gentle, confidential kiss. He didn't understand it, but it felt good.

He climbed into his Mustang and started the engine. It was a powerful machine. He felt powerful, too. He thought again about Lotta's gorgeous, full-figured body and her voracious appetites. *If I have to be separated from the people I love, I guess this isn't a bad way to do it.*

He drove out of her driveway. If he hit all green lights, he would just make it to his appointment on time.

"Here it is," said Ray Martinez, opening the door to a large and sunny, two-bedroom apartment.

"I'll take it," said Razz.

"But you haven't seen it yet."

"I've seen enough. I'll take it. How much did you say it was?"

"I didn't."

In his desperation, he hadn't asked any of the financial details. *How could I be so stupid? This guy's going to ream me. He can charge whatever he wants now. I'll have to take it or start all over again.* "Okay, how much?"

"It's a thousand dollars."

"A week?"

Martinez laughed. "By the month, of course."

"I don't have to share this with anyone, do I?"

"Ha-ha, no. It's all yours, if you want it," said Martinez, his light brown face turning red from amusement.

Razz smiled, until another doomsday thought crossed his mind. "What's the fee?"

"Huh?"

"How much will it cost me to get the lease?"

Martinez laughed again.

He's really enjoying this. That means it will cost a lot, probably ten thousand or more. Maybe Sarah will lend it to me. No, that's a recipe for disaster, especially after this morning. If she ever finds out, the only money she'd lend me would be for a one-way ticket to Yemen.

"The owner pays me, there's no fee. There are no strings, no nothing." He waited. "So, do you want it?"

"Yes." Now Razz was laughing. "When can I move in?"

"Today, if you like."

It seemed too good to be true, but Martinez pulled out a rental agreement and Razz didn't question it further. Before signing, he did take a full tour, however.

The place was perfect. There was plenty of room for his kids. They would have to share a bedroom, of course, or one could sleep on a foldout couch in the living room. *Hell, better yet, they can both sleep with me.*

He had not felt this hopeful since before Sarah dropped her bombshell. He stepped out a sliding glass door from the living room onto a nice-sized flagstone patio and saw a grassy, fenced-in yard. He immediately took the agent's pen and signed the agreement. He now had a place to live and a place for his children.

Next, Martinez showed him the one-bedroom for his parents. It was a charming, Spanish-styled bungalow, similar to thousands of guest houses scattered around Los Angeles on the grounds of private homes, but this one was totally self-contained. His parents wouldn't have to share a walkway, a yard, a hallway, or anything with anyone. Their fenced-in yard even had an orange and an apricot tree. Razz knew his mom would love that. She loved to garden, but she'd never had the space to do much of it before. She would offer those trees and whatever flowers she could plant an abundance of love.

"Uh, I know you gave me a great deal on the other place, but, see, my folks don't have a lot of money and I'll need to help them pay for this one. Would it be possible to get this for around a thousand, too?"

"It's only six hundred and twenty-five. That's per month, no sharing."

"Where are the papers?"

His parents came over shortly after he called, though his dad had to move up his lunchtime one hour. They fell in love with the place.

"There, didn't I tell you? Things happened for a reason," Sally McNeil said, beaming. "Now we'll live in the same neighborhood. I mean, until you and Sarah are back together."

Razz hugged her. "I'm glad you like it, Mom."

His pop chimed in next. "Well, it's not as big as Enterra," he said, before he burst into a big grin. "But it's a hell of a lot nicer. I love it, son. Thank you."

Tom McNeil grabbed his son around the waist and lifted him off the ground.

"Pop, be careful."

"Don't you worry; nothing's going to hurt me. I've got the best woman in the world, the best son, and, now, the best home."

As cheerful as he was naturally, Tom McNeil exceeded his usual good nature ten-fold. He was a proud Irishman and he felt like he could provide for his loving wife again.

The three of them danced, hugged, and cried. They dreamed of what they would do and the joy their new homes would bring them.

Even real estate agent, Ray Martinez, had happy tears in his eyes.

"I pushed that project through for you and I expect the same results from you." Mayor Hidalgo was livid, but his audience, Richard Gold, was unmoved.

Gold studied him, his back to the wall in his usual power position at Primo's. Hidalgo looked almost boyish, despite his forty-seven years. His threat seemed like that of a whining five-year-old boy who badly wanted candy.

"How does three hundred thousand sound?" Gold asked.

"What do you mean 'how does it sound?' For what?"

Gold was feeling on top of his game and was going to use the opportunity to remind the Mayor how much he needed him. It was actually a two-way street, because they needed each other, but, tonight, Richard Gold held the car keys.

"Three hundred thousand for the first deposit to the 'Re-elect Mayor Hidalgo Fund.'"

All of a sudden, Jaime Hidalgo was as docile as a puppy dog being scratched behind his ear. "Three hundred?"

His reaction was laughable, but Gold held back. Hidalgo had gone from petulant five-year-old boy to docile puppy to sixteen-year-old girl thrilled to be invited to the senior prom all in three hundred thousand dollars.

Gold nodded. Never mind that he hadn't raised the money yet; he'd been so busy with Natalie Wesson he'd forgotten all about it. If he had to, he could front Hidalgo the money, but he knew his sources wouldn't dare refuse him and most supported Hidalgo anyway.

"Three hundred?" Hidalgo asked again. "Already?"

"We're on target for a million."

In a city the size of San Margarita, a million dollars could garner a sea slug fifty per cent of the popular vote. It would ensure a competent man like Hidalgo a resounding victory.

Hidalgo took a bite of his Caesar salad, then a drink of wine. He was trying to compose himself, but he really wanted to jump up and down like Tom McNeil had when he'd seen his new home.

"Thank you, Richard, that's great. I'd still like to announce you as my finance chairman. I think it will win me votes."

Gold savored a spoonful of minestrone soup. Normally delicious, it tasted even better now that he had Hidalgo back under control.

"Talk to my assistant, Natalie Wesson, tomorrow. She'll set it up."

"I'll have Dan Manley give her a call."

"I'll have her take it."

Richard Gold smiled, as did Mayor Jaime Hidalgo. They understood each other perfectly. There was no need for small talk. Hidalgo rose and took Gold's hand, again sealing their partnership. Between men of power, it was always a balancing act between immediate ego needs and long-term symbiosis. They would be in balance for a while now.

"Can I expect that in my bank account tomorrow?"

"You'll have it on Friday."

That was enough for Hidalgo. He started to go, and then realized he hadn't paid for his salad and glass of wine.

"I'll get it," Gold said.

The Mayor excused himself, and then went to perform every politician's sacred mission—win votes. He glad-handed through the restaurant on his way to the front door.

As Gold watched him leave, he was uncertain whether Hidalgo would sway as easily the next time. He knew only one way to get to him. It was that time-honored technique that he understood better than most—offer large sums of money to get what you want in exchange. He figured it would be wise to find another way to influence him. *Perhaps, it would be a good project for Natalie,* he thought. *Yes, of course. Natalie would know just what to do.*

She certainly had a way with men.

19

Robbie didn't have time to explain even if he'd understood the man for he was busy dodging his first piling. As he glided easily past, he wondered if his ride might be easier than he had first thought.

"Hey, it's me," Razz said into his office phone. He was at work, as usual, on a Friday night, but tonight he was tipsy from too many celebratory scotches with his mom and dad. They had helped each other move into their respective new homes that afternoon, so congratulations were in order, but when it came to drinking, he couldn't keep up with his old man. He couldn't even keep up with his mom. He'd set them up at the bar hours earlier where they remained, knocking back scotches, laughing, talking too loud, and bragging about their son.

Sarah Gold McNeil hesitated. She was exhausted from that week's work, from taking care of her kids alone, and from trying to answer their endless questions about where their daddy was. But she didn't want to appear like she missed him. "Hi."

"Can I speak to the kids?"

"Are you at work?"

"Huh? Yeah, uh, can I speak to them?"

"They're sleeping, Razz. It's ten o'clock."

He looked at his small wall clock, but could barely tell the big hand from the little hand, his eyesight blurred from alcohol. "Sorry, I guess I lost track of time."

"Uh-huh." She waited.

It took a moment for him to remember the main reason for his call. "So, you think I could see the kids tomorrow? I got a new place and I'd like to have them over. We've been moving all day."

"We?"

It had come out automatically. It was an involuntary reflex, but she wondered who else might be in her husband's life after only three days away from her.

"Mom and Dad and me."

Had he listened more carefully to her tone, been less drunk, or been more manipulative, he might have played with her. He might have asked why she cared or might have tugged on her heartstrings to make her miss him, but it was way above his capacities at present. Besides, he was happy just to hear her voice.

"Oh, well, that's great."

There was a long pause as Razz tried to sober up, and Sarah tried to figure out how to proceed.

"So, can I see them?"

"Yes, of course. They ask about you all the time."

Despite his drunkenness, he was moved. "Thank you."

Sarah struggled for the right words, words that could change her life by changing her relationship with her estranged husband, words that could maybe put everything right. But, try as she might, "What time?" was the best she could muster.

He hadn't thought about a time. He looked at the clock, but it was still a blur. "Uh, ten?" He remembered hearing that number recently and thought it sounded good.

"Okay, see you tomorrow at ten. Sleep well."

'Sleep well,' she'd said. It was another thoughtful gesture from a thoughtful woman, wishing him pleasant dreams. She needn't have bothered. Razz would sleep very well tonight, but not for many more hours.

Razz made his way downstairs, holding on to the handrails. He could hear his father laughing too loud in public. When he got to the bar, Tom McNeil was in the middle of a crowd telling jokes and weaving tall tales. Rick, the bartender, was laughing and it appeared his father was good for his business. Even Tom, the sometimes-persnickety server, was laughing. His dad seemed to bring good cheer wherever he went. His mom didn't look quite as bubbly.

"Honey, your dad's not going to get you in trouble, is he? I think he's had too much to drink."

"Oh, he's just having fun. Thanks, though, Mom."

To worry was part of a mother's job and Sally McNeil did her job well. "Well, if you're sure."

Her concern didn't begin to match his, though, when Louis, Lotta, and several colleagues marched through the front door.

"Oh, shit." Razz saw his job, his apartment, and life as he knew it disappear before his eyes.

Louis was surprised by the sight of this ruddy Irishman standing on a bar stool, holding court, in his restaurant where he'd come to enjoy a nice, quiet evening with friends.

Lotta looked at Razz and her eyes told him he should do something quickly, so he went to his father.

"Hey, Pop—"

"Hey, everyone, this is my son, Robbie McNeil, the best son in the whole wide world." The rowdy crowd cheered him on.

"Dad, it's time to quiet down. My boss is here."

"Invite him over. Let me buy him a drink."

"Thank you, I'd like that." Louis calmly raised his hand toward Tom McNeil.

As if they'd seen a very powerful ghost, the crowd backed away.

"Hey, Laddie, you've got a nice place here." Mr. McNeil climbed down from his perch to shake hands, but pulled up short. "Hey, who are you?"

Razz was no longer worried about his job. Now he was worried about his father's health. Tom McNeil wasn't one to censor himself, especially in his current condition, and Razz could tell he was getting ready to say something someone would deeply regret.

"Come on, Dad, it's time to go." He grabbed him and led him away. It was rude, he knew, but he hoped he could deal with Louis later. Right now, he didn't want his father to do any more damage.

Confused and drunk, Tom McNeil didn't put up much struggle.

"Robbie, wasn't that the man people are always talking about? The bad man. Is he really your boss?" his mother asked.

Razz' heart sunk. She was displeased and that hurt him as much as any physical torture could. *Why had Louis come in tonight?* Not only might he lose his job, it appeared he had lost his place in the softest spot of his parents' hearts.

"What the hell is going on?" his father asked, catching on. "Isn't that the drug guy?"

"Come on, dad." Razz hustled his dad out, not nearly ready to explain his working arrangement. "Can we talk about this tomorrow, please?"

"But he's that man, the bad man," his mom said, fixated on an image of Louis gleaned from rumors and front page headlines.

"He's not a bad man, Mom."

Razz was surprised he was defending Louis, but he was mainly trying to defend himself. He wouldn't have considered supporting Louis a month ago, no matter what the situation; but now he was Razz' gravy train.

At least, he hoped he still was.

After he finally got his parents into a cab, over his father's heated protestations, he was so tense his ribs hurt. He looked down the Pier and saw the Friday night revelers at Sea Breeze Park enjoying ring toss games and water balloon shoots, as well as the Ferris wheel and bumper cars. He wished he could feel so carefree. He thought about what he would do now. His father standing on a stool could be excused, but Razz being drunk could not. At least, he had hustled his father away before he could say anything too derogatory.

Louis is bad, just like my mom said. Where's my morality gone? How can I work for such a man? Razz struggled with those questions and more, but he figured he wouldn't need to struggle with them much longer. He was sure he'd be fired.

He crept in the Surf's Up's back door. He considered going directly to his office and cleaning out his desk to save Louis the trouble of shit-canning him. He had insulted him by not introducing his parents. Worse, he'd shuffled them away as if ashamed. Louis was not one to slight.

"What the hell are you doing?"

It was Lotta. When his organs stopped tumbling, he said, "I'm just sneaking up to my office with my tail between my legs. How angry is he?"

"He's fine. I talked to him."

"What do you mean 'he's fine'? Isn't he pissed?"

"He was. I thought you knew how to handle people better than that."

"I thought my dad was going to say something I couldn't take back, so I maybe overreacted."

"Your dad sure knows how to have a good time." Lotta smiled. "Listen, Louis will understand; he's seen pretty much everything. People either grovel, run from him, or want to yell at him, but he's really just a regular guy."

Razz wasn't ready to believe Louis was "just a regular guy," but, at least, he was less inclined to run from him in fear. "Do you think he'll still let me work here, short of washing dishes, that is?"

"Why don't you ask him?"

He thought about his new apartment, about his kids coming over in the morning, about his livelihood. He knew he didn't have much right now without his job. He would ask, beg, and grovel, if he had to. He would do the same with his parents tomorrow, but he suspected they wouldn't be as forgiving.

He approached Louis' table with trepidation, but thrust out his hand, attempting to take as much control as possible, because he knew he had very little. "I'd like to apologize for my behavior and the behavior of my father."

Louis waited, not responding, and all the control was back in his possession.

Razz' hand was shaking itself now, but he did his best to hold his resolve firm.

Louis finally took his hand. "Tell your father he is welcome here any time, no matter what he may think of me." Louis could see Razz was embarrassed. He didn't want to fire him, but he needed to be sure such a scene wouldn't happen again. "Lotta tells me business has never been better."

Razz was grateful for the change to a more pleasant topic. "I think our success has a lot to do with our new ownership and our staff. Lotta's done an amazing job; I couldn't do it without her."

As he locked eyes with her, Razz thought he saw her blush, though he knew that wasn't her style. Although he felt magnanimous right now, he knew he really couldn't do it without her. Without her, he wouldn't have a job.

The remainder of the night went more smoothly. Louis and his friends came and went without further incident. Razz sobered up, forgot about his parents' disappointment in him, and considered instead how lucky he'd been, about how lucky he was.

I've got to be more careful. I've got to stop taking things for granted. I've got my job, my kids, my health, my parents, and my wife. Well, I've still got a chance at my wife. I've got to remember who signs my paycheck and who my allies are.

He couldn't help but think of Lotta, his biggest ally and one of his biggest concerns. He had to keep her on his side without allowing her to be too close. He certainly couldn't allow her to be as close as she'd been that morning.

When he got into his car after his long hard night, he knew he had his work cut out for him.

The next morning Razz found out just how much. When he went over to help his parents rearrange some furniture, they barely spoke to him, ashamed he could ever work for a man like Louis Marcayda.

"Be careful, son, be careful," was all his father would say.

He and Sally had been on the phone with friends since early that morning asking questions about Louis. They'd heard rumors about him, had read about him in the *Monitor*, but had never known who he was. They would have been happier never knowing.

"I don't work for him. I work for a corporation," Razz explained. Never mind that Louis was currently the corporation's sole stockholder.

The elder McNeils were unmoved. They thought they'd raised their son better than that. They didn't want him associated with such filth as drugs or sex for hire or any people that might be associated with such things. And they rightly suspected Louis was tied up tightly in both.

Razz didn't tell them about how he'd smoked pot, snorted cocaine, and bought hookers during certain bleak times in his past. He was still the perfect son in their eyes, at least, until last night. He desperately wanted their unconditional acceptance again. But it was clear he would not get it today.

When Razz picked up his children, they were also decidedly frosty, no more forgiving of his four day absence than were his parents of his professional associations, so he let them stew during the fifteen minute ride back to his new home. He already felt beaten up, and it was only a little after ten o'clock. But, by the time they'd reached his place, his kids had softened considerably and were just happy to be with their dad again.

The situation wasn't totally his fault. Sarah had kicked him out of the house, after all, but those facts get lost in the confusion of little minds. And there is no woman in the world, no matter how generous and good, while angry at her estranged husband, is going to tell his point of view better than her own. Later, he would tell Caitlin and Ronnie his side of the story or, maybe, he would just relax, enjoy their company, and save it all for another day.

Caitlin and Ronnie walked uncertainly into his apartment. They were going to check it out very carefully before giving their seal of approval.

"Come and see your new bedroom," Razz said and the kids followed him warily.

Caitlin poked the queen-sized bed from arm's distance, as if it might spring up and bite her. It didn't. She jabbed it again from closer in. The mattress bounced back appropriately and she decided it suited her just fine.

"Where's Ronnie sweep?" she asked, already having commandeered this bed.

"Sweep? Oh, sleep." It had been a few days since Razz had heard such a creative use of the letter "w." "Well, either he can 'sweep' with you—"

Caitlin's vigorous head shake alerted Razz that his proposal was a non-starter.

"—or he can sleep in my room."

Now little Ronnie shook his head, but it was up and down, not sideways. "Yeah! Yeah!"

Caitlin was mortified. She wanted some of that daddy sleep action, too. "I want to sleep with Daddy!"

"Me! Me!" countered Ronnie.

"You sleep here," she said, fairly tossing Ronnie onto the bed. She hugged her daddy's leg.

"Hey, be careful with your brother."

It was too late. Ronnie was already bawling and looking for revenge. He hit his sister with a closed fist right in the side of her cute little head.

"Hey, Ronnie, stop that!"

Now Caitlin was crying and Razz was getting a taste of single fatherhood. It wasn't a great taste, but compared to his last few days, he was still happy to be holding his angry kids at arm's length from each other.

"Let's go out in the yard."

The yard was hidden behind a curtain that hung over a sliding glass door in the living room. When Razz ceremoniously drew back the curtain to reveal his ace-in-the-hole, huge smiles lit his children's faces. It wasn't a big yard, but it reminded them of home. It would be enough for them to run, to play, and to fight in.

He opened the sliding door and his kids flew out like sparrows chased by an eagle. They ran across the lawn as fast as their tiny legs would carry them. It didn't take them long to reach the other end, but they were happy. They sprinted back into their father's waiting arms and Razz was the happiest of them all.

The three of them spent the rest of the morning chasing each other around the yard, playing a version of children's tag with ever-changing rules, until they all retired, exhausted, to the kitchen for lunch.

Razz' culinary efforts were meager, but ham and cheese sandwiches and bags of potato chips, with a root beer for Ronnie and a Coca-Cola for Caitlin, were more than enough to please them.

"How about a nap?" he asked, hopeful.

No kid in the world wants to take a nap during the middle of a sunny day, especially if they can still keep their eyes open and their legs moving.

"Everyone in my bed."

That did it; he'd broken down their natural kid defenses.

"Yeah! Okay!"

Caitlin and Ronnie ran to his room and flung themselves onto the bed. They jumped up and down, laughing. Razz took longer to get there, but when he saw them, he laughed, too. This wasn't the type of nap he had in mind, but he lay on the bed anyway as they jumped and laughed and laughed and jumped around him. It wasn't like one of those relaxing massage beds, but it still didn't take long for him to fall asleep.

Once he had settled in, snoring slightly, Caitlin stopped jumping and snuggled against his back protectively. Ronnie tried to snuggle against his dad by way of his sister, but she'd have none of it and pushed him away. He was about to cry in protest, but, instead, got up off the bed and circled round to the other side. He climbed up in front of his father and now both kids were happy. Razz was sandwiched. He smiled contentedly as he slept, undoubtedly having some very sweet dreams.

On this Saturday afternoon, Sharky was still struggling with the words of his mystery caller. The man had told him in no uncertain terms that he should go back to the Hempstead, but Sharky wasn't sure how to do it secretly. He could strong-arm his janitor friend again, but he didn't want to push his luck. The less he saw of that man, the less likely the janitor would mention his presence to any curious cop, such as Robert Donati. He could pretend he was looking to rent an apartment, but he worried the leasing manager had already gotten a good look at him despite his homeless disguise.

Terri could almost hear his wheels grinding and couldn't bear much more. "Why don't we get out of here? Let's take a walk."

"Okay." He dragged himself up from his chair and could feel a burden lift. "That's a damn good idea."

"I was afraid you were going to blow a gasket."

"I was. You saved me again." He kissed her cheek and went to the door. "You coming?"

She grabbed her sweater and joined him outside. It was a beautiful day, but the partly cloudy skies and light breeze compelled her to wrap the sweater around her. For her sake and his enjoyment, Sharky wrapped his arms around her as well.

He wasn't in disguise today. He wasn't even on duty. He forgot all about Wally for a moment and he was amazed at how Terri's companionship could do that for him. In years past, he'd focused solely on his police work. His focus had helped him be a good cop, but had made him a miserable human being. He enjoyed himself a lot more in her presence, so Wally and Chief Wilson would have to wait.

As they rounded the corner of Rosewood and Seventeenth streets, Sharky stopped short.

"What's the matter?" Terri asked.

"Uh, nothing."

After a moment, he continued walking. She'd seen so much odd behavior from him in such a short time, she didn't think much about it. His eyes danced a jig and his head swiveled from side to side. He was looking for something, because the picture in front of him didn't seem quite right. He saw Razz coming out of an apartment with two kids in tow.

"Hello," shouted Sharky. "Are you following me?" He said it with more gravity than intended, worried Razz could be on the other team, whatever team that might be.

"Hey, Sharky, uh, Gerard, what's going on?"

Sharky considered Razz, his kids, and the apartment, and he wasn't sure where to begin. Fortunately, Terri still had manners.

"Hi, I'm Terri."

"Razz. Nice to meet you. This is Caitlin and Ronnie."

His kids held tighter to him, wary of these strangers, but mostly wary of Sharky.

"Oh, they're beautiful." Her face positively glowed as she bent down toward them. "Hi, Caitlin. Hi, Ronnie."

The kids weren't terribly interested in anything but their dad, but Terri was enraptured with them. Like many childless women in their early forties, it was clear she wished she had children of her own. It was so clear that even Sharky could see it. He just wasn't sure why his legs hadn't buckled at the thought.

"Uh, sorry, this is my new girlfriend," Sharky said. He could tell she wasn't satisfied with that description. "My partner, I mean."

"Congratulations," Razz said. "What happened to Johnson?"

"What do you mean? Why do you ask?"

Razz paused while trying to figure Sharky out. He didn't try long, though, figuring it was impossible. "I was just kidding. Nice to meet you, Terri. Come on, kids, let's get you back to your mom's."

Each clung to a leg as he dragged them to the car. He didn't want them to go, but he'd promised to have them home by three-thirty. Besides, he had to get to work. After last night's debacle, he didn't dare be late. He lifted his kids into the convertible and, after some struggle, got each strapped in.

"Do you live here now?" Sharky asked.

"Yeah, nice place, huh? If I had more time, I'd show you around, but I'm running late."

"It was a pleasure to meet you," said Terri.

"You, too. You guys walk around here often?"

Sharky went in for the kill; he'd had enough of Razz' innocent act. "We live around the corner on Eighteenth, but you knew that."

"Oh, okay. Yeah, I remember now. I brought you home the other day, didn't I?"

Terri was fascinated. Razz seemed harmless, but her man was treating him like a possible enemy of the state.

"Daddy, let's go."

"Okay, guys, one second," he said, trying to mollify them. "Hey, hope to see you again, Terri. I guess we're neighbors. Of course, I'm just glad I found any place to live; staying on the floor of one's office isn't suggested for good health. Take it from me."

Sharky recalled the morning Razz had stumbled sleepily from the Surf's Up and realized his paranoid tendency had again reared its ugly head. "Sorry, Razz. Welcome to the neighborhood. I hope you got a good deal," he said, more friendly now.

"Yeah, actually, it's unbelievable. I found this great agent. He even found a cheap place for my folks nearby."

"That's great," Terri said.

Sharky chuckled, somehow amused by Razz' simple explanation. "Yeah, that's great."

"What? What's so funny?"

"How much do you pay?"

"Jerry, don't be noisy," said Terry.

"No, it's okay, I'll play," said Razz. "I pay a thousand a month; my folks pay less for a one-bedroom."

"Wow, I wonder how you got such a good deal?"

"I guess I got lucky. An owner can ask whatever rent they want. Right?"

"They sure can." Sharky was full-on laughing now. "You have no idea who owns this, do you?"

"No, why? And who cares? I needed a place to live."

Two of his reasons for needing the place, his kids, were squirming in the cramped back seats of his Mustang. "Daddy," they pleaded.

"Well, you have to go," Sharky said. "Anyway, welcome to ..." He paused, creating the right tension for his climactic finish, "... to Louisville." His emphasis of Louis Marcayda's preferred pronunciation made Razz understand immediately.

"That's right," he continued, "Louis Marcayda, your boss, owns most of this neighborhood. He owns your place and probably your parents' place, too. Louis is your landlord."

Sharky took Terri's hand and led her down the street, his piece spoken.

Razz didn't have time to ponder the implications; his kids were yelling. He would likely be late getting them home and be late for work, but those prospects paled in comparison to the one big fact Sharky had just heaved at him. Louis Marcayda was now his landlord. *No wonder my rent is so low. Louis is subsidizing me.*

He felt himself spiraling deeper into the well that Louis had drilled for him. He desperately wanted to climb out and run far away, but he didn't have any place to go. Once again, Razz decided to deal with all of it later. He'd follow a temporary course of inaction, but he knew that inertia and the enjoyment of having a place of his own would mean he probably wouldn't try to change a thing.

One thing was certain—he wouldn't mention their new landlord to his parents.

20

"Hey!"

Robbie teetered on his board before regaining equilibrium. This was no time for surprises. Thinking the yell was a warning, he surveyed his situation, but it had simply been a general alert from one of the nearby surfers that this was indeed THE DAY. Robbie was too busy navigating his board to notice the tumult he was causing.

Tuesday, January 18, 2005

"No, no, no, no! I'm too old to play cops and robbers. All I want is to go to work, see my kids, surf once in a while, and get my wife back," Razz spewed into the phone. Like a telemarketing call from hell, someone on the other end wouldn't take no for an answer. "And I don't give a shit about your fucking job!"

At the other end, Sharky took a deep breath. The straightforward approach didn't work, so he tried another tack. "What if Richard Gold was involved? Better yet, what if he wasn't and he was wrongly accused? Wouldn't you like to help him? It might help you get your wife back."

"Gold's guilty of being an arrogant, smarmy asshole, but we both know he isn't guilty of murder."

"Actually, I don't know. He's my only suspect right know. I'd like to find something on someone else, anyone else."

"Whatever, I don't care. Send the bastard to jail."

This tack wasn't working particularly well either, but Sharky kept moving. "What about your kids? You think they want a jailbird for a grandfather?"

"You stupid bastard—"

"I'm just saying, Razz, he's all I've got right now. Maybe I can find a clue pointing to someone else, but I need your help."

Razz' silence raised his hopes.

"All I need is an hour."

Finally, Razz responded. “All right, you son-of-a-bitch.”

“I don’t know what the fuck I’m doing here,” Razz mumbled as he approached the Hempstead. “I’m not a fucking cop.”

No, he wasn’t, but he did know why he’d succumbed to Sharky’s entreaties. He enjoyed the action. He already knew a lot about Wally’s murder. He’d been in his apartment before with Sharky. He’d looked through the Sol a Sol’s viewing glass and seen where Wally’s body was discovered. He’d even played along with Sharky’s undercover machinations just days earlier. He knew he could easily drown, if he wasn’t careful, but he was determined to stay near the shallow end of this investigative pool. He’d dip a toe into detective work here and there, but when the going got rough, he’d get the hell out of harm’s way—in a hurry.

His role wouldn’t be difficult anyway. All he had to do was ask Susan Berne to show him Wally’s apartment. He’d tell her he would get some help to pay the rent or some other bullshit, but he had to convince her to let him in. Then Sharky would arrive covertly, slide in when she wasn’t looking, and that would be that. Sharky could comb the apartment for clues all night if he liked, but Razz’ job would be over. Regardless of the exciting intrigue, Sharky was going to owe him big for this one.

When he and Susan Berne reached the door of Wally’s apartment, Razz instinctively looked back down the hall.

“Anything wrong?” she asked.

“No, nothing, nothing at all.” *Easy, big fella. Thou doth protest too much, methinks.*

Berne didn’t seem to notice his nervousness, but he felt like he was dripping sweat like a leaky faucet. She opened the door.

Razz tried hard—too hard—to view the apartment as if for the first time. “Wow, spacious,” he said, admiring his ad lib.

“Twelve hundred square feet. Plenty of room,” she responded, without a hint of enthusiasm.

“How much did you say this was again?”

“Forty-two hundred, non-negotiable.”

“Sure, sure, not a problem.”

It wouldn’t be a problem as soon as Sharky arrived, so he could get out of there, but, right now, his nerves were starting to get the best of him. “So, everything looks new,” he said, stating the obvious as though it were a revelation.

She didn’t bother to respond.

He began to think she wasn’t very good at her job, and then remembered he wasn’t there for a sales critique. “So, is that the master bedroom?”

Berne rubbed her eyes, exhausted by years of looky-loos like Razz, and then followed him to the bedroom.

He paused inside, stalling, before proceeding to the balcony. “Wow, now I see why it’s so expensive. What a view.”

She half-smiled, the kind of smile you’d see from an automaton. She didn’t have high hopes for a commission, so she wasn’t going to waste her energy.

Razz turned back and gasped when he saw someone he didn't immediately recognize. He caught himself, but not quickly enough. Berne turned and saw Sharky, sneaking in the door as planned, except that he was dressed like a Transylvanian transvestite right out of *The Rocky Horror Picture Show*.

"Wait there, I'll be right with you," she said faux sweetly. "Where do they get these guys?" she said quietly to Razz. "This place is a fucking fag magnet."

"Helloooo," Sharky said sounding like a cross between Katharine Turner and Mr. Ed. He sort of looked like it, too.

"These guys are such fruitcakes," she whispered, now a co-conspirator with Razz.

He smiled, glad to have her on his side for now, as if she were an anchor to reality.

"Oh, I'm with him. Hi, Razzy," Sharky continued, waving his fingers in greeting like he was tinkling vertical piano keys.

Razz' smile left him. Berne was too appalled by Sharky's behavior to be embarrassed by her own. She backed away from both of them.

"No, uh, you don't understand, this is, uh, this is ... my brother. Yeah, my brother ... Bruce," Razz said.

Sharky took it all in stride, having too much fun in his new role. "Oh, honey, don't be embarrassed. It's the new millennium. She's seen gay men before." He sashayed through the room like he owned it and starting re-decorating.

"We can put the red velvet couch over there, the piano near the wall there. Oh, this place needs plants, lots of plants. It's like death in here. We need life. Life." He threw his hands in the air as if he were invoking the *Chorus Line* gods. "Too bad we can't have kids. Maybe we can adopt. I always wanted to adopt."

Had Razz not been so embarrassed, he would have busted a gut at Sharky's act.

"Are you going to be staying here as well?" asked Berne.

"You couldn't keep me away with ten firemen, honey. Actually, my Razzy will live here by himself, but expect me to visit often." His winking eye and rising vocal inflection implied more than just visitation, which discomfited both Berne and Razzy. "I'll help him with the rent, though. I hear it's a bitch here."

Berne recoiled. "Listen, I think I'll let you "guys" work out the details. Look at the apartment, discuss it. Feel free to take as much time as you need. I'll be downstairs, if you have any questions."

When the door slammed behind her, Sharky broke into laughter until Razz smacked him hard on his shoulder.

"Ow! What'd you do that for?"

"What for? I have a wife and kids. I live in this town."

"I live here, too."

"Yeah, but you're unrecognizable. She doesn't even know your name. That's it, I'll go tell her your name, that this was all a gag," Razz said, and he moved toward the door.

Sharky grabbed his arm, still laughing. "Hold on, hold on. Terri used to be a fashion stylist and suggested this. In case Berne caught me, I had to make sure she wouldn't recognize me. Maybe I got carried away with the act, though. I'm sorry. But you have to admit, it worked."

Sharky looked so silly, Razz finally broke down and laughed, too.

"Hey, I don't look that funny."

"You crazy son-of-a-bitch, where did you get a sense of humor, all of a sudden?"

"Love does crazy things to people."

Sharky was pleased with himself, but Razz was more somber.

"Sorry, Razz. You'll get your wife back." Sharky put a comforting hand on his shoulder.

Razz didn't understand this new, improved version of Gerard "Sharky" Sampson, but Sharky had already moved on, exploring the apartment for clues.

"Well, you don't need me anymore, so—"

"Stay. It will help my cover."

"But I—"

"Listen, ten minutes, that's all I'll need. I'll owe you, anything you want."

"You already owe me."

Razz figured he'd now be known as a wife-cheating pervert. *Well,* he thought, *I guess I can't argue with the wife-cheating part.*

He didn't feel like laughing anymore.

Sharky stretched far out over the balcony railing, looking for something that seemed just out of sight. He squinted against the glare of the afternoon sun as it reflected off the multi-storied buildings of San Margarita.

"It's been ten minutes. Let's go," Razz said, but Sharky ignored him. "What the hell are you looking for anyway?"

Sharky pulled himself back onto firmer footing. "If I tell you, you'll just be further into this." He walked past into the living room.

Now Razz had a dilemma. Should he let it go, not ask, and maybe miss out on something big? Or should he ask and risk falling into the deep end without a life jacket?

Sharky seemed not to care a whit about Razz' predicament; he was chasing clues. Unfortunately, he wasn't finding any.

Razz rubbed his brow as if he could bring mental clarity to his thoughts like wiping a dirty windshield brings visual clarity to a truck driver. It didn't help. He sighed and dove in, head-first. "What do you mean? Tell me what?"

Sharky turned, grinning like a Cheshire cat. He had a secret he badly wanted to share, and he needed help, because he wasn't getting anywhere alone. "I got a call on Friday that I was looking in the wrong apartment."

"Then why are we here?"

"No, the guy meant Gold's apartment. That was the wrong apartment. I was there Friday."

"So, who knew you were in Gold's apartment?"

"That's just it, I don't know. Other than the janitor, no one saw me."

"Ah-ha! The janitor did it. Case solved. Let's go home."

Razz moved toward the door, but Sharky grabbed him.

"Okay, okay, I assume he told you to look here," said Razz.

"I'm guessing that's what he meant, but I don't know. He said something about being able to see everything, even the time."

With a child's simplicity, Razz reached up for a clock hanging from the living room wall. He turned it around, took out the two AA batteries, checked the case closely, put the batteries back in, and then hung the clock back on the wall. "Well, nothing here. Let's go."

"Good try, I already thought of that."

"Hmm, great minds. Well, you can see everything from out there." Razz went out onto the balcony and looked north. *Nothing.* Then south. *Nothing obvious there.* He looked west to the Pacific. *No clocks out there.* He looked down at the Pier and was ready to give up detective work entirely, aware that holding onto his restaurant job was difficult enough.

"Well, that's it for me. Good luck," he said, before noticing something shiny about a half-mile to the south. He shielded his eyes against the sun's reflection. "What's that building?"

"Which one?" Sharky struggled to see.

"Is that City Hall? It looks like a clock tower. Does City Hall have a clock tower?"

"Can you really see that far?"

"Yeah."

"Shit, I got to get my eyes checked. Yeah, there's a clock in the tower of City Hall."

Neither was sure what that meant, but it didn't sound good.

"So, what's at City Hall?" Razz asked.

"Just the Mayor's office, the main police headquarters, the Town Council, every elected official in San Margarita, as well as the whole judicial system, judges, the DA, everyone, everything."

"Well, he did say you could see everything from here."

"Fuck, fuck, fuck," Sharky muttered.

"I couldn't have said it better myself. Well, good luck with your investigation, Officer Sampson. Razz Q. Public has to go to work now. You keep them safe, I'll keep them fed."

He began to leave, but Sharky stopped him with only words this time. "You can't tell, you know."

"Tell? I don't know what any of this means. What am I going to tell?"

"This could go pretty high up, Razz. Be careful."

As if on cue, a loud knock on the front door nearly sent Sharky out of his knee-highs and Razz into incontinence.

"Are you all right in there?" It was Susan Berne. "I'm going to have to ask you to leave now. What are you two doing?" She opened the door cautiously, terrified of what she might interrupt.

"I told you, mauve would look marvelous with splashes of yellow. You never listen to me," Sharky said, not missing a beat. He walked past her into the hall.

Razz missed several beats, however. He just stood there, unsure what to say.

"Have you seen enough?" Berne asked.

"Uh, yes. I certainly have."

Razz didn't figure he'd get a call from Susan Berne real soon. He'd seen more than enough of the Hempstead and Wally's apartment anyway. But Sharky wasn't going to let him off the hook easily.

"Damn it, Sharky, will you just leave me alone?" he spewed into the bar phone at the Surf's Up. He slammed down the receiver, but the phone rang again almost immediately. "I'm serious, don't call here again!"

His vehemence turned heads at the bar, but interest didn't last long. It being Los Angeles, the patrons were far more interested in themselves.

"Just tell me anything else you can think of, anything that might help," said Sharky from the other end.

"I already told you! Leave me alone!"

"Is everything all right?" asked Rick.

Razz noted his bartender's concern, but was fairly certain it had more to do with the negative effect on his bar business than worry over his welfare.

"Call me back in three minutes," Razz said and slammed down the phone. He never answered Rick and never explained his behavior, but as soon as he left the bar and was making his way toward his office, business was back to normal.

Rick smiled his winning bartender's smile as he delivered pints of Budweiser to thirsty patrons.

Razz had barely sat down at his desk when the phone rang. "Hello," he said quickly.

"Easy, Razz, you may be too uptight for this kind of business."

"I'm not in this kind of business, you are. I'm in the restaurant business. That's all."

"Yeah, sure, of course." Sharky paused, a calculated move that succeeded in raising Razz' tension level. "What else did you see?"

"Nothing, nothing at all. You know everything. I mean, you are the cop, aren't you? How fucking dare you put me in that position? Make me look like an asshole in front of that Berne woman—I should have punched you right in the nose."

"Uh-huh. What else?"

"Nothing, other than the fact she hates my guts because she thinks I'm queer, she clearly has no problem letting people know how she feels about gay people, and that you hung me out to dry!"

"She what?"

"Huh?"

"She what?"

Razz didn't know what the fuck he was talking about. "What what?"

"You said Berne had no problem letting people know how she felt about gays."

"I guess."

"Why did you say that?"

The fog of memory lifted and Razz saw her words emblazoned against a dark recess of his mind. "She said, 'Where do they get these guys? This place is a fucking fag magnet. These guys are such fruitcakes.'"

There was a long pause while Sharky considered. "She said all that?"

"Yeah."

Another pause, more brief this time. "That's great, great. Thanks, Razz. This may be the break I was looking for. I'll let you know."

Click.

Razz had no idea what he'd meant by "the break" he was looking for, but he preferred to be kept in the dark from here on out. *That's the only break I want. Just leave me alone.* But try as he might to calm it, his mind raced. *What did I say that got him so excited? So Berne hated gay guys, so what? She's not the only bigot in town, and why would Sharky care? Could she have something to do with Wally?*

His mind spun itself further into confusion, like a drill bit drilling toward the blackest center of the earth, before he came to his senses and a light appeared. *Berne wasn't even around when Wally was murdered. She'd been on leave. It must have been something she said that interested Sharky. But what was it? What did she say again?*

He struggled to shine the faded image of her words. Finally, they were again recognizable. *"Where do they get these guys? This place is a fucking fag magnet. These guys are such fruitcakes."*

With blinding clarity, he understood. Wally lived in a "fucking fag magnet." Berne was referring to his apartment. That had to mean Wally was gay. For the briefest of moments, Razz was extremely proud of himself, having figured out the puzzle. Then his pride faded and discouragement took over. He couldn't care less about Wally's sexual preference and didn't know why anyone else would either. He had no idea why that information might be important.

Sharky knew why, though, and he'd gone directly to the morgue after his conversation with Razz to re-examine Wally's decaying body. Sick from reeling in the surf while retrieving the body, he hadn't been at the initial examination, but had been filled in secondhand on the details.

They'd found nothing that had shocked him. Dirt under the fingernails meant Wally had first been buried somewhere the police still had to determine, but they knew he'd been dead for days prior to his lashing under the Pier. He had suffocated to death, not drowned. There were no indications of a struggle, but it was unlikely he'd been a willing sacrifice. The details of Wally's death had been a profound mystery, never mind the confusing extracurricular events of his retrieval from a gravelly grave and his watery display under the Pier. Why was he killed, where, and by whom were the questions that mattered most to Sharky. Now, he at least had a theory.

Wally had been suffocated while having sex, likely in his own bed with his own pillow. That's probably why there were no bed sheets when Sharky first inspected the apartment. They'd been discarded to remove any possible DNA evidence. That's also why the place had been wiped clean of fingerprints. He guessed the perpetrator had been Wally's lover and had been in his apartment before, probably many times. *But why had no one seen anything?*

He went over the details of the Hempstead's floor plan. One couldn't repeatedly come in the front without being seen; Berne noticed almost everything from her office perch. Maybe Terri was less diligent; he'd ask her again if she'd seen anything suspicious. Maybe the lover/killer could have come up the side way, through the door from the poorly-lit alley, and walked up the emergency stairwell. Wally lived at the end of the hall, near the stairwell, so it was possible someone could sneak in that way. But he questioned whether it could happen over and over again. *Why would Wally's supposed friend go to all that trouble? And what the hell did City Hall have to do with this?* There was no shortage of gay men there; he'd have to try and track them all down, but he couldn't exactly take a census. *Or does City Hall hold any relevance? Did the caller want to send me off track? Or have I just not found the right clue yet? Is there another place that shows the time that can be seen from Wally's apartment?*

Sharky reeled from the possibilities and was saved only by the entrance of Medical Examiner, Danielle Pierson.

21

A gaggle of surfers paddled madly toward the Pier like baby ducks running over water to catch up to their mother. Others ran along the beach to cheer him on and to pick up the scraps if there would be anything left of Robbie/Razz to pick up.

Danielle Pierson was five-feet-two-inches tall, blonde haired, and looked delicate, like a china doll, or perhaps a shorter version of Barbie, but when she unzipped Wally's body bag and flipped his dead body over on the examination table, she looked more like a pumped-up Malibu Ken. Her triceps danced as she pushed and pulled Wally into position, ass-up on the table.

The stench was terrible, the view was worse, but Sharky wasn't fazed. As long as there was no water involved and his life wasn't in danger, he figured he could handle almost anything.

Wally was purple-blue, stone-cold, and decaying by the second.

"You want to do the honors," asked Pierson, cotton swab in hand.

"Very funny," he replied.

She went to work. "You look like you've been working out, Sergeant." She lined up several glass sample slides on the table beside the body.

"Maybe a little."

Sharky liked the flattery, but knew it was just small talk, not a come-on, because Pierson was a talker. He figured she did it because, by talking, she could divert her attention from the fact she was now probing a dead man's asshole with a cotton swab.

"Did you color your hair? You look younger," she continued, pulling the first swab from Wally's orifice.

The peppermint oil Sharky had placed under his nose came in handy when the stench was elevated several notches by the liquid now oozing from Wally's body. Its grotesquely red-green color made him wish he'd also had some very dark glasses.

"Yeah, I'm going out with someone, too. Man, can that boy fuck," she said as she thrust a second swab into Wally.

Sharky winced. She wasn't gentle, but Wally wouldn't notice.

"Hey, it's obvious you're in love. In this job, you notice things, you know? I bet she's a nice girl."

He smiled, in spite of himself. "Uh, yeah, she is."

"It's good to know where your next lay is coming from." Pierson laughed a masculine-sounding laugh, incongruous coming from her petite frame.

She pulled out the second swab and it looked much like the first. She wiped it against a second slide, and then dropped the swab into a hazardous waste container. She reached for number three. "You know, it's been a while; he's pretty decomposed. I'm not sure what this will tell us."

Sharky was glad to be back on familiar ground, familiar to his case and less personally familiar with Danielle Pierson. "I don't know either, but it's worth a shot. Why didn't you do these tests at the autopsy?"

"Because no one told me he was a butt-pirate!" She roared with laughter, very proud of herself.

That he didn't laugh didn't bother her in the least.

"Seriously, until you told me he was Liberace's sister, there was no reason to check."

She is one odd little duck.

She pulled out the last swab and looked at it for a moment before wiping it across slide number three. "That should do it. Don't forget to sign."

"Huh?"

"I noticed you didn't sign in."

"Oh."

Sharky approached the visitors log book. He purposely hadn't signed in. Pierson didn't know he was no longer officially on the Bumper's murder case, but she'd quickly find out if she suspected him in any way. It would only take a phone call. Then all Hell would break loose and it would break all over him.

He looked at the names on the log. Chief Wilson's name was there as was his and Donati's, among others. He smiled self-consciously, and then with a whoosh of the pen, he scribbled an illegible facsimile of Robert Donati's name into the log.

"You want to see what we've got?" she asked.

"Sure."

Pierson hunched over her microscope. "Hmmm. Uh-huh. Oh, my, that's interesting," she said quietly.

Sharky drew closer and closer, drawn in by secrets yet revealed.

"Oh, gosh. Huh. Hmmm."

He could barely stand the suspense. "Do you see anything?"

Pierson stared into the microscope for several seconds, then lifted her head. "I see some things."

"Really? What? What do you see?"

"The first thing I see ... is shit." She cackled.

He knew it wasn't right to strike a woman, but she was pushing him.

"Ha-ha-ha. Whew, that was a good one." She wiped laugh tears from her eyes.

Oh, my God, even the Medical Examiner wants to be a comedian. Life is one big audition in LA.

She looked again into the periscope. "Wait, I see ... I see ..."

Sharky leaned in, anticipating.

"... more shit." She roared like a good ol' boy after a twelve-pack.

He started to leave.

"No, wait, wait. I do see something."

"Yeah, I know. More shit."

"Yeah, there's plenty of that, but there's something else."

He waited, no longer hoping for much.

"I see ..."

"What? Dead people?"

She looked up at him. "No. Dead sperm."

She'd said it with such a straight face that he thought it might be part of her act. "Sperm?"

She nodded affirmatively and Sharky's case took a decided turn to the left, but, at least, he now had a definite direction.

"Shit," he said.

"Yeah, we already established that." She cackled again.

"So, he was gay."

"Well, unless he could fuck himself. Then he might not be considered gay, just really fucking lucky!"

He'd heard enough. Wally was gay and was being bumped by someone in City Hall before he was permanently bumped. "Have Harvey run some DNA tests. Let me know when you get the results."

He walked out of Pierson's office and down the hall and could still hear her laughing.

Little Ronnie wasn't laughing, he was wailing at the world's injustice. He'd come to Harrington Park with his sister and mom and he wanted to play baseball with the older boys. Never mind that he was only three and all he'd ever done was swat a Nerf ball off a T-Ball stand with a big, plastic bat, and they were ten- and twelve-year-olds playing hardball. Ronnie had high aspirations, just like his father. But now he was on the bench, watching, fighting back sniffles, while the other boys chose sides, snickering at the little kid who thought he was big.

Sarah fought the urge to go rescue him and embarrass him further. She was pushing Caitlin in a swing, but it broke her heart seeing Ronnie cry and she couldn't bear it any longer.

"Wheee! Higher, Mommy, higher."

"That's enough, honey. I've got to go see your brother."

"No!" Caitlin's blood-curdling response left little doubt where her concerns lay. "I want to swing higher!"

Sarah wasn't about to be bossed around today by a six-year-old or anyone else. She'd had enough of playing doormat to Razz, her father, anyone, but before she could respond to her obstinate daughter, she saw a young boy approaching her son. Her focus wandered to them, and she let Caitlin fend for herself.

"Mommy?"

"How you doing?" asked a shy, ten-year-old boy. It was Patrick Marcayda.

Ronnie quickly wiped a tear away and straightened up. He wasn't about to act his age now. "Okay." He punched his tiny mitt, ready for action.

"Guess you wanted to play ball, huh?"

"I don't care." Ronnie's high, squeaky three-year-old voice gave him away, but Patrick didn't let on.

"How about playing catch with me?"

Ronnie's eyes lit up. "Sure." He grabbed his plastic bat and ball, then, realizing, got embarrassed. "Do you have a baseball?" he asked with as much bravado as he could muster.

"Hey, Patrick, you playing?" asked a blonde haired boy from the pitcher's mound.

Patrick looked at the boys, sides now chosen, getting ready to start their game.

"Let the kid cry, come on," yelled another.

Ronnie dropped his head, ashamed.

"No, you guys go ahead. I'm going to play catch with this guy," said Patrick.

Ronnie's chest puffed up like a circus strongman's.

"What are you talking about? He's a kid," said blonde boy.

Patrick waved off his buddies and grabbed the plastic Wiffle ball. "Come on, we don't need a baseball." He tossed the ball to Ronnie who caught it unsteadily in his glove.

"No wonder you suck, loser," said one of the older boys before blonde boy punched him hard enough to shut him up.

Patrick and Ronnie tossed the plastic ball back and forth, ignoring the older boys who soon ignored them back. Ronnie giggled gleefully when he fired a fastball that Patrick couldn't handle. Truth be told, Ronnie was really good for his age and Patrick wasn't good for his, but they weren't thinking about impressing any baseball scouts. They were just having fun.

"Is that your boy?"

Sarah whirled, surprised, and saw Merice and Melanie Marcayda, standing hand-in-hand. "Uh, yes." She smiled and turned back to watch Ronnie, and then turned again. "Oh, is that your son?"

Merice nodded.

"That was so nice of him. What a nice young man. Thank you. I'm Sarah McNeil."

She offered her hand and Merice was pleased to take it.

"Merice Marcayda. Nice to meet you."

"It's a pleasure meeting you."

Melanie didn't care for small talk or niceties, so she climbed into a swing next to Caitlin. Caitlin checked her out, not sure she wanted to share her turf, then started to swing. When Melanie struggled to get her swing moving, Caitlin hesitated, then jumped off and gave her a push.

"Thanks," said Melanie.

"That's okay," responded Caitlin before she climbed back into her seat.

Caitlin tried mightily to catch up, as Melanie was already rolling, and soon they were both swinging high and laughing loud. Neither needed any help from their mom.

Something nagged at Sarah. "I'm sorry, but have we met before? Your name seems familiar."

"No, we haven't, but I think I saw you from across the room on New Year's Eve."

"Oh, my God, that wasn't one of my better nights. Wait, Marcayda? You didn't send the Champagne and flowers, did you?"

"My husband was going to just send Champagne, but I told him that would be like a bad joke, so I picked out the flowers."

"Thank you, that was so sweet. I asked my ..." Sarah hesitated, then continued, "... husband, because I didn't recall meeting anyone named Marcayda. Of course, I can't recall anything from that night."

Merice laughed. "It's good to have a good time."

"Yeah, but it's even better to remember it."

Over the next two hours, Sarah and Merice laughed and talked like old friends as Caitlin and Melanie and Ronnie and Patrick quickly became new ones.

The next day, Razz rolled over in bed and reached for where his wife should have been. He opened his eyes, disappointed. He looked at his bedside clock. It was eight a.m. He grunted and pulled the covers over him, shielding the daylight. He was exhausted from another successful night at the Surf's Up, so he wouldn't surf that morning, but he didn't want to get out of bed at all. It felt so comfortable after his nights in the office and on Lotta's couch. So safe. He began to drift off.

Knock! Knock! Knock!

He looked again at the clock. It was still eight a.m. and someone was knocking on his front door. He pulled his pillow over his head.

Knock! Knock! Knock!

He jumped out of bed, ready to tell whoever this person was what he could do with whatever he was selling. He threw on a robe before he tore open the door.

"Hi, neighbor."

"Who the hell are you?" asked Razz.

He would have been nastier had it not been a woman, dressed in heels, skirt, and alpaca sweater, standing in front of him. She was about five-feet-nine-inches tall in heels, not counting two extra inches for her puffy blonde hair. Not the prettiest and clearly on the masculine side, she made Razz wonder what kind of neighborhood he'd just moved into.

"I'm sorry, but I'm trying to sleep," he said and he swung the door toward closed.

The woman caught it mid-swing and walked in past him. "Can't sleep, we've got work to do," she said in a bad vocal imitation of Marilyn Monroe.

Razz knew this could only be trouble, but had no idea yet just how much. But as he watched the person enter his domain uninvited, his anger rising, he noticed the slightest of limps in the person's gait. "Sharky?"

Sharky/Jerry/Gerard/Marilyn whirled and his/her skirt twirled around him. All he needed was air from a subway tunnel beneath him to complete the effect.

"What do you think?" he said now in his usual voice. "Isn't it amazing? Terri is great at this stuff." He admired himself in a mirror, practicing his walk as if he were modeling for Victoria's Secret, his flesh-toned nylons masking his leg scar.

Razz thought he must be in a time and gender warp. Sharky was dressed like he was straight out of *The Adventures of Ozzie and Harriet*, but it was tough to decide which of them he looked like most.

Finally, he spoke with the delicacy the situation called for. "Have you lost your fucking mind? Why are you dressed like that? And what the fuck are you doing here?"

Razz pulled his Mustang into a parking spot in front of City Hall and turned to Sharky who was still dressed as the Mystery Woman.

"I mean, who do you think we are, Starsky and Hutch? I'm not a fucking cop. Oh, excuse me; I guess you're one of Charlie's Angels now."

Sharky ignored him. Getting out of the car, he caught his nylon, causing a run. "Fuck!"

"That's lady-like."

Sharky preened, straightened his dress, fixed his faux hair, and waited.

Razz sighed. "Yeah, 'fuck' is right." He dutifully followed him into City Hall.

It was only nine a.m., but the place was buzzing, San Margarita's tax dollars hard at work. A sixty-something black man argued with security guards about needing to talk to the Mayor, but he wasn't making much progress. A forty-something white woman argued with a disinterested clerk about a parking ticket and wasn't getting anywhere either.

The crime-solving comrades breezed through the security gate and moved toward the stairs.

"Hold it."

Razz turned to see two not-very-happy security guards. Sharky kept walking, hurriedly sashaying onward as if heading to a Manolo Blahnik half-price sale.

"You! Stop right there."

Sharky turned back with attitude to spare. Although he didn't want the attention, he was going to give these men a piece of his mind and relish it.

"Hey! Stop!" said one of the guards as they both rushed forward.

What the fuck, thought Sharky. *I stopped already, I stopped.*

When the guards, guns flopping in their holsters, ran past him to accost a young woman wearing headphones, he was almost as surprised as she was. But his cover was still intact.

"Just look around for anything suspicious," whispered Sharky.

"The only suspicious things here are you and me."

"Maybe, but we didn't kill Wally, did we?"

Razz did his best to be inconspicuous, reading a *Ten Most Wanted* poster and government-sponsored brochures on the benefits of living and working in San Margarita, while he looked for something that might actually be useful. The problem was he had no idea what it might be. He felt oddly excited by his proximity to the Wally murder mystery, but irritated at the same time, because he knew Sharky was using him.

His feelings were quickly overwhelmed by one clear-cut emotion—fear. Sgt. Robert Donati was headed straight for him.

Razz averted his face and slinked behind a six-foot Areca Palm, thinking frantically about how he'd respond to this police goon. He was fairly certain he wouldn't get beaten to a bloody pulp in front of onlookers at City Hall, but he didn't want to find out the hard way. Besides, the bump on his head had only recently disappeared after their first run-in.

When he peeked out from behind a palm leaf, Donati was gone. He'd forgotten the City Hall building also housed the main police station. Donati had been going to work and hadn't even noticed him.

When he moved out from behind the plant, he was less sure than ever what he was looking for. And Sharky was nowhere in sight.

Sharky was already on the second level balcony, which overlooked the first floor entry way. He sat outside the Mayor's office on a hard wooden bench, which must have been purposely designed so people wouldn't get too comfortable and linger. Legs crossed, not-so-demurely, he watched people of all types, shapes and sizes come and go from this hub of city government, but he didn't see anyone overly suspicious. Although he was trying to be inconspicuous, his nylons itched like crazy and he couldn't help but scratch. He wondered how women put up with the nylons, mascara, and makeup while his tissue-stuffed bra chafed his underarms.

"May I help you?"

He turned too quickly to the voice and his blonde wig shifted slightly. "Uh, who are you?" he asked, now favoring a pale imitation of Renée Zellweger over Marilyn.

"I'm Dan Manley, the Mayor's assistant."

The guy looked and sounded anything but manly, but, right now, Sharky couldn't exactly compare notes. From his perfectly coiffed hair, manicured nails, and tie-pinned, white-collared, blue shirt down to his highly-polished Bally wing-tips, Manley looked right out of *Queer Eye for the Straight Guy*. But he clearly wasn't the straight guy.

"Uh, no, thank you," Sharky cooed.

"Are you here to see the Mayor?"

"No." The Mayor was the last person he needed to see.

Manley seemed intrigued and sat down next to him. "You've been sitting here for several minutes, you must want something." He smiled and Sharky swore he was flirting with him/her.

Sharky dove in. "Do you know a Wally Bumpers?"

"Who?"

"Wally Bumpers. He worked as a clown at the Pier."

"No, sorry." Manley readied to leave.

"He was murdered around Christmas time."

"Gee, I guess he didn't have a very jolly holiday."

After a moment, Sharky blurted, "Was he one of your lovers?"

Manley waited and it made Sharky nervous."You are gay, aren't you?"

"Isn't everyone? Some people just don't know it yet," said Manley, mock-flamboyantly, before moving toward the office door.

"Was he your lover?"

Manley turned, his good humor now gone. "A Pier clown? Please, honey, if he didn't go to Harvard, Yale, or Princeton, I wouldn't fuck him with your dick. And I know you have one. You don't dress in drag and fool a fag. I've seen too many drag queens in my day not to know one when I see one, but I can tell you're a first-timer. You're doing this for some other show. Maybe I should call the police and see if they—"

"No."

He smiled, but it wasn't flirtatious this time. "My, my, scared of the little old cops? Hmm, let's see who's around this morning." He went to the balcony railing and looked toward the first floor. Someone caught his eye below and he waved, a smile broadening across his face.

"Hey, I thought I lost you."

Manley and Sharky turned to see Razz who was winded from his run up the stairs.

"Uh, Shar-Sheri, don't you think we should be going. We've got to pick up the kids. Remember?" Razz wasn't convincing, but he was trying.

Manley burst out laughing. "Oh, you two better take some acting lessons or something."

A well-dressed and better-muscled, Brad Pitt look-a-like reached the top of the stairs.

"Hey, baby," said Manley, and he moved to him. They kissed, lip-locked, for many seconds.

"Yeah, good to see you, too," said faux Brad, good-naturedly, surprised at Manley's passion.

"Honey, I want you to meet some people," said Manley as he dragged his lover over. "I'd like you to meet Marge and Homer Simpson."

The man chuckled and offered his hand to Razz. "Hi, I'm Jeff. Just a hint, you don't want to piss him off. Hey, if you ever need a mortgage or a refi, call me." Jeff offered his business card and Razz felt oddly flattered, but Manley would allow no flirting unless he was the one to do it.

"Come on, baby, let's leave these two to their silly charades," he said, taking Jeff's arm to lead him away.

"One more thing," said Sharky, "do you know who else might be gay?"

After the briefest pondering of the insipid question, Manley said, "Only ten percent of the world, darling, twenty percent of the military, and forty percent of City Hall." He moved in, confidentially. "It's just a fuck-fest here."

The lovers walked toward the stairs, before Manley turned back. "Remember, don't ask, don't tell." He grabbed Jeff's ass as an exclamation point to the conversation.

"So, what's the straight guy dressed like a woman for?" asked Jeff.

Manley whispered, "Identity crisis."

They smiled until a man's angry voice boomed from the first floor lobby.

"Too late, Attila the Hun's here," said Manley.

Jeff kissed him, briefly this time. "Go on, get back to work. I'll see you later."

Mayor Jaime Hidalgo stormed up the stairs, screaming into his cell phone. Two large, mean-looking Mexican men that Razz recognized as the bodyguards who had throttled him at the Gold Shore groundbreaking followed. He hoped they wouldn't recognize him back.

"Well, why don't you just hire another maid?" bellowed Hidalgo. "You've got three already, what's one more? That is, if you have time between manicures!"

Sharky slunk into the men's room and watched through a slit in the door.

Manley was too busy playing sycophant to notice. "Good morning, Mr. Mayor, we have a couple of your constituents here to speak with you."

Hidalgo clicked off his phone without saying good-bye. He thrust out his hand, smiling instantly. "Wives, can't live with them, can't live without them." He chuckled politely, turning on the charm that had gotten him elected. "Have we met?"

Razz wasn't about to remind him where. "No."

"Well, I hope I can count on your vote in the upcoming election. We still have a lot of work to do in San Margarita and I need your help."

His cloying, manufactured smile almost convinced Razz of his sincerity, but when he whizzed past, his pitch for another vote over, Razz knew it was all for show.

"Manley!"

"Yes, Mr. Mayor." Manley fell into lockstep behind and they disappeared into the Mayor's office.

The bodyguards stationed themselves at the door. No one would get to Hidalgo now unless invited.

Over the years, Razz had often felt adrift and confused, but after his experiences that morning, he felt refreshingly normal. And when he saw Sharky, dressed in his crepe skirt, gesturing frantically from the men's room, he felt downright superior. As nonchalantly as he could, he walked into the men's room, averting his eyes as he passed the guards.

They couldn't have cared less.

"Hey, lady, don't you know you're in the men's room?"

"Shhh," whispered Sharky. "Keep your voice down."

"We've got to stop meeting like this." Razz was jovial now, but Sharky was all business.

"So, what do you think?"

"Huh?"

"Do you think the killer could be Manley?"

"Why? Because he's gay? Like he said, forty percent of City Hall is gay. Wow, who knew?" He went to the urinal and unzipped his fly. "God, this place is disgusting. Look at all these hairs and shit."

Indeed, there were human hairs and filth on the urinals, used paper towels overflowing their basket, and urine splattered on the floor, but Sharky was focused on one thing. Staring, he walked closer as Razz urinated.

"Sharky? Sharky, what the fuck? I'm pissing here."

He crept closer still, his eyes fixated on the urinal.

Razz quickly finished his business and backed away. "Has wearing that dress gone to your brain, man? Or should I say wo-man?"

Sharky didn't respond, but reached toward the urinal.

"Dude, your grip is long gone."

Actually, his grip was firmer than ever, and he was holding tightly to a tiny, black pubic hair retrieved from the urinal. "Here it is," he said, triumphantly. "This is how we're going to find our killer."

"What, by looking at guys' pubic hairs?"

Sharky smiled. "Yes."

22

Robbie cut back just in time to avoid a two-foot-in-diameter piling that snuck out from behind the glare of the sun. It was harder to see under the Pier than he'd expected. Either the weathered wooden pilings blended in against the water or he lost them when he inadvertently looked into the sun.

Thursday, January 20, 2005

Razz' job was simple. He had to collect every specimen of human hair he could find from every single men's room at City Hall. Then he would do the same at the courthouse. He had vehemently declined to collect hairs from the police station and Sharky hadn't pressed that issue. If the killer was in police ranks, Wally's unknown assailant might have to remain unknown. Razz didn't want to get anywhere near Donati and Sharky couldn't go near him either, not even in a dress.

So, there he was, once-famous surf dude, Razz McNeil, the man who had conquered The Pier, toiling away in toilets. At the peak of his earnings power and height of his professional career, holding down a full-time job with benefits and potential equity, a job where several people depended on him for their livelihoods and many others for their gastrointestinal pleasure and safety, Razz McNeil was gathering human hairs, mostly of the pubic variety, from public toilets. It wasn't a picture he'd ever imagined on his darkest days, but he kept telling himself it was for the public, not pubic, good.

He humored himself as best he could, playing on words like public and pubic and making up stories with successful endings from the stalls where he waited until men had finished their business, before he scampered out to see if they'd left any follicular evidence. He had to have a solid fantasy life to handle a job like his, because he knew his actions went way beyond the border of perverse. But, after a while, he had to pull out all the stops. He dreamed of being with Sarah and his kids again, of being Sarah's attentive, doting, appreciative husband. If he ever got another chance, he was determined to be all that and more. He dreamed of loving his kids more, though he didn't know how it would be possible. But he knew he could love them better by being more patient and more generous with his time. He vowed to do so and that was the only successful ending that really mattered to him. Somehow, through his spy efforts, he hoped to win his family back, to prove himself a hero worthy of their love, and prove Richard Gold had nothing to do with Wally's murder. Those dreams and rationalizations kept him going amidst the filth and stench, but there was one other thing at work, he was becoming addicted to the thrill. Granted, picking up pubic hairs was mundane, but having to duck into a bathroom stall to avoid discovery made an average guy like Razz feel like he was an agent for the CIA. That's where he was now, in a toilet stall in the second floor men's room near the Mayor's office.

He crouched, hovering inches above the toilet seat, and watched two men through a seam between the stall and its door. The Mayor and one of his bodyguards stood side by side at their respective urinals, wordless. The immense bodyguard cast a shadow over the average-sized Mayor making him seem petite. The Mayor flushed first. He walked by the stall and Razz swore he looked straight at him. His heart racing, Razz turned away and crouched lower. He could hear water flowing from the faucet, then the cranking of a paper towel dispenser, then both again when the bodyguard went to wash up. He watched through the other door seam, but he couldn't see the sink area. After a moment, he heard nothing—no voices, no movement, nothing. It seemed as if the men had frozen, as if they were lying in wait for some prey. Razz trembled. *They're waiting for me!*

He stood up, his thigh muscles burning, and pondered his options. He felt the men approaching now, surrounding his stall. The bodyguard could crush him like an over-ripe grape; he made Donati look like a wimp. With no escape route or alternative, Razz decided to face them. He took a deep breath, bucked up his courage, and opened the stall door, expecting the worst.

But there was no one there. The men had gone. *Maybe they didn't notice me. Or maybe they're outside, ready to tear me apart like hyenas killing a helpless zebra!* His fantasies were getting the best of him and he took another long, slow breath to try and calm down. As he did, he remembered what he'd come there for. He went back to check the urinals and found one tiny black hair. He picked it up between his rubber-gloved thumb and forefinger and put it into one of several plastic bags along with scores of other specimens. He removed his gloves, folded them together, and then buried them in the trash bin. He washed his hands with scalding water and lots of soap, and dried them carefully. Then he bolted out the door.

Razz didn't care that the bodyguards stared as he hurried past. He just wanted to get out of there, hand over the hair samples to Sharky, and take a long, hot shower to remove the residue, if not the memory, of that morning's experience.

His sleuthing was done for the day.

Although Razz felt bad, Richard Gold felt far worse. He stood in the middle of the Gold Shore Hotel and Resort construction site in a spot where, in normal circumstances, he would have been run over by cement trucks or men carrying rebar. But these were not normal circumstances. The Ironworkers Local

Union 416 had walked off the job. No rebar would be set, so no concrete forms would be placed. Because other unions were sympathetic to worker actions, there would be no dump trucks, no backhoes, no nothing. Gold was in a panic.

The project's numbers had never been pretty, but now they would be a disaster. Despite Natalie Wesson's assurances to the contrary, Gold knew he was close to triggering a default notice on his construction loan. *Why didn't I listen to Sarah?* She had always been a voice of business reason, primarily because she espoused the sound financial lessons he'd taught her over many years. This time, greed had gotten the best of him, as had his dependence on a sexy young siren named Natalie Wesson. He knew he had to be more careful, he had to pay more attention to the project and less to fucking her every chance she gave him. And she had given him plenty. Coquettish at times, tough as nails at others, she played Gold like a concert master playing a Stradivarius.

But now he felt way out of tune. He had to diversify his risk on the project, but now he had few, if any, options, just as Sarah had warned. No reasonable person would want to become involved in a financially underwater construction project being struck, no matter what the price. Because of his personal guarantee, he was facing a potentially bottomless financial pit. There had been no hint at labor strife, his relations had always been good, and Gold hadn't made any contingencies for such an event. Although the work action was officially still only a walk-out, the legal technicality didn't soothe him.

Only Natalie Wesson could. "Richard, Richard, please, this isn't how to handle this."

He turned to her, ready to lash out at anything and anyone, but, when he saw her, he knew he couldn't ever lash out at her. She wore a determined, supportive look, without a hint of condescension, and Gold fell in love with her all over again.

"What are we going to do?"

"We'll fix this. We'll find an investor."

He wanted to scoff at her naiveté, but he didn't see a trace of naiveté in her. She looked like she knew exactly what she was doing. It scared him, but her certainty also excited him. He had known that certainty before. He'd known it most of his adult life, and he wanted to feel it again. And he wanted to feel her.

"Let's get back to the office and get to work," she said gently.

She took his arm and he instantly went from a doddering, frothy-mouthed, impotent old man, to a man of dignity, strength, and virility. He marveled that she could do that for him so quickly. Yes, he believed her when she told him they would find an investor.

Now, they had to figure out how.

Sharky was a changed man because of a woman, too. He woke up early in the morning now, often before seven a.m., even though he wasn't officially on duty. Before Terri, he might have slept till noon, awakening only upon Rosie's arrival or when he finally ran out of REM. Whether Terri woke him to have sex, and he gave her explicit instructions to do so whenever she had such urges, or he woke simply to watch her put on her makeup, brush her hair, dress, or make him breakfast, he woke happy. Almost everything she did gave him pleasure, sexual or not.

By noon, they'd both been up for several hours and Terri had been primping and prepping since she'd wakened. She was going on a job interview and wanted to make a good impression. Sharky assured her that Nordstrom's would be lucky to have her applying their overpriced cosmetics to wannabe starlets and housewives.

"Look what you did for me," he reminded her, only partly joking.

She laughed, but only briefly, because she was starting to run low on savings, and it felt too serious for much levity. "I've been working since I was six. I'm not about to stop now."

He loved having a love partner, especially one who wasn't interested in sucking him dry financially. His trough wasn't that deep, but what there was in it, he hoped to keep. As he watched her now, scurrying, unfocused as some women under pressure get, he thought she seemed so cute. A stressed-out woman had never evoked that thought before and his mind inexplicably wandered to the idea of marriage. He couldn't remember when he'd entertained such a concept, except for one brief moment when he first met Rosie.

He was drunk when he met her in a bar a few years back. While watching her bend deliciously over a pool table during a game of eight-ball, his thoughts drifted toward love and life partnership until he learned he would be paying for her services that night. That fact dashed his romantic fire and decidedly sobered him up, though it didn't stop him from striking up a business relationship. Even in his haze, he knew that love, alcohol, and hookers did not mix.

But this was different. There were no payments and no alcohol, just lots of love and desire. His feelings were frightening, but thrilling. They seemed like a roller coaster ride without a safety harness; sometimes the coaster turned upside down, and he just had to hang on for dear life. And, when Terri pulled her keys from her purse, preparing to go out into the world, the coaster flipped over and went into a free fall.

"What's that?" Sharky asked, staring at her hands.

"What?"

He shook his head, trying to shrug it off. "Aw, never mind, you'll be late." But he couldn't help staring at her hands.

"Sharky, what is it? What are you looking at?"

He turned away. "You'd better go."

She'd seen enough odd behavior from him not to be alarmed, so she reached for the door. When she did, her keys jangled together and he couldn't resist any longer.

"Where'd you get that key?"

She turned, no longer a sweet loving partner, but an irritated woman who had somewhere else to be. "What key, Sharky?" She said the words slowly, enunciating each one carefully, warning him to tread lightly with his response.

He didn't get the hint. "That one, the large, silver one. I haven't seen that before."

"Have you been counting my keys? Do you trust me that little?" She bit off each word so sharply that she reminded him of his ocean nemesis from many years earlier. He didn't like the comparison and he back-pedaled.

"No, I mean, I'm a cop, I notice things. I just noticed it, that's all. I hadn't seen it before."

"It's a key from the Hempstead."

His coaster was upside-down, hurtling backwards now, and his grip was weakening. "The Hempstead?"

She didn't respond except with a constant glare. She would leave it to him to dig his own grave and shovel the gravel in over him.

"Is it to Richard Gold's apartment?"

Terri sensed his vulnerability, because, under his bravado, he'd always been a quivering mass of vulnerability. "Can we talk about this when I get home?"

Not knowing when to graciously accept an out, Sharky said, "No, is it to his apartment?"

"Yes, it is."

She said it simply, directly, in response to a simple, direct question and it decimated him.

She is a shark, after all. They live in the water and on the land and they all seemed to be after me. He gasped for air and a sharp pain inexplicably shot though his scarred calf.

"Yes, it's to Richard Gold's apartment ... as well as to every other apartment. It works in every door, interior and exterior. It's a master key, Sharky. I was a leasing manager. Remember? I found it when I was unpacking my things and I've got to get it back to them. I put it on my key ring, so I wouldn't forget. Can we talk about this later? I'm going to be late."

His coaster was righted and slowing with every word. It finally ground to a halt and his bare knuckle ride was over, at least, temporarily.

"A master key?"

At times like these, most men would grovel and beg forgiveness, knowing they had been way out of line. They'd be embarrassed and they'd shuffle, but they would apologize. But Sharky was already thinking about other matters.

"Can I have it?"

Terri took the key off the ring and threw it onto the carpet in disgust. Then she slammed the door after her, rattling the apartment and tilting a couple of newly-hung pictures.

He thought of going after her, but he didn't. Instead, he retrieved the key. He knew needed to mend his selfish, jealous ways, that he'd have to apologize profusely, that he'd have to make it up to her somehow, but right now, he was focused solely on solving the Wally Bumpers murder. A key to the Hempstead could come in awfully handy, and he was more determined than ever to solve the case, even if it killed him. And he knew there were plenty of people that might want to arrange his demise.

Razz was pissed off. He was pretty sure his recent irritability had everything to do with Sharky coming more and more into his life. Although he'd collected hair samples all morning and he had only a few hours to relax before a long night at work, Sharky wanted him to bring the samples to him.

"My work is done. Christ, you live almost next door. Why don't you just pick them up like you said you would?"

He didn't receive a satisfactory explanation. Sharky said something about being busy, something about the Hempstead, a key, and something else, but, by that time, Razz knew he wouldn't fight the inevitable.

"Just meet me at the morgue," Sharky said, before hanging up.

Click. It sounded so final. There would be no more arguing, no attempt at suasion or reasoning. Although Razz shuddered at the thought of dead bodies, even if tucked away in their storage bins, he'd seen too many episodes of *CSI You-Name-The-City* not to be intrigued. He wondered if crime investigations really worked like they did on television, then he caught himself. *Nothing happens like it does on television. That's why it's called television.* But, just the same, and as ghoulish as it seemed, he began to look forward to his visit. He even began to fancy himself a crime fighter.

Sharky met him in the parking lot with such uncharacteristic enthusiasm that Razz figured he must be on Paxil or Zoloft after years of doing without—a pharmaceutical high.

"Do you have them? How many did you find? What do you have? Let me see."

Maybe he's doing meth, thought Razz. *He sure seems to be on something.* Turning his body to shield anyone else's view, like a street drug dealer showing his goods to a buyer, Razz revealed five plastic bags with varying numbers of hair samples. Each bag was marked. One was for the second floor bathroom at City Hall, one for the first floor bathroom at the Courthouse, and so on. The latter bag contained the most hairs, but was probably the least useful, because many of the hairs undoubtedly belonged to members of the public and not to government employees.

"That's great, terrific. Great job. Guess what?" Sharky asked, smiling broadly.

"Uh, you got a lobotomy?"

Sharky laughed and Razz was now certain he had.

"Guess again. Come on." Sharky sped forward toward the Courthouse steps.

Only yards away from City Hall and Police Headquarters, in a parking lot shared by occupants of both, with Sharky skating on thin, dubious ice professionally, Razz had expected him to be more careful, but he was brimming with confidence.

"Uh, did you get laid or something?"

Sharky roared. "Better than that."

This was no Sharky he had ever seen before. *He's a methamphetamined, Paxiled-out, sexually satisfied alien. That has to be it.* Razz caught up to him at the bottom of the Courthouse steps.

"I found a hair sample in Wally's apartment," Sharky said quietly, finally sharing his secret.

Now Razz understood why he'd been so giddy. He had something to match against the hairs Razz collected. With this new sample, they just might find a suspect.

"Wow."

"Yeah. Wow," Sharky responded just as eloquently. "Let's go see who we're looking for."

Their positive feelings were short-circuited when Sergeant Robert Donati confronted them after exiting the Courthouse. Razz' sleuthing didn't seem nearly as glamorous as it had a moment earlier, but Sharky kept on smiling, unfazed.

"Hey, Officer," Sharky said in his faux-friendliest way.

"Sergeant to you, asshole. What the fuck are you doing here?" was Donati's genuinely not-so-friendly response.

"Just taking care of a few parking tickets."

Razz had to hand it to him; Sharky was smooth. He smiled until Donati sneered at him. His throat tightened as if Donati's big mitts were again squeezing the blood from his neck.

"See you around," said Sharky, and he disappeared through the revolving door.

But Razz didn't move quickly enough and Donati stopped him with one stiff index finger to the chest.

"You watch yourself, bud. I've got my eye on you," he said as he ground his digit into a soft spot between Razz' ribs.

My God, this guy could beat me up with one finger! He's a pain-inflicting machine!

Razz felt betrayed by Sharky's disappearing act, and Donati didn't intend to comfort him. Then he realized several things. First, they were in a public place, and there wasn't anything terribly harmful Donati could do. Also, Donati wasn't any bigger than him, was only a few years younger, and probably wasn't any stronger given that Razz had paddled thousands of miles over the years through difficult surf. He did have a gun, but he couldn't use it. What Donati had over him was attitude. So, Razz decided there was only one thing to do—fight back.

"Dude," he began, mustering his courage, "why don't you go fuck yourself?"

He walked past a stunned Donati into the building. And, although his legs were still shaking when he reach safe haven inside, he felt good. He felt almost as happy, relieved and proud as when he had conquered the Pier. In both cases, he had lived to tell about it.

He caught up to Sharky half way up the stairs that led to the crime lab. "Hey, thanks a lot for your support back there. I thought that goon was going to put a permanent dent in my chest."

"Huh? Oh, we won't have to worry about him much longer. As soon as I solve this case, I'll get promoted and his ass will be fired."

Razz took offense at his use of the possessive. He wanted some credit, too. He had, after all, risked his health in various ways to further the cause. But he didn't have a chance to argue his point, because, like a tiny bull in a china shop, Danielle Pierson stormed out of the morgue, face buried in some paperwork, and ran smack into him.

"Why don't you watch where the fuck you're going?" she said before she looked up. "Oh, you're kind of cute. Maybe we'll have to bump into each other more often." She made suggestive hip movements and cackled loudly before she saw Sharky. "Oh, hi, Sergeant, you've got to work on your penmanship. I could barely read your signature the other day. Who's the stud?"

"Danielle Pierson, coroner, meet Razz McNeil, married."

"Hey, if you ever want to watch me carve up dead bodies, call me."

Razz had never experienced a Teamster's mouth in a ballerina's body before.

She slapped him on the back. "Ease up, Turbo, that's just a little morgue humor." She turned to Sharky. "Doesn't say much, does he?"

"No, not much."

"That's all right. I like them dumb and cute." She cackled before heading down the hall, nose back in her report. "One more thing, we got a DNA sample from your boy's butt."

"Great!"

"Talk to Harvey," she said, continuing down the hall.

Sharky's grin resurfaced. "Things are finally turning our way."

It didn't appear that way when they got to Harvey Howells' office. Howells was decidedly cool and didn't seem to care a whit about Sharky's "big case," hair samples or anything else.

"If I had known the tests were for you, I wouldn't have bothered."

That attitude didn't bode well, because they needed Harvey Howells' help. Howells was the police's DNA specialist, but because he'd had a falling out with Sharky several years earlier, he wasn't too keen on lending his talents to the present cause.

"So, let me get this straight. You want me to check hundreds of hair samples, try to find a match with the suspect DNA, and do it all on my own time, just because you're not officially on the case?"

Sharky nodded weakly.

"Gee, I wonder whose case it is. Let's see. Oh, it's Donati's. Well, I'll just have to give him a call."

"Please, don't."

Howells enjoyed that the balance of power had shifted decidedly in his favor. "If you think I'm going to help you after what you did to me last time, you've got another thought coming."

"Harvey, that wasn't my fault."

"Oh, sure, you get promoted and I'm stuck in an office staring into microscopes. I wanted to be a detective, you know."

In truth, Howells didn't look like the detective type. In the movies, they're usually handsome, strong-chinned, suave, or, at least, off-beat and dangerous. But Howells was skinny, weak-jawed, and weaselly-looking. His glasses were Coke bottle thick and they made one wonder how he could ever see a DNA strand, let alone tell one from another. Despite whatever brain power he had, he was not confidence inspiring. His nasally twang made every word sound like it was filtered through a high-pitched echo chamber. A maniacal fun house clown couldn't have sounded more eerie.

"Maybe you will if we solve this case. Come on, I need your help, Harvey."

Sharky's plea almost worked, but Harvey caught himself.

"No, no, you'll take all the credit, just like last time. You'll get the promotion, the medal pinned on your chest. Uh-uh."

Razz felt a strong undertow pulling their hopes out from under them. What he didn't know was that Howells had helped Sharky solve the infamous murder of the Swiss tourist years earlier. He'd helped pin the murder on a gang member through the use of what was then a relatively new method of DNA matching. At the time, there had been some questions as to how and where Sharky had gotten his suspect's DNA sample, but solving the case had cured the city's image problem, so the questions weren't probed too far. And Sharky had gotten a medal.

Harvey Howells was, in a word, jealous. The fact that Sharky's promotion was short-lived did nothing to mollify him. He wanted one day to get up on stage and have a medal pinned on his chest, too. He wanted the excitement of being in the field, facing danger, not the four drab walls of his work space.

"They just needed a face, Harvey. Someone they could trot out for the cameras. I was the lead detective."

Everything Sharky said seemed logical to Razz. He wasn't sure why this Howells guy was so upset. Maybe it came from being cooped up inside for years on endless end. Maybe the guy had lost a bit of his grip, however clever he was with a microscope. Or maybe he just needed some attention, like everyone else.

Sharky was getting nowhere fast and his prospects weren't looking good, until Razz found a stroke of genius he hadn't known was in him.

"Are you one of those CSI-type guys?" he asked with enough hero worship that it got Howells' attention.

"Humph! That stuff's all fake on TV. But, yeah, that's the kind of stuff I do. DNA evidence, fingerprints—"

"Wow, cool, man." His words weren't convincing, but his enthusiasm was. He knew without this guy's help, they were sunk.

"Yeah, it is pretty cool," Howells said, thawing noticeably. "You want to see my lab?"

Razz nodded vigorously and Howells led him toward a closed, nondescript wooden door. Razz caught Sharky's eye and thought, *maybe we aren't Starsky and Hutch, but we're not such a bad team.*

Sharky was thinking the same thing. He followed the men into the lab.

It was dreary and small, barely a hundred and fifty square feet, not at all like the spacious, fancy crime labs you see on television or in the movies, but it had all the necessary bells and whistles—the microscopes, the refrigerators to keep blood samples cold, the centrifuges. The equipment appeared expensive and up-to-date, but, otherwise, the place looked like it was outfitted from the Salvation Army, circa 1950. There were two small wood desks and one cheap, wheeled desk chair, with nary an Aeron in sight, rusting metal file cabinets, a faded and worn linoleum floor, and two disintegrating, pull-down window shades in varying colors which ran between deep green and dirty tan.

No wonder this guy Howells is ornery, thought Razz. *Anyone who could be responsible for keeping him holed up in this place deserves his wrath.*

Showing him around the lab was so clearly a bright spot in Howells' day that Razz felt obliged to let him, despite needing to get to work soon. And it was interesting. Howells showed him how the centrifuge worked to separate blood components, where he stored human tissue samples, and he even let Razz look into a high-powered microscope at the building block of life—DNA.

As he peered into the slender tube, seeing life magnified to the thousandth power, he couldn't help but think of his kids and how their genetic make-up sprang from his curlicued DNA somehow magically linking up with Sarah's. The thought was too powerful and he backed away from the microscope.

"Wow."

"Yeah," said Howells, seeming to understand the profound ramifications.

Thinking about his kids, his wife, and DNA had subdued him, so Razz handed Howells his business card, readying to leave. "Thanks for the tour, Harvey. Come down for a free meal. Anytime."

Howells stared at the card, and then blushed like a school girl asked to the prom. "I'd like that."

The two men shook hands. Howells double-handed him in avid appreciation, then walked him to the office door.

"When will you have the results?" Sharky asked, getting back to business.

Howells scowled. "Soon."

His grin returned full force when he turned back to Razz. "See you at the Surf's Up."

Razz waved as he exited and Sharky followed him out. Howells closed the door, looked around at his depressing, windowless office, sighed, and went back into his tiny, depressing lab, sat down at a desk, and went to work.

Outside an effusive Sharky threw his arm around Razz' shoulder. "There might be hope for you yet, 'Detective' McNeil. Great job."

He was happy he could help, but unhappy to have been reminded of his kids and wife who were so separated from him.

"You okay?"

He really wasn't sure.

"What's up? What's the matter?"

"Nothing. I was just thinking about DNA."

He walked ahead, no longer focused on Harvey Howells, Wally Bumpers, or in solving a murder case, he was only thinking of the part of his life that had been amputated without anesthesia. Worse than losing a limb, it was like losing his heart, his soul, his very DNA.

Sharky left him to his thoughts, walking behind. He had his own troubling thoughts. He still had a case to solve and he knew it could be tricky. There were lots of moving parts and he didn't want to get caught in the machinery.

They were both rescued, in a manner of speaking, when Danielle Pierson walked around a corner and again ran smack into Razz.

"We've got to stop meeting like this, people are beginning to talk. How about my place? Eight o'clock?"

Most men would die for such an invitation, but, under the circumstances, Razz was horrified. "Uh, um, I, I don't think—"

"Ha! Easy, Sparky, don't blow a gasket. Ha-ha. I was just going to suggest dinner, Champagne, and some bathtub sex."

Razz was thinking about how he'd had sex with Lotta only days after getting kicked out of his home. He felt worse than ever, but Pierson didn't stop.

"Come on, buddy," she said, slapping him on his ass like a football player congratulating a buddy after a good play. "Jeez, if you can't get fucked at City Hall, where can you get fucked?"

A switch seemed to turn on for both men.

"Jeez, where'd you get this guy?"

"What did you say?" asked Sharky, beating Razz to the same question.

"Where'd you get this guy?"

"Before," blurted Razz.

"He speaks. It's not much, but it's something." Pierson laughed again, but the men had moved far beyond her.

They looked at each other. Sharky spoke first. "You thinking what I'm thinking?"

Razz nodded. "Fucked by the government."

As if two separate minds were joined to work as one, like computers connected to create a more powerful one, the men began to solve a piece of the Wally Bumpers riddle.

"The little old guy—"

"In the alley, the homeless guy—"

"Outside the Hempstead—"

"He wasn't talking philosophically—"

"No, he meant it literally—"

"Fucked by the government—"

"Yeah, fucked every day—"

"He knows who it was—"

"Uh-huh. He knows who the killer is."

Danielle Pierson was speechless until she conjured the obvious question. "What the fuck are you two talking about?"

The men turned and seemed surprised she was still there.

Sharky started. "There was a little, old homeless man in the alley next to the Hempstead apartments where Wally Bumpers was murdered.

Razz joined in. "He was talking gibberish about being 'fucked by the government.'"

"But it wasn't gibberish at all."

"No, we thought he was talking about himself, how he'd been screwed over somehow, but he was really talking about Wally."

"He must have seen the killer coming and going through the alleyway door."

"Exactly."

"We've got to find him."

"Come on, let's go," said Sharky.

Razz looked at his watch and was already late for work. "Okay." He wasn't about to miss the action now.

They sped down the hallway.

"Gentlemen! Wait!"

Sharky turned back, impatient. "We've got to find the guy—now!"

Before the men made it to the stairs, Pierson stopped them in their tracks.

"I think you already did."

They looked back and, as one, said, "Huh?"

When Pierson motioned for them to follow her into the morgue, neither took it as a good sign.

Pierson pulled out a drawer from the wall and began to unzip a body bag. The men watched, hoping against hope it wouldn't be their little homeless man. The stench of rotted flesh spread through the room and Razz winced. In their haste, the men hadn't bothered applying any peppermint oil. The bag opened further. Finally, they saw the man's bluish-white face, staring vacantly back at them. His head had been shaved on one side and there was an indentation where his skull had been crushed by the metal pipe. Their hopes were crushed, too, because it was clear this man wouldn't be offering any more help on the Wally Bumpers case.

It was back to the drawing board and the body count was rising.

23

Smack!

His board scraped into the side of a piling, almost throwing him, and he began to think this wasn't such a good idea after all. He could drop down onto his board, but he would lose maneuverability and crash into a piling for sure. He thought of jumping into the water and letting his beloved board fend for itself, but he would be totally at the waves' mercy. Even before the waves could dash him again and again into pilings and rocks on his bloody path to shore, he would probably drown.

Friday, January 21, 2005

Despite the comfortable, new, six-foot-long leather couch in his Sol a Sol office, Razz couldn't sleep. He tossed, turned, and almost screamed for mercy, because his thoughts wouldn't stray from an image of Wally Bumpers' spread-eagled dead body tied to pilings almost directly under where he lay. Hamlet's sleep patterns couldn't have been worse than his on this night.

He had slept there after work because he was determined to get into the water that morning whether the waves were weak or not. He had to get back to his roots, back to where he felt safe. Murder investigations could do serious damage to a man's comfort level. Discovery of the homeless man's death had spooked him, raising his already high fear levels. Sleeping, or trying to sleep, in strange surroundings on a rainy night hadn't helped matters.

It was still dark when he went outside. He had brought his suit and board in last night in preparation for an early start, but it was even earlier than he'd expected. The sun hadn't begun to hint at its arrival, but Razz couldn't wait any longer.

He ignored a *No Trespassing* sign and stepped over a chain barrier onto a steep, steel gangplank slippery from dew that led down to a small wharf. Each barefooted step rattled the walkway making it grate against its metal hinges, the resultant sound rang in his ears like an irritating alarm clock. Although the wharf was intended for official Harbor Patrol business and use by anyone else was illegal, it was too early for cops, members of Harbor Patrol, or anyone other than a few homeless stragglers who happened to have insomnia as bad as Razz. Of course, most self-respecting surfers would enter the water from the beach, but he wasn't concerned with his self-respect just yet. It was still too early.

He could barely make out the water it was so black, because a full moon was hidden by cloudy skies. *Nothing feels clear in my life right now. Everything's overcast,* he thought. The wharf barely moved, so he knew the sea was calm. Though that was mildly disappointing, he knew waves could kick up at any time. *That feels like my life, too. Emotional tsunamis kick up instantaneously.* The metaphors were beginning to piss him off, and he desired sleep. *To sleep, perchance to dream.* He felt like screaming.

"Aaggh! Fuck!"

Pain shot through his left foot into his shin, up his leg, and into his brain where it exploded like a stick of dynamite. He'd slammed his foot into something solid. At least, the pain cleared his mind of metaphors.

"Fuck! Ow."

He put down his board indelicately, and felt around for a place to sit. He could just make out the object he'd walked into, a small rescue boat turned upside down on the wharf, awaiting use. As the pain subsided, he sat on the culprit's keel and massaged his big toe.

"What a fucking day already. Well, it's got to get better." He could only hope.

Though he felt the slipperiness of fresh blood pulsing from between his big toe and nail, he was pretty sure nothing was broken, so he picked up his board and carefully hobbled to the wharf's edge. He slid into the water and finally felt safe. Between the painful stubbing of his toe and the invigoratingly cool waters, he was also wide-awake. *Hamlet can go fuck himself.* Razz didn't care one iota about sleep now.

He paddled his new Wegener long board, his Christmas gift from Sarah, and hoped it hadn't been scratched. He wondered if he wasn't a glutton for punishment—something in his life always seemed to be getting banged up. He wished he'd used his Corky Carroll Signature or his Town and Country, but neither held for him the meaning his new board did. It was too late, anyway, so he resolved to deal the best he could with whatever bruises his Wegener had suffered, just as he would his own bruises.

As he stroked through the smooth waters, he calmed. Soon it would be just him, his board, and the waves. That is, if there would be any waves. Maybe it would just be him and his board, but Razz knew that would be enough.

He skimmed swiftly over the water's surface and was surprised when he became winded. He considered that it might be time to start working out, then decided his best health cure would be to surf more often. *No need for gyms yet; don't do anything drastic.* He smiled and rose off his belly to straddle his board, legs dangling off each side, as he caught his breath.

The black water glistened, every now and then casting reflections from the street lights onshore. Razz looked back at the Pier, quietly ominous, then at San Margarita, its steep bluffs imposing in the distance.

Hints of daylight appeared at the horizon's edge, and the gentlest of waves lapped at his board. It was exquisitely peaceful. He decided he didn't care if there would be surf or not, he'd gotten what he came for—some peace. Life was good again.

A cool breeze blew past, chilling him as it rippled the water around him. It reminded him it was still wintertime. Sometimes, it was hard to tell in Southern California.

He zipped up his wet suit a few inches to its top. He felt something brush against his left foot and a wave, seemingly out of nowhere, rocked his board. He steadied himself and looked around, but it was too dark to discern much. *That's weird. The wind must have kicked that wave up. But just one? And what the hell touched my foot?* He raised his still-bleeding foot from the water and felt it was throbbing, which sufficiently answered his last question. He had reason enough to be jumpy without any extra help, but, when another wave rocked his board from the landside and he felt something brush against his right foot, his imagination worked overtime.

He brought both feet up onto his board and blood mixed with the fresh layer of board wax he had applied to improve his footing. He paddled carefully, circling, but he didn't see anything unusual. There had been no reports of sharks, but that didn't mean they weren't out there. *What else could it be?* He'd never had a run-in with a shark before, but he'd heard enough stories about them. He couldn't help but think of Sharky.

Razz wasn't exactly scared. He was more curious than anything, but, when he noticed droplets of blood falling from one edge of the board into the water, he decided not to tempt fate. He paddled toward shore, roiling the water as little as possible. He hadn't gotten far when he looked up at the Pier. Suddenly, fate seemed to be tempting him and his own waters became extremely roiled.

He saw someone he'd never expected to see at such an hour. It couldn't have been much past six a.m., but there, under a lighted lamp post at the end of the Pier, stood Louis Marcayda with three men. He was carrying a suitcase and seemed to be admiring the view.

Razz stopped paddling, paralyzed by his choice between two potential man-eaters as his board's momentum carried him closer. Even from this distance, he could see Louis' self-satisfied smile, the type of smile he'd seen before. It appeared supremely confident, crossing over into arrogance. It was the look he'd seen on his father-in-law's face on Christmas day when Gold told him about the Gold Shore Hotel and Resort land purchase and Razz had nearly been eviscerated. It looked like Louis Marcayda was very happy with himself.

The rich keep getting richer, Razz thought. *I doubt he's happy because he finished this morning's crossword puzzle. And those men aren't there to ride the Ferris wheel with him. He must have a lot of money in that suitcase. No wonder he's happy.*

There were two safes at the Sol a Sol, a small one in his office and a large one in Louis'. Razz used the small safe to store each night's receipts and petty cash, but had no access to the large safe. He'd only seen it once in passing when he'd surprised Louis and Lotta one night. She had quickly shut and locked the door indicating that office and that safe were off limits. It hadn't bothered him before, because it was reasonable that larger sums of money would not be under his control. It was only good accounting practice. But, as Louis stood there with his smile and his suitcase, surrounded by the three men, Razz couldn't help wondering how much money was in that suitcase and how much more was in that safe.

He paddled closer as the men moved toward the Sol a Sol. Once they were out of sight, he paddled faster. He didn't know for sure why. Louis had a safe and wanted to put money into it or take money out of it before dawn while under heavy guard. The fact that he didn't use Brink's or the Pinkertons didn't comfort him though. It just reminded him that he didn't know much about Louis or his businesses, but the rumors of drugs and prostitution sounded louder in his brain.

He stopped paddling and coasted in. He held onto the wharf and looked up at the Sol a Sol. On the second floor, a light flashed on, and he could see the back of a man's head through one window. Razz ducked when Louis peered out a second window, but he only seemed interested in the police substation, still closed only a hundred yards away.

"Come on." The command was muffled, but insistent, a clear order from Louis to hurry things up.

What's his rush? Wouldn't it be safer if the cops were there? But Razz didn't feel safe around cops either, especially one particular cop named Donati.

He heard a commotion above, the shuffling of feet and something being rolled across a wooden floor. He heard muffled talking and then there was silence. He looked up at the office window and saw Louis staring back at him! He ducked and pulled his board closer to the wharf. It was still dark, but not like before. *Did he see me? And what if he did? I'm just here for a morning surf; no need to worry.* But he did worry, because he was suspiciously spying on his naturally-suspicious boss.

He breathed easier once he paddled under the Pier out of sight. Feeling tense again, he was more determined than ever to surf now.

His tension level elevated when the light from the Sol a Sol's viewing glass flashed on and illuminated the water. Razz scooted behind a piling and struggled to keep his board from drifting into view. It seemed like minutes before the light finally went off. Still, he didn't move. The light flashed on again, as if playing a game, trying to entice him into the open and capture him with its rays.

Finally, the light went off again and, this time, he didn't hesitate. He paddled furiously toward the south side of the Pier to get as far away from the Sol a Sol as possible. Although small rolling waves were kicking up now, he managed to navigate through dangerous pilings into open water.

Breaking into a swim sprint, he stroked quickly and powerfully, as if trying to catch a wave, but he kept at it for three hundred yards before resting. His arms were limp and exhausted, his breathing was labored, but he felt safe.

As the sun kissed the horizon, he looked back at the Pier and saw no sign of Louis or his men. Relieved, he sat up on his board and checked his left foot. The blood had stopped. A two foot wave surprised him and almost made him lose balance. He looked around nervously for a dorsal fin, but all he saw were more two foot waves coming toward him. He smiled, because he knew there would soon be bigger, better waves. He would be able to surf today and he soon forgot about anything else.

Louis backed away from one of the Pier's many sightseeing telescopes, the kind that for ten cents will give you an up close and personal view of things far away. He still wore a self-satisfied smile, and now he knew exactly who'd been watching him, who had tried to avoid being seen by escaping on his surfboard, just like he knew practically everything else that went on around him. He had many eyes watching for him, some with seemingly telescopic powers. Ten cents was a bargain for this information. He was used to paying much more.

"Let's go, boys. Don't forget my luggage."

The three bodyguards, Mexican men no bigger than him, laughed. No, they wouldn't forget. As one man rolled the suitcase toward their waiting bulletproof Mercedes, another popped open the trunk. Then the three of them wrestled the bag into the trunk.

That suitcase was heavy.

When Razz dragged himself from the water three hours later, he was physically spent. He felt like a wet dishrag that had been wrung out several times too many. He laid his Wegener board gently on the sand and unzipped his wet suit. He strained to peel the top of his suit from his arms and torso, and then let it hang from his waist as he rubbed his tired, goose pimpled arms to regain feeling. The goose pimples that had protected him in the cold water melted away in the warm morning sun that peaked from behind rapidly dispersing clouds.

He looked upward, enjoying the sun's rays, and hesitated. *What time is it?* He'd only planned to take a few runs, but three- and four-foot swells with nice consistent breaks had impelled him to ride fourteen waves that morning.

Sarah was waiting in her driveway when he got there. She wore a form-fitting, blue pant suit and a look that no man wanted to see—the "you can't do anything right" look. It's a look that can make big, strong men feel impotent and infantile. Razz felt both.

He got out of the Mustang wearing a hang-dog expression and hoped she'd take pity on him, though he knew he didn't deserve it. He was late to pick up his kids. He'd agreed to take them to school, because Sarah had to work that morning.

"I'm sorry, I'm sorry. Where are they?"

He could tell her disgust was immense. She picked up her leather briefcase and reached into the Range Rover to lay it on the passenger seat. He stared as her coat rose up revealing her pant-suited ass. Her two lovely cheeks seemed to laugh at him, increasing his torture. "*This body is what you can't have, what you'll never have again, because you're a fuck-up!*" those cheeks seemed to say.

"I'm sorry, it will never happen again."

As soon as he said it, he knew he was the one speaking out of his ass. Of course, it would happen again, they both knew it. Sarah had overlooked his many shortcomings for years, because she loved him. Now, she didn't have to.

She drew her body out of the Range Rover just long enough to say, "I've got to go. I'm late," then she climbed into the driver's seat.

"Are the kids in the house? I'll get them." He headed for the door, but she cut him short.

"They're already gone."

"But I was going to take them."

"But you were over an hour late."

No logic existed that could win Razz this fight, so he wisely backed off. "I'm sorry."

"You said that. I have to go."

"I miss you."

She started the engine. "I have to go. Please move your car."

Razz looked at his Mustang parked just inside the driveway entrance. It was blocking her path to freedom.

"Sarah, just give me two minutes, Richard will understand. Please."

She looked at him and through him. "Talk. Quickly."

It wasn't much encouragement, but it was enough. "I didn't do this to insult you or to dismiss you. Your time is valuable, your job is valuable. I screwed up, that's all. I won't do it again."

This time, he almost believed it, but it didn't sway her.

"I still have to go."

"Sarah, I love you."

"Don't."

"But I do."

"I don't have the time for this, Razz."

He could see her armor dissolving as she tried to hold back tears. "I just want you to know, and I'm going to do everything I can to win you back. I don't want to live without you."

With that, her armor was gone and she turned off the engine. "I miss you, too," she said quietly.

"You do?" He wanted to scream with joy. "It's not the same without you."

"You just miss the kids."

"I miss all of you, but I didn't know how much I needed you until I didn't have you."

Tears streamed down her face. "I've got to go."

"I know. Thank you for hearing me out."

She dabbed at her eyes with a tissue. "Oh, my mascara's a mess."

"You look beautiful." Despite her runny mascara and swollen, red eyes, he meant it.

She smiled. "Talk later?"

"Count on it." He pulled a business card from his wallet, wrote something on the back and handed it to her.

She surveyed both sides. "A cell phone? You're finally joining the twenty-first century?"

"Grudgingly."

Despite their smiles, it was an awkward moment. He so much wanted to kiss her and she desperately wanted to go, for self-protection as much as her need to get to work. But he wasn't ready to let her go.

"So, who took the kids to school? My folks?"

"No, a new friend."

In most languages, "a new friend" was code for "boyfriend" or "lover." "What 'new friend'?"

Razz was panicked, frightened, and she was in control. But, as usual, she was kind and good and never considered abusing her power.

"A woman I met in the park the other day."

He sucked in air like he hadn't taken a breath in a week. "Oh."

"Her name's Merice, Merice Marcayda."

Now, he was in a vacuum again, his lungs begging for air.

"She has two young kids, too. I think they're all going to be friends."

"No."

"What?"

"No, you can't, you can't be friends with her."

Sarah's warm fuzzies were gone; her husband was back to his controlling tricks. "Razz, I've got to go."

"You can't, it's dangerous, for the kids."

She shook her head in disbelief. "Move your car, please."

"Promise me you and the kids won't have anything to do with the Marcayda's. Please."

"Razz—"

"Just promise me!"

Sarah saw the fear in his eyes and heard it in his voice, but she was too angry to comfort him. "Just move your damn car. I have to go to work."

"They're dangerous, Sarah. I don't want them near my kids."

"Oh, they're your kids? Well, they're mine, too. Why on earth would the Marcaydas be dangerous? Have you gone totally insane?"

He hoped her last question was rhetorical. "They just are."

"Yeah, she's a hit woman and the kids are drug dealers. Okay, fine. Just let me go before I have to call someone. Like the men in the white coats."

"Sarah, please—"

"What, Razz? What? You've tried to control me since we were married. You didn't want me to work. Okay, so I didn't work until recently. You made it clear in not-so-subtle ways that you don't think I'm bright or capable. I've let it slide, chalking it up to your own insecurities. And now, you don't trust my judgment in choosing friends for me or my children. Now I know I've made the right decision about you."

"No, it isn't like that. You can work. You can do anything you want. I'm sorry if I ever made you feel less than what you are which is a wonderful, bright, beautiful ... God, I'm sorry. I need you, Sarah. And I do trust you. I do. You just don't know these people."

"And how do you know them?"

He hesitated. "I work for her husband."

Sarah pondered this information, uncertain why it made her new friend and her young children dangerous.

"He's a dangerous man," he continued.

"Then why do you work for him?"

"I mean, he could be dangerous, if anyone crossed him. I just don't feel comfortable being too close to them."

"It sounds like you're already pretty close. What the hell's gotten into you? If he might be dangerous, why do you work for him? And you dare to question my father's ethics? Fuck you, Razz. Fuck you."

"What did you say?" He was getting sucked under, drowning with her every word.

"If you're working for someone that could put our children's safety at risk, or mine, fuck you. And if you're not, but you're trying to tell me who I can have as a friend, fuck you again. I'm leaving. Now move your car."

"No."

"Razz."

"Promise me you won't see her again."

"Razz, move your car."

"Promise me."

She started up her Range Rover and put it into forward gear.

"I'm not moving till you promise me."

Sarah floored it, screeching forward, and pulled a one-eighty in the drive. It was a move of which many a Hollywood stunt driver would be proud. Her vehicle hurtled back toward Razz and he leapt out of the way. She sped past him and he anticipated the collision.

"No!"

The Range Rover crashed through the rose garden at the edge of the drive, flying past the waiting Mustang without serious incident, then sped down the road.

Razz was relieved his car was still in one shiny piece, but he worried he'd ruined any chance he might have had of winning Sarah back. *Boy, I can really fuck things up in a hurry.*

This time, he was right.

24

Though several people had died on the Pier over the years, many more had died while swimming in the waters around it, caught in rip currents or undertow that didn't care if their victims had mothers, fathers, or small children waiting for them at home. And they especially didn't care about some crazy kid trying to ride a wave underneath the length of the Pier into history. Robbie/Razz didn't want to be the next to die.

Sarah wheeled her Range Rover into the underground parking structure at Gold Tower, barely acknowledging the attendant as she cruised past, then skidded to a stop in her reserved parking spot two spaces down from her father's. That Natalie Wesson's late-model Chrysler Sebring convertible sat between her vehicle and her father's seemed only fitting. Wesson had driven a wedge between father and daughter since she'd arrived on the scene.

Sarah grabbed her briefcase and keys and hurried to the elevator. She checked her watch for the hundredth time that morning and saw it was five minutes to ten, just enough time. She pressed repeatedly on the elevator call button despite knowing once was sufficient. When it arrived and the door opened, she was glad to find it empty. She was hoping for a solo ride this morning. She pressed twenty-seven, the button for the penthouse floor where Richard Gold's office hovered over San Margarita, and the door slowly closed.

At the third floor, a maintenance man got on and Sarah checked the time. Four minutes till ten. The man pressed seven, then changed his mind and pressed eight, and she felt like screaming, *"Get the fuck out of my elevator!"* By the time several more people had gotten on and off, she'd stopped checking her watch and was resigned to being a few minutes late.

An elderly man, stooped over, supported by a spindly cane and spindlier legs, said, "Have a good day," when he stepped off at the twenty-fourth floor.

She barely squeezed out a small smile, because that morning's row with Razz had thrown her off balance. She was groping inside her briefcase for some papers when the elevator door finally opened at her destination. Focused on her paperwork, an updated financial analysis of the Gold Shore Hotel and Resort, she almost walked into a tanned, well-dressed man, also carrying a briefcase.

"Oh, sorry," she said, only glancing at him.

"No problem," he said, smiling, and he got on the elevator.

Sarah looked back at the handsome man in his late thirties, dressed in a navy pin-striped suit, blue shirt, red power tie and wing-tips. *A little conservative for Los Angeles,* she thought, *but cute.* She returned his smile as the door closed.

Her brief flirtation over, she hurried down the hall. "I'm so sorry I'm late," she said as she entered her father's magnificent office. There were mahogany credenzas, ceiling high bookcases, wall-length windows and expansive views of the ocean, but all Sarah could see was Natalie Wesson sitting cross-legged on the desk with her father sitting below her in his chair. They appeared to be master and servant, but not in the hierarchy she expected.

"You're late," said Gold.

"Two minutes. I'm sorry; I had some trouble getting the kids to school. So, where's the other side?"

"He just left," offered Wesson.

Sarah froze as if the slightest misstep would send her onto a massive land mine. Finally, she said, "The meeting was at ten. It's two past ten."

Gold stepped carefully. "It got changed. Didn't you get the message?"

Each of them looked at the other, waiting for someone else to go belly-down on the explosive.

Natalie Wesson spoke first. "I'm sorry. I thought Richard was going to tell you."

Gold's surprise and the smarmy look on Wesson's face told Sarah there had been no such agreement, but that Wesson had frozen her out.

So Gold detonated the charge. "I'm sorry, Sarah, it was my fault. I forgot I was supposed to call you. Forgive me?" He went to her with pleading eyes and outstretched arms, trying to limit the collateral damage.

Sarah thought he seemed weak for the first time in her life. He'd never succumbed to her mother's pleas or desires, always going his own way on his own time. He'd never catered to Sarah except in money and meaningless gifts. He'd always been selfish and self-involved, and now he was apologizing for something he didn't do, humbling himself in a way he'd probably never considered before—all for a twenty-something assistant.

She nodded, but couldn't hide her hurt feelings. She turned to go.

"Aren't you happy we got the deal done?" asked Wesson.

Sarah looked back and saw the Devil standing in front of her. "Done? Already?"

"Yes," Gold chimed in, happier now, moving onto safer ground. "Three million dollars, just like that."

"At a premium. Right, Richard?" Wesson was grinding it in with all her might now.

"At a premium. Natalie was right. They paid three million dollars for only a ten percent stake. It values the total equity at thirty million and the project at one hundred and five. It's quite a profit and I didn't put up a dime." Gold was giggling now, a Scrooge who had found a dollar.

The analysis in Sarah's hand felt heavy. "But, how? Who?"

"Like I always say, 'location, location, location.' They knew it was the best spot in San Margarita. They don't make any more land, you know."

She had heard him say "location, cash flow, quality" and other real estate development buzzwords for years and they had always made sense before, but not this time. "Did they look at the numbers? I mean, we have a work stoppage and we're almost in default."

"Not anymore," said Wesson, as if her words explained everything.

Sarah was too numb to fight back, her arm exhausted from her now-leaden analysis.

"They just wanted to be involved, Sarah. They feel it's a great project. And they're going to help mend fences with the union, though I still have no idea why they walked out."

Sarah couldn't muster words, but Gold's next comment told her all she needed.

"Natalie made it all happen."

He glowed like a proud, if lecherous, father. Natalie Wesson was now his pride and joy, not Sarah. The psychological umbilical cord between father and daughter had been tenuous for years, but now it was severed for good.

Sarah heard self-satisfied giggling as she walked back to her office, but she couldn't tell who was giggling more, Wesson or her father. She fell into her desk chair, pressing deeply into it, the analysis still in her hand. She dropped the papers into the waste basket, all her work for naught. It should have made a loud noise, it felt so heavy, but she heard nothing. Of course, it was great they'd found an investor, but these matters usually took weeks or months, not hours. Negotiations often drag on over fine points and this investor didn't even want to look at the updated financials. It was clear someone had deep pockets and a shallow mind or, more likely, deep motives to rationalize such an investment.

She felt alone. Normally, she could talk to Razz in situations like these, even though he was never the most understanding, but the thought of a discussion with him right now sickened her. Her mother wouldn't understand or care, saying, "Oh, that's your father," before moving on to another cocktail. And her father was out for obvious reasons. Sally McNeil probably wouldn't understand the financial issues and, under the circumstances of her recent estrangement from her son, wouldn't be the best choice for a heart-to-heart talk.

Sarah decided to call her new friend, Merice Marcayda.

Razz dragged himself to his front door. He'd taken a circuitous route home as if he were trying to lose his torment in the winding back streets of San Margarita. He closed the door behind him and looked at his new residence. He knew he was lucky to have it, but it didn't feel like home unless his kids were there. It was just a place where he could hope for better things.

The flashing light on his answering machine focused him, until he considered the machine might hold an irate message from Sarah, which sped his mind a million-fold. *Maybe I over-reacted. Will she ever forgive me? How can I regain her trust? Will I ever be happy again? Was I really happy?* He sighed and tried to clear his convulsing brain. There were no current answers or solutions to his problems. Other than ingesting a bucket of Valium, he had few options for attaining peace of mind today. He wasn't a meditating type of guy.

He was relieved and disappointed when he heard Lotta's voice on the first message. "Hey, Razz, there's a guy here said you were going to meet him. He's looking for you."

Oh, shit. Who's looking for me? James said he was leaving town. Could it be Donati?

Because of their run-in yesterday, Razz knew he'd need to watch his back. It had felt good telling him to "fuck himself," but now he questioned the wisdom of his bravado. He clicked to the next message and it was Lotta again.

"This guy keeps asking for you, says he doesn't want to order till you get here. I didn't think I should give him your home number, but he's beginning to annoy me."

The next and last message was again Lotta. "This guy's starting to piss me off. He won't give his name, but he said he met you yesterday. Call me."

I met him yesterday. That was that. Donati was waiting for him at the Surf's Up. He was sure of it. Donati was going to pay him back, probably several times over, for yesterday's episode. *Well, at least, it will be in a public place. How much damage can he do?* Razz internally answered the question several times over in increasingly maudlin ways, and then escaped out the front door.

For reasons of courage, foolhardiness, or exhaustion, Razz walked into the Surf's Up prepared to face whatever came his way. At least, the danger took his mind off Sarah.

The place was busy, just as it had been since Louis took over. He braced himself as he approached the bar. He couldn't help but look behind him and side to side. If he saw it coming, he might be able to ward off the attack. He reminded himself that he was big as Donati and, though exhausted by his morning paddle, strong enough to put up a good defense. Unfortunately, he suspected that Donati knew every dirty fighter's trick in or out of the book and Razz wasn't really in the mood for a tussle. Sarah had taken most of the fight out of him.

His head was on a swivel, but he couldn't find Donati. He figured the guy couldn't be hiding, it wasn't that crowded, not like on a Saturday night. It was the lunch hour, for God's sake.

"All right, where is the son of a bitch?"

Lotta and several customers turned to the voice that was too strident for the time and place. She indicated to his left.

Razz turned, prepared for the worst, but didn't see Donati. "Where?"

She motioned again and couldn't believe he didn't see the guy.

Razz felt like he was being played for a patsy. "Is this some kind of bad joke? Just tell me where the prick is and he and I will have it out, right here, right now."

"He's right next to you, Razz."

He spun, his fists cocked and ready, but when Lotta opened her palm, as if presenting what's behind door number two, he finally noticed a squirrelly-looking man standing next to him. He looked vaguely familiar.

"Who are you?"

The man recoiled, insulted and scared. "Harvey Howells. You invited me for lunch."

"I did? When?"

Harvey Howells. Harvey Howells. Where have I heard that name? Then it came to him and his black cloud lifted. "You're the guy that's been looking for me?"

Howells nodded, smarting from his reception.

Razz burst out laughing, and Howells retreated like a cowering dog. He was a fragile little man.

"No, wait!"

Howells wasn't about to wait for more abuse and embarrassment.

"No, no, you don't understand. I'm sorry. I was expecting someone else, someone I didn't want to see. I'm glad it's you."

That stopped him. "You are?"

Razz bordered on giddy. "You have no idea. Come on."

He took Harvey Howells' arm and, after some hesitation on Howells' part, led him toward a corner table, the one Paul and Scruffy used to frequent. "Lotta, bring Mr. Howells the salmon special. You like salmon, Mr. Howells?"

Howells looked as proud as a boy who'd just lost his virginity or a baseball player who'd hit a grand slam to win the World Series. "Yes, yes, I do. And you can call me Harvey."

"You got it, Harvey. Lotta, bring two salmons, a bottle of Perrier, and two Cokes, please. You like Coke, Harvey?

"Sure."

He was smiling now, because he felt like a big shot. He strode proudly to the corner table. "I thought for a second you didn't recognize me."

Razz brushed aside the notion, but, in truth, he had forgotten all about his nebulous invitation. He certainly hadn't expected Howells to take him up on it so soon and so unannounced. "How could I forget?"

There was an awkward pause, normal for two strangers with little in common.

Razz asked, "So, what did you want to see me about?"

Howells scrunched his face as if in pain. "You invited me for lunch."

"Oh, of course. I just didn't expect you so soon, you know. It was just kind of a general invitation."

Howells face was scrunching like a dried prune now.

It looked painful, so Razz tried to help. "I mean, sure, I'm glad you could make it."

That sentiment apparently made Howells feel better, because his face normalized, such as it was. He felt better still when Lotta delivered the Cokes and Perrier.

Razz hoped the salmon would get there soon. Although relieved he didn't have to deal with Donati, this lunch didn't appear like it would be much more enjoyable. He pawed at his silverware and forced a smile.

"So, tell me about yourself, Harvey."

Forty-five minutes later, finished with the salmon, an ice cream brownie dessert, and way too much information about the lonely life of Harvey Howells, Razz was beyond exhausted. He struggled to keep his eyes open and his head aloft.

"And that's how I got into the crime-solving business."

Howells capped his story with a proud smile, but it was easy to see that it covered a deeper pain. This guy was clearly attention-deprived. And he wasn't done talking.

"Those guys in the field, they don't even know what they're doing. Like Officer Sampson, I had to solve his last murder case."

Razz perked up, back to a topic he cared about—solving a crime. "Oh, that reminds me, when do you think you'll be done with the hair analysis?"

"Already finished."

"Huh?"

Razz had listened to Harvey Howells' laments of his childhood, of his teenage years, of his early adulthood, and of how he'd been teased and beaten because he was weak and intellectual instead of strong and athletic, while all he had really wanted was to find out how the analysis was going.

"What do you mean, you're done? I thought these things took days."

"Not if you're good and if it's clearly not a match. I knew right away it was the victim's hair, not the perpetrator's."

Razz wished he had known right away, too. He didn't have time to play amateur shrink. He was too busy playing amateur husband, amateur father, and amateur private investigator.

"Well, that's it then," he said.

"What do you mean?"

He wondered if Howells was really so smart. "We needed the hair match to find a suspect. Now we're back at square one."

"Tell me about the case. Maybe I can help."

Razz scoffed.

Howells ignored the condescension and pressed on. "Tell me."

Razz considered his nebbishy lunch mate. Although he didn't want to encourage more conversation, he figured offering a condensed version of the case wouldn't hurt too badly. At least, he'd be talking and not Howells.

Three minutes later, when he stopped, Howells was smiling.

"What?" asked Razz.

"All you need is another hair from the crime scene."

"That's right."

"Why don't we go get one?"

"Like I said, the place has been searched several times. It's been painted, re-carpeted, cleaned, you-name-it. There are no more hairs there."

"Yes, there are."

Razz couldn't tell if Howells was mocking him, but he felt like knocking the ambiguity off his slack-jawed face. "Sure. Whatever."

"I bet I could find some."

"And what would you like to bet?"

"Another lunch."

Razz almost gagged on his Coke. *Needles under my fingernails, the desert for days without water, reality TV, anything but another hour with this guy.* But he decided to take one for the cause.

"Okay, you're on. So, under the circumstances, knowing the apartment has been combed over several times by a number of qualified people, how would you propose to find a hair sample that might lead to the killer of Wally Bumpers?"

"You said that the killer had probably been in the apartment many times before, right?"

"Yeah. We think they might have been lovers. So?"

Howells waited, giving his best interpretation of a pregnant pause, and then said, "You got a wrench?"

The question wasn't at all what Razz had expected. *Is this non-sequitur the rambling of a crazy man or a piece of idiot savant wisdom?*

When Howells giggled in a grating, high-pitched tone, Razz knew why he'd been beaten up as a youth, why his mother had dressed him up in girl clothes, and why he hadn't had a lady friend for the past twelve years, but he also began to believe him.

He went to his office to find a wrench.

When they got to the Hempstead, Sharky was waiting in the alley. Harvey Howells wasn't pleased.

"What's he doing here?"

"Just here to check your work, Harvey," Sharky said only half-jokingly.

Finding nothing funny about it, Howells did an about-face and walked toward the street. Razz' hopes sank. He looked at Sharky, piercing him, until he relented.

"Harvey, I'm sorry."

Harvey Howells seemed to grow taller and broader. His ego puffed to twice its normal size. "What did you say?"

Sharky frowned. He had said it once, saying it a second time felt like it might kill him. "I'm sorry, Harvey. You don't need my help."

It wasn't a convincing performance, but it was enough to get Howells moving back toward them.

"Though you might need my key," Sharky mumbled so low only Razz could hear.

"Now, watch how a pro does it," Howells said, wrench firmly in hand and figuratively crashing it into Sharky's skull.

Sharky felt the bruise, but a grateful look from Razz reminded him they needed Harvey Howells.

The three men entered the alley door with a copy of Terri's master key. Although such keys weren't supposed to be copied, Sharky didn't let the law stand in his way. He knew a shady locksmith who owed him a favor, so getting his new key had taken all of thirty seconds.

Sharky looked inside and found the stairway empty. He started in, but Razz gently held him back to allow Harvey Howells to climb the stairs first. He felt his power usurped at every turn and did not like it one bit, but Razz was playing a careful game of mediator. His ego would have to wait.

They climbed the metal steps as quietly as possible, hoping no one else at the Hempstead needed to hide and use the back stairs, too. They were a motley-looking crew that would arouse any normal person's suspicions, but, despite a few disconcerting hallway noises, they made it to the seventh floor without incident.

"Come on," said Sharky, reasserting his authority as he led the others into the hall.

At this point, Howells didn't mind that Sharky took over. He was sweating and Razz was beginning to worry he wouldn't hold up.

"You okay, Harvey?"

Howells nodded feebly. "Never better," he said as a sweat drop fell from his forehead.

Razz felt badly for him. Harvey Howells was a man who yearned to be a detective, who lived for it, but because of his human shortcomings, would likely never make it. It painfully reminded Razz of his own situation with his wife, but, fortunately, they were already standing in front of apartment 703.

It seemed too easy. There had been no one in the stairway, no one in the hall, and Sharky's key fit like an original. Howells was still sweating profusely, but it looked like the men were home free. Sharky turned the master key, then the door handle, and they went inside.

"What are you doing here?" The question froze them and its feminine softness unnerved them.

When a thirty-something Caucasian woman, holding a beautiful, sleeping baby girl, inched into the living room to confront them, the men wondered the same thing. Furniture, paintings, plants, and mother and daughter now filled the supposedly empty apartment. Razz hoped an irate husband and father wasn't waiting in the wings.

Howells looked ridiculous, his hands and wrench held high in the air, as if under arrest, but Sharky and Razz looked only slightly less so with their mouths agape.

The four looked at each other, uncertain, but the sight of three nervous men with a wrench understandably frightened the woman.

"I'll scream," she threatened, backing toward the bedroom.

"No, no, it's not like that. We didn't know anyone had moved in," said Razz.

The woman waited and the men hoped her baby wouldn't wake, screaming, to complicate matters.

"We're here to clean your pipes, uh, there's something wrong in your bathroom," Sharky offered.

"Oh," she said. "Sure. Wow, that's great service. I just called it in an hour ago. The manager said it would take till tomorrow."

The men breathed a collective sigh of relief over the fortunate coincidence. Razz helped Howells lower his frozen, airborne hands, and barely held back a laugh.

"Service is our business. We'll have it fixed in no time," he said, dragging Howells toward the bathroom.

"Jump right on it," said Sharky, following them.

Before they made it to the bathroom and relative safety, the woman asked,

"Why does it take three of you to fix a toilet that won't stop running?"

The men looked at each other, but, this time, it was Howells who spoke. "Union rules."

They escaped into the bathroom and closed the door.

Fifteen minutes later, the men had what they'd come for. From the bathroom sink drain, they'd retrieved a hair ball big enough to choke a horse and one that might offer a hair match and clue to Wally Bumpers' killer. As they hurried down the back stairs, very pleased, the tenant in apartment 703 was already on the phone complaining to Susan Berne about the inept plumbers she'd been sent. She griped that her toilet was still running and, now, her bathroom sink leaked, too.

Susan Berne had no idea what the woman was talking about.

25

So, he kept going. The wave was strong, but manageable. The wind was swirling as expected, buffeted by the pilings, but not strongly enough to knock him from his perch. That wasn't his problem. Nor was the increasingly loud yelling as people ran toward where, if he were supremely lucky and supremely good, he would land safely on the beach. Not even the wail of the Rescue Squad's siren bothered him. No, it was none of that. He simply had to pee.

Saturday, January 22, 2005

Razz had tossed and turned most of the night, fixated on what Harvey Howells might find in their collection of mucky hair strands, and he couldn't wait to learn the results. He yearned for the simpler days when he was a relatively happily married, unsuccessful restaurant manager. His avocation as a detective's sidekick was fascinating, but nerve-wracking and wearying. And today was clearly not going to be a low-stress, high-energy day. It was only six a.m. and he already needed a nap.

He thought of going surfing as a way to take his mind off things, and then remembered the previous day's outing. From his almost-confrontation with Louis at the Pier, to his driveway confrontation with his wife, his problems seemed to keep mounting. *At least, I'm alive to have problems,* he thought, trying for a positive spin. He knew he couldn't say the same for his wife's massacred roses.

When he unfolded that morning's edition of the *Monitor*, any thoughts of surfing died like the roses. On the front page, in big, bold headlines read, "Beach Closed! Shark Sighting!"

Thankfully, no one had been reported hurt, but Razz realized how close he'd been to becoming breakfast. Something had brushed his leg—twice. He'd downplayed both instances, but his fears had proven true. A shark was cruising the waters off San Margarita. And maybe there was more than one.

Normally, he would worry about the deleterious effect a shark sighting would have on his restaurant business, but there was too much else vying for his limited attention span. Though it seemed a drastic action this early in the day, there was only one thing for him to do—get ready to go to work.

Sharky had read the newspaper, too, but his reaction to news of a shark sighting was far different than Razz'. No, he did not anticipate going anywhere near the Pier today or anytime soon, if he could help it. After reading the story headline, he had ensconced himself in bed and was determined to stay there until he was sure every shark within a thousand miles of San Margarita was dead. He planned to stay in bed a long time.

"Baby, are you all right?" asked Terri when she noticed him shivering under the covers.

He tried to answer, but he couldn't control his mouth. Noise came out, but it was unrecognizable.

"Huh? What's the matter, honey?"

He barely managed raise his hand to motion toward the newspaper.

"Oh, no," she said when she read the headline, immediately understanding his dilemma. To her credit, she didn't dismiss his feelings or tell him to face his fears, trust in the universe, or any other well-intentioned, but meaningless, mumbo-jumbo. She just held him in her arms.

After a few minutes, he stopped shaking enough to speak intelligibly. "Thank you."

"Of course, this has to be hard for you with what you went through. I think you're very brave."

Sharky didn't look or feel particularly brave, but he was enormously grateful.

"Do you want me to stay home with you today?"

He wanted that very much, but, for one of the few times in his life, he put someone else's welfare first. "No, it's only your second day. You need to go to work."

"I'll call you later to check on you."

He almost screamed for her to stay, but, instead, whispered, "Okay."

She nodded encouragingly, gave him a kiss on the forehead, and walked toward the front door. Halfway there, she turned back. "You sure there's nothing I can do? Can I get you some breakfast before I go?"

He wanted to say, *"Yes, stay with me, feed me, keep me safe! Protect me from the big, bad shark and my big, bad thoughts,"* but the only words that came out were, "I'll get something at Mae's."

Terri grabbed her keys and purse. "Okay, honey. Have a good day." Then she walked out.

He trembled, but it wasn't due to the cool breeze entering from an open window. No, the thought of being alone scared him, so there was only one thing for him to do. As soon as he could drag himself out of bed, he would go to Mae's for coffee, donuts and distraction.

Harvey Howells knew what he had to do, too. He had to find a match between one of the hairs found in the bathroom drain at Wally's old apartment and one of the hair samples from the City Hall bathrooms. He also had to trust that

Sharky knew what he was doing, and that there might possibly be a match, or all of his time would be wasted. The first task was difficult, believing Sharky about anything was next to impossible. He didn't respect his methods or his intelligence, but the truth of the matter was that Howells wasn't terribly busy with his regular work anyway. San Margarita was way too safe for Howells' career aspirations. One didn't need to study DNA to convict jaywalkers and speeders. Helping Sharky solve this murder might be the only way he would ever become a hero, so he had a vested interest in the case. He had, after all, discovered the hairs in the apartment. But after a long morning of peering into microscopes and analyzing samples, he found himself questioning his desire for fame and a detective's badge.

He remembered climbing the stairs in the Hempstead while sweat beads formed on his forehead, then slid in tiny rivulets down his face. He remembered how he'd acted, shaking from fear, hands frozen in the air, when confronted by a harmless-looking woman and her baby. He considered that maybe he wasn't cut out to be a police detective, and the thought dispirited him so much he was ready to quit police work altogether.

Tedious lab work with little recognition over many years had strengthened his fantasy life, but had done nothing to help him cope in the day-to-day world. Dreams of solving crimes, writing investigative novels, going on book tours surrounded by adulating fans had kept him going during the bleak, lonely times, but yesterday's experiences had shown him personal weaknesses that were irreconcilable with his grandiose dreams. Tweezing out scalp and pubic hair from drain muck in order to solve a crime would have seemed glamorous to him years ago, but now it just seemed disgusting. He wanted to wash his hands of all of it. The only thing that kept him at his microscope was his new, if one-way, friendship with Razz McNeil.

He felt Razz had listened to him, had believed in him, and had trusted him. Howells didn't even know his interest in the Wally Bumpers case, but it didn't matter. Sharky could be damned, but Howells was determined to help Razz, so he would keep going, hair by hair. He removed his glasses and rubbed his tired, red eyes, then looked at the wall clock. It was almost noon. He considered his bagged lunch of a tuna sandwich and potato chips sitting on top of his desk and decided he needed to have a real lunch and needed to see a friend. He decided to go to the Surf's Up.

Sharky felt hung over when he shuffled into Mae's, although he hadn't had a drink in days. He went straight to the far end of the counter and was relieved to find a seat, because the place was already lunchtime busy.

"Are you all right, Sweetie?" asked Mae, her brow wrinkled with concern. She held a greasy spatula and wore a greasier apron. "Burger and fries?"

"No, thanks, I haven't had breakfast. Uh, coffee… and maybe a couple honey-glazed."

"Sure thing." She turned to go, but then turned back. "I'm sure it's nothing. Probably some stupid tourist saw a dolphin and freaked out."

He nodded gratefully and she went to get his order. Several regulars reading newspapers looked at him blankly, and then looked back at the offending headline about a shark in San Margarita. Although many were vaguely familiar with his ordeal years ago, no one other than Mae knew Sharky well enough or cared enough to reassure him. But, almost as one, they folded their papers and went back to their meals.

"It's on the house," Mae said when she returned with his coffee and doughnuts.

"Thanks, Mae."

"How's that woman of yours?" she asked, trying for a happier subject. But when he didn't answer right away, she got nervous. "Oh, no, everything's all right, isn't it? I'm sorry. Me and my big mouth."

As if to prove it, she opened her mouth wide and stuffed her whole right fist into it. It was just one of the tricks Mae used to loosen up the clientele. If a new patron laughed, she knew he was her type of customer. If he didn't and, instead, stormed out, appalled, she didn't need his business anyway. But, this time, she worried she truly might have broached a touchy subject.

"Everything's fine. She's at work."

Mae took her fist out of her mouth, grabbed her chest, staggered backwards, and bumped into the railing that guarded the hot, fry grill. "Ow!" She grabbed her ass cheek and hopped around, as if in pain.

Sharky had seen this act before, as had most of the customers, but he couldn't help laughing anyway.

"That's better," she said. "As long as you've got that girl, you've got nothing to worry about. But my ass will hurt for a week!"

She cackled at her joke, continuing long after everyone else had stopped. Only when Mayor Hidalgo entered the restaurant with a well-dressed man did she stifle herself. Although she wasn't easily impressed, she was smart enough to know that keeping the Mayor happy couldn't be bad for business.

As she worked her way from behind the counter to greet Hidalgo, Sharky sank lower on his counter stool. His face mostly hidden behind a metal napkin dispenser and a lunch menu, he watched the Mayor greet a suddenly well-behaved Mae and then glad-hand constituents on his way to his table. Though his charm was obvious, he seemed distracted. The man with him didn't wait for niceties, but moved directly to a corner booth and slid into the bench seat facing Sharky.

He didn't recognize Hidalgo's lunch partner, tall, dark and handsome, but he turned away when the man glanced in his direction. Only after the Mayor had finally sat down, his back to him, did he look back in their direction.

He could only see the back and side of Hidalgo's head and, from time to time, his left arm. He watched the men between his bites of doughnut and sips of coffee and they appeared cordial, yet competitive, friendly, yet tense. He figured they were having the type of business lunch that was taking place in hundreds of restaurants in Los Angeles. One person wanted one thing, the other wanted another, and they had to find common ground. Perhaps Hidalgo was raising money for his campaign, trying to win support from one of San Margarita's power brokers, or maybe they were working out the details of a new zoning ordinance.

Whatever he thought the meeting's purpose might be, those thoughts crumbled when the mystery man reached across the table and nestled his hand against Hidalgo's. This meeting seemed to be about much more than business. He stared at their hands, hoping Hidalgo would jerk his away, but his hand didn't move. *No, I'm too far away. I can't see what's happening from here. The angle's bad, they can't be touching.* But, when the man smiled warmly and caressed the top of Hidalgo's hand before drawing back, Sharky almost choked on his doughnut.

He didn't know what it all meant, but he knew heterosexual men didn't normally act that way. He also knew there was no way this new information could be good for him. He had to get out of there. Hidalgo already hated him and wouldn't appreciate being spied upon.

Sharky slid off his stool and bent toward the ground as if picking up loose change. He was readying to make a break for it, when Mae piped in, "Done already, Sarge?"

Her voice seemed to echo through the small diner. Subtlety was never her strong suit. Sharky hesitated as heads turned toward him, then he scurried toward the back, still bent over, trying to hide from the Mayor's view behind the cover of the service counter.

"No need to run. I said it was on the house!"

She roared with laughter and patrons joined in when they saw Sharky scramble, but he didn't stop to explain. He bolted out and closed the door behind him, muffling the guffaws inside. Outside, he leaned against the old plywood door and took a breath, finally feeling safe.

When he looked up, his safety bubble burst. Two big, burly Mexican men were staring right at him. He recognized them from the Gold Shore groundbreaking as well as the Mayor's office and they recognized him right back. They didn't seem pleased.

The larger of the two enormous men moved toward Sharky. "How tough are you without your gun, maricón?"

Sharky assumed it was a rhetorical question, but, when he tried to leave, the men blocked his path. "You guys don't want to fuck with me," he said as menacingly as possible.

"No, gringo, you don't want to fuck with us," warned the larger.

"You're so big and strong," said the smaller. "You lift so much weight."

The larger man backhanded his partner's arm, silencing him, and Sharky seized his opportunity. He escaped past them and broke into a sprint down a side alley. Only when he looked back over his shoulder and saw no one, did he slow his pace. He walked backwards for several steps, checking the alley, to make sure he was in the clear.

That's just my luck, he thought. *Sharks, a mayor with a secret, and big, nasty Mexicans, all lurking ready to hurt me if I'm not careful.* He couldn't wait to get back under his safe and comfy bed covers.

He turned to go home, then saw something that froze him in his tracks—a long, black limousine. Leaning against a fender, another large Mexican man watched him. Sharky backed away, his eyes locked on the chauffeur's, and then he turned to run.

"Nadie se ríe de un payaso muerto," hollered the man.

Sharky's legs went limp. *"No one laughs at a dead clown."* It was the same thing his almost executioner had said in the gym on the night of his almost execution. Here was one of the men that had warned him against pursuing Wally

Bumper's murderer in a most life threatening way. He did the math. Two bodyguards in front of Mae's and the chauffeur made three. There were two bodyguards plus a driver at the Gold Shore ceremony. There were only the two guards at Hidalgo's City Hall office, but the chauffeur had probably stayed with the car. There had to have been at least three men at the health club on New Year's. One, two, three. And one, two, three large Mexican men in Mayor Hidalgo's employ. And, despite having a wife and three children, Hidalgo seemed to play on the other side of the sexual street.

Could he have had anything to do with Wally Bumpers' murder? The mystery caller had seemed to imply someone at City Hall had killed Bumpers. *Had the two men been lovers? Did Hidalgo have his men threaten me to keep me off his track? Did he force the Chief to take me off the case and then fire me?*

"*Nadie se ríe de un payaso muerto.*" The words echoed in his brain, magnifying in volume until he thought his gray matter would explode through his ears.

He walked back toward the chauffeur; his legs would only carry him in that one direction. The driver looked nervous, not ready to be confronted, certainly not by a man who acted like he had nothing to lose. He didn't understand Sharky's maneuver any more than Sharky did. It just was. Inevitable. And there was nothing either could do about it.

Sharky was within ten feet. "¿Qué dijiste?"

The man no longer seemed to understand his native tongue, so Sharky tried again. "What did you say?"

Both men were like cornered animals, unable to back away or back down.

The chauffeur glared at Sharky, towering over him and outweighing him by a hundred pounds. "I said you're a clown. Dig the shit out of your ears. You don't know who you're up against."

Sharky tensed, ready to jump up and claw, kick, gouge, whatever-it-took this man to death. Whether he would have had a fighting chance or been squashed like a bug, no one will know, because, at that moment, the Mayor, his friend, and his two bodyguards walked around the corner.

Sharky jumped back just as the chauffeur lunged for him, and then sprinted down the alley. The bodyguards arrived to help the chauffeur up, but Sharky was long gone.

"Who was that man? What did he want?" asked the Mayor.

"Just a bum begging for money, sir. He insulted me. Nothing serious," said the chauffeur.

The two bodyguards were silent, but they knew it hadn't been a bum. The man was a police officer and, from the chauffeur's worried look, they guessed he now had a good idea who had nearly killed him, ironically, at a health club on New Year's morning.

But the driver's explanation was enough for the Mayor, so he and his friend climbed into the back seat of the car. His Mexican protectors looked at each other uncertainly, knowing they would have to be more cautious in the future and that it might already be too late.

It was fortunate Razz had come in early, because the Surf's Up was busier than ever that morning. He'd helped out serving, bussing tables, even chopping ham, tomatoes, and onions for omelettes. The work had helped keep his mind off weightier matters.

He and Lotta had just sat down at the bar for well-deserved respites when Harvey Howells entered.

"Hey, Harvey, any news?" Razz asked.

"Not yet.

His hopes crashed. "Oh."

"Ready for that lunch?" asked Howells, so eager he reminded Razz of a child expecting a Christmas present. That thought made Razz think of his children, which made him think of his wife, and suddenly he wasn't pleased to see Howells.

Lotta felt the attitudinal shift and energized herself enough to make a quick exit to the kitchen, leaving Razz to fend for himself.

"Burger and fries, okay?"

Howells scowled. "That salmon was good."

A Burger and fries cost the restaurant about a buck-seventy-five while the salmon cost six dollars, but he wouldn't argue. "One salmon special coming up."

That brought a happy grin back to Howells' face and he went to sit down at what he considered "their" table. Razz went to get him a Coke.

Razz wasn't in the mood to hear all about the lonely life of Harvey Howells. He just wanted to hear about a hair match and how they had solved the puzzle of who had killed Wally Bumpers, and then he wanted to go on with his life—his old life. After delivering one Coke, he headed back toward the bar.

"Aren't you joining me?"

"Uh, well, I'm working. I'm busy." Unfortunately, a momentary lull had left several empty tables, so Razz' excuse felt empty, too. "Maybe for a bit."

An awkward silence almost convinced him to go back to work, but, when an agitated Sharky entered, Razz decided he wasn't going anywhere. If Sharky was at the Pier when a shark had been sighted nearby, something had to be very important.

"You won't believe it," said Sharky. "You just won't believe it. It's incredible."

Razz and Howells waited.

"I mean, it's unbelievable. You won't believe it. I don't believe it myself."

Razz had never seen him so animated, but he was animated almost into incoherence and seemed unable to finish verbalizing his thought.

"What, Sharky? What?"

"Sit down," he said, apparently not noticing the men were already sitting. "You won't believe it."

"What the fuck are you talking about?"

The outburst helped focus Sharky. "The mayor."

Razz bit his lip, trying to maintain patience. Howells' opinion of Sharky was too low to get much lower, so he wasn't expecting much anyway.

"Gay ... bi, whatever. The mayor."

"*Gay. Bi. The mayor.*" Razz struggled to decipher the cryptic message and was ready to toss in the towel and toss the messenger out.

"Maybe he knew Wally," offered Howells, indicating he'd seen a light that remained pitch-black to Razz.

Now Howells and Sharky were united, excitedly sharing a secret that Razz still couldn't fathom.

"Mayor Hidalgo, gay, bi, whatever, maybe knew Wally," he said, piecing their words together, but not quite their import. "Are you guys out of your fucking minds?"

Lotta poked her head out of the kitchen, impelling Razz to herd the men to the back patio for more privacy. "What the fuck are you two talking about? Have you gone totally fucking bananas?"

Now Sharky and Howells were like school kids, giggling best friends guarding a secret. Sharky looked at Howells, implicitly asking permission to tell. Howells nodded.

"I saw him with another man. They were touching hands."

"I'd heard the rumors," said Howells. "So he's our killer?"

Sharky nodded. "I think so."

Razz felt like he was the only sane man in an insane world. But he was mistaken, there was no sanity anywhere.

It took Sharky ten minutes to explain about the bodyguards and their New Year's threat and about the Mayor's tête-à-tête at Mae's. Howells listened excitedly to every word, very much back in the cops and killers world. He could already picture the award ceremony and his medal.

Razz took it in, resistant at first, but he began to see the picture that Sharky painted. It appeared Sharky and Howells already had the Mayor electrocuted, but he wasn't as convinced.

"But Harvey hasn't found a match yet."

His logic only briefly dampened his comrades' spirits.

"Well, I'll find it. If it's there, I'll find it," said Howells.

Sharky smiled. "Yeah, he'll do it. He's the best."

Razz was surprised to feel a tinge of jealousy at their budding friendship, but he re-focused on the puzzle. "Harvey, what floors have you checked?"

"Huh?"

"Which hair samples, from which floors?"

"I've finished all but the second floor bathroom next to the Mayor's office."

Sharky patted Howells proudly on the back and Razz felt like he'd entered another dimension. *Mayors and street clowns fornicating. Sharky Sampson and Harvey Howells becoming best friends. What's next?*

When Razz flashed back to the day he collected hair samples, he flashed to the second floor bathroom. He flashed to the stall from where he'd watched the Mayor and his bodyguard. He flashed to his picking up a pubic hair from the urinal where Mayor Hidalgo had just finished his business. Then he too saw the light. *Maybe the Mayor could be the killer.* And, with blinding clarity, he saw their problem.

"It sounds like you're already in danger, Sharky, but if Harvey finds a hair match placing the Mayor at Wally's apartment, we could all be marked men. The Mayor has powerful friends. And none of them are going to be happy about this."

The three men looked at each other more soberly now. No, the Mayor and his friends wouldn't be happy at all.

26

He had planned to pee when he first got in the water, but he'd gotten so wrapped up in his preparations, he'd forgotten. To relieve himself now would be at least as disconcerting as holding it in.

Wednesday, January 26, 2005

Although Richard Gold was ostensibly a friend of Hidalgo's, he was not unhappy. He was ecstatic. He had been laid that morning by one of the most beautiful women in the world, his assistant, lover, and budding business partner, Natalie Wesson, but his good mood transpired from much more than that. In a quick turn of fortune, he was making money on his Gold Shore property and there was nothing better than making money in Richard Gold's world. By selling ten percent of the equity for three million dollars, he had effectively priced his zero dollar investment at twenty-seven million. From having his empire at risk one day to marking to market an additional twenty-seven million the next day, it was just another incredible deal in the amazing life of a real estate mogul. During boom times, people made real estate fortunes daily, and during busts, you could find developers and bankers lined up together in bankruptcy court. Today, it was another fortune made for Richard Gold.

He was so happy he actually whistled as he walked down the hall with Wesson clinging affectionately to one arm. He could not recall the last time he whistled. He thought it was probably when he was a young kid or, perhaps, when he was on shore leave from the Navy and was trying to impress young women. He didn't really care, because he'd never been the reflective sort. He had always looked straight ahead to the next deal, to the next million dollars, and to the next sexual conquest.

He looked at Natalie Wesson and marveled how one so young and so exquisite could have turned a budding disaster into such a financial windfall so quickly. Whether it was due to a rigorous curriculum at NYU Business School or to something else, she had learned a lot in her tender years. He smiled thinking about all the things she'd already taught him in the bedroom. He bent to kiss her cheek appreciatively as they turned into his office.

"Oh, I'm sorry."

Surprised by Sarah's presence, Gold jerked away, his elation turned to anger.

"I thought I'd organize your desk before you got here," Sarah continued, embarrassed by her father's dalliance with this woman much younger than herself. "I'll just ... I'll be in my office."

As she hurried past them toward the door, Gold regained his enthusiasm. "Thank you, Sarah."

She turned, a smile of relief uncertainly cracking her lips, and nodded.

"Don't you want to see the paperwork?" Wesson asked, aiming the razor-sharp words straight at her heart.

Sarah deflected the words and they landed harmlessly on Gold's Berber carpet. "Why, yes, I'd love to."

Though the smile on Wesson's face never wavered, her eyes revealed her disappointment when Sarah met her challenge.

"Great," said Gold, oblivious to the drama playing out in front of him. "Sarah, could you get me a cup of coffee, please, while Natalie prepares the papers?"

Wesson's smile grew perceptibly now, but Sarah stayed cool and said, "Sure, Daddy."

As Sarah turned to leave, Wesson hesitated, either impressed by her show of control or busily planning the next move to eviscerate her.

Gold broke her spell. "Natalie? The papers?"

"Yes, yes, of course, Richard." She opened her four thousand dollar Hermes leather briefcase, a small token of Gold's appreciation, and gracefully removed a folder containing two copies of the sale agreement for ten percent of the equity in the Gold Shore Hotel and Resort.

Wesson ceremoniously laid one fresh, clean copy in front of Gold, then handed him a gold, limited-edition Tibaldi pen as he studied the first page.

"Oh, Richard, it's the same document you read ten times last night."

"But I didn't sign it last night."

A deal of this size and importance deserved several reads anyway, but because they had changed a few words at the advice of Gold's legal counsel that had only been approved by the investors earlier that morning, it needed one more read to ensure everything was letter perfect.

Sarah entered and set his coffee in front of him, but Gold was fixated on the document. As if this particular choreography had been danced many times before, he handed each finished page to Sarah for her review. Their synchronicity was impressive, but if Natalie Wesson was jealous of their business intimacy, she didn't show it.

Every now and then, Gold exhaled a burst of air that bordered on laughter, very pleased with the deal. Sarah read with impressed incredulity, almost disbelieving the deal terms could be as favorable as had been described. But there they were in black, twelve-point courier type—three million dollars for ten percent of the equity, purchased by Cardinal Investments, Inc. of San Antonio, Texas.

When Richard Gold finished reading, he looked up and saw two beautiful women watching him, awaiting his command, his loving daughter and his sexy young lover. The world seemed very good to him at this moment.

He took a sip of the hot, black coffee, savoring it even though it was only Folgers. Gold could spend a thousand dollars over lunch, but wouldn't splurge for decent coffee for the office. He began signing and initialing the relevant pages.

"Well, congratulations," Sarah said. "To both of you."

"Thank you, dear," he said, not looking up. Wesson barely nodded an acknowledgment.

Her dismissal complete, Sarah turned and left the office.

Wesson edged closer to him, her long bare legs now obliquely in his view. He tried to concentrate on signing the papers, but his eyes kept wandering to her thighs. *They are magnificent thighs,* he thought. *My thighs. And I can't wait till they're wrapped around me again.* His pen hand went limp when his delicious thoughts overpowered his motor control, but she touched his hand to steady him.

She brushed her breasts against him and whispered, "Hurry."

Richard Gold understood and had she been his Chief Petty Officer, he wouldn't have held firmer attention. He sped through the remaining pages while Natalie went to lock the door. He was like a fumbling teenage virgin hurrying to finish his homework so he could go out and play with the neighborhood tart, but he finished the last page as Natalie returned to his side.

He grabbed her and tried to lean her against the desk.

"Wait," she said, "sign the second copy first."

"It can wait." It could, but Gold couldn't. He tried to lift her onto the desk, but she was dead weight and wouldn't budge.

With a stern look, she backed a chastened Gold away, and then she smiled coyly and moved in, kissing him. Again, he rushed like a virgin schoolboy until she held up her hand and said, "Sign first. Then we play."

She held out the second copy and handed him the pen. "This way we won't have to worry about it. Don't you think that's a good idea, Richard?"

Had she suggested he jump from the roof top, it might have seemed a good idea, because she now held his cock in her right hand, working it and working him as she had for the last few weeks, always in control and making Gold lose his.

He seemed confused, unable to do two things at once. "I've got to read them."

Wesson squeezed harder and he gasped from the painful pleasure. "It's the same contract. Don't you trust me?"

With her hand on his crotch and her breasts in his face, Gold didn't care if he could trust her or not. He signed the papers, moaning as she jerked him off, and didn't read a word.

"Mmm, this is sexy," she purred, working him harder.

He was getting more cross-eyed by the moment, but he kept signing and initialing.

"Sign it, Richard, sign it."

He could barely control himself and, just as he finished signing the last page, he came. It was complete, a fitting climax.

Natalie Wesson wiped his semen from her hand with a tissue, a repulsed look on her face now, as he recovered.

"Oh," said Gold, catching his breath, "you're amazing. Just amazing."

She had already grabbed the signed papers and was moving to the door.

"Where are you going?"

She turned back and her look was no longer sexy and supportive, but cold and hard. She looked like someone who had seen and done far too much in her years and was thoroughly disgusted with all of it. The fresh-faced, young woman was long gone.

An inexplicable chill ran down his spine.

"I'm just going to take care of these," she said coolly, forcing a smile. With that, she took the papers outside and closed the door behind her.

Gold was confused, but, whether it was due to the aftermath of orgasm, or the appearance of this strange new version of Natalie Wesson, or a combination of both, he didn't have time to ponder. He had to clean himself up.

The test results were official and, just as Sharky, Harvey Howells, and Razz had hoped and feared, someone who had used the second floor bathroom at City Hall had known Wally Bumpers intimately. Howells had worked long hours to find matching hair samples and to match their DNA to the DNA recovered from Wally's anus. Exhausted, he was sleeping off his ordeal, so it was up to Sharky and Razz to carry on the investigation today. That Sharky and Harvey Howells were certain who the killer was, and that Razz worried they were right, wasn't enough. They needed more than a threat on Sharky's life by some men who worked for a possibly-gay, possibly-guilty mayor.

This time, though, Sharky didn't have to coerce Razz to help; he was already a step ahead. Razz not only drove the two men to the Hempstead, but he suggested they interview Susan Berne and anyone else who might have ever seen Mayor Hidalgo on the premises. They needed a witness, someone to place Hidalgo at the scene of the crime. They also needed an independent DNA sample from Hidalgo, but they'd worry about that once they knew they were not totally off-base.

Berne was not pleased when Razz walked into her office, but she was genuinely confused when Sharky walked in behind him. He looked vaguely familiar, but she couldn't place him.

"The apartments didn't get any cheaper in the last week," she said.

Before Razz could defend himself, Sharky did it for him. "I'd suggest you try to be nice, you fat hag, and I'll try to remember you helped us, assuming you do." Flipping open his police ID folder with his fake badge inches from her face seemed to make an impression upon her.

"How can I help?"

"That's better," said Sharky. "Have you ever seen San Margarita's mayor, Jaime Hidalgo, in this apartment complex?"

"The Mayor? How would I know? And why do you want—"

Sharky flipped open his ID folder again and, this time, clipped the end of her nose, startling her. Razz almost burst out laughing, but Sharky was dead serious.

She understood. "Sorry. No, I don't think so."

"You don't think so?" He hovered over her, not letting up. "What do you mean, 'you don't think so?'"

Berne hesitated and looked to Razz for solace, but he enjoyed watching her squirm.

"I mean, I ... no, I haven't seen him."

"Are you sure?"

"Yes, no ... maybe. Maybe I saw him."

"When?"

The men moved imperceptibly closer, leaning in, as if to hear the news that would implicate Mayor Jaime Hidalgo a fraction of a second sooner, because they couldn't wait any longer.

"I think it was about a year ago."

A year ago? Sharky doubted she would be much help, but that didn't deter him.

"Wasn't Hidalgo here the night of December 21st?"

His question seemed not to fully register, so he pressed on—harder. "Didn't you see him that night? Didn't you see Hidalgo? Tell me!"

"No! No! I wasn't even here!"

A flash of recognition came to him. He'd forgotten that Berne had been away during the time of Wally's murder. He took a deep breath and began again, more calmly.

"So, when else did you see him here?"

"Just that once."

"Just once? Come on. You're sure?"

Berne nodded affirmatively and it was as if a giant vacuum had sucked most of the air out of the room.

He struggled to regain momentum. "Okay, okay. It's all right. When you saw Mayor Hidalgo here, where was he?"

"What?"

"Who was he here to see?"

"I, I can't say."

"Can't or won't?" Sharky grabbed her arm roughly.

"Ow!"

Razz thought about intervening, knowing his tactics were crossing the line, but he held himself back. This was Sharky's turf.

"Who was he here to see?"

"Richard! He was here to see Richard Gold!"

Any remaining air left the room in a whoosh. Sharky pondered her answer, but Berne soon made her meaning crystal clear.

"They were discussing the Mayor's re-election. Richard was going to support him. I mean, he and I were close at the time, so I was with them in Richard's apartment, number 310. That was the only time I saw the Mayor here, I swear."

Sharky believed her and wasn't pleased. Not only wasn't his case being solved, he was reminded Terri had once been Richard Gold's mistress, and that he had met her in that same apartment. Then he remembered something else.

"You said 'Richard's apartment.'"

Berne nodded uncertainly.

"It's not in his name," Razz said, unable to stay on the sidelines.

She looked at them both, trying to understand their meaning.

Sharky continued, "It's in Emma Northrup's name and Gold's illegally renting it for way below market. Who's Emma Northrup?"

As his question sank in, she smiled, and it threw Sharky.

"What's so funny?" he asked.

Now, even Razz wanted to rough this woman up.

Berne sensed their frustration, but started to laugh anyway. "Sorry, but this seems like such a perfect time to get back at him for dumping me for that blonde bitch." Her nasty comment leveled directly at the love of his life didn't move her closer to Sharky's good side, but when her laughter turned to sobbing, Sharky softened.

"What is it?"

Both men seemed to wilt at the sight of her tears, just as men have done in the face of women's tears since time immemorial. Razz handed her a tissue.

"Thank you," she sniffled. "I'm sorry. It's just that, despite everything, I loved Richard. He wasn't all that kind or attentive, he wasn't even particularly good in bed, but, underneath it all, he was a little boy crying out for love and attention. I guess I wanted to take care of him."

Such self-revelation was foreign ground for Sharky and Razz, descendents of Neanderthals as they were. And, despite their vaguely sensing its truth, they didn't appreciate the implication that men could be like needy children.

"Emma Northrup was his wife's mother. He kept the apartment after she died. It's totally legal.

Razz shook his head, sighing. "She's right, I should have remembered. Northrup was the name of my wife's maternal grandparents. I never met them."

"Okay, okay. We'll keep asking around," Sharky said. He was disappointed, but used to cases that didn't solve easily. "Listen, as far as anyone's concerned, we aren't here and we haven't been here."

She was too emotional to argue.

"Will you be all right?" Razz asked.

When Berne managed a tiny nod in the affirmative, the men went back to the hunt.

At her desk, Sarah went over every clause of the contract in her mind. It was just as Natalie Wesson had predicted. She said she'd find someone to buy equity in the properties at a premium despite all the obvious problems, and she had. But Sarah had a nagging feeling that something was wrong. As her father had told her many times when she was growing up, if something seemed too good to be true, it probably was. But, try as she might, she couldn't find any flaws. The contract was clean and ironclad. Signed by both sides, it would be as strong as the word of God, except that even God's lawyers could bicker over the subtlest shades of meaning until Hell froze over. But the big print and big meaning were all that really mattered here. They'd found an investor that paid too much for a piece of the Gold Shore. And Sarah wanted to know why.

She wasn't going to get any clues from her father. He was happy to count his money and have some breathing room with the project. And what would Wesson tell her, other than "I told you so"? Despite Razz' limitations, in happier times, she would have talked to him, just so she could hear the circumstances of the deal aloud. Sometimes, that helped her clarify complex situations.

The problem nagged at her as she reviewed numbers for a potential condo project in Las Vegas. She peered at the generous estimates for sales prices of two-bedroom, two-bath, sixteen hundred square foot apartments and wondered why anyone would pay a million dollars for two bedrooms and two baths of airspace in a sweltering desert surrounded by tacky tourist attractions, drunken tourists, and bad entertainment. It made her glad to know that what happened there, stayed there, because as far as she was concerned, they could keep it. She plopped the condo proposal into a deep desk drawer promising never to revisit it, and gave her weary brain a rest.

She dragged herself over to a window. The view wasn't as expansive as from her father's office, but she could still see a slice of the Pacific Ocean and the Pier. The Pier made her think of Razz, which alternately angered her and made her nostalgic for happier days, and made her feel even wearier. She considered going out for a walk, but, as she had begun to do more and more when she needed a pleasant distraction, she called Merice Marcayda instead.

The phone rang once, twice, then three times and, disappointed, Sarah began to lower the receiver. Just as it rang for the fourth time, Merice answered.

"Hello? Hello?"

"Oh, hi, it's Sarah. I'm sorry. Did I catch you at a bad time? I can call back."

"Hi. No, I was just out in the yard. How are you? We miss you."

Her enthusiasm cheered Sarah immediately. "God, I wish I had your wonderful energy."

Merice laughed. "You do, that's why I like you so much."

The two women talked for fifty minutes about their kids, the weather, and about nothing in particular. They talked the way men hardly ever do, free, easy, and, seemingly, without agenda, just happy to be hearing a friendly voice.

"I think I'd better go. I still have some yard work to finish," Merice said during the fifty-first minute.

"Of course, and I should go back to work myself."

"Hey, why don't you come over for dinner tonight and we can start up where we left off."

"Oh, I'm sure your husband would love that."

"What do you mean? He loves you. Come over, please."

"I don't know, it's late and I don't have a sitter."

"No, bring your kids. Patrick and Melanie miss their new friends."

A rush of warmth and good feeling coursed through Sarah and she felt better knowing that Merice was there for her, and that she could depend on her.

"Thanks, we'd love to."

Sharky and Razz weren't having much success at the Hempstead. Although Sharky had interviewed everyone before, because of his latest run-in, he felt a greater urgency now. But many people weren't home, or they pretended not to be, and those that were didn't offer any useful information.

"Maybe it's all a big coincidence. Maybe the Mayor's got nothing to do with it," offered Razz.

"So, why would his goons almost guillotine me?"

"Are you positive they were the same guys?"

An annoyed look gave him his answer, but Sharky elaborated anyway. "You saw them. They were with him at City Hall yesterday; they were with him at the groundbreaking; they were with him—"

"Yeah, yeah, I know. And 'dead clowns.'"

"That's right. 'No one laughs at a dead clown.' You think that could be coincidence?"

Razz shook his head, without enthusiasm.

"Come on, five floors down, only two to go."

Although Sharky seemed confident, Razz couldn't even fake it. He dragged himself forward anyway, like a soldier dedicated to performing a mission even though he knew it might be his last.

"Wait," said Sharky, looking back up the hallway.

"Wait, what? Let's go. You said 'only two to go.'"

But Sharky was already making his way back to apartment 310, Richard Gold's apartment via his wife's mother, Emma Northrup.

"Oh, crap," was all Razz could say.

Nothing seemed odd about the apartment to Razz, but Sharky was fixated on the bedroom's picture of Richard Gold, the one that had spooked him when he'd first met Terri.

"Christ, Sharky, all I need is for Gold to walk in now. I'm lower than low in his eyes already. Breaking and entering wouldn't raise my stature."

He felt like a novice skier navigating a treacherous slalom course. He was going dangerously fast and hazardous bumps were everywhere to throw him off-balance and, perhaps, hurtling towards a precipice.

"We didn't break, I've got a key. And I'm a police detective."

"Yeah, without a warrant. And who's not even officially on this case. I don't know who'll be more screwed."

"I've got a key," Sharky repeated.

Razz waited for something more substantial, but Sharky said it again, more slowly, as if pondering every syllable. "I've got a key."

"Yes, you do. Very good. Key. K-E-Y, key."

Sharky wasn't listening, because he'd gone back into the living room. Razz sighed, and then followed him, but when he reached the living room, Sharky was already at the front door.

"Seen enough?"

Razz had seen more than enough and did not ask why the sudden change of heart, he was just happy to get the hell out of there.

They quickly worked through the last two floors. The routine was the same at each apartment: Sharky flashed a badge, showed Hidalgo's picture, and asked whether Hidalgo had ever been at the building. When pressed, Sharky gave his name as Robert Donati and hoped no one would know the difference. No one did. Razz was relieved to stay in the background and take notes.

By the time they finished, they had spoken to about fifty percent of the residents, presumably the unemployed ones, but no one had seen anyone resembling the mayor at the Hempstead. That left fifty percent they would have to contact later.

Normally, Sharky would have rounded everyone up and made a huge fuss until he got what he wanted, but it was Donati's case now and he had to be careful. He wondered why he hadn't seen more of Donati, but chalked it up to his cohort's inferior work. If Donati had a clue, any clue at all, he reasoned, they would have crossed paths more often. It made him glad Donati was a moron.

"Is that it? Are we done for today?" asked Razz. "I mean, I still have a couple restaurants to run."

Sharky caught Susan Berne watching them from her office, then led Razz down the hall while he thought of his next move. Near the hallway exit, it came to him. "Let's check the basement."

Razz decided he would have plenty of time to get to the Surf's Up.

They hurried down the dimly lit metal stairs, making no attempt to be quiet. Each clanging step echoed off the concrete walls. At the bottom, Sharky opened a windowed door and the men went into a small basement hallway. It was darker than the stairwell, but they could see it didn't run the whole length of the building. There were three doors.

Sharky reached for door number one. Razz held his breath in anticipation, and when the door opened to reveal the parking garage, he felt let down. Sharky shut the door, pondering the building's layout. After a moment, he threw open the same door, startling a young woman about to climb into her Jetta. He examined the knob from the garage side, but there was no keyhole. He tried twisting the knob, but it wouldn't budge.

"Do you ever enter the building this way, through this door?" he asked the woman.

"No, it's always locked."

He considered her answer and again jostled the doorknob. He watched a few people enter and exit the garage, and then he nodded and closed the door behind him, dismissing it as the killer's likely access point.

In the hallway, the men discovered door number two was locked. Sharky inserted his master key and swung the door open, revealing an array of electric and water meters busily humming away. "One more and you're free to go."

Three weeks earlier, Razz would have been happy to go, but now he was hooked on the thrill. "May I?"

Sharky gave him the key. "Sure, Detective."

When Razz slipped the key into door number three, he felt a rush of excitement. He'd never understood why anyone would want the hassle or danger of being a cop, but he did now. It was about power, yes, but it was also about the excitement and satisfaction in solving a seemingly insoluble puzzle. He turned the key.

He slowly pushed open the door and entered with Sharky protectively close to his right shoulder. The low light from the hall crept into what seemed to be a storage closet and revealed rows of paint cans, a garden hose, sundry mops and brooms, and various paraphernalia for apartment building upkeep. His thrill was gone.

"Oh, well." Disappointed, he turned to go, but a light touch from Sharky's left hand stopped him.

Sharky was staring at something. Razz followed his sight line and when he found the target, he gasped. There was a man sitting on a cot. It was the janitor.

"We've been looking for you," said Sharky.

The man nodded. "I know what you want. You must protect me."

Sharky looked at Razz. They had hit the witness jackpot.

The janitor's name was Manuel Jose Rivas. He'd come to Miami from Guatemala five years earlier to visit his cousin and stayed. He moved to California shortly thereafter and held a series of odd jobs before landing at the Hempstead three years ago. With a fake identification card under the name of Jose Rigas, no one ever questioned his background. As long as he could work and would work cheap, none of his employers seemed to care about anything else.

Sharky tried to comfort a distraught Rivas. "It will be okay. I'll protect you."

"Señor, you don't know these people. They will hurt me. They will send me back."

"Not if you help me. Not if you help me." He leaned in, touched the man's shoulder, and nodded confidentially. "Trust me."

Off to one side, Razz watched, wanting to believe his partner's sincerity, but he knew Sharky had no more power with the INS than he did. In his brief experience, he'd learned police work could be a dirty business.

After a long moment, Rivas looked up and nodded uncertainly. "I trust you." He shifted his position, trying to get comfortable on the hard cot, then gave up and began his story. "He'd come in from the alley, go up the back stairs, almost every night."

"Do you know who he was?"

"No, but he seemed important. He wore nice suits."

"Is this the man?" When Sharky flashed a picture of Jaime Hidalgo, a deathly look came over Rivas' face.

"Yes."

"What time did he come here? Was there any particular time?"

"Usually around seven o'clock."

"Good, you're doing good. When did you first see him here?"

Rivas hesitated. "I don't know, a year ago, maybe two. I'm not sure."

"Why didn't anyone else see him? Why only you?" He prodded Rivas harder now, his good cop routine quickly giving way to the real Sharky. "You're lying!"

"No, señor, no! I wouldn't lie to you!" The man shuddered, on the verge of tears. "I wouldn't lie to you."

"Okay, it's okay."

Sharky looked for help. From Razz' vantage point, the man seemed to be telling the truth, but he only shrugged, uncertain, so Sharky pressed on.

"Why didn't anyone else see him?"

"I don't know."

"What do you mean, 'you don't know'? Who else uses these stairs?"

"No one, señor! No one!"

Razz didn't know if Sharky was schizophrenic or just really good, but the interrogation almost made him want to confess just to get some calm, some sanity, back in the world.

Agitated, Rivas continued, "No one uses them. The alley, it's too dark, it's dangerous."

Razz caught Sharky's eye and knew he, too, was thinking about the little homeless man and the danger that had befallen him.

"The man lets himself in, with a key. I've watched him. No one else uses these stairs and the apartment is at the end of the hall. No one would know."

No one would know, Sharky thought, *except a dead, little homeless man and a Guatemalan janitor. Two witnesses, but only one is still alive. No wonder the man is scared.*

"What happened on the night of December 21st, the night of the murder?"

Rivas looked like he'd just seen the Devil. He shook his head, and then his body shook with it. "No, señor, no."

"What happened?"

"No, señor."

With lightning speed that would have made Billy the Kid proud, Sharky thrust his right hand onto Rivas throat, then squeezed. Rivas's eyes bulged and his carotid artery popped from his neck, but Sharky only squeezed harder.

"What happened?"

Rivas thrashed trying to loosen his grip, but Sharky was undeterred.

Razz looked away. He knew the game, but didn't have the stomach for it.

"What happened?"

Holding onto Sharky's hand, which was still firmly attached to his throat, Rivas was literally holding on for dear life. His head flopped to the left, and he began to lose consciousness.

Razz couldn't bear it any longer. "You're killing him."

Sharky tightened his grip further and Rivas's eyes went blank.

"Let him go!" Razz ripped his hand from the man's throat and Rivas gulped a huge breath.

Sharky nodded and Razz realized he'd been an unwitting accomplice, playing good cop without even knowing it, but the bad cop had made his point.

When Rivas had regained his breath, he said, "I'll tell you anything."

He not only told them anything, he told them everything. In ten minutes,

Sharky and Razz knew they had the Mayor.

On the night of December twenty-first, around seven o'clock, from the darkness of the storage closet, Rivas watched a man he now recognized as Jaime Hidalgo through the door window. Hidalgo entered from the alley and walked upstairs, just as he'd done many nights. Nothing seemed unusual, so Rivas rested on his cot where he sometimes took refuge while at work. Thirty minutes later, when he heard the clanging of metal stairs, he went to the door and saw the Mayor, in a panic, run outside.

He said he'd been tempted to follow him to see what was wrong, but before he could muster his courage, two large Mexican men he'd never seen before rushed in and hurried up the stairs, so he stayed in the shadows behind the door. Normally, at seven-thirty, he would leave for home, but on this night, because of the curious circumstances, he stayed. Ten minutes later, he knew his curiosity had put him in danger when the men returned, carrying something large and heavy wrapped in blankets and bed sheets.

After Rivas watched the men go back upstairs a few minutes later, this time empty-handed, he waited over an hour for them to return. Finally, he grew tired and decided to go home where he'd feel safer. He returned to work the next day as if nothing had happened, not daring to tell anyone what he'd seen for fear he would be sent back to Guatemala—or something worse. He had hoped that it was all nothing, that everyone was fine, that the large, awkward, heavy something wrapped in blankets and bed sheets wasn't what, or who, he thought it might be.

Days later, when dumping trash into an alley dumpster, Rivas saw the front page of the *Monitor* and the picture of a dead Wally the Clown. That's when he knew the incident had definitely not been nothing.

When Rivas finished his story implicating Mayor Jaime Hidalgo in the death of Wally Bumpers, no one spoke for several minutes as the three men contemplated their futures. Neither thought theirs looked bright.

27

He forgot his urinary dilemma when, once again, he looked into the sun, which momentarily blinded him. He had decided against wearing shades because they would be dangerous in the shadows under the Pier, but not wearing them created another problem entirely. Just as he regained his sight and his bearings, he found himself greeted by a two-ton piling smiling at him from only eight feet away.

When Razz arrived late for work at the Surf's Up, he was proud of his efforts to find Wally's killer, but he was also scared. And when Lotta told him, just after he walked in, that Louis wanted to see him that night, his fear level increased. She did not know the reason for the meeting and he couldn't think of anything new he'd done wrong work-wise; the restaurants were doing well.

Maybe Louis heard about my nosing around and doesn't appreciate it. I'm not paid to investigate, but to run restaurants. My focus should be on my job, any employer would demand that. And if an employee can't do that, why should he keep his job or any of the perks, like cheap apartments, which might come with it?

In about three and a half thoughts, Razz had himself fired, him and his parents homeless, and himself without a professional future. And he still had to worry about possible public fallout from the impending arrest of Mayor Jaime Hidalgo.

"He wants you there at six, 1313 Oak Street, park on the street."

"Thirteen-thirteen?"

Lotta simply nodded and walked into the kitchen.

Thirteen-thirteen, that can't be a lucky number.

When he left at five-forty-five, it appeared it would be a busy evening at the restaurant. Chad had called in sick, so they were already short-handed, and Razz knew Lotta would be in for a difficult night. Although he had restocked the bar and kitchen and tallied the lunch receipts, he felt guilty. That guilt almost overpowered his dread over his meeting with Louis, but, once he wheeled his Mustang out of the lot, he forgot about Lotta and dread took over completely. *What does Louis need to speak to me about? Why don't we just meet at the restaurant? What's so important it can't wait?*

He was so focused on his meeting that he almost rear-ended a Jaguar stopped at a red light at Ocean Boulevard. Its handsome, silver-haired driver scowled at him through his rear view.

Razz waved sheepishly. "Sorry."

The man wrinkled his brow, clearly unimpressed, and, when the light turned green, he squealed his tires and sped away, as if he could erase his unpleasant experience through burning tire rubber.

Insulted, Razz considered flipping him the finger, then remembered that was just one of many ways you could get yourself shot in LA. *Man, it's an angry town. Everyone's on edge.* He knew he was.

As he drove up Westerly Boulevard away from the ocean, he began to calm. Though the sun was already down, he felt the unseasonably warm Santa Ana winds whip his still-full head of hair. *It's not as good as surfing, but, if you have to be on land, driving a convertible is the next best thing.* He'd never driven a motorcycle and didn't plan to. He considered that an activity for reckless, crazy people, and he didn't notice the least bit of irony in his attitude.

By the time he turned onto Oak Street, his edge had dulled, but, as he counted address numbers, it started sharpening again. *Thirteen-fifty-seven. Thirteen-thirty-nine. Thirteen-twenty-five.* Then he saw thirteen-thirteen.

The house looked like a normal, suburban home, not too big, not too small. It was not what he had expected, then he realized he hadn't expected anything, because he'd been too busy worrying. He pulled into a parking spot behind a Mercedes with darkened windows. Had he known there were armed men inside, he would have been even more nervous. Then he saw something as he crossed the street that sharpened his emotional edge so much it could have cut titanium.

Parked in front of the Marcayda home was Sarah's Range Rover. He fought the urge to sprint the other way. It was not that he didn't want to see Sarah. He just didn't want to see her here and under these circumstances. He had told her to stay away from the Marcaydas, but it appeared she was getting more deeply involved. He was unsure he'd be able to hold his temper when he saw her, but before he could consider it further, Louis opened the front door.

"Hola, amigo!"

Razz looked behind him for an "amigo" until he realized Louis had meant him.

"Glad you could make it," he continued.

Razz couldn't tell if he was drunk, but he sure seemed happy. He hurried up the drive and Louis shook his hand like they were long-lost, best friends.

"Hi, uh, thanks for having me. I thought this was a business meeting."

"Business, pleasure, it's all the same. If you can't have pleasure in your business, why do business?"

Razz thought of several inappropriate responses concerning some of

Louis' pleasure-oriented businesses, but this time he kept his poker face. "I mean, that's my wife's car."

"Oh?" Louis seemed confused. "I'm the only one here."

That was her Range Rover and her license plate number, Razz was sure of it. *But where's Sarah? Is she at another one of these homes? And why? And where are our kids? Did she leave them with a sitter so she could go on a date? Already?* Now, his poker face was gone.

"Come in," said Louis.

"Yeah, thank you."

Louis led him through the living room, pointing out Marcayda family memorabilia as he went. "Those were taken on our trip to Hawaii two years ago," he said, indicating toward photos of his kids playing in the Hawaiian waves.

Good surfing waves, Razz thought, as he reviewed the photos. But when Louis handed him a photo of Merice in a bikini, he lingered.

"Beautiful, isn't she?"

He couldn't exactly say no, that would be impolite, but he felt awkward telling Louis just how beautiful he thought his wife was. "Yes, she is," he said, trying to navigate the fine line between compliment and insult he'd created by lingering.

"She's a wonderful wife and I'm a lucky man." As soon as Louis said it, he knew he'd struck a sour chord for Razz. "Let's go to my office."

He put his hand gently on his shoulder and it created an intimacy that Razz wasn't ready for. It felt strangely like male bonding. Louis led him down a long hallway with rooms on both sides.

Razz looked through a crack in one slightly ajar door and saw vestiges of male childhood—a basketball, scattered books, an unmade bed, model airplanes, and a full-length poster of a baseball player he couldn't quite make out. It looked a lot like he hoped his son's room would look in a few years. Suddenly, he missed his kids terribly.

Louis pulled the door shut. "This way, please."

He led him into his home office where Razz got enveloped by an amazingly plush leather couch and waited.

"Cigar?" asked Louis, opening a box of contraband Cubans.

"No, thanks. I need to get back to work, that is, unless you're firing me or something."

Louis looked at him, very serious, and for a moment, Razz thought firing him was exactly what he'd do. Then he laughed. "You, my friend, are truly paranoid."

Razz remembered he'd said that about him before, though, under the current circumstances, he felt any level of paranoia justified.

"Relax, I just wanted to give you this." Louis handed him a bulky, letter-sized envelope.

To the touch, it felt full of dollar bills. Razz waited for an explanation.

"It's just a thank you for a job well-done. Open it."

When Razz counted fifteen one hundred dollar bills, he almost gagged.

"The restaurants are doing better than expected and I like to share my success with the people who help make it happen."

Razz wasn't used to having so much of his own money in his hand. "That's very generous, but there's no—"

"There's more where that came from. Just keep doing what you're doing. You can declare it, or not. It's up to you. You know, there's a lot of cash in the restaurant business."

Though he appeared bemused by his joke attempt, all Razz could wonder was where else this cash could be coming from.

Louis sensed his hesitance. "Listen," he said, more serious now, "half of the people in this town work for me and the other half want to. You're my guy in the restaurant business, if you want to be. Don't hesitate to use that phone I gave you. I'm here to help you. Do you keep it with you?"

"Oh, sure." Razz patted his right front pocket as if to prove it.

"Good." Louis pushed back his chair, the meeting over. He had said what he wanted, offered his incentive, hooked Razz by the gills and reeled him in.

Razz thought about this money, this gift, this bonus, this bribe, whatever one wanted to call it, given to him in return for his hard work and allegiance, and he thought about all the money the restaurants were now making. He deserved his fair share. He thought about Louis, his home, and his family, and realized they shared much in common. Then he considered Louis' background, businesses, and the violence he'd allegedly used, and he decided to give the envelope back, his better self again in charge. He was determined not to be a part of such cash payments, whether declared for taxes or not, but before he could complete the act, there was a noise at the front door.

The sounds of happy children, Ronnie, Caitlin, Patrick, and Melanie, filled the home. Then he heard Sarah's voice and all thoughts went to his family.

"Come, let's say hello," said Louis, smiling a winner's smile.

Razz stuffed the envelope into his pocket next to the cell phone, his better self ignored for now, and he walked into the hall.

"Dad! Daddy!"

Ronnie and Caitlin raced to their father and gleefully jumped into his arms, almost bowling him over.

"What are you doing here, Daddy?" asked Caitlin with the innocence only a child could possess.

The irritated look on Sarah's face was anything but innocent, and she wanted to know why Razz was there, too.

The profound joy he felt at seeing his kids left him. Though deep down he was pleased to see Sarah, his surface told her he wasn't pleased to see her here. And that only irritated her more. Without a word, they were fighting again.

He lowered his adoring and adorable children down to earth and kissed each one. "I was just talking with my friend here."

"You're fwiends with Melanie's daddy?" asked Caitlin, voicing the question on her mother's mind as well.

He looked at Sarah, Ronnie, and Caitlin, at Louis, Merice, and their children, then back to Caitlin. "Yes, I am."

"Yay! Yay!" yelled Caitlin, and then Ronnie joined in. Soon, Patrick and Melanie were jumping and laughing with them without understanding or caring about the cause for such celebration.

First, Louis laughed, then Merice, then Razz and then, grudgingly, Sarah laughed, too.

"Who wants a drink?" asked Louis.

Razz looked to Sarah, silently forgiving her and asking for her forgiveness. She looked away and his hopes waned.

"I'll have a Chardonnay, if you have it, please," she said. "And I think my husband still likes beer."

They had declared a truce for now.

Razz had been easily convinced to stay for dinner and, after several courses of delicious, homemade Mexican cuisine, pleasant small talk, and one-too-many beers, he was bursting at the seams to tell his crime-fighting secret. Sarah had been cordial, but noncommittal, all night, and he was dying to improve his position with her. When the kids scrambled for supper remnants in a quesadilla free-for-all, they were sent to the playroom, and he couldn't hold back any longer.

"I've got a secret," he said, eschewing all subtlety or story technique.

The others looked up, expectant.

"You know the thing in the paper a few weeks ago, about the clown that was tied up under the Pier?"

"Oh, that was so terrible," said Merice.

"I can't believe anyone could do something like that," Sarah chimed in, united in disgust with her friend.

"Well," he said, pausing for effect and because he knew he needed to be careful about how much he told them, "we found the killer."

His audience shared in surprise, but for decidedly different reasons.

"And you won't believe who did it."

Louis and Merice appeared intrigued, but Sarah had one question on her mind. "We?"

Razz hesitated, not quite understanding.

"You said 'we.' Why are you involved in something like that?"

Hoping for a more appreciative response, he backpedaled. "Well, my friend, he's a cop. Uh, I helped him."

"But why would you get involved?"

"Well, my cop friend, I mean, because the clown guy had lived at the Hempstead, he thought your father might have had something to do with it."

"What? My father wouldn't hurt anyone."

"I know. I know he wouldn't. That's why I got involved, to help him, to help Richard. Anyway, you'll read about it in the next couple days."

She didn't know what to say, but it was clear she wasn't as proud of Razz as he was of himself.

Louis tried to help. "That's impressive, amazing, really."

"And I didn't do it during work hours, only before and after. Just so you know."

"No, no, that's fine. Citizens should help law enforcement officials whenever they can. I'm surprised, that's all."

"Me, too," added Sarah, but her tone indicated her surprise wasn't as pleasant.

"Well, congratulations," said Merice. "Would anyone like dessert?"

Sarah had no interest in dessert. "So, while you and I have been dealing with certain issues, you've chosen to neglect your family—"

"I haven't neglected—"

"—to play cops and robbers," she said more forcefully. "Is that right?"

"No, yes, I mean, no. What do you want me to say? I was trying to help Richard, to help you."

She stared in disbelief. "You just don't get it, do you?"

He had no idea why she was upset. It just proved to him again that men and women were entirely different species.

Sarah stood up. "Thank you for dinner, but I need to be going. I have to work tomorrow." She directed "work" toward Razz to grind its blunt point in as painfully as possible. "And Caitlin has school."

"Of course," said Merice, disappointed, "I'll get your kids."

"No, I'll get them, Merice."

"I've got to get mine ready for bed anyway. You finish things with your husband."

She caught herself, but it was too late, her words hung in the air, inviting a response, and Sarah took full advantage of it.

Razz could see his wife's mouth move at normal speed, but her words sounded distorted, as if they were spoken by an alien, by that very different female species he often couldn't understand. But, this time, her meaning was all too clear.

She said, "We already are finished."

Before he could respond, Ronnie ran in. "Mom! Dad! Look what Patrick gave me!" He beamed as he displayed a special gift from his friend and he wanted everyone to appreciate it as much as he did.

Sarah glanced at the baseball card of Albert Pujols, St. Louis Cardinals, 1999, but she was far less enthusiastic. "That's nice, Ronnie. Thank you, Patrick. Now get ready, we're leaving."

"Look, Daddy! It's a baseball card."

Razz knew it was an impressive gift for a three-year-old, that it might become quite valuable one day, and that he couldn't care in the least. He turned to his wife. "What did I do wrong this time? Come on, I was trying to help. Please."

Ronnie's sudden moping would have broken the heart of an ogre, but it couldn't budge that of a parent in the middle of a spousal argument.

"Thank you, Merice. Thank you, Louis. It was very kind of you. Sorry, I have to run." She didn't even look at Razz, but grabbed the hand of a despondent Ronnie and confused Caitlin.

"What's the wush, Mommy?"

The jerk of her little arm was the only answer she received as Sarah dragged both of her children outside.

"Sarah! Wait!" He could only watch as she helped their kids into the Range Rover.

"Sarah," he said, more softly, as she drove away. Caitlin looked at him from the back seat, helpless, and he could tell little Ronnie was crying. Razz' heart was now officially broken.

"Th-thank you," he sputtered to his hosts.

"It will all work out. I'm sure of it," said Merice. "I'll talk to her."

"You two have done so much already. Thank you."

For the second time that night Louis placed his hand on Razz' shoulder. "We're here when you need us. Just ask."

Razz looked into his deep brown eyes and almost fell in. "Thank you for everything," he said, forgetting now all the dubious circumstances surrounding Louis and his restaurant takeover. "Excuse me, but I've got to get back to work."

"No, no, take the night off. I'll call Lotta. She'll understand."

Razz wasn't as sure she would, but he didn't relish the prospects of dealing with difficult customers all night. After the night's run-in with his wife, his patience reservoir was severely depleted.

"Maybe you're right. I promise I'll make it up to you."

"I'll count on it." Louis slapped him on the back in the way men do, as if a bit of painful camaraderie can somehow cure the deepest of hurt feelings.

Oddly, it seemed to work this time. Razz did feel better. He shook Louis' hand and hugged Merice, and then walked across the street to his car.

His hosts waved as he drove away, then Louis nodded acknowledgement to his men hidden in the ever-present black Mercedes.

"Let's go get our kids."

He put his arm around his wife lovingly, and they walked into their home and closed the door.

Once again, Razz had angered his wife and did it without knowing how. *She got mad because I tried to help her and her father, for God's sake. It's not like I threw a cognac glass. I didn't call him a rotten bastard. I just proved he didn't murder a Pier clown.* He believed it might really be over between them and was surprised the possibility no longer crushed him.

He drove aimlessly, turning down streets at random, first toward the beach, then away from it, then north, then south. He wasn't ready to sit, alone, in his apartment this early in the evening. He'd worked nights for the past ten years, but had seen enough thirty-second television commercials to know he'd probably shoot himself if he was stuck in front of a television all night.

If my marriage really is over, maybe it's time to see other women. Maybe I should see Lotta. Thinking of her softness, her beauty, her sex, excited him. *There could be a lot worse things than to have her as my fallback position,* he mused.

Then he thought about his relationship with Louis and Merice. They were treating him better than anyone else in his life right now, even his parents. He remembered how negatively his mom and dad had reacted when told of his new working relationship. *What do they know? My father's worked hard for forty years and all he has to show for it is a bad back.*

With his left hand on the wheel, he squeezed his right hand into his front pocket and took out the money envelope. He was soon fixated by it. *Fifteen hundred dollars. Cash.* He wondered if he'd receive that much every month and he did the multiplication in his head. *Fifteen times twelve is what? Ten times fifteen is fifteen thousand, plus three thousand equals eighteen thousand dollars. With my salary and equity build-up, maybe I'll be able to buy a house in a couple years. Have room for a yard for the kids, maybe a small pool.* He knew they'd love that.

It was a beautiful evening, warm with clear skies. He marveled at the rocky ride he'd been on in his personal life, but he saw better things ahead, with or without Sarah. For the first time in a long while, he felt like he could make it on his own. He felt like a man. *It's funny how money in your pocket will do that for you.*

When he looked up from his treasure, he found himself veering over the centerline and only a hundred feet from the Pier's connecting bridge. He jerked the wheel to center the Mustang in his lane, and then turned toward the Pier. It seemed relatively quiet, normal for this time of year. Still, he knew the restaurants would be busy and Lotta would be exhausted. He considered going for a drink at the Vista del Mar Hotel less than a quarter mile down the beach to try his hand at meeting attractive, lonely women, but guilt and the recognition that Lotta held more interest for him made him pull into the Surf's Up parking lot.

The outside patio was busier than it should have been, and the sight made Razz hesitate. That drink at the Vista del Mar sounded better and better. Torn, he took the easy way out and decided to walk down to the Sol a Sol. He'd check on things there, knowing Julio had everything under control, but it would give him time to gather his thoughts.

Red, green, and blue colored lights from the Ferris wheel danced on the side of his face as he walked past the amusement park. A child's shriek of joy from the roller coaster made him turn and he saw a mirrored image hanging from the side of a French fry stand that made him cringe. Looking back at him was a person he barely recognized. Distorted by the flickering colored lights, his face looked like that of a clown. A Pier clown.

He turned and sped toward the Sol a Sol. Despite his efforts to run from his memories, a fair-skinned young woman languishing on a bench reminded him of Sarah. An old, grizzled fisherman reminded him of the fateful day when he dodged fishing lines to conquer the Pier. The shiny new police substation reminded him of Robert Donati.

By the time he'd reached the back door of the Sol a Sol, he was winded and sweating. He ducked inside and snuck upstairs, avoiding any employees that might need his attention. His jaunt down the Pier had been anything but relaxing and he questioned his decision to return to work. *I'll just rest a while, maybe do a little paperwork, and then go home.*

Walking down the hallway, he noticed a light peeking through the slightly opened door of Louis' office. *Louis couldn't be here. Could he?*

Razz wondered how much time he'd spent driving aimlessly and would have looked at his watch had he ever worn one. He'd never bothered as a youth, because he hadn't cared whether he was early, late, or if he even got to where he was headed most of the time. As an adult, he was usually close enough to a clock to know the time if he wanted to, though he often still didn't. Not used to carrying a cell phone, he forgot he was a walking, breathing time machine. But thinking of a clock reminded him of the clock on top of City Hall, which reminded him of collecting pubic hairs from the second floor bathroom, which reminded him of the Mayor.

It was hopeless. He didn't possess the concentration to add two plus two, let alone resolve invoices. *Maybe I'll just say hello, and then go home like Louis told me to do in the first place.*

He reached out to knock when he noticed the chain lock attached on the other side. Curious, he peaked through the opening and saw that it wasn't Louis inside. It was Lotta, and she was counting money. Then Razz saw the huge open safe and the stacks upon stacks of bound bills filling it. The two restaurants operating at many times capacity couldn't generate that amount of money.

He watched her count bills, stack them, bind them with rubber bands, and place them in the safe. She appeared well-practiced and in a hurry. He wondered how much money had gone through her pretty little fingers and how much of it had been illegitimate. He touched the envelope in his pocket filled with hundred dollar bills and felt sick to his stomach. He backed away into the shadows, but, as he did, a weakness in the old floorboards made them creak.

Lotta whirled. "¡Mierda!" she spewed, then pushed her chair away and strode to the door.

Razz froze. He heard her approaching and saw her hand reach for the chain, and, finally, he sprang into action. He deftly sidestepped a mop and broom and hid behind an old metal locker where the mop and broom were supposed to be stored.

So he wouldn't breathe too loudly, he imagined being pummeled underwater by thousands of gallons of pounding surf after wiping out on a big wave. In such a situation, there was nothing to do but hold your breath and wait until you could rise again to the surface or they found you washed up on the shore. He was in the same situation now. He would hold his breath until he could escape or until he was discovered and interrogated for spying.

He heard the chain slide lock unlatch and the door open. He focused on tons of water cascading over him as office light spilled into the hallway. He imagined himself pinned against a sandy beach bottom and it felt like he was there for longer than any human could possibly survive. Finally, the light from Louis' office faded. He wondered if he might not be passing out, but, when he heard the door's bolt lock click shut, he knew he'd outlasted the imaginary water and the very real Lotta. He'd survived. He drew several quiet, deep breaths, and then tiptoed down the hall, past his office, down the stairs and out into the night air.

Razz McNeil would not be working this evening.

28

Robbie violently shifted his weight to his back left foot (he was a goofy-footer which made this day's task all the more difficult, having to cut back facing away from shore) and swerved his board to the left just in time, the end of his board barely nicking the surprised and disappointed piling.

Friday, January 28, 2005

The next morning at ten o'clock, when Richard Gold walked down the hall of the twenty-seventh floor of Gold Tower, morose didn't begin to describe him. In fact, walking didn't begin to describe how he moved. He seemed to creep, not out of stealth or motive, but because there wasn't enough energy in his body to move any faster. His vacant eyes blankly followed the path of his shuffling footsteps and his shoulders stooped forward and down, as if he'd given up his battle with gravity.

He approached Natalie Wesson's office and his gaze shifted to the empty office. A tiny, pathetic sigh escaped into the air. If he slowed, it was imperceptible, for he hadn't expected to see her. He hadn't seen her since he'd signed the documents handing over ten percent of the equity in the Gold Shore two days earlier.

"Daddy, are you all right?" Sarah had seen him in various states of elation, anger, and depression over the years, but had never seen him quite so broken.

Gold raised a corner of his lip slightly, as if to smile in reassurance, but he didn't speak. It was obvious he wasn't all right. She took his arm, her heart breaking, despite the pain her father had caused her. He'd continually sided with Natalie Wesson, but now, all she could think about was how to ease his anguish. Although it's always difficult for a child to see parents age, in this case, it had happened virtually overnight. If he'd had a stroke, heart attack, or some rapidly debilitating disease, she might have understood. It would have made sense in life's random sort of way. But Richard Gold's disease was love. And it had struck him down quickly.

Gold wearily lowered himself into his chair with an assist from his daughter. He looked up at her. "Has she called?"

When Sarah hesitated, he continued, knowing she hadn't, "I hope she's all right."

"I'm sure she's fine," she said, looking out toward the street below. She turned to him, affecting enthusiasm, "I'll make some calls to find her."

"You do that."

She walked to the door and briefly looked back.

Her father was already asleep.

Mayor Jaime Hidalgo's day wasn't starting any better than Richard Gold's. However, when Sharky Sampson, Johnnie Johnson, and two San Margarita police officers showed up at City Hall with a warrant for his arrest, he reacted with defiance.

"You have no idea what you're getting into, Officer. You will never work in this town again!"

"Tell it to the judge," said Sharky as he slapped cuffs onto Hidalgo's wrists. "Where are Larry, Curly, and Moe? We'd like to talk with them."

When Hidalgo hesitated, Sharky explained. "Where are your bodyguards, your driver?"

"I don't know."

Sharky tightened the cuffs and the Mayor winced. "Suit yourself. Want to try again?"

"I don't know, I told you."

Just a threat to tighten the cuffs again convinced Hidalgo to be more cooperative. "They didn't show up this morning. My wife brought me to work."

"Sure she did." He yanked the Mayor toward the door. "We'll find them."

When they exited the back door of City Hall, a hundred cameras seemed to flash at once, blinding Sharky. "Get them the hell out of here!"

The genie was out of the bottle. The press had learned of the Mayor's impending arrest and had arrived within minutes of the police, followed closely by a local TV news crew. Although San Margarita was a small city, it boasted seventeen daily or weekly rags, in addition to the main source of news, the *Monitor*. Most were located within a five-block radius of City Hall. No one jaywalked in San Margarita without someone noticing and putting it in writing somewhere, but, even for such a major event as a mayor's arrest, this outpouring seemed excessive, especially because Sharky had gotten the warrant only thirty minutes earlier.

It became less suspicious seconds later when Chief Wilson's car sped down the alley toward them. Wilson hopped out wearing a camera-friendly smile amidst more flashing. Sharky wasn't sure, but he even thought he saw the Chief wink.

At first, the press attention irritated Sharky, then he was annoyed at having to share it. He was happier moments later, however, when Wilson Chief quieted the crowd and said, "We should all be grateful for the good work of police detectives like Sergeant Gerard Sampson in helping to keep San Margarita one of the best and safest places to live."

With that, the cameras flashed again catching Wilson, Hidalgo, and Sharky within their frames. Hidalgo glowered, Wilson smiled confidently, and Sharky beamed a hero's smile.

This time, he would look very good on the front page.

"Yes, a Natalie Wesson. Uh-huh. She graduated from the Business School. Within the last five or six years, I think." As Sarah waited for a response through the phone line from thousands of miles away in New York City, she looked over Natalie Wesson's suspiciously spotty employment record. There was no address listed, only a P.O. Box number. She had called Wesson's phone number and received a disconnection message, though she doubted it had ever worked. Natalie Wesson had begun work at Gold Development Corp. only four weeks before, and, although she'd left a lasting impact in those weeks, she'd disappeared into the ether from which she seemed to have come.

"Hello? You still there?"

The woman's voice jolted Sarah back to the present. "Yes, I'm here."

"I'm sorry, but there's no record of a Natalie Wesson graduating from the Business School."

"Maybe she didn't graduate. Maybe she only went one year. Could you check?"

"Actually, according to our records, there's never been a Natalie Wesson enrolled at the Business School. Ever."

Sarah leaned back in her chair and pondered her next move. *Maybe Wesson exaggerated by claiming an MBA. People lie on resumes all the time.*

"How about undergraduate business? Maybe she went to the college."

After a moment, Sarah heard "I'll check" offered with little enthusiasm.

Almost immediately, the woman responded again. "There's no record of a Natalie Wesson here in the last fifteen years."

The little hope Sarah had left her. It looked like Wesson may have lied about everything, and she wondered what other unhappy surprises she'd find in her wake. "Well, thank you for checking."

Sarah waited for the woman to hang up, but she didn't right away. "Hello?"

"There is one listing of a Sharon Natalie Wesson."

"Oh?"

"But it's from nineteen-eighty-eight, so I doubt she's who you're looking for."

"Eighty-eight?"

"And she studied theatre arts, not business. Sorry I couldn't be more help."

"Thanks for trying."

An actress? That makes sense. Whoever she is and for whatever reason, she fooled all of us. But could she really be almost forty? Sarah felt jealous of her all over again, then realized she'd never been around Wesson long enough to dispute her claimed age of twenty-eight.

She looked again at Wesson's employment card. The company knew nothing about this woman who had so influenced her father. Sarah couldn't ask the person, who hired her, because Masterson had not been seen since the day he left. His departure had led to the downfall of Wendy, which had led to the rise of Natalie Wesson. Cause and effect, in microcosm. Sarah knew the cause, but still wasn't sure of the full force of the effect.

A web search yielded information on a number of Wessons, but not on anyone resembling their target. Several internet background checks utilizing first names, Natalie and Sharon, cost forty-nine-ninety-five each, but, after hopeful phone calls, each lead proved fruitless. Sarah believed she'd reached a dead-end until, while rifling through her Rolodex, she came across a business card that gave her pause. On it, read the name, *Herbert Winston, Esquire*, and a Los Angeles phone number.

She dialed.

Jaime Hidalgo made bail of a half million dollars and walked out of the Ninth Street police station a free man, at least, temporarily. Sharky had wanted to hold him at a small, out-of-the-way station to avoid a public spectacle, but his recommendation had been rejected. A huge crowd awaited Hidalgo's release after Judge Hiram Askew set a bail amount against the District Attorney's wishes, because Askew didn't consider Hidalgo a flight risk. He also figured Hidalgo didn't have access to that kind of money, but he'd been wrong. Although Jaime Hidalgo was of relatively modest means and was now damaged goods to lenders and bail bondsmen, he still had one wealthy supporter, his lover, Graydon Lord, super-agent to Hollywood's mega-stars.

Sharky recognized him as the mystery man he'd seen with Hidalgo at Mae's. And when a smiling Lord accompanied Hidalgo out of the police station, it was clear Lord wasn't representing a new client in hopes of selling some tell-all memoir. No, they walked down the station steps holding hands. The cameras captured everything. The press was clearly intent on making big news of Hidalgo's sexual orientation, but Hidalgo didn't seem to care. Perhaps, he was relieved he'd never again have to meet a lover surreptitiously. His secret was out and split wide-open for mass consumption, and he strode proudly, his head held high.

When he and Lord reached Lord's waiting limousine, he turned back and waved his hands, imploring quiet from the crowd. "Thank you. Thank you all for being here today to capture this travesty of justice. I want you to know I will fight all accusations, all charges, all falsehoods. I am innocent."

Had his wife been there, she might have disagreed with his innocence claim. Marie Hidalgo had been her husband's wife in name only for several years, since shortly after their third son was born. She had played the good wife, partly because of his budding political career, but mainly for her sons. She knew she couldn't change him, even though she'd fought with him constantly in trying, but she could still offer a semblance of a normal family life. It would all be for naught when the papers hit that afternoon's newsstands.

Hidalgo waved to the crowd, offering a broad, confident smile only a politician could muster under such dire circumstances. Then he and his partner got into the limo's back seat and closed the door behind them, momentarily escaping public scrutiny.

Razz wore a path in his apartment's newly laid carpet, pacing from living room to bedroom and back again, contemplating his task that night. In his right hand, he clutched the fifteen hundred dollars Louis had given him, and, occasionally, he stopped to gaze at the hundred dollar bills. They reminded him of the stacks of bills he'd seen in Louis' safe and that troubling memory impelled him to want to find out from where all that money had come. But to do it, he'd have to find a way into Louis' office without leaving a trace that he'd been there.

He could get in by hiring a locksmith to make him a key, but that information would get back to Lotta and then to Louis. He could remove the screws to the door's lock assembly and temporarily remove the lock, but that would crack the surrounding paint and leave a telltale sign of entry. The only windows overlooked the water and the first floor patio, respectively, and neither opening could be reached in any inconspicuous way. As he checked off his options, it looked as though he had only one choice. He'd have to climb through the tiled ceiling into Louis' office and hope he didn't knock a tile to the floor or fall through himself.

Razz had repeated this pattern for over an hour, living room, bedroom, stop, think, bedroom, living room, stop, think, and he'd begun to tire of the scenery. He stuffed the money into his pants pocket and walked out into the hazy sunshine.

He meandered down a side-walked street, breathing deeply, happy to clear his head of stale thoughts in the fresh air. But, when a Kenilworth diesel hauling a load of organic produce blasted him with its noxious exhaust, he realized that fresh air in LA was a misnomer.

He soon found himself outside a small home he vaguely recognized. It had been several days since he'd spoken with his parents, so he was pleased to find himself outside their new home. But when he saw his mother admiring her tiny rose garden, he hesitated. His life history coursed at hyper speed through his brain, his carefree youth to his now troubled adulthood, and, finally, he thought of Sarah and his kids. When he did, he knew his opportunity had passed. He just didn't have the strength. Razz dropped his head, and then realized his right hand was clutching his fifteen hundred dollars, squeezing the tender as if strangling it would prevent it from telling its sordid secrets.

"You want some coffee?" Sarah asked as brightly as she could muster. She put a full cup on her father's desk in front of him.

His only response was a grunt and a slight shift of his head, but he didn't look up. It seemed as though his head were steel and the earth a huge magnet, and it took all his strength to keep from crashing to the floor.

"Daddy? You want to look at the Heaven Crest deal?"

She hoped that by tantalizing him with his first love, money, she could lure him out of his funk, but Richard Gold gave no indication of interest. She turned away, beaten again by Natalie Wesson, the mystery woman who, even in her absence, was more powerful. She was glad when the office suite's front buzzer sounded.

Sarah made her way down the hall. Although there were plenty of secretaries and assistants, it gave her some relief to create distance between her and the oppressiveness of the corner office.

"Hi, sign here, please," said an excessively cute, twenty-something UPS man holding an electronic signature pad.

She wouldn't have even noticed his excessive cuteness had the man not maneuvered to look up into her face.

"Are you all right? You're too beautiful to be sad."

She found herself gazing into the deepest brown eyes she'd ever seen. And those eyes were surrounded by perfect, pouty lips, a piercing jaw line, and an enticing, brilliantly white smile, all supported by a taut, seemingly fat free body.

She smiled back. "Thank you. I needed that."

He smiled more broadly and, if you had asked her what name she had just signed into the register, she wouldn't have been able to say for sure. But she smiled a bit wider, too, and took the package from him.

"I've noticed you here before. I just never had a chance to speak with you," he said.

Sarah subconsciously twirled her wedding band, her hand at her side, crossing her same-hand thumb over to her ring finger. It appeared she had an itch and was trying to scratch it.

"Too bad." She turned away, embarrassed, when she realized she was actually flirting.

The man watched her, eager to play this game of cat and mouse, but she cautiously avoided him by tearing open the envelope from the County Recorder and leafing through a notice of recordation. A look of shock came over her and, suddenly, she didn't care about anything the handsome UPS man might say.

"Daddy!" She tore down the hall and into his office like a downhill racer whizzing past a gate. "What the hell is this?"

Despite the monumental effort it required, Gold lifted his head. "What is what, dear?"

"This, Daddy! This!"

He took the document. When he read the cover page, a perplexed look came over him. He turned to the next page and his body tightened, his teeth clenched, and his face turned crimson. He leafed through the rest of the document until he came to the final page and his signature, where he paused.

"Tell me you didn't sign this, Daddy. Please!"

Gold was wholly confused. It wasn't the document he thought he'd signed when Natalie Wesson was having her way with his manhood. But all that mattered was that the recorded document gave Cardinal Acquisition ten percent of the equity in the Gold Shore Hotel and Resort as well as, which was the unexpected problem, the right to one hundred percent in the case of default on the project's construction loan. All Cardinal Acquisition had to do was cure the defaulted loan. Without knowing it, Gold had potentially signed away his ownership in the Gold Shore for a hand job. And the document was recorded for the world to see.

"What were you thinking?"

He wasn't about to tell her what he'd been thinking or with what he'd thought it. But he was no longer a frail old man with nothing to live for. No, now he was an angry old man that lived for revenge.

"That fucking bitch! That slut!"

Sarah resisted stating her concurrence as Gold paced randomly about the office. His anger had jump-started his brain and he was already thinking of the myriad ways in which he could create an ugly death upon Natalie Wesson's beautiful body.

"I'll kill that fucking whore."

She wasn't sure she liked his tone, but would hardly have stopped him in the act.

Gold shifted smoothly into business mode, survival mode, and Sarah shifted into high gear with him. "Find her. Find anyone who knows her. Call Herb Winston, have him check—"

"He's working on it." She waited, pad and pen in hand, ready to take down his every word, so she could execute them to his satisfaction.

Gold studied her for a moment, and then smiled proudly. "That's my girl."

She blushed, but he gave her no time to wallow. "Get Harold Baines on the phone. I'll collateralize the project, maybe refinance this building, and see if he'll stretch out our term. Call Dave Manning and tell him to speed up the job, to do whatever it takes. Oh, and get a hundred thousand dollar check drafted for Local 416. I don't want any more trouble."

When he took time for a breath, Sarah knew that was her cue to move. She hurried to a secretary's station outside his office. Whatever had happened to make her father sign such a flawed agreement, he was back to the Richard Gold that she, despite his failings, loved. She would be right by his side working to save his namesake resort.

Harold Baines on three," she hollered through the open door, and then she dialed another number.

Gold picked up the line. "Harold, how are you? How's the golf game? We've got to play—"

Cut-off in mid-ingratiating-sentence, Gold's surprised look turned sour, then horrified. A moment later, he hung up the phone, sprang from his chair, and met Sarah hurrying in the doorway.

"We've got a problem," they said simultaneously.

"Come on," said Gold. Then they raced down the hall and out the front door.

One person who didn't appear to have a problem was Louis Marcayda. Surrounded by stacks of hundred dollar bills in his Sol a Sol office, he smiled, satisfied, then hung up his telephone. He looked over at Lotta. "It's started," he said.

She nodded. "Things could get ugly."

"Yes, but not for us." He kissed her on her forehead gently, the kind of kiss one gets from a dear friend. "Take care, cousin."

Lotta considered their journey to this point, from the difficulties of growing up in and out of the gangs of Tijuana through Louis' rise and business success in America. They'd been through a lot together. "You, too, cousin."

"Don't worry. Everything will be fine." He placed ten of the one-inch stacks of cash in his briefcase. "Put down "ten" for petty cash, Surf's Up, please."

He walked out, briefcase in hand, and Lotta locked the door behind him. A worried look on her face, she moved toward the large safe. Its heavy steel door was ajar, but, instead of locking it, she strained to open it wider. She looked inside and smiled, instantly mesmerized by millions of dollars in exquisite cash.

Her reassurance was complete.

Richard Gold wasn't reassured; he was horrified. By the time he and Sarah reached the Gold Shore job site, every single union had struck and construction workers were leaving the job en masse.

"What the hell are you doing?" he asked, as if he could not believe the all-too-obvious facts. "We've worked together for thirty years. When haven't I been fair to you?"

Although many of the men had worked on his projects before, and Gold did grudgingly pay union wages, today wasn't yesterday, last week, or thirty years ago. And none of them seemed to care anything about loyalty. "Hey, old man, good luck building the rest of it," said a twenty-something-year-old man with long blonde hair and a sunburned face.

A tough-looking Latino with weathered skin peppered with tattoos was more personal. "Maybe your girlfriend will help you," he said, staring at Sarah.

Gold sprang toward the man, directing a clenched fist straight at his face.

"Daddy!"

The instinctive attack was an impressively athletic maneuver for a man of his age, but the tattooed man sidestepped his punch and Gold fell onto the dry, gravelly ground.

"Daddy! Daddy!" Sarah knelt to help him as a chorus of catcalls and taunts grew. He shoved aside her hand, his embarrassment winning out over his appreciation.

"Daddy, daddy," said another worker, laughing.

"Help, Daddy, help!" mocked the tattooed man in a falsetto voice, his hands clasped at his chest.

Gold rose slowly, gathering himself for another attack.

"Don't bother with them," Sarah pleaded, but he was too proud. A woman could bring him to his knees, but he'd fight a man, or many men, to his death. Gold clenched his right fist, drawing it back, preparing to strike again, but before he could leap at the laughing, hateful brown face, someone yelled, "Stop!"

Amazingly, everyone did. The crowd of callous, work-hardened men stopped their taunts and meekly turned away, and Gold unclenched his fist.

A man of Mexican heritage, in his sixties, with silver-hair and a clean, crisp, beige uniform, strode forward. He wore his immense dignity on his sleeve and in his voice and in every move he made. He stood before Sarah. "Are you all right, Miss Gold?"

She nodded gratefully and reached for his extended hand.

"I hope you can forgive these men. Some people have no appreciation for those who have helped them over many years. But I do, Miss Gold."

He bowed respectfully, gently released her hand, and then approached Richard Gold. He grasped Gold's right hand in both of his as if he could double his already-absolute sincerity.

"Mr. Gold, my friend, I pray you will accept my sincerest apologies. My men seem to have forgotten the great respect they owe to you."

"Don Julio, what happened? I don't understand."

"Nor do I, sir. You have always been fair to me and to my men, but I no longer know the people who control our union. Nor do I understand what drives them. And I am sorry, for I know, in previous times, this would never have happened."

"But you don't understand. Just not now, it can't happen now," Gold pleaded.

Don Julio straightened, taller, as if to remind Richard Gold of his own pride and stature. "You are right, sir. I do not understand much about this world anymore. You were wrong on one point though; all any of us have is now—right now. I'm sorry."

With that, Don Julio Marquez, the Laborer Foreman, led his now-obedient men through the gated fence and out of the yard, before turning back. He raised his hand to wave good-bye to Richard Gold. Both men sensed he was also waving good-bye to an era and that neither of them would be the same again.

Richard Gold did not respond, again weakening into the helpless old man he had been earlier that morning. He looked around him, surveying his construction site, once gloriously humming with activity, but now like a deserted ranch town after the water has dried up. "I'm going to lose everything."

Sarah's silence confirmed what they both knew—Richard Gold's empire was in jeopardy. His personal guarantee on the Gold Shore bank loan could bankrupt him, because his great wealth wasn't liquid, it was in real estate. It would take time to raise cash and time was not something that Gold had in abundance.

When vultures start hovering, sensing death, they don't wait for their prey to die, but only until it's defenseless enough not to fight back. Bankers and businessmen were no different than vultures, and Richard Gold appeared primed for picking.

Whimpering, face down in the dusty earth, his helplessness seemed complete. From impotent young child, to growing adolescent, to powerful adult, to feeble old man, his life had arrived full-circle.

Tears gushing, Sarah looked toward the sky as if pleading for Divine guidance and strength. Or, perhaps, she was just looking for vultures.

29

Indeed, the Pier seemed to have come to life, with each piling making its attempt to humble this foolish, young history-seeker. Only halfway through his trip, Robbie had already bumped two pilings, which would have thrown a lesser surfer into the water, or worse, into the pilings themselves. He had twice been temporarily blinded. He had dodged fishing lines and withstood surprise yelling and siren wails. And he still had to piss like a racehorse.

"Come again," Razz said without enthusiasm as a young couple walked past toward the front door of the Sol a Sol.

"Thanks, it was great," said the perky, feminine half of the couple, but Razz had already turned away, disinterested in small talk and distracted by larger matters.

His was rude behavior, for sure, but it was unintentional. Fortunately, Miss Perky's masculine partner wasn't as offended as she was and, despite her mild protestation, she was led out the door, probably never to return.

It was only four-thirty and Razz knew he was in for a long, difficult evening. Covering for Julio on his night off, he didn't expect it to be overly busy, the difficulty would lie in his need to feign interest when his real desire was to run upstairs and break down the door to Louis' office.

"You okay?"

Razz almost jumped out of his skin when he heard Lotta's voice. "Uh, yeah, sure," he said, too strenuously. He'd forgotten that she'd been upstairs working on the restaurant's books.

"More troubles at home?"

It seemed an innocent question, but, when Razz saw her moisten her lips alluringly, he remembered that "innocent" and "Lotta Gugliotta" should never be used together.

"No, yeah, no." He felt like a faucet had been turned on under his armpits. "I mean, everything's fine. Thanks for asking. I'll see you tomorrow."

Lotta was used to him acting strangely so she didn't question his current weirdness, and walked out onto the Pier.

Through a window, he saw her bundle her black leather coat protectively around her and he couldn't help but wonder how much cash she was trying to hide, then he remembered it was winter and a cold front had plunged temperatures down into the mid-fifties. She was probably just trying to stay warm.

Razz looked at the antique brass clock hanging from the far wall. It was now four-thirty-two.

"I just want to see it. It was going to be so beautiful."

Richard Gold was no longer crying prostrate upon the dusty ground. He had risen, sturdier now, and wanted to go up into the skinless structure of the Gold Shore Hotel and Resort.

Sarah worried her father wasn't strong enough. They walked together toward the construction elevator, but he refused her assistance.

"It still can be. We'll work it out, Daddy. It will be okay."

"I know, dear. Thank you for everything. You've always been the best of daughters." He squeezed her hand gently. "I hope you'll forgive me."

"There's nothing to forgive."

Richard Gold surprised her by leaning in to kiss her forehead. "Always my little girl. My precious, loving little girl."

She blushed, but Gold had already moved onto the open-air elevator platform. She proudly and obediently followed.

Huge steel I-beams and girders, welded together in supportive mazes, loomed above them. The structure looked like a huge, adult Lego play land, almost random in its sequencing, but it was the by-product of careful planning, great minds, strong backs, rugged machines, and mounds of money.

The platform groaned as the elevator cable strained against the winch's powerful insistence and then lurched upward, almost knocking Sarah over. At the controls, Richard Gold didn't notice. He was staring intently above him.

As they passed the first level, a gusting breeze blew the platform sideways. Sarah held tightly to a makeshift handle, fighting the urge to lie on the platform floor and close her eyes until it was over. Gold pressed on, full speed.

They passed the second level and, again, a gust of wind shifted the platform sideways making it screech against a steel guide pole. Sparks flew.

"Daddy? Could you slow down, please?"

If he heard her, he didn't let on. He kept his palm pressed hard against the control handle and looked skyward.

Although construction had begun only weeks earlier and the crew had lost hours to a slow-down, because of American ingenuity, hard work, and overtime, the structure still had risen to over forty-four feet above ground level and was sunk over thirty feet into the earth. It was an engineering and workmanship marvel, but it was still behind an aggressive schedule. With interest accruing on principal and interest accruing on interest, the Gold Shore had been a potential financial burden from the beginning. It was now an albatross, hanging heavily around Richard Gold's wealth, dragging it downward. But Gold kept looking skyward.

Sarah felt better when the platform finally clunked to a standstill four stories above San Margarita. When she stepped onto what was to be the fourth floor, she staggered against the swirling winds like a Saturday night drunk, still reeling from her ride in the elevator from hell. Because of the site's location on a cliff overlooking the Pacific Ocean and the Pier, even at only four stories, the view was impressive. She watched, mesmerized, as the flaming red winter sun extinguished itself into the Pacific. Despite the wind, the cold, and everything that had happened that day, it almost seemed peaceful.

"Daddy?"

She hesitated, her senses dulled by the intoxicating view. She couldn't quite believe her eyes as Richard Gold marched toward the western edge of the structure.

"Daddy?"

She tore into a sprint across the concrete decking covered randomly by orphaned two-by-fours, scaffolding supports, and power cords, which created for her an untimely obstacle course. She hurdled over a couple of steel beams like a high school track star.

"Daddy! Stop!"

Gold didn't speak, but seemed to shudder under the weight of what he was about to do and his daughter's love. He was only six feet from the edge and Sarah was still twenty feet away. She wouldn't get there in time.

"Stop! Please!"

Four feet. Three feet. Two. From here, Gold could see the ground below and just make out, through the dimness, where he would land. He took another step.

"Daddy, I love you!"

His right foot planted itself only inches from the structure's open western edge and it would take only one more step with his left foot to end all his pain, his feelings of betrayal, everything. The muscles, the tendons, every fiber in his foot strained, but Gold couldn't move, as if he were pulling against an irresistible force.

Sarah slowed to a walk, not daring to rush him and, perhaps, scare him into jumping.

An involuntary sob rose, escaping from deep inside Gold's being, and his shoulders heaved.

"Please, Daddy," she said softly.

His feet stayed planted as he turned to face her. His visage ripped at her more than her two childbirths had. Where his eyes used to be there seemed a void. He had done his cost/benefit analysis just as he had thousands of times during thousands of deals, and he'd decided the cost of living was greater than the benefit. It was simple economics.

The equation changed when Sarah said she loved him. Now Gold was at equilibrium, a Supreme Ambivalence, teetering in an uneasy truce with life. She could see it wouldn't take much to tip the balance the wrong way.

"We'll be okay, Daddy."

A gust of wind, stronger than those before, pushed her from the back. She took a step to steady herself, and then dread overcame her.

Her father twisted in the wind, like he was performing some strange, slow motion, Cosmic dance. He struggled to avoid that one extra step that would normally help, but, in this case, would be the step that would take him over the edge to his death. The breeze seemed to lure him, just as it pushed him, toward his Last Step.

"Daddy?"

Gold teetered forward, like a swimmer anticipating the starter's gun. Then he swayed backward, his legs splayed and he collapsed. "Aaggh!"

"Daddy!" She saw her father splayed on the concrete and she ran toward him.

"Stay away!" He dragged himself back from the precipice.

She stopped short, relieved and hurt at the same time. "Let me help you."

"Stay away from me!"

His anger and exertion seemed to drain whatever energy he had left. He had reached the depths of impotence. He was so feeble, so inept, that he couldn't even kill himself. He mumbled something.

"What, Daddy? What did you say?"

"I want Elizabeth."

Richard Gold wanted to see his wife.

It was only six-fifteen, but Razz couldn't wait to test his plan, so he was in his office attempting a dry run. Later that night, he hoped to climb up through a roof tile, down into Louis' office, find irrefutably damning evidence, and have everything well by morning.

He teetered on a wooden chair with one wobbly leg, straining to reach a ceiling tile. Standing on the chair's seat wasn't going to take him high enough, so he stepped onto the desk.

The well-worn oak desk, expensive when first made during the nineteen-fifties, was a remnant left over from previous ownership. Now barely worthy of a yard sale, it reminded him of his days with Paul, when he'd had to make do with a budget annoyingly close to zero. Louis had offered to replace it with a shiny, expensive new one befitting his position, but Razz declined, preferring not to have to worry about scratching it.

He pushed a few magazines to the floor to create foot space and climbed onto the old desk's scarred top. The fifty-year-old legs creaked beneath his weight. Razz' almost fifty-year-old legs creaked, too, and now he was more depressed than nervous. Being forty-five automatically meant you were on the downhill slide to fifty and, every now and again, his body did something to remind him of that fact. This time, it was as simple as his knee joint cracking. He tried to tell himself it didn't mean anything, but it did. Because no matter what your outlook about reaching the age of fifty, in ninety-nine percent of human lives, being fifty means your life is more than half over. If you hadn't accomplished your goals and dreams by then, it was unlikely you ever would. The world stacked the odds more and more against you once you arrived at the dreaded 5-O. Razz didn't have much time left.

He nudged at a faded ceiling tile and a cloud of dust and tile fiber puffed outward. The tile probably hadn't been changed since the restaurant was first built back in nineteen-sixty-two. It was heavy, almost an inch thick, easily breakable, and probably contained asbestos. It was a tile-type so prevalent from the fifties and sixties that most people preferred to ignore the fact its contents had been proven to kill them.

He coughed away as much of the pollutants as he could before lifting the tile carefully up out of its frame and setting it to one side. He was relieved the wall didn't go all the way up to the rafters, but left several feet through which he could maneuver. In the darkness above the dropped ceiling, he could just make out the two-by-eight inch rafters into which were nailed old, rusting wires, which supported the flimsy metal frames that held the crusty tiles in place. He reached for something solid by which he could pull himself up for a closer look, but he wasn't high enough to grab anything substantial.

"What are you doing?"

Razz almost fell off the side of his desk when he heard the male voice below. When he'd steadied himself, he looked and saw Julio watching him from the doorway.

"Hey. Uh, the tile was out of place, you know, kind of askew. It's been bothering me since I moved in." Razz laughed in the false way that hardly ever fooled anyone.

"Oh, I hadn't noticed," Julio said in the innocuously innocent way that hardly ever fooled anyone either.

It was an awkward standoff, but mostly for Razz, so he moved first. He repositioned the ceiling tile and it fell perfectly into place creating a wind current that spread more killer dust to attack any live lung tissue in its way. Because Julio had a direct line to Lotta, who had a direct line to Louis, killer dust didn't seem to be Razz' biggest problem.

"There, that's better," he said, stifling a cough. He inspected his handiwork a little too carefully, before turning his attention back to Julio. "So, what are you doing here?"

"I had to get something."

"Oh."

Again, each waited for the other's move, but Julio lost interest in their chess match. He opened a battered, gray metal locker, grabbed a DVD-sized package, and thrust it inside his leather bomber jacket.

Though he saw it for just an instant, Razz could tell it was wrapped in heavy brown paper. It reminded him of the mail-order pornography he used to receive every few weeks during his single days. A guy has a night off and needs some company, so he shares it with several sexy, naked, two-dimensional women. It all seemed pretty natural to him.

"Well, have a good night," said Julio.

"Yeah, you, too," said Razz in an overly personal way, but Julio avoided the innuendo and was already making his way toward the stairs.

Razz looked up at the ceiling tile and felt exposed and guilty. He jumped down from his desk, shaking the building's skeleton as well as his own, locked the office door as he left, and hurried back downstairs.

Elizabeth Gold hadn't flinched when Sarah told her that her husband of over forty years needed her nor had she when told just why he did. She hadn't flinched when she rode up the rickety construction elevator operating the controls herself, and she hadn't flinched when she stepped onto the open-walled Gold Shore fourth floor into a gusting wind. But she couldn't help herself when she saw her husband cowering at the edge of the precipice, shivering. The Ice Queen was genuinely moved.

"Richard?"

She glanced at Sarah, offering her the briefest reassurance that everything would be all right, but she kept moving toward her husband. Her daughter had done what she could. It was now up to her.

"Richard?"

Gold didn't respond, but stared straight ahead into the night. Lights from the Pier hundreds of yards away offered some illumination as did nearby street lights, but it was still dark on the fourth floor. It should have been treacherous travelling for Elizabeth Gold, but her steps seemed unusually sure as she made her way toward him.

When she'd gotten within ten feet, she stopped. Then she smiled a broad, confident smile. It seemed incongruous, like laughter at a funeral. Then Gold turned, as if just noticing she was there.

"Hi, Richard. May I join you?"

Gold hesitated, and then screamed, "No! Get away! I'll jump!"

Startled, Elizabeth's smile vanished, but it quickly returned along with her courage. "It's all right, dear. I'll wait. I'm right here behind you, just like I've been for forty-three years."

Sarah knew her mother had always stood behind her father, only sometimes it appeared she was holding a long, sharp knife to his back while standing there.

"It's beautiful up here, isn't it, Richard? What a view. It reminds me of your first project. Remember that? You built the first ten-story building in San Margarita. You could see for miles from the top of that building. Everyone was so skeptical at first, they fought against you tooth and nail, but you won them over. Then you invited them to view the building's progress and they were all so impressed to see firsthand how these buildings are created. It was a brilliant public relations move on your part. It helped you the rest of your career, because people knew you would create buildings that would last and that they would be beautiful. It wasn't a mysterious process anymore, so they weren't scared, not once they'd touch the steel girders, the concrete, had worn a hard hat. People trusted you after that, and that's why San Margarita is what it is today. Because of you."

"That was your idea," Gold said quietly. "It was your idea to let everyone see the construction."

"Was it? Well, you made everyone believe. You made them believe in their town. You made them believe in you."

Although still crouched inches away from oblivion, Gold no longer seemed like a coiled spring ready to leap.

"This town owes you a lot," Elizabeth continued.

"It owes us a lot," he responded, louder now.

As cynical about her parents' relationship as Sarah had been over the years, she started to become a believer. Her mother knew her father better than anyone, knew what he needed, how to motivate him, how to scold him, and how to give him enough hope and self-respect to keep him from jumping forty feet to his death. After all her father had put her through, his mistresses, his anger, and his selfishness, Sarah could see her mother still loved him. She didn't know why that made her feel so uncomfortable.

"I'm in trouble, Liz."

Sarah had never heard him refer to her mother as "Liz" and the familiarity surprised her. It seemed far more personal than the "Elizabeth" or "honey" or "dear" that she was used to.

"You've been in trouble before, Richie. You always found a way out."

Richie? Sarah felt like she was in the middle of her parents' bedroom watching their most personal of acts, but knew she couldn't turn away.

"Not like this, Liz. I could be ruined. I could lose everything."

"No, Richie, not everything. You'll always have me."

Sarah heard her father sob and saw his back heave upward. Then his body stiffened, as if to protect itself from an unbearable pain, as if the slightest movement would bring torture upon his person. Though it was only seconds, it felt to her like agonizing minutes before he responded

"Yes," he said. With that, his body seemed to relax again. He turned to his wife. "You look like an angel ... my angel."

"It must be the coat. It's Chanel." She was wearing a knee-length, white, wool Chanel coat that was outrageously expensive, but hardly angelic.

Sarah's spell was broken. Her father was struggling with life and death and her mother was discussing her designer coat. She wanted to scream so loudly that some sense, some understanding, might infiltrate her mother's head. Then her mother laughed. Sarah was about to argue, but then her father laughed, too. Then she knew everything would be all right.

Her parents had their own code, their own language. In any loving relationship, the right word at the right time can cut like a machete or bring giddy, uncontrollable laughter, even in a crisis. It made Sarah think of words she'd used to cut Razz, and she started feeling ill.

"May I join you?" asked Elizabeth, moving forward.

"You might get your angel coat dirty."

"That's okay. You'll buy me another one."

Sarah could not recall the last time she saw them enjoy each other, but here they were, laughing like school kids on a first date. Her mother sat down next to her father, white Chanel on dirty concrete, with her legs dangling over the edge. She didn't hesitate, didn't try to spare her Chanel, and didn't complain; she just wanted to be near her man. Richard Gold watched her every move proudly. Then he took her hand. Together, they looked out over the San Margarita Pier, over the Pacific Ocean, beyond the horizon, and reflected on their lives and their love.

It made Sarah want to cry. It made her want to see her husband.

30

He could see an excited crowd gathering on the beach and a rescue truck racing to join them, but he had more important things on his mind. To continue traveling under the Pier, he had to cut back again, but he wasn't sure this wave was going to let him. It was still strong enough on its right side, but was breaking early on its left, which meant Robbie was in danger of being carried through the Pier, not under it to shore.

"See you tomorrow," Razz hollered without looking up, intent on retrieving that night's take from the bar's cash register, as Matthew, the new Sol a Sol bartender, was leaving for the night.

Matthew, a nice-looking, dark-haired guy in his twenties, turned back. "I'm not here tomorrow. I'll be back on Sunday." He waited for a response to his revelation.

Razz didn't give a rat's ass when, or if, he'd see Matthew again. In his day, Razz would have had the bar jumping all night, telling jokes, laughing with his clientele, handing out free drinks to all the right people, usually beautiful single women, and would generally do whatever it took to help increase business for his bosses. However, Matthew wasn't much of a bartender; he didn't know half the drinks he should have, nor had he a scintillating personality. Though Razz had an urge to reveal to him these truths, he had something more important to do.

"Great," he said, his attention back on the register. He'd offered to count out for the night, so he could be alone that much sooner.

Matthew was slow, not only behind the bar, but also on the uptake, so he continued to wait.

With a handful of twenties and a head full of worries, Razz blurted, "Yeah, see you Sunday. Christ."

Though his response dripped with disdain and would have made most men bristle, it satisfied Matthew. "Yup, see you Sunday," he said, beaming. He closed the door behind him, proud he had cleared up any potential scheduling error.

Razz stuffed the register's contents into a moneybag and walked toward the stairs. He guessed the tally would be light for a Friday, but the bag felt weighty nonetheless. He went to lock the front door and noticed his legs felt heavy, too. He realized the heaviness had nothing to do with weight, but had everything to do with gravity.

His was a grave situation. Louis was not a man to cross. To attempt to legally, or illegally, take him down could be suicide. And there was nothing that would send a man to the grave sooner than that.

The click of the front lock gave Razz some relief, confirming as it did that he was safely alone, until he remembered Johnson and Donati's surprise visit a few weeks earlier. He flipped off a light switch and the place went dark save for spillover from the exterior floodlights. With just enough light to navigate, he took a step toward the stairs. That step seemed to reverberate through the restaurant, making the old oak flooring creak as if it were speaking to him, warning him against taking another. But Razz didn't wait to listen, chat, or argue. Instead, he sprinted as fast as his heavy legs would carry him, past brightly colored tablecloths, vases of silk red roses, and rows of glass windows through which one could see the police substation and the mainland beyond, up the stairs. Within moments, he was in his office, the door was locked behind him, and he was breathing heavily. It was an inauspicious beginning to his night's spy work.

He dropped the moneybag onto his desk, its impact muffled by a pile of invoices, stepped up onto his chair, and then onto the desk. He'd had enough of thinking, he needed to move quickly or he might lose his last remaining nerve. He lifted the ceiling tile and it came out surprisingly easy, without resistance. Even the killer dust seemed to make way for him this time, with only the smallest puff emanating outward.

He moved the tile to one side, careful not to bruise it. Because the office's main light hung from the ceiling in the middle of the room, little illumination made its way through the opening. He reached into the darkness toward the rafters, grasping for anything that might support his weight.

"Ow!"

Razz yanked his right hand back, balled protectively into itself. He grimaced as he unfurled it and was disappointed to find that a small scratch had caused him such distress. He resolved to get a tetanus shot in case he'd brushed a rusty wire.

As a droplet of blood formed on his index finger, he marveled at how he could think about needing a tetanus shot at a time like this. It reminded him that humans are survivors, that they're programmed to do whatever they must to survive. That thought reassured him until he realized that Louis had the same innate programming and his might be stronger.

He wiped his bloody finger against a dark pant leg, and then pressed against it with his thumb to stem the bleeding. To get more light into the crawl space, he pushed up an adjacent ceiling tile and killer dust rushed toward him. The dust reminded him of a film he watched in the fifth grade on the dangers of smoking. Like in the movie, each death particle appeared magnified a thousand-fold in vivid, gross detail, and moved in slow, unstoppable-motion.

Then Razz recognized what seemed to him the ultimate irony. Not only was he programmed to survive at any cost, Death in all its forms was chasing him inexorably, waiting for him to make a mistake, to give It its opening. As the dust penetrated his nose and mouth, he envisioned each molecule making its way deep into his lungs, into every brachium, and rapidly spreading through his bloodstream to attack every cell.

But his body fought back. He coughed huge, hacking coughs, attempting to reject the foreign intruders. Again, his survival instincts had taken over without his explicit permission. He just wished his hacking wasn't so loud. He felt like he was a foghorn alerting Harbor Patrol to an oncoming shipwreck.

Slowly, his coughing subsided, the thousand-fold-sized particles decreased to normal, infinitesimal size, and the dust cloud disappeared. He shifted the ceiling tile to one side and light streamed into the space above the tiles. He reached for a now-visible rafter, but it was just out of his grasp. He briefly rested his heels back onto the desk, then bent his knees and sprang forcefully into the air. His hands flailed upward. He didn't jump as high as he used to, but he knew he'd jumped high enough when his fingers grasped the top of the rough-hewn beam. Wood splinters sunk into his hands, but he ignored this new pain and pulled himself up.

With strong lat muscles from years of swimming through heavy surf, getting up into the crawl space was easy. But when he did, he found there were only a few feet from rafter to roof, and much of that space was filled with electrical wires and wooden cross-members. He would have little room to move.

He maneuvered his arms over the beam to support him, and a new round of splinters entered his forearms. He began to think his plan wasn't very well considered, despite the hours he'd spent dwelling on it. Mainly he'd dwelled on the danger, however, not about how to mitigate or navigate it. He could let go, drop down to the desk, maybe figure out a better plan, then try again, or he could hang there for minutes more, or he could try something. So he tried something. He swung his legs behind him, and then thrust them forward into a jackknife like a gymnast. The momentum helped him lift himself upward. When he extended his arms, his head banged into the underside of the roof.

"Oh, shit. Ow."

Razz pushed back and landed his ass on an adjacent beam and the rafters shook on impact. He massaged his head to ease the pain, and then squeezed his legs through the two-foot space between the beams and extended them forward. His goal was directly in front of him. Unfortunately, he'd forgotten a flashlight, so maneuvering through the wall opening, not so difficult in the light, would now be tougher. He wondered how he'd gotten as far as he had in life and then realized he really wasn't very far at all. *That explains a lot. No wonder I'm ten feet off the ground, in the dark, about to look for something, but I don't know what.*

Supporting himself on his hands, Razz drew his butt toward his feet and landed his ass on top of the next beam. He extended his legs forward while pushing off with his hands to complete the movement. He felt like a Chinese acrobat contorting himself for the Cirque de Soleil, but, after two more sets of movements, he was sitting on the office wall in position over his target. All he had to do was raise a ceiling tile and drop down to the floor. He reached down on either side of his legs and tried to lift the ceiling tile, but he couldn't get his fingers underneath the edges.

"Fuck."

His epithet echoed against the tiles and roof and cascaded back at him. What he thought had been a whisper sounded more like a security alarm. Trying again, he nudged the tile to the left and barely squeezed his right index and middle fingers between the tile and frame, then lifted the tile's edge. Excited by his success, he squeezed too hard and dented the composite material. He froze, then relaxed his grip and felt the tile almost return to normal. *Maybe it won't be noticeable. No one ever looks at a ceiling anyway. No one, that is, except someone who never misses anything!*

Fear almost caused him to hyperventilate, but he pressed on. He grasped the left edge of the tile with his left hand, gently this time, and moved the whole panel aside, then folded at the waist to look down into the room. Moonlight filtered through two windows, though it was still dark. He could just make out the safe across the room and the desk next to the wall on his right. Below him, there looked to be a small sofa.

Emboldened, he twisted onto his front and scrunched in his legs to release them from their perch. His stomach landed on the wall's top and his back and hamstrings strained to keep his legs from crashing into the wall as they fell. After catching his breath, he inched his way down the wall. His shirt and pant legs slid against the smooth wood paneling, and he was happy he was no longer gathering splinters.

Before touching down on the sofa, he paused to survey the area beneath him. Hanging by his fingertips, forearms braced against the wall, elbows bent, he thought he saw clear floor space to his right. To avoid leaving footprints on the sofa, he decided that should be his target. He shimmied to his right as far as he could without disturbing another tile, then swung his legs to the left and pushed off to the right.

Crash!

"Aaggh!" His legs buckled when his feet hit the floor. Momentum carried him off-target, and he slammed into something solid. Splayed on the floor, he reached for his right ankle with one hand and his head with the other.

"Shit. Fuck. Shit." He leaned against the wall and looked toward the dark corner to see what he'd hit. It appeared to be another safe.

"Fuck, how much money do they have?" The more money Louis had and the more safes he needed to hold it, the more trouble Razz would be in if caught.

"Shit," he grumbled as he stepped gingerly on his right foot. He shifted his weight onto his left, and then stepped again with his right. Pain shot through his ankle.

"What the fuck was I thinking?" He sat on the couch to rest and wiped wetness from his now-bulging skull. His fingers felt slippery.

He convulsed, jumping up from the couch as quickly as his wracked body allowed. When his feet hit the floor, pain from his right foot again overtook the pain from his head.

"Aaggh!"

Go right, instead of left, and it can make all the difference. Jump to the floor, instead of the couch, and it can be your downfall. One false step easily leads to another.

He thought back to his argument with Sarah about her working for her father and all the wrong that had happened after that. He thought about his childish fireplace christening at Richard Gold's, his accepting a job from Louis, his dalliance with Lotta, his being late to pick up the kids and he couldn't tell what led to what. His false steps led so far back and over and around again, he couldn't even tell where his downfall had begun.

Razz limped over to the window next to the desk and peeked out. He was never so happy to see the Pier so empty. Then he looked at his hands. His heart sank when he saw blood.

A lighted desk clock read three-twenty-five. Sunrise would take place around six-fifty, but he had to be gone long before then. That gave him little more than two hours to find his evidence, erase his tracks, and get the hell out of there.

He rubbed his hands on his black cotton trousers so hard the heat friction hurt them. Focused now, like his life depended on it, he twisted a desk lamp's neck so the light housing kissed the wall, then turned on the lamp. Streams of light escaped, but not so much that they'd alert a Pier denizen to his presence.

He was depressed to see the mess he'd made. Though the couch, made of a dark purple material, wouldn't reveal much, he'd left a streak of crimson on the maple-colored paneling when he'd slid down the wall.

Razz removed his blood-spotted buttoned-down and found the origin for some of the blood. His forearms were scraped and bleeding. His right index and middle fingers were bleeding, too. Adrenaline coursed through him, dissipating his pain.

He found a clean spot on his shirt and began wiping down the wall, but the blood had dried. With no water easily at hand, he spit on the cloth to moisten it and the blood. He cleaned as high as he could, and then pulled over a wooden desk chair to reach higher. When he finished, he angled the lamp to get a better look. The wall looked normal, but another fifteen minutes were gone and he considered abandoning his sinking ship. He figured it could take ten minutes to climb back into his office, hopeful his return would go more smoothly than his initial voyage. He didn't know how long it would take to search the office, and that was the problem. He wanted to be far from the Pier before any hint of sunrise.

He put his dirty, wrinkled shirt back on. He looked rumpled on the outside and felt rumpled inside, probably like many of the hard-living homeless persons on the San Margarita streets. Right now, he would have changed places with almost any of them.

He scrutinized the desk. Invoices he'd approved for payment, payroll checks ready for signing, credit card receipts, and vendor letters, all organized neatly in appropriate piles, monopolized the desk's top. It was much more organized than his desk ever was or would be and it didn't tell him a thing other than what he already knew. They were running a restaurant downstairs.

A search through several desk drawers yielded little other than where Lotta kept her staples and paper clips. As Razz opened the last drawer, the bottom right, a stack of papers revealed itself and lifted his hopes. Sorting through them, he found receipts and invoices from previous weeks and an unaudited financial statement for the first month of Louis' ownership. After carefully extricating the financial statement and marking its place, he inspected it like it was a newly discovered Picasso. Unfortunately, unlike a Picasso, it was straightforward. There were no hidden secrets, just the performance numbers for the Surf's Up and Sol a Sol and the combined numbers for both. The surprising numbers suggested Louis' aggressive purchase would prove extremely profitable and they reminded him that he, Razz McNeil, was a mere mortal and would probably never become a wealthy businessman. He started counting the bonus money that would come to him if they continued their strong performance, before he caught himself. He knew that, one way or another, there was blood attached to this money. Though he still had the fifteen hundred dollars and felt the sting of his own culpability, he was determined to redeem himself. But there was nothing in this financial statement that would cleanse him.

The Sol a Sol had grossed almost one hundred and four thousand dollars and the Surf's Up had grossed just over eighty. Combined net earnings were around forty-three thousand dollars. It probably wasn't a lot of money in Louis' world, but it was more than Paul had cleared in seven years with the Surf's Up. And Razz couldn't even feel a sense of accomplishment for his part in it.

He positioned the statement carefully back in place and evened the surrounding paper edges to remove traces of his presence. He closed the drawer and looked at the clock. It was seven minutes after four.

He went to the window as fast as his bum ankle would allow and looked out. Fortunately, the Pier was still empty save for one unkempt soul wrapped in a raggedy blanket who was wandering back toward the police substation.

Razz searched for clues near the big safe, but there was nothing on top of it, beside it or behind. As a lark, he grabbed hold of the safe's handle and lifted, but it resisted. No, it would not be that easy.

On the other side of the office, he looked under the couch and around the smaller safe and copying machine, and on the bookshelf. He found several books on accounting, a couple on the restaurant business, and a biography of John D. Rockefeller, but nothing more incriminating than that. *Where haven't I looked?*

Then it hit him. It was staring him right in the face. A computer monitor sitting innocently on the desk might reveal all to him. Though Razz wasn't a whiz, technologically speaking, he knew how to search files because he was always misplacing them. Maybe he could find something.

He located the computer underneath the desk and pressed the "on" button. He heard a buzz and a couple of clicks from inside the machine, but the screen stayed blank.

"Shit." *Just my luck, it's broken.*

He was about to give up when he realized the monitor wasn't even turned on. Feeling barely brighter than the dim room, he pressed the monitor button and heard a whir of life. Success!

The screen erupted and light poured through the room and out the windows. He scrambled to shield the screen with his body and the room went dusky. He maneuvered his shirt off and draped it over the monitor. Again, he was semi-naked and still very vulnerable.

Razz could see a gauzy image of the word "Windows." He clicked the "enter" key on the keyboard, but nothing happened. He poked his head underneath the shirt for a better look and the problem became clear. He needed a password.

He typed "solasol", but was told that the "password is incorrect". He typed "surf'sup", then corrected himself and retyped "surfsup". Again, no luck. He tried "Louis", then "Carlotta". He wracked his brain trying to think of a magic word or letter-number combination, but it was no use. He shut down the computer and the screen went dark. It was four-forty-seven.

He bent over, his elbows propped on his knees, exhausted of energy and ideas. He stared blankly at the unyielding machine, and then noticed paper edges peeking out from beside it. Tucked between the computer and the inside of the desk sheathing, he found a tattered accounting ledger.

When he looked inside, it told him little, but confused him greatly. There was page after yellowing page of relatively small numbers, ranging from one to three thousand and -four, and none made any sense. Each page had a heading of only letters. One page was headed by "S", another by "W". Several were headed by "C" with another letter or two following it. There was a "CA", "CE", "CR" and "CRE". *"CA" could stand for California,* he thought, but there was no similar pattern for other states, so he dismissed the idea. Entries were numerous, but there were no dates anywhere and Razz began to think the book was a child's play thing, possibly for Patrick or Melanie, and not a meaningful ledger at all. But the entries were not written by a child's hand, and he'd never seen Louis' kids anywhere near the restaurants. No, there was something very adult about this book. It had to have significance, only he couldn't imagine what it might be.

He thought back to high school mathematics and vaguely remembered something about correlation, but there didn't seem to be any patterns or correlation to the numbers. There weren't even any totals or running tallies.

The only number he understood was on the clock—it was already five. Razz blinked, disbelieving. *How the hell? I have to get out of here.* Sunrise might not be for another hour and fifty minutes, but early morning activity on the Pier made his presence there too dangerous. Transients were already on the move and the police substation would open in an hour.

He hopped over to the copier. Fortunately, it was in rest mode, so he didn't have to wait long for it to warm up. After positioning the fragile ledger, he retrieved his shirt from the monitor and covered the copier glass with it. He pressed the button and a brilliant light raced back and forth across the glass and through his shirt's fibers.

He adjusted the ledger to copy the next page, and then hopped to the window. He hoped, at worst, to see a stray vagrant or early morning fisherman, but he saw something much, much worse. Making its way down the Pier toward him was a black car that looked exactly like Louis' Mercedes 500 CL. It was only two hundred feet from the Sol a Sol's front door!

Think. Think!

Razz looked at the copier and ledger, both ready for round two. Despite a heavy dose of panic, he was determined to make another copy. If Louis had noticed anything suspicious, it was already too late. If he hadn't, it might be too late for him to escape anyway. And if he did escape, he wanted his trouble to be worth it.

He fought the urge to hurry across the room and press the copy button. Instead, he waited. And he listened. After a moment, he peeked outside just as the

Mercedes was passing out of view. Then he hopped into action. He went to the copier and pressed the button. The copier light no longer mattered; Louis was outside on the other side of the building.

Razz soon realized his was wishful thinking when the back door cracked open downstairs. Louis wasn't outside; he was already in the restaurant!

He heard several footsteps enter, but, with danger imminent and every reason to panic, a strange thing happened. Instead of running for cover, leaving the office in a shambles and hoping for the best, he carefully, methodically made another copy. Then he made another.

He heard feet plod across the creaky wooden floor below and could tell exactly how fast they were approaching. He didn't have much time.

Razz balled up his shirt and flung it toward the rafters. It disappeared from sight somewhere above the ceiling tiles. He took his copies from the copy tray, folded them twice and slid them into his back right pocket. He removed the ledger from the glass and carefully folded it closed, then hobbled over to place it back between the computer and the side of the desk. He clicked off the desk lamp and moved it back into place, twisting the flexible neck into its original position. Then he surveyed the room. *Something's not right. But what is it? What is it?*

The feet were at the base of the stairs. He figured there were at least three sets, but he knew only one pair mattered.

He was out of time, so he stepped up onto the sofa arm. The first pair of feet reached the top of the stairs just as his fingers grasped the top of the wall. He strained to draw himself up toward the ceiling opening, and then he hesitated. He turned, still suspended, and looked behind him. He hadn't moved the chair back into place!

Despite his limited math skills, Razz probably performed a million probability calculations in a microsecond. *Would Louis know its original position? Will he notice? Is there time to do anything about it?*

The footsteps were just a few yards from the door, so close he thought he could hear their owners' breathing. Instead of fleeing, Razz made an unlikely decision. He dropped softly to the sofa and then to the floor. Despite the shooting pain in his ankle, he grabbed the chair and tiptoed halfway across the room with it. As a key chain tinkled outside, he gently placed the chair beside the desk where he'd found it. He turned to look at the door, then at the wall, and, when he heard a key enter the door's bolt lock, he did the fastest four-yard, ankle-sprained tiptoe in history.

With no time for subtlety, he performed a one-legged hop up onto the couch cushion. And, as he did, the bolt-lock clicked open. He was sure he wouldn't make it.

The key chain tinkled again as the person outside fumbled to unlock the door handle. "Mierda."

A shudder coursed through Razz when he heard Louis' voice, but it spurred him forward. In a maneuver worthy of Mary Lou Retton, he stepped with his good foot onto the couch arm and leaped toward the ceiling. He caught the top of the wall with his hands and pulled himself upward in one fluid motion to lift his torso into the rafters. He twisted his body to land his butt on the wall, raised his legs to the adjacent rafter, and bent forward to grab the ceiling tile. As the door handle twisted open, the tile fell into place.

He listened as several men entered. He worried that a cloud of ceiling dust might give him away, but, if there was one, they seemed not to notice.

"Rápidos."

Razz knew enough Spanish to know Louis was commanding his troops to hurry. The wall beam dug into his ass cheek and his ankle throbbed, but he didn't dare adjust his position. He allowed himself only the tiniest of inhalations. He felt a sweat bead travel from his hairline to his eyebrow and he silently implored it to stay there, dammed up by a bushy brow. But his brow wasn't bushy enough and it fell onto the ceiling tile. It seemed to explode on contact and echo through the rafters.

He froze, holding his already-tenuous breath. Then a strange and worrisome thing happened—absolutely nothing. Five seconds went by without a sound or sign of movement below. Then five more went by and five more after that, but each single second felt like a minute. Razz could almost feel Louis the Superman's X-ray vision boring into him.

I put everything back. Didn't I? The light's off. The copier's in rest mode. I cleaned the wall. What did they find? What are they waiting for? What are they doing?

He heard a single footstep, and he allowed himself a tiny breath. Then a picture shot through his head. And the image sickened him. It was a footprint, his footprint, and it stood out distinctly against the dark fabric of the couch cushion.

I wasted too much time. I should have cleaned up. I should have been more careful. I should have just gotten out of there!

"Mil treinta y siete, entretenimiento, doscientos y siete, adquisiciones, veinticuatro, restaurantes, quinientos ochenta y tres, bienes raíces."

Razz knew the Spanish word for "restaurant" because he'd worked with Spanish-speaking Mexicans at the Surf's Up for years and recognized some of the numbers, one thousand something as well as twenty-four, but he didn't know what Louis meant by any of it. At least, there was activity beneath him, which led him to believe the men were thinking about something other than an intruder hovering above them.

As the sound of suitcase wheels, presumably carrying heavy loads of cash, rolled across the office floor, he allowed himself to shift his weight to relieve some of the pressure on his behind.

Creak!

The wheels stopped rolling and again Razz stopped breathing. Rivulets of sweat ran down his forehead and they seemed to bombard the ceiling tile like water flowing over Niagara Falls crashing into the rocks below.

His wait seemed interminable, but the next sounds were of the door closing and its bolt-lock clamping shut. He worried it was only a trap to lure him out and, when he did, Louis would be there waiting for him. Then he heard footsteps going down the hallway.

Relief spread as those footsteps continued downstairs, along with the *clump-clump-clump* of heavy suitcases. The steps continued across the restaurant floor, and Razz began to breathe normally again. He shifted his weight and stretched out his legs. His relief was palpable, but something still felt wrong. He hadn't heard the car drive away.

It took several minutes for him to feel safe enough to leave his perch. With every movement, he half-expected a gunshot to pierce a ceiling tile and him, but he knew Louis was too smart for that. Besides, death by gunfire would be too painless. It would be too clean, too quick. If he were caught, his demise would be anything but quick, clean, or pain-free.

He flipped onto his stomach and reached out for the next rafter. Vertebrae in his upper back popped in relieved approval when he stretched to look down into his office. No one was lurking in wait, so he moved forward until he could position his hips over a rafter and drop his legs into his office space. With a firm handhold, he lowered himself.

Razz was thrilled, despite the pain that shot through his ankle when his feet hit the desktop. He sat on the edge of the desk and was comforted to find his filthy button-down lying next to him. He rested while his foot, hands, forearms, and mind pulsated, then a satisfied look came over his face.

He closed his eyes and pressed a hand against his forehead to relieve some pressure and his head fell back. A comforting beacon of light filtered through his eyelids, soothing him.

After a moment, his eyes shot open and every shred of satisfaction and comfort disappeared. *How could I have been so stupid? The office light was on the whole time!*

Razz saw light escape under his door and knew that Louis couldn't have missed it. He realized, in more depressingly vivid detail than ever, just what a fool he was.

He was alone, stupefied under a glaring light, and it somehow seemed fitting. He was alone and clueless in his life, and his every action seemed illuminated. He seemed transparent, totally visible, to everyone but himself. After all the effort he'd expended that evening, after all the danger he'd encountered, he was worse off than before.

Now Razz wouldn't feel safe anywhere, anytime. And there didn't seem to be anything he could do about it.

31

If he cut back under the Pier too far, he would lose momentum with the wave and tip into the dangerous surf. If he didn't cut back, the wave would carry him through the Pier and he would fail. He had only ten feet in which to decide whether to be a hero and further risk his life, but it only took him three. He cut back sharply against the wave into the Pier's underbelly, picking up speed past several expectant pilings.

Saturday, January 29, 2005

Though he hadn't yet gotten out of bed, Sharky was already flying high this morning. He was pictured on the front page of the *Monitor* alongside Police Chief Wilson and captured murder suspect, San Margarita mayor, Jaime Hidalgo. Sharky's beaming face, Wilson's kind words, and the newspaper's grateful headline all proclaimed him a hero.

He listened to the sound of running water emanating from the bathroom where Terri was brushing her teeth, looked around him at freshly painted walls and a newly decorated bedroom, and reflected on his tumultuous past few weeks. From Wally's discovery to Hidalgo's arrest, he had been through a lot. There had been ups and downs and all-arounds, but he'd finally made it to the top. And he wanted to enjoy it while he was there.

"Babe, what do you want to do tonight?" he asked, raising his volume to trump a noisy faucet. "Let's have some fun. My treat."

It was clear she hadn't heard him, so he continued the conversation himself. "Oh, I want to stay home and make mad, passionate love to my big hero man," he said in a sultry voice, puckering his lips as if he could kiss himself.

Now, standoffish and masculine, like John Wayne in a Western saloon, he said, "Well, so will everyone else, little lady. Why shouldn't I share myself with all the pretty girls in town?

Sharky giggled, enjoying his conversational fantasy. Then he made the mistake that countless men have made over the ages, he pondered his own ridiculous, rhetorical question. *Why shouldn't I share myself with all the pretty girls in town?* He was a bona fide hero, after all, his picture and deeds splashed all over the front page of the local newspaper. His dangerous investigative work had led to the capture of a murderer. Surely, people would be impressed, especially impressionable young women.

He looked around him again and the walls didn't seem quite as bright. The new lamp didn't seem to fit the room as well as it had moments ago. The new mattress felt lumpy. Insecurities and doubt were beginning to overtake him.

Then a strange and wondrous thing happened. Words escaped from his mouth, unplanned and spontaneous, almost disembodied, as if he were channeling. He said, "Because I love you." And he believed to his bones that, somehow, Terri had answered him.

He looked toward the bathroom from which now came the sound of a flushing toilet. Terri hadn't said anything, but he believed the words just the same. His fantasy of college-aged girls begging for his autograph and more disappeared. He choked up when he realized her love meant more to him than anything and that she was the only woman he wanted.

He tried to remember if he'd ever felt this deliciously scary feeling before, but he knew he hadn't. He couldn't remember much of anything that had happened in his life before he met Terri.

The walls brightened again, the lamp was perfect, and his mattress felt like a puff cloud, but he climbed out of bed anyway, because he now had something important to do. He landed his feet on the floor beside his bed, naked, but laser-focused, and walked to the bathroom door.

Although they had an unspoken rule to allow each other privacy for their most personal of functions, Sharky opened the door as Terri was finishing her business. She pulled up her underwear and pushed down her skirt.

"Jerry, what the hell?"

He stared at her, beaming a broad, zombie-like smile, fully exposed.

"I'm sorry, but I don't have time to play this morning."

His countenance didn't waver.

"Are you all right? I'm kind of busy here. I've got to get to work."

"Will you marry me?" he asked.

"Huh?"

That wasn't the response he'd hoped for, but he kept on smiling, convicted in his truth. "I'm sorry I had to ask you like this, but I know I want to marry you. I want you with me always. Nothing else matters."

Her face flushed and she began to cry. Someone wanted her in sickness and in health, wanted her more than anything or anyone else, and wanted her for life. Then, inexplicably, she hit him on his chest with her tightly balled, bony fists. And she kept on hitting him. And she kept on crying.

To most men, a beating like that would indicate a distinctly negative response, but Sharky hung in there and took blow after blow. "Don't you want to get married?"

After several more blows, Terri finally exhausted herself and she draped her arms around him. She clung to him, sobbing into his naked chest, and then looked up at him. She appeared helpless, her make-up was battered, tears were streaking down her face, and he'd never seen her more beautiful.

"Sure, Jerry. Sure, I'll marry you."

Before he could kiss her and carry her in his arms across the bathroom threshold, she broke away and said, "Now, I've got to get to work."

She turned to the mirror to fix her make-up. Though her reaction wasn't overwhelmingly positive, Sharky's smile hadn't left him. She had said "yes." She had agreed to marry him.

"I'm late; I'll do this in the car." She breezed past him out of the bathroom, then came back and kissed him on the cheek. "See you tonight?"

He wondered why her inflection had created a question. "And every night."

She nodded, then ran to the front door, tore it open, and closed it behind her harder than she needed.

Sharky pondered his morning's experience. It felt like it had already been a full day. He looked down at himself, naked, skinny, and scarred. He decided he'd propose to her again, but next time, he'd do it right. Firstly, he'd be clothed. Secondly, they would be somewhere romantic, he'd have a ring, and he'd be on one knee when he popped the question. His romantic vision brought him another huge smile.

That smile didn't leave even when, moments later, Harvey Howells called to ask when he should expect his promotion.

Razz McNeil wasn't smiling. He'd awakened early, too, but only because of haunting thoughts. He'd had plenty to do with the success of finding Wally Bumpers' killer, but he would not be pictured on The *Monitor*'s front page. He couldn't even impress his wife with the news as evidenced by their fiasco at Louis' home.

His options turned over like ping-pong balls in a lottery drawing, only he didn't have nearly as many. He actually only had a few and they essentially boiled down to two: drop any intention of pursuing Louis, strive to win his family back and keep his job, and hope to live a long, guilty life; or confront the truth of Louis' guilt, try to help justice be served, and maybe live only long enough to regret his choice.

Razz wasn't a hero by nature. Not even on his historic day under the Pier so many years ago did he feel remotely like a hero. He'd just been a silly surf dude driven to do what no one else had. Although he knew he might risk his life during his attempt, he felt like he had some control on his board whatever conditions he might face. He felt no control whatsoever during his current endeavor.

It was eight o'clock and he had nowhere to be until four when he had to walk into the Surf's Up with a straight face and go about his business, all the while knowing there was way too much money sitting in the Sol a Sol safe for any honest restaurant business. He rolled, trying to ignore the pain that coursed through his body, and curled the covers around him as if they could shield him from his unappealing choices and from Louis Marcayda. He completed a full one-eighty turn, then realized hiding in his bed wouldn't be terribly useful. Louis knew where he lived.

He hobbled to the bathroom. Bruises covered both forearms and shins and there were multiple abrasions scattered across his body. Looking in the mirror, groggy from lack of sleep, and physically and emotionally scarred, he barely recognized himself.

He shifted over to the toilet to relieve himself, leaning most of his weight on his good left foot. He considered the fact he could now leave the toilet seat however he wanted, up or down. It's something that most men wished for at one time or another, until they realize the consequence of its meaning. That simple freedom simply meant Razz was a bachelor again.

As his liquid waste flowed into the bowl, he closed his eyes to rest them and listened to the monotonous patter. Despite his aching muscles and throbbing shins and right ankle, the sound almost lulled him back to sleep. Then the phone rang, startling him, and made him miss his mark. Yellowish urine drops splashed onto the tile floor.

"Shit."

Whoever wanted him so badly and so early would just have to wait. On the fourth ring, he was doubly relieved when his message machine picked up and his flow trickled to a halt.

"Hi, you've reached Razz McNeil. I'm busy, so leave a message and I'll get back to you as soon as I can."

"Hi, it's Sarah."

Razz didn't bother to flick off, rinse off, or clean up, he just hopped as fast as his left leg would allow toward the phone.

"I wanted to apologize for the other night. I mean, I saw the paper. That's amazing, Razz. I guess I was a little stressed—"

"Hi," he gasped into the receiver. "How are you?"

"Oh, I'm good. I didn't think you'd be there. The paper said there were waves."

He smiled. She still knew his routine. "I worked late." He refrained from telling her the many reasons why he had little energy or interest in the water this morning.

"Well, congratulations about catching the Mayor. I mean, that's what you were talking about, right? It's really incredible. Maybe it's the start of a whole new career."

He could tell she was making small talk, forcing enthusiasm into the conversation so it wouldn't lapse into more treacherous territory, but he had something much bigger to discuss. "Thank you, Sarah, I'm glad you called. I need to talk to you."

"Razz—"

"No, no, I need your advice. I have something to show you."

"Oh."

He sensed a trace of disappointment in her voice that gave him a glimmer of hope for their relationship, but that wasn't what he wanted to talk about right now.

"It's an accounting thing," he continued, "I need your help."

"Well, next week—"

"No, I've got to see you today. It's important."

"Razz, something's come up. I have to work and it's just not a good time."

"Please."

The urgency in his voice overcame her reluctance. She knew her father would be out, being nursed back to emotional health by her mother and, in truth, she was curious to find out just what accounting issue could be so important. "How about ten o'clock at the office?"

"Ten o'clock is fine. See you then."

"See you—"

Razz hung up the phone before she could finish and he hurried back to the bathroom for his own unfinished business. He wasn't sure what he would do for the next two hours before their meeting, but one thing was certain. He was going to spend as little time in his apartment as possible.

After one of the quickest showers in history and an equally swift teeth brushing, he threw on jeans, a long-sleeved sweatshirt, and flip-flops, stuffed work clothes in a duffel bag, and headed for the front door. But before he departed, he grabbed the copies of the old accounting ledger he'd discovered last night in Louis' office.

He needed to know exactly how those numbers added up.

Sharky had easily dispatched with Harvey Howells' phone call. He had gushed over his contribution to finding Wally Bumpers' killer and assured him he'd speak with Chief Wilson regarding a commendation. The phone call lasted shy of forty seconds, and for the moment Harvey Howells was satisfied.

Sharky wanted to keep his phone line free for congratulatory calls. He wanted to bask in what he felt was well-deserved adulation, but a problem soon became apparent—no one other than Howells called him. He decided that, if an adoring public weren't going to seek him out, he'd go find one.

He slid open the bedroom's mirrored closet door to retrieve some clothes. Because of Terri's organizational skills, the closet was normally immaculate—his pants folded over hangers, crisp, lightly starched shirts lined up in a row, and shoes placed on the floor, toes out, ready to go. Her garments were usually spaced apart to prevent wrinkling with seldom-worn, long dresses near the wall on the left, skirts in the middle, and blouses and tops toward the right.

But, as he reached for a dark blue pima cotton shirt with thin, light-blue stripes, an attractive-looking shirt he felt suitable for his new, improved station in life, he noticed the closet was askew. He scanned the line of Terri's clothes and several garments were missing. The usual order was upset.

He dismissed any lingering concern when he remembered how often she took clothes to the dry cleaner. And she had rushed out this morning in order to get to work on time. So, Sharky smoothed out a rumpled blouse and re-positioned several skirts to even out a gap. Then he laughed.

She's really starting to rub off on me. I can't wait till she gets home to rub some more.

He added a pair of black cotton slacks, leather belt, and black loafers to his ensemble and checked himself in the mirror. He appeared the picture of success. And he wanted to show off that success, so he called his erstwhile friend and associate, Razz McNeil, to help him.

Razz was only too happy to meet Sharky in a highly public place somewhere other than the Sol a Sol or Surf's Up. He wanted to let someone know what he was planning, he just didn't know yet whether that person would be him. Sharky was a cowboy and Razz felt his situation required subtlety. But he knew he needed to leave some tracks, because if something went wrong, those tracks might help save him.

He was already on his third cup of coffee when Sharky arrived at the News Cafe around nine-thirty. Watching him swagger in only made Razz angrier. "Where the hell have you been?"

"I stopped by Mae's and she wouldn't let me leave until I took pictures with her and all her staff. Then a few customers wanted pictures. You know, they wanted to be near a hero."

On edge from a caffeine overdose and his previous night's adventures, Razz wanted to knock his arrogant smile right off him. "Whatever, asshole. Fuck, I've been here an hour already."

If Sharky was insulted, he didn't let on. Like a narcissist to a reflecting pool, he went to search for stories about his exploits. In the twenty-foot-long rack at the News Cafe were magazines and newspapers from around the world. Editions of *Newsweek*, *Le Monde*, the *Wall Street Journal*, the *Times of India* and numerous other important world publications were on sale.

Several local rags were also represented and those were all Sharky cared about. The *San Margarita Bee*, a daily paper known more for its plentiful and cost-effective fictional business statements than hard-hitting news, had a picture of him on its cover. He held the paper up, as if he were reading something inside, but it was really only so everyone else could see. That no one noticed only made him try harder. The *Windward*, a daily paper apparently owned by a sailor, made no mention of him and he cast it aside. The *San Margarita Daily*, printed, strangely enough, only three times a week, was also void of that day's big news.

"These papers suck," said Sharky when he returned to the table.

"That was a nice picture of you in the *Monitor* though."

"Thanks. Yeah, that's a good paper. I couldn't have done it without you, you know."

Razz wasn't comforted by the compliment, because it only served to remind him of his troubles. And he blamed those troubles, in part, on his recent association with Sharky. Ignorance had meant relative bliss until recently, but now he knew too much for his own good.

"I know, but I sure wish you had."

"But you're a hero."

"Not to anyone that matters, I'm not."

"But we won, Razz."

"No, you won. I'm losing everything."

"What are you talking about? Your wife? This will help you win her back, you'll see."

He didn't share Sharky's confidence on the matter and didn't feel like sharing the myriad reasons why not. "I'll see you later."

"Stay." Sharky reached out to reassure him, but made him wince when he gripped his left forearm. A purplish spot poked out from under a sweatshirt sleeve.

"What the hell? Are you doing drugs?"

Insulted, Razz ripped his arm away. "Ow. Shit." He lightly massaged his bruise to ease the pain.

"What's going on, man? Were you in a fight? Tell me who it was. I'll bust their ass."

"No, no fight, no drugs." Razz hesitated. "I, uh, I can't tell you, not till I'm sure. But I may need your help."

"Sure of what? Hey, if you're in trouble, I'll help you, like you helped me. We're partners, right?"

Although Sharky's enthusiasm to kick someone's ass for him was oddly reassuring, he wasn't so sure he'd describe their relationship as a partnership. He'd been a barely willing accomplice over the course of the past few weeks, not his partner. It was like the difference between casual dating and marriage. Razz didn't think he was ready for a full commitment.

But he knew he needed help. "Uh, I think I found something last night."

Sharky silently encouraged him. From interrogating suspects, he'd learned there were times when you just had to give someone enough rope to hang himself.

Razz took the rope. He motioned Sharky to come closer, bent towards him, then whispered, "I think Louis Marcayda may be laundering money through the restaurants."

Sharky digested the news, held back as long as he could, then burst into laughter loud enough to send aural shock waves through the room. Heads turned, but their interest lasted only until they realized the matter didn't matter to them.

Razz turned to leave, but left him with one parting thought. "Fuck you."

"Sit down, Razz. I'm sorry, I'm sorry."

Razz ignored him and hobbled toward the door. He was only steps away from it when Sharky stopped him without taking a step himself. "Everyone already knows that!"

Whether everyone actually knew it or not, he wanted to find out just why Sharky thought they did. He haltingly returned to the table. "What the fuck are you talking about?"

"Everyone knows."

"Shhh."

"Oh, look around, Razz. None of these people give a shit about you or me, the self-absorbed idiots."

Despite Sharky's pitiable lack of awareness of his own self-absorption, he was right. Two body builders were sucking on protein shakes and admiring their bulging biceps. A young woman with too much make-up was busy applying more. Several other patrons had their heads stuck in newspapers or magazines, either deep in thought, avoidance or both.

"Have a seat, Razz."

He reluctantly did, but not before he led Sharky to a far corner, several tables away from their nearest neighbor.

"Look, why do you think you're paying as little rent as you are?"

A glimmer in his eye revealed Razz was beginning to comprehend.

"Yeah, exactly. Louis subsidizes Boys' Town, so he can bring other money into the system. He declares more than he makes in rent, pays the extra taxes, and legitimizes the cash from his illegitimate businesses."

"What businesses?"

"Come on, Razz. What are you, five? You ever hear of drugs? Prostitution, maybe?"

"You know that? For sure?"

"Yeah, you could say that. I know, for sure. I mean, I can't prove the money laundering part, and I don't think I'd want to, but it's not a novel idea. Why do you think he wanted to own restaurants?"

Razz shook his head in disbelief. "So, we're all in on it. Great. Selling out for cheap rent."

"Hey, there are worst things to sell out for." Sharky cracked a doubtful smile, knowing he'd been selling out for a weekly economy-priced hooker for years.

"But you're a fucking cop."

Sharky struggled to decipher his meaning.

"Don't you think someone should do something?"

"Oh, yeah, Razz. Someone sure should do something, all right. And I guess you think you're that someone. Wow, this hero stuff has gone to your head. I've created a crime-fighting monster."

Razz resisted his desire to rearrange his face.

Sharky wasn't about to apologize. "Are you out of your fucking mind? Are you?"

"Fuck you."

"No, tell me, because I'm thinking you must be. This shit's gone to your head, man. Taking down the Mayor, that's one thing, but Louis Marcayda? You're out of your league, rookie."

"And I thought you were a good cop."

"I am, but I'm not a stupid one."

"You're not an honest one either. You look the other way when you know you shouldn't; that's a lie. You run when you know you should stay; that's a lie. You're as crooked as the rest of them," he said, jamming his right index finger repeatedly into Sharky's chest.

Flustered by his own outburst, Razz pulled back and tried to gather himself. He wasn't sure why he was so disgusted, because he knew Louis was dangerous. Anyone confronting him was likely to lose. He had taken money from him more than once, accepted a job running restaurants likely used to launder money, and accepted unusually low-priced apartments for him and his parents. And he'd done it all in the name of money. Louis had bought him, and he had come cheap and easy.

That is when he realized why he was so disgusted with Sharky. It was because he was so utterly disgusted with himself. He hated himself for being weak, for needing Louis' job, money, and apartment. He hated himself for getting into such a dubious situation, for feeling so impotent, for cheating on his faithful, loving wife, for hurting his beloved, always-supportive parents, for letting down his perfectly-imperfect children, and for not fully appreciating all the good he'd once possessed in his life. Though he did not feel he'd accomplished much good other than the creation of those children, he hated himself for having given up on his potential to do so.

"I'm sorry, I had no right," he said.

Since Terri entered his life, Sharky no longer felt he had to lash out over every perceived slight, but he didn't have to just sit there and take any either.

"Good luck, Razz." With that, he walked toward the door.

"Sharky, I'm sorry."

But Sharky didn't acknowledge him and Razz didn't chase him. Their partnership, acquaintanceship, friendship, or whatever one might call their relationship, appeared over.

Razz leaned back in his chair, balancing precariously on two legs just like his life was balancing precariously. The slightest wrong move and his person and his life could both come crashing down.

It had been a rough morning, a dismaying second act following his exciting, but dangerous, first act last night. And he wasn't looking forward to a possible act three climax. But when he noticed the long hand of a nearby wall clock nicking the four of the clock face, he knew he had another problem to resolve before he'd have a chance at a curtain call.

He was twenty minutes late to meet his wife.

Sarah didn't seem surprised when Razz, trying hard not to limp, walked into her office at ten-thirty-three for their ten o'clock appointment.

"I'm sorry. Sorry, I'm late."

She'd been so busy trying to save her father's empire, and her inheritance, that she'd lost track of time herself. She had bigger issues than what she thought were going to be Razz' tax questions. But when he showed her the odd-looking ledger copies and explained from where they'd come, even while he was leaving out the most worrisome details, she suspected big things were afoot.

"There should be two sides of any real accounting ledger, debits and credits, but there's only one here," she explained. "That probably means this ledger keeps track of money coming or going, but not both."

When he nodded in understanding, she asked, "Do you know why anyone might do that?"

"I have some ideas, but I'm kind of hoping I'm wrong. What do you think?"

"Are you in trouble, Razz?"

"No, no trouble," were his precise words, but his body language and furrowed brow revealed his flagging confidence.

"Please, be careful. You told me he could be dangerous."

"Oh, so now you believe me," he said, hoping to lighten the mood, but neither of them felt terribly light this morning. "I know. I will."

"Why don't you just quit? We don't need ... I mean, you don't need the money that badly. No one does."

That she had momentarily included him with her, at least syntactically, raised his spirits. "I'll be careful."

"Your kids need you, you know."

Now, what little confidence he had vanished. Sarah had played the kid card, reminding him of the huge stakes attached to any move he might make. If he were to perish, the larger world wouldn't skip a beat, but his kids' smaller world would skip several. And if he were to endanger his children or wife, there could be no forgiveness.

"I know what I'm doing."

She wasn't buying it. "No one keeps these kinds of books unless they're hiding something, Razz. And they probably wouldn't like you knowing that they're hiding something."

"What do the numbers mean? Why are they so small?" he asked, trying to change the topic away from himself and his potential culpability.

Though her concern was sincere, it came with the implicit warning, "*Don't you dare do anything to endanger our children!*" But she gave him a pass for now and continued, "They probably represent larger numbers in some kind of formula. Maybe you just add a couple zeros."

"Or several zeros," he blurted, before he realized he should have kept his thought to himself.

"Just how many zeros do you think go behind these numbers?"

"I don't know. Just a couple, I'm sure. Look, it's nothing."

"What's going on, Razz? Tell me." Her steely glare knifed through what little resolve he had left.

"I think, I mean, I'm worried Louis might be laundering money through the restaurants."

After a moment of reflection, Sarah dropped her head into her hands. "Oh, Razz."

There, it was official. She was now as disgusted with him as he was with himself. "Oh," plus a man's name spoken by a woman with the appropriately appalled inflection is enough to cut a man at the knees and send him crawling on his belly for the nearest hole, impotent in the knowledge that he'd let that woman down once again.

He scanned the office, as if there might really be a hole in which he could hide, but Sarah caught him. She let him squirm, but now it was her turn to appear more confident than she really was.

"Yes, that could make sense," she said. "They probably keep another ledger for money coming in. I'm just guessing, but they wouldn't want to keep anything official, like a real accounting system. And they wouldn't keep all the information in one place. These pages, or even the whole ledger, by themselves, don't mean anything. Except to you and, now, to me."

"I'm sorry. I didn't mean to involve you, Sarah. Please, forget I said anything. I'll drop the whole thing."

"Ha! No, you won't. You can't."

"Sarah, I'd give my life before I'd let anyone hurt you or the kids."

"I know that. Thank you, but I also know you. I know you'll have to try and do the right thing. It's not that you always do, of course, but I know you'll try."

"Well, the right thing is to protect my family, that's all that matters."

"True, but you know too much. Face it; you're an idealistic risk-taker,

Razz. It's one of the things I love about you."

"You still love me?"

Though that was not what she meant, she did still love him, despite everything he'd put her through. She squeezed his left forearm to reassure him and Razz had all he could do not to cringe in pain. "Can we talk about this later, please? My father's run into trouble on one of his deals, so I need to get back to work."

"Sure. That's all I needed to hear anyway." He so much wanted to hold her, but he could tell she wasn't ready for such overt affection, so he touched her hand. "Thank you."

He got up to leave, but couldn't resist one comment. "I thought your dad never lost in a real estate deal."

Sarah didn't flinch, largely because she was so angry over the deal herself. "Yeah, so did I. There may have been extenuating circumstances on this one."

Her sarcasm led him to wait for further explanation.

"Someone got him to sign a terrible contract and, even though it was clearly done fraudulently, I don't know how to prove it."

"Who was it?"

"It doesn't matter," she said, dismissing the notion that he could help in such a complex business matter.

"Come on, tell me."

"Razz ..."

It was clear he wasn't leaving that easily, so she continued. "Okay, it was a company called Cardinal Acquisition, but they probably formed it just for this investment. The name doesn't really matter."

"Did you say 'Cardinal'?"

"Yeah. So?"

"Albert Pujols," he said, as if it explained everything.

But it explained nothing to Sarah. "Who?"

"Albert Pujols. He plays for the St. Louis Cardinals. It's a baseball team."

"Look, I'm busy, Razz." Politeness over, she opened a manila folder, took out the suspect Gold Shore contract, and studied it, searching for any inconsistency that might offer them wiggle room in court.

He leaned in closer, as if it would help her understand. "Remember the baseball card Patrick Marcayda gave to Ronnie? It was of Albert Pujols."

"Razz, my father could lose everything!"

That her office door was wide open made her revelation more revealing by her loss of control. She went to the door, wordlessly imploring him to leave.

Implore, beg, or bribe, he had no intention of going anywhere now. It was a standoff that Sarah knew she couldn't win, so she shut the door. "Make it quick, Razz. What are you talking about?"

"Sarah, 'Cardinal' is the name Louis uses for the restaurant holding company, Cardinal Restaurants. He clearly likes the name, the team, the bird, something. Don't you think that might mean something?"

Now he had her full attention. "You think Louis Marcayda paid three million dollars for a piece of the Gold Shore?"

"The Gold Shore? Three million? Wow."

"That's an awful lot of tacos, Razz."

"Yeah, but I don't think this is taco money."

He thought about the two safes in Louis' office and about all the money he'd seen stuffed into the larger one. "Wait a second," he said, scanning through the ledger copies.

"See here? 'CA,' 'CR,' and 'CE.' 'C' could stand for 'Cardinal.' So, 'CR' might mean 'Cardinal Restaurants.' Right?"

She nodded, encouraging him to go on.

"Then 'CA' might mean 'Cardinal Acquisition.' But what's 'CE?'"

"Electric?" she offered.

"Maybe. Elevator?" He shook his head, knowing he was off base. "Wait a second." He paused, his eyes subconsciously shifting as he searched for a stubborn memory. "Entre ... entretent ... uh, it's Spanish ... entremento—"

"Entretenimiento?"

"That's it! Yeah. What's it mean?"

"It means you should have studied harder in school. 'Entertainment', Razz. It means 'entertainment'."

"Of course."

"Let me see those."

She took the papers, and he was only too happy to have her help. She studied each page, trying to make sense of the seemingly random numbers, but she knew they weren't random at all. In her world, numbers hardly ever were. They usually told a story and she was sure these did. "Look at this entry, Razz. Three thousand from the 'CA' account."

"Okay. And what's that mean?"

"It means you're probably right. That could be the entry for the Gold Shore stake. Just multiply every entry in the ledger by one thousand and that will tell you how much money Louis is tracking."

"Holy shit. So, two hundred and seventy must mean—"

"Two hundred seventy thousand."

"Yeah," Razz said, annoyed she hadn't let him finish his calculation. "There's an entry for two hundred and seventy under 'CR,' but we haven't made that much money. Two hundred and seventy thousand dollars could take most of the year."

She hesitated before telling him what he already suspected. "Unless he owns a whole bunch of other restaurants, you may have found your evidence he's laundering money."

Though Razz wanted to rejoice at finding the solution to the ledger puzzle, he knew the information could only complicate matters for him, so all he could say in response was, "Oh, fuck."

Oh, fuck, indeed.

32

Despite his increased velocity, Robbie knew it wouldn't be enough to carry him to shore. He cut to his right, but was once more faced with the dilemma of going outside the cover of the Pier. To most people, even to most surfers who, at their worst, are more idealistic than normal humans, that would seem a small technical point when faced with possible death at every turn, but it made all the difference in the world to Robbie/Razz.

Only after Razz promised profusely not to do anything stupid or rash had Sarah let him leave. And this time she made no bones about whose lives he would endanger, if he weren't careful. She wanted him to quit his job as soon as practicable and promised that, if he did, they could try to work things out between them. To say he was feeling better by the time he left her office would have been an extreme understatement.

He would have been happy to quit that night, but he didn't want to arouse any more suspicions than he probably already had by snooping around in Louis' office. No, he'd lay very low for a while, stay out of Louis' way, then fade off into the sunset and gracefully retire from the restaurant business.

That was his plan and, though it gnawed at him to have to look the other way when it came to Louis Marcayda's shady dealings, he knew it was the only logical choice to make. Besides, they say that every man has his price. His price was his wife and kids.

He wanted to call Sharky and apologize now that they were in the same "look the other way" camp, but he knew it could wait. He'd have plenty of time to say his mea culpas to Sharky, his parents, his kids, and, if things worked out well, his wife. He wondered what his next career would look like, and then realized that was the least of his concerns. A bigger problem was what he would do for the next few hours before having to go to work.

Razz couldn't see his kids, because they were with his parents and he wasn't ready to face his dad. He didn't want to go home for the same reasons he hadn't wanted to stay there that morning. Normally, he'd just go to work early, change clothes in his office, and go about his business. But spending extra time at work didn't sound like an appealing scenario either.

So, he drove north. His powerful, shiny Mustang convertible was a far cry from his underpowered, dilapidated Volkswagen Bus of almost thirty years ago, but driving up the coast surveying wave patterns still reminded him of his youth. Surfing was out of the question for him, given time and shark constraints, but that didn't stop him from examining wave breaks. Wave patterns today, along with upcoming weather and tidal information, could tell a veteran surfer the likelihood, size and type of waves tomorrow and for several days to come. With four-foot swells and a rainy cold front coming in tonight, along with heavy offshore winds, he knew larger, stronger waves were on their way. As soon as he felt it was safe, he definitely wanted to get back into that water.

A little over three miles north of the San Margarita Pier, as he rounded a curve, Razz noticed a small group of surfers waiting for waves. Though he no longer had the stomach to ignore shark warnings, that didn't mean every surfer would heed them. In his younger days, he'd ignored more than his share of warnings. He slowed his car to let a Dodge minivan pass, then pulled a U-turn and parked on the opposite shoulder, facing back toward San Margarita and the Pier, both visible in the distance. A gravelly knoll partly obscured his view, so he got out and scrambled up the man-made barrier created to prevent wayward drivers from hurtling over the cliff.

A brisk, salty breeze met him when he reached the top and it felt good, refreshing. Although his family and professional circumstances, his body, and his fondness for risk had evolved over the years, the feeling he got being near the ocean hadn't changed. He still loved it.

When one of the surfers caught a wave, he couldn't resist checking out the young man's technique. Though he no longer competed with every surfer in town, it was still difficult for him to appreciate another surfer's style. But he admired this young surfer, because he reminded Razz of himself in his early, aggressive days. Slashing a wave back and forth, speeding down the face, and reversing course to confront the wave at the end of the ride were reminiscent of how he used to do it. And of how he still tried to on his good days.

But Razz would settle for being a spectator today. Even if he'd had the time and nerve, his sprained ankle, bruised muscles, and scraped, open skin needed a few more days to heal. Salt water could help cauterize his wounds, but would also sting him unmercifully. He felt he'd endured enough pain recently.

He lay back on the earthen mound, settling his head on a lonely tuft of grass and watched as his young doppelganger sliced up another wave, daring it to throw him at every vicious turn. But the young man held firm to his board until the wave surrendered in foamy capitulation.

As the surfer sank into the waist-deep water, triumphant, Razz' eyes closed contentedly. With the mid-day sun warming him and gentle winds caressing him, he fell asleep to find the most peaceful dreams he'd had in a long time.

Sharky wasn't anywhere near peaceful. He sought an admiring audience and wasn't having any luck finding one. He'd stopped at every coffee shop within walking distance of the News Cafe, but few people recognized him, let alone cared about his triumph. In a world where wars could start without protest and whole species could be wiped out before anyone acted, blasé cynicism had become an art form. In a narcissist-filled town like San Margarita, one cop's good deed and one mayor's bad one hardly rated consideration.

All was not lost, because Sharky knew of two places where people still appreciated him: Mae's and his own home. He'd already basked at Mae's, so he could barely wait for Terri to get back from work to give him a heaping helping of adoration.

Driving back to his apartment, he took a shortcut through the heart of Boys' Town. He considered throwing his weight around the neighborhood to cheer up, but realized he didn't have enough heft to have any impact or fun here. He sank in his seat as he passed Louis Marcayda's red-doored clubhouse brothel.

A minute earlier or three minutes later and he might have passed by without incident, but his timing had never been fortuitous and it wasn't now. Out of the corner of his eye, he saw something that made him slow, and then stop, his car. It was a train wreck in the making, and he was the train. He backed up to get a good look at a man lounging on the brothel's front steps smoking a cigarette. It was Jaime Hidalgo's chauffeur, the man who had warned him that dead clowns weren't particularly funny.

Leaving his car idling in the southbound lane, Sharky gripped his billy club at his side as he crossed the street. He should have called for backup before making contact with a suspect, but, even in the best of circumstances, he barely followed protocol. Besides, he wanted to get a few whacks in before anyone, especially the suspect, knew what was happening. He remembered well how he'd worn a hundred-and-eighty-five pounds of iron on his Adam's apple the morning of the New Year, and he wasn't above seeking revenge. He wanted to wallow in the oozing muck of it.

As he began to raise the club only steps from the languorous man, two smaller Mexican men wearing earpieces and mirrored shades, dressed in conservative blue suits, one wearing a red tie, the other a blue one, exited the brothel. Both held .44 caliber handguns by their sides. Their actions were subtle, but their meaning was loud and clear.

"Te dije que te quedaras adentro," the red-tied man directed to the chauffeur.

"Necesito aire," the chauffeur responded before noticing Sharky. Shaken, he quickly recovered his bravado. "Hey, its clown man."

Sharky took a step toward him, but the two men raised their guns, which were mostly hidden by suit coats too long, just as quickly to stop him. Each man suffered from the curse of bad tailoring or, more likely, benefited from a smart design sense gained from years of having to hide firearms in public.

A raised eyebrow from the red-tied man on Sharky's left indicated toward the roof. Sharky's eyes followed until they rested on a video camera mounted above the door.

"It will be self-defense, señor. The camera doesn't lie."

The chauffeur rose to stand on the second step, towering above Sharky on the sidewalk. "What are you going to do now, clown man?"

Before Sharky could respond, the red-tied man interrupted. "Get inside. The boss wants to see you. Now."

The chauffeur's eyes drifted up toward the all-seeing camera. His smile vanished and he vanished with it behind the red door.

Sharky wanted to follow, but knew it could be suicide to go behind those well-guarded doors with or without backup.

"Let it go, señor. The mayor is yours. You're a hero. Enjoy it while you can."

The meaning was clear. The boss behind this door could take it all away and more, if Sharky wasn't careful. As scared as he was of Louis Marcayda, this time the threat made his desire greater. He moved toward the door, but the two men stepped in front of him.

"I'm sorry, but this is a private club," said the red-tied man, pointing to a conspicuous sign on the exterior that indeed read, "Private Club."

"So, I'll join."

"I don't think you're our type of member, señor." He laughed and was joined by the blue-tied man.

"So, you don't like white guys? Tell your boss I'll sue him for discrimination. Remind him of that unfortunate raid a few weeks back. That must have been bad for business. It can become a regular occurrence, if he likes."

Though he was blowing smoke, the threat garnered him some small measure of respect. He again moved toward the door, and this time, surprisingly, the men parted.

"The boss sends his regards and invites you to sample the club and the benefits afforded to our VIP members. No charge," said the red-tied man, now as solicitous as a concierge at a high-priced hotel, though he did appropriate the billy club.

The man opened the door and Sharky looked inside to darkness. With great trepidation, he entered what he hoped wasn't a doorway to Hell.

He passed through a velvet red curtain and two more Mexican men in suits and earpieces detained him. He couldn't help but wonder if there was a convention in town. One man frisked him, patting him on parts of his body even Terri hadn't discovered, while the other watched.

"Enjoy yourself," said the frisker, dismissing him into the room.

And what a room it was. Behind the simple red door of the nondescript stucco building in the heart of a middle-class residential neighborhood, a magnificent ballroom spread out before him. Though only fifty-feet wide, the permissible building width for an average sixty-foot-wide San Margarita lot, the room appeared to go on forever. On his right sat an ornate oak bar that seemed right out of a twenties' speakeasy. Tending bar in a see-through negligee was one of the most beautiful women he'd ever seen. Appearing to be in her early thirties, she sashayed toward him, her perfectly crafted D-cups fiercely resisting gravity.

"What can I get for you, big guy?" she asked, smiling flirtatiously through full, red lips.

Hers was an inviting package, but he reminded himself he wasn't there for a drink or flirtation, so he turned away without comment. He saw a row of semi-discrete booths curtained in red velvet for men and women of varying numbers along the opposite wall. Beyond the knee to shoulder high curtains, Sharky could see that the women were, invariably, in some level of undress and were writhing over, near, or on top of a man's body. Some men required two such women. Another required, and could clearly afford, three.

Laughter and Latin jazz permeated the great room along with marijuana and cigar smoke. It was an exhilarating mixture. Although it was only two o'clock in the afternoon, normal work hours for Sharky, this party appeared to play twenty-four hours and he was struggling to maintain focus.

Two young women, more gorgeous and scantily dressed than the bartender, approached and silently offered themselves. And they made it clear he wouldn't have to choose between them. He scurried away before he could do something he might regret.

Another beauty, a well-kept forty-something with blonde hair, approached with a silver tray filled with drinks and assorted paraphernalia. She offered a glass of Cristal Champagne, which he politely declined. He was more interested in the bowl of white powder that sat in the middle of her tray surrounded by marijuana joints in golden ashtrays.

Sharky stared at the powder, locked in a losing battle with the dispassionate substance. He shuddered, his resistance ebbing, and without much in the way of options, he looked to the woman for help.

None was forthcoming. "Would you like a taste, sir?" she asked, holding out a tiny silver spoon.

He stared at her, the spell of the powder momentarily broken. She reminded him of someone, but he didn't dare linger to try to figure out whom.

Bombarded by pleasurable possibilities, he escaped to a dark, empty nook to regroup. Although he had passed on the enticing offerings thus far, it hadn't been easy and it wasn't getting easier. If it was Louis' plan to woo him with sex, booze, and drugs, it was working. The place was intoxicating in every way.

Sharky decided to flee before he caved in to his desires, but in his confusion, he moved further into the debauchery. The room seemed to spin around him, and he wondered if he'd gotten a contact high. He looked back at the front door over one hundred feet away and doubted he could make it again through the sybaritic obstacle course without giving in. More than halfway into this great open room governed only by free choice and Louis, he felt trapped.

He ran clumsily toward the back. He brushed past several impressively endowed working girls, almost knocked down a fat, balding patron, and barely noticed any of them. Normally, a plethora of ever-present guards would not condone his boorish behavior, but when he reached the back, a guard, similar in attire and skin tone to the front door guards, simply opened the door.

Outside, Sharky collapsed to his knees onto the concrete steps and breathed heavily. He felt someone staring at him and turned, but no one was there. Then he noticed two cameras, like in the front. He was sure whoever was watching was having a great laugh, but he didn't care. He had escaped.

He brushed off his pants and hoped to brush away the whole episode until he saw a black limousine heading south. It looked like Jaime Hidalgo's limo, the one he'd seen at the Gold Shore groundbreaking, at City Hall, and at Mae's. *Is that Hidalgo's chauffeur escaping?*

Several black limos lined the street. He raced from car to car knocking on windows, but always the wrong man greeted him, and usually not very kindly. When he finished searching, without success, he walked back toward the brothel. He wondered why the chauffeur, under the circumstances of his boss's arrest, had been hanging around such a visible establishment, but given his newly acquired appreciation of the brothel's allures, that question was easily answered. *But why was the man protected?*

That question gnawed at him until he reasoned that Louis wouldn't want patrons hassled at his place of business, regardless of the cause. *Maybe Louis is just protecting one of his own.*

The guard held the brothel door for him, but he decided on a safer path. Perhaps he could enjoy an invitation to this pleasure palace at another time, but right now he needed to get off Louis Marcayda's turf.

Sharky walked toward a side alley that led back to Twentieth Street. Another guard blocked his way, but a nod from the doorman convinced him to step aside. As he walked down the alley, he saw a BMW idled at a drive-through window and cash exchanged for something in a nondescript brown paper bag. His guilt already weighing heavily, he tried not to think about it.

His car was as he had left it, double-parked and idling, and he realized there weren't many areas of town where you could leave a car unattended, keys in the ignition, and not have to file a police report. And his billy club was sitting on the front seat. His property's protection was just one of the many ironies associated with Louis Marcayda and his enterprises. Boys' Town had the lowest reported crime rate in all of Los Angeles, because few dared to commit crimes here, unless they were officially sanctioned by a higher authority.

Sharky stared back at the cameras that gawked at him from above the front door. He knew Louis was watching and that his impertinence would be taken as a challenge. His meaningless point made, he jumped into his car and sped away.

Razz gazed at the Pacific Ocean, the sunny, cloudless sky, and a bevy of surfers slashing through picture-perfect waves, and wondered if he would be late for homeroom. He smirked, realizing he didn't care if he was. He'd been late to class more often than not lately and he always got away with it, especially since his feat of surfing underneath the Pier. Everyone in San Margarita had heard about it. He was a folk hero at seventeen and life was good. He was given free burgers at Pete's Eats and free gas for his Volkswagen at Phil's Fill 'er Up. He relived his big day as if it had happened yesterday, feeling in his body every twist, turn, and danger. It was the greatest feeling in the world, and his self-satisfied smile kept broadening until he woke with a start.

Confused, he raised his head and pain seemed to split it open, threatening to allow the contents to spill out. His whole body ached and his right ankle throbbed from pooling blood. The wind had picked up, dark clouds shielded the sun's warm rays, and he shivered. He rolled to one side, saw the Pier a few miles to the south, and regained his bearings. Harsh reality had interrupted his sweet dreams. His simpler, earlier time had been replaced by his current complicated and perilous one. Sun had been replaced by clouds, warmth by cool, perfect waves by foamy early-breakers unworthy of any self-respecting surfer. Razz was forty-five again, not seventeen, and he was far from carefree. He was still separated from his wife and kids and was still in a whole heap of danger. He lay on his side trying to weather the painful storm that truth and his body rained down upon him until he realized he might also be late for work. This time, he did care about being late, because it made him think of Louis. He sat up too quickly, but fought through the pain and reached into his pants pocket for his cell phone. It was three-forty-two.

If he hurried, if he physically could, he would just make it to work on time.

Sharky hadn't needed to rush. When he left the brothel, Terri was still a couple hours from coming home, but he'd gone straight to their apartment anyway. He had barely escaped temptation at Louis' and didn't want to tempt himself with more. Only in the safety of his home behind a locked front door did he feel sure that he wouldn't screw up.

He passed time picking up his clothes, in a sort of poor man's penance for his almost-transgressions, and cleaning the kitchen in anticipation of her return. He hadn't noticed before the toast crumbs and coffee stains she'd left that morning, so used to everything being spotless now that she lived there, but he didn't think much about it.

With the short hand of the kitchen clock nearing five, Sharky worried in earnest. It was four-forty-six and Terri was usually home by now. Her shift ended at four and she worked only seven miles away at the Gallery Mall, but because of the volume and vagaries of Los Angeles traffic, he knew a seven-mile trip could sometimes take a lifetime. Although she had asked him not to call her during the workday, afraid her supervisor would take exception, the workday was now over. So, he dialed her cell number. After four rings, her voice mail picked up and a bright, cheery voice responded.

"Hey, you've reached Terri. Sorry, I can't take your call, but leave a message and I'll get right back to you."

The message was short, sweet and to the point, just like her. She hadn't hesitated the day they met; she'd gotten right to his point, and it had been very sweet. He was aroused by his fond memory, but caught himself.

"Hi, honey, I'm just wondering where you are. I was a little worried." When his eyes misted over, he realized how worried he really was. Despite his fleeting longings of that afternoon, his powerful love for her could make him cry at the drop of a phrase or image. It felt almost unbearable. He continued, his voice wavering, "Let me know you're all right. I love you."

He put the portable phone on its base and sat back to recover in his new chair. On his throne, he was the king in his castle, but it didn't feel right without his queen beside him. He turned on the television news, praying he wouldn't hear about a fiery freeway car wreck involving a green Grand Am. He resolved to buy her a new Volvo to help keep her safe, but, on further reflection, he knew that would not be possible. With his expected raise at work, maybe he'd be able to afford a Nissan.

As the four o'clock news became the five o'clock news, the proverbial "no news is good news" made Sharky feel better. There were no accidents of note, but he tried Terri's cell again anyway. When he heard her voice recording, he hung up. But, at five-thirty-five, he was near his breaking point. It wasn't like her to be this late. After one more unsuccessful effort to reach her on her cell, he decided to call her work number, before realizing she had never given it to him. *Where does she work again?* One department store was the same as another to him, but he finally remembered. She worked at Neiman-Marcus at the Gallery Mall in the Valley.

After retrieving the number from information, he dialed. Each of the five rings echoed uncomfortably through his brain and he was relieved when a young woman answered.

"Hi, could I speak to Terri Howard, please?"

"Which department?"

"Uh, I don't know. She does make-up, you know, selling cosmetics."

"Then that would be the cosmetics department."

Embarrassed by the obviousness of her response, he became annoyed when she continued to wait on the line. "So, may I speak with her?"

"Well, you could if there was anyone here by that name."

Her cheeriness was really beginning to piss him off. "Do you know when she left?"

Another pause almost sent him through the roof, but the young woman's next response brought him crashing back to earth.

"I'm sorry, sir, but no one by that name works here."

"No one by that name works here." Sharky repeated the phrase internally trying to comprehend its meaning. "Well, transfer me to the cosmetics department. Someone there will know her."

"Sir, I run the cosmetics department and have for four years. The phone rings here after office hours, because, frankly, we're not that busy. I've never met anyone by that name."

"I must have the wrong Neiman-Marcus. Is there another store nearby?"

"There are a few, but I hire for every cosmetics department. I don't know anybody by the name of Terri Howard."

Now he was becoming frantic, grasping at the slightest straw available. "Maybe she used another name. She's blonde, early-forties, maybe five-foot-three. She would have started about three weeks ago."

"I'm sorry, sir, I don't know what to tell you. Good luck."

The woman hung up with a finality that made him think she'd been confronted with such questions before and the answer was always the same—the person you think works here, doesn't, and whatever she told you, for whatever reason, it isn't true.

It's all been a lie! But how? We were together, laughing, making love, even shopping! She said she loved me! She has to love me!

However hard he rationalized her being late, he couldn't calm down, so he poured himself a glass of Scotch. After he downed it, he poured himself another. Soon, with the numbing effects of alcohol on his side, he began to feel less suicidal. After drink number three, he felt like throwing up. Not succeeding, he hoped for sleep. Myriad morbid thoughts drowned that hope, so he poured drink number four.

Exhausted, he collapsed into his La-Z-Boy, but then sprang up, as if burned by the new upholstery. Though his head was spinning, he vaguely remembered the chair's connection to Terri, so he wanted nothing to do with it now. He stumbled to a far wall and slumped to the floor, propping himself against the wall while the television spewed forth now-unrecognizable sounds.

Yards away from the portable, he struggled to pull his cell phone from his pocket. He fumbled with the keypad, threatening to call Terri again, but he couldn't press the proper buttons in his current state. He couldn't even see them; the phone was a blur.

Fading in and out of consciousness, Sharky alternately sipped and spilled his Scotch until, finally, the glass fell harmlessly to the carpet and he fell, thankfully, asleep.

33

"You can do it, man!"

"You got it, dude! Whoo!"

He looked at the crowd ahead, knowing most of them wouldn't care a whit if he strayed outside his intended path, while a few probably hoped he'd crash and burn. With only inches to spare, he cut back under the Pier toward the wave's foamy edge, again picking up speed. But he knew it wouldn't be enough to get him to shore. This journey was over.

Two hours into Razz' shift at the Surf's Up, all was well, except for the persistence of a splitting headache. Though four Tylenols and work adrenaline had numbed his body, his head continued to torment him. Every step and every thought sent another shooting pain to the back of his right eye. He'd always had more faith and use for his body. Until recently, it had rarely let him down, but his head was another matter. Thinking had often seemed to be his worst enemy, and now he was certain of it.

Fortunately, despite approaching storm clouds, a good-sized, after-work crowd was well-behaved and spending freely. His experienced staff had the situation firmly under control. Even Petra had become relatively competent. He hadn't seen Lotta, Louis, or anyone that looked like they might be a compadre in crime, so he'd been able to forget about those troubles for minutes at a time. But his comfort never lasted long. His head reminded him of pain and his mind reminded him that his potential tormentors could show up any second to inflict more.

He wished he could go upstairs to his office, curl up into a protective ball, and sleep until the headache and danger went away, but he was more wired than tired, so he kept working the floor. When two stunningly attractive fortyish women, dressed in business suits, entered the restaurant, he was happy he had. They moved like dancers, graceful, but purposeful, and he couldn't remember when he'd seen women of more beauty and class at the Surf's Up. He seated them at a front window table, a strategic table in every restaurant where attractive patrons were seated in order to lure other attractive patrons.

"Thank you," said an olive-skinned brunette.

Her friend, a lighter-skinned blonde, said, "Thank you so much," then touched his hand.

All of a sudden, his headache was gone, as was his ability to form intelligent sentences. "Are you two from around here?" he asked. It wasn't much of a comeback, but it was the best he could do under the circumstances.

"No, we're here on business. Just for the night. We're staying at the Vista del Mar." The brunette continued, "My name's Suzanne. This is Helga."

"Razz." He knew it was a time-honored tradition, when flirting with strangers, not to give more information than necessary and each side was playing exactly by the rules.

He took Suzanne's offered hand and it was the softest, yet firmest handshake he'd ever experienced. He couldn't help but linger and she didn't seem to mind that he did, but when Helga offered her hand, he took it. Then he couldn't decide which hand was nicer and wondered if they used the same aesthetician.

Freeing himself from Helga's heavenly clutches and his inane thoughts, he said, "What can I get you?"

"Well, for now, we'll have your best Bordeaux. We'll see about later," said Suzanne.

"Our finest Bordeaux, coming right up."

With that, Razz was off to retrieve a bottle of Rothschild 1987 from the wine closet. It was an eighty-five-dollar bottle wholesale that he'd likely have to write off as a "customer appreciation expense", but the pleasant interlude with the women had done what the Tylenols couldn't. He had forgotten about his headache.

It was six-thirty, well past the time Sarah would normally pick up Ronnie and Caitlin from day care. She'd asked Razz' mom to take care of them and Sally McNeil was only too happy to oblige. She had almost asked for Merice's help, but Razz' warnings, however exaggerated they seemed, had taken their toll.

She watched from her twenty-seventh floor office as storm clouds closed in and threatened to engulf her. The churning, black clouds mirrored her thoughts as she searched for a viable solution to her father's financial problems. Because those problems were automatically hers, the situation was even more dire. Her father's net worth directly affected her net worth and she wasn't willing to become middle class without a fight.

One fact was obvious—her father had signed a flawed contract. The reason for him doing so was not clear; she only knew it had something to do with Natalie Wesson. Wesson apparently had something to do Cardinal Acquisition, which apparently had something to do with Louis Marcayda, who had a lot to do with her husband, Razz McNeil. She didn't like the inadequate degrees of separation, and could only hope there would soon be multiples more between her and Razz and the rest of them. As much as she had warned him this morning, she worried he was in over his head and he didn't know how far. She didn't question his intention to quit his job, just his decision-making in getting there. She prayed a wrong decision wouldn't get him into the type of trouble from which he couldn't recover.

She studied the words, *In case of loan default by Seller and subsequent cure of said default by Purchaser, Purchaser shall be entitled to one hundred percent of Company Equity.* Those words and their meaning seemed unassailable and, after thousands of dollars in legal fees, her lawyers could only agree.

She studied the document's signature, hoping she could prove it was a forgery, but she knew it was her father's. She had seen his distinctive scribble hundreds of times on hundreds of deals.

There were no copies of the previous contract, the one she had read and approved, from which to argue. Natalie Wesson had apparently destroyed them all. And whoever wrote this contract, with its appended and offending portions, knew exactly what they were doing. To litigate its legality might buy the Golds time, but it would drain the company's coffers, and Sarah's inheritance, further.

The company had plenty of equity in other buildings, of course, but most of the buildings were held by partnerships. As the General Partner, they could pledge their interests in the partnerships for a bank loan, but going through all the documents might take more time than they had and any subsequent loan would be very expensive. Bankers always know how badly a client is bleeding and usually prefer to suck out their share rather than offer a tourniquet.

She pushed the papers aside, partly so she wouldn't have to look at them and partly so they wouldn't be stained by her now-falling tears. When her phone rang, she glanced at the caller ID and saw the call was from Merice. Despite her ambivalence, she picked up the receiver.

"Hi. Sorry I haven't returned your calls, it's been a busy day. How are you?"

"Me? How are you? I'm worried about you."

"I'm fine," she said, but her voice betrayed her.

"Oh, God, Sarah. Are you okay?"

"I'll be fine, thanks. You're a dear friend."

Sarah's pronouncement had slipped past her broken defenses, and despite everything, she still wanted to believe in their friendship.

"Look, I won't take 'no' for an answer. Come over tonight for drinks and bring the kids. We'll let them wreak havoc on the house and we'll drink till everything looks better."

Sarah laughed and then realized it was her first laugh of the day.

"That's better," Merice continued. "Thank God the men are working, so they won't bother us."

She stopped laughing. A reference, even an oblique one, to her husband by someone associated so closely with Louis Marcayda made her nervous.

"You all right?"

"Yes. I'm sorry, Merice, but I've got so much work to do tonight. How about tomorrow night?"

When she hesitated, Sarah's nervousness grew.

"Of course, tomorrow night, it is. Hey, do you want me to watch the kids while you're working? You can pick them up later on."

"No, no, they're fine. They're with my parents. See you tomorrow night."

"Great, see you then."

Sarah hung up the phone and pondered their conversation. It had felt forced, unlike previous conversations between them, unlike normal conversations between friends. There were subtexts, things unsaid. She knew her own involved a question of trust, that's why she lied about her kids' whereabouts, but she didn't understand Merice's.

Before she could feel too bad about her deceit, the phone rang again. It was Herb Winston, her father's most trusted legal advisor. Herb Winston was a man who knew his way around Los Angeles' power circles and how to get things done. He had been on Richard Gold's team unofficially for many years, and he knew where more than a few business skeletons had been buried. He'd buried several of her father's, for substantial fees, himself.

"Hi, Herb. How are you?"

"Better than you, it sounds. How's your dad?"

"Fine, he's at home. I'm sure he'd love to hear from you."

Despite her attempted brush-off, she rather enjoyed Winston. He was loud and opinionated, but also jovial, brilliant, well-read, and well-traveled. He had made a wonderful dinner companion on those not-so-rare occasions when Razz opted not to join her at one of her parents' soirees. But today was no dinner party.

"Actually, what I've got is for your ears. You can decide what to do with the information."

Her curiosity was piqued, but she was still annoyed Winston wouldn't tell her father directly. "Okay, shoot."

"Funny you should put it that way," he said with no implication that the phrase was worthy of laughter. "Look, we got some information on Natalie Wesson."

Sarah sat bolt upright, ready. "Great, what did you find?"

"Her body, actually. The police found her in the LA River. Looks like she died of an overdose, there were needle marks in her feet. Did you get the impression she was a junkie?"

Although she'd often wished for an ugly demise for Natalie Wesson, now that her fate was sealed, Sarah felt no satisfaction whatsoever. But she understood why Winston told her first, because her fragile father would be devastated by the news.

"Uh, no, I didn't."

"Neither did I, not from what Richard told me. I did get the impression she was a hired hand though."

"What?"

"She worked for someone, Sarah. When that someone had gotten what they needed, like a signed contract for equity in the Gold Shore, they got rid of her to keep her quiet. She left little trail behind, which is how employers of such people want it. Your tidbit about her attending NYU helped, but she kind of disappeared after that. She had been 'off the books' for years. The police said she overdosed on almost pure heroin and there isn't a real junkie in the world that has access to that."

"Are you saying this was all a set-up? That she was … like, a prostitute?"

"Yes, I believe you could say she was very much 'like a prostitute.'"

Sarah's stomach did somersaults at the thought of that conniving whore with her father. In her world, drug overdoses and prostitution didn't happen. They belonged in crime/romance thrillers and pulp fiction novels; they were not supposed to exist in her insular, protected Fairside world. But then, many things had happened recently that she hadn't expected.

"Someone shot her up to shut her up and tried to make it look like she'd done it before. I thought you should know."

"Are you sure it's her?"

"The police found her company ID." He paused, as if he needed to consider carefully before releasing his next words. "And your father, uh, he gave me something she'd used for a DNA sample. He didn't ask why I needed it. It's her, Sarah."

Shocked though she was by the news, there was one more important question she had to ask. "Did you find out anything about Cardinal Acquisition?"

"Not much." Winston's tone suggested failure, something to which a man like him was not accustomed. "It's run by some guy named Ramirez out of San Antonio and looks to be funded offshore through Antigua. The money trail is a black hole from there. It could come from anywhere. Ramirez is probably a front for somebody, but the contract appears valid. Sorry, I don't have better news."

"No, that's helpful. Thanks." Sarah was busy thinking about offshore accounts, Mexicans, and money laundering. She thought about baseball, Albert Pujols, Patrick Marcayda, and his parents. "Uh, don't tell my father just yet."

"Of course."

Although Winston was willing to share more information and to explain further the details of Natalie Wesson's demise, he was, after all, paid handsomely by the hour, Sarah had heard enough. She added Winston's information to her own and she understood why Merice needed to see her so badly. Louis Marcayda wanted his wife to keep an eye on her. *Merice is part of it!*

The disappointment Sarah felt because of her friend's betrayal faded when she realized what all of it meant—her family was in danger. And Razz might be in grave danger. She had to warn him.

It was rainy and cold, the sun had set behind the cloud-ridden horizon two hours earlier, but after a couple glasses of Bordeaux with the two gorgeous visitors, Razz was feeling nothing but toasty. Though he was ignoring much of his work, things were going smoothly in the restaurant. Guilt-laden though he was for his flirtations, the two beautiful strangers played powerfully with his fantasy life and seemed happily willing to make it more than fantasy.

"Come on," said Suzanne, "we're just here for the night. Come with us. It will be fun."

Razz had no doubt how much fun it could be, he'd already mentally played through several rendezvous with the women in their penthouse suite at the Vista del Mar, and they got better with each showing. "Believe me, I'd love to, but I've got to work."

"I'm sure this place can live without you for one night," said Helga.

He was oh-so tempted, but ignoring his duties on-site was one thing, going AWOL would be entirely another matter. He could rationalize socializing with guests, it was part of his job, but Louis wouldn't forgive him if he left his post, not even for these two women. It was not a good time to make Louis angry.

Despite that very good reason against it, he might have gone with them had he not kept thinking of Sarah. Although they were officially, if not yet legally, separated, arguably allowing him some wiggle room with morality, his slowly developing conscience told him a rendezvous could never be worth it. He had already cheated on Sarah, his kids, and on himself through infidelity and selfishness, and he needed the chance to make it up to everyone.

After running through his fantasy one more time, he rose from the table and said, “Ladies, thank you, you’ve made my night, my month, my year, but I’ll have to leave you to your wine now.”

“Oh, that’s so disappointing,” said Suzanne. “How’s that for a whine?”

The three of them laughed, before she continued, “We’ll be here, in case you change your mind. Could you bring another bottle, please? And please join us when you can.”

Razz didn’t understand their determination, but he certainly did appreciate it. *Perhaps, I can get away later*, he thought, before catching himself.

Suzanne reached out her hand and he took it. This time, instead of feeling the smoothness of soft, perfect skin, he felt the roughness and dryness of paper. She was handing him money and she could tell it bothered him.

“Don’t be offended, sweetie, it’s just a tip. You’ll be coming for free.”

The two women giggled alluringly, but when Razz looked at a folded hundred-dollar-bill in his hand, he felt cold inside and could not explain why. He only knew that he’d felt this way before and he didn’t like the feeling. He put the bill back on the table.

“Thank you, but there’s no need, ladies. I’ll bring your wine. Please, enjoy yourselves.”

“We still hope to,” Helga said, but he had already moved out of earshot.

The women did not look happy, but as he walked away, his back to them, Razz looked petrified. Before he could figure out exactly what had scared him, another unpleasant sensation accosted him.

“Hey, Razz. Hey! Over here!”

Things had looked so good only minutes ago, but now his headache had come back full force, and he was confronted by another headache standing near the front door—Harvey Howells.

“What’s up, Harvey? I’m kind of busy.”

“I could tell. They’re hot,” said Howells, lasciviously eyeing the women. “You need some help with them?”

Normally, Razz would have broken into helpless laughter at such a remark from such a man, but in this instance, it didn’t even raise a chuckle. “Uh, no, they’re all yours. Knock yourself out. What are you doing here?”

“I’m celebrating. I’m going to get a promotion.”

“Hey, congratulations. I’ll buy you a drink—”

“Sure.”

“—tomorrow. How about tomorrow? Tonight’s not a good night.”

“I bet. You just want them for yourself. I can’t blame you. They’re hot, really hot.”

Razz considered Harvey Howell’s limited vocabulary in describing the opposite sex and suspected his vocabulary was greater than his experience. "Yeah, they're hot, Harvey. So, I'll see you tomorrow?"

"Great!"

The enthusiastic response could have been considered a compliment, but, when Howells sat down at his usual table, Razz didn't feel any appreciation whatsoever.

"Just one drink tonight, though. And how about that salmon?"

Razz reluctantly resigned himself to Howells' company tonight and probably for tomorrow, as well. His own night had taken a decidedly-drastic turn for the worse in the past few minutes, but when he saw Louis' black Mercedes roll slowly down the Pier toward the Sol a Sol, his velocity around that now-dangerous turn increased a hundred-fold.

"Fuck," he said to himself, but Harvey Howells felt the curse's prick.

"Okay, just the burger then. Jeez."

Razz didn't hear him, he was already moving toward the front door. He walked out into the rain and watched the Mercedes' tail lights fading into the fog that was rapidly rolling in.

What the fuck is he doing here? Whatever it is, it can't be for anything good.

He leaned against a sign post for support as water soaked through his thin cotton shirt. He barely noticed, still fixated on the car lights that were now merely tiny, red specks.

"What are you doing out here? It's wet."

He turned and saw Sharky whose ruddy face and bleary eyes gave away the fact he'd already had a rough night. "You look like crap," said Razz.

"Thank you. I feel like shit." Sharky threw his arm around him in an overly-friendly gesture and said, "Just thought I'd have a drink with my best buddy."

Razz looked back down the Pier, but the tail lights had disappeared. A rapping on a restaurant window drew his attention and he turned to see the women eyeing him. Suzanne gestured for him to join them inside. The sensory overload was nearly too much and he briefly considered escaping with the women anywhere they liked, just to get far away from the Pier.

He looked back at Sharky, who could barely hold himself upright, his eyes at half-mast, and sighed. "Come on, let's get you some coffee."

"Whiskey."

"Whatever."

Razz put his arm around his mid-section and helped him inside, not looking forward to hearing the inevitable story of what had brought him to his lowly state. He hoped he would pass out in a corner quietly, but then a brilliant idea came to him. He walked Sharky through the restaurant and deposited him next to Harvey Howells.

"Hey, Harvey," mumbled Sharky who looked happier to see him than vice-versa.

"What's he doing here?"

"Salmon dinner and a Coke coming right up, Harvey," said Razz, then he headed for the bar, leaving Howells to figure out the answer himself.

Razz handed off the duties for the care and feeding of his crime-fighting buddies to Petra, and clung to relative safety behind the bar. Although the beautiful and mysteriously tenacious women continued to woo him, he held firm by keeping his distance. Harvey Howells waved him over several times, but he deftly sidestepped that trap, pretending not to notice him. Rick, the regular bartender, tolerated his presence as long as he put all the tips in his jar.

Making drinks, making dollar tips, and making jokes felt like the good life to Razz. Managing restaurants, a family, his emotions, and a so-called grown-up life seemed too difficult for any mere mortal. *How do other men do it?*

He felt bad for not offering Sharky more moral support, but when Howells put a consoling hand on Sharky's shoulder, he felt that pressure ease. He would make sure Petra kept feeding him whatever he wanted.

Out of the corner of his eye, he saw Suzanne and Helga rise from their table. He grabbed a towel and wiped down the bar, trying to ignore the dual temptation that was now approaching him.

Shit, shit, shit, he screamed internally. *I should run while I can. I'm weak, weak! Run now, run!*

He didn't have the courage to run, so he went to the opposite end of the bar and turned his back, hoping the women would leave him to his spinelessness. He rubbed the bar hard, concentrating on that one tiny aspect of his life he could control. He heard footsteps behind him. They grew like thunder as they approached, then they stopped.

"Razz."

His heart leapt into his throat, out of his mouth, and halfway down the Pier. He turned and was relieved to see Lotta.

"Are you all right? You don't look good," she said.

You wouldn't either without a heart or a spine!

"I'm fine, fine. What are you doing here?"

"Louis sent me to give you the night off. I think I got here just in time. You look like you could use it."

The two women seemed to lie in wait, ready to pounce like hungry lionesses, and he warmed to the idea, easily forgetting his foreboding of only moments before. *I'll give them some flesh*, he thought, and, before he knew it, he was smiling.

Suzanne and Helga smiled back enigmatically, as if equally happy and sad about their likely success. He turned to Lotta who wore a strangely similar expression. He backed up three steps so he could take them all in simultaneously, so he could see the whole forest instead of only the individual trees. What he saw frightened him more than Suzanne's hundred-dollar handshake.

The three women looked like clones—beautiful, sexy, scheming clones. Though not exactly alike on the outside, when he looked into each one's eyes, he saw the same thing. *They're killing machines!*

He leapt back against the bar.

"Are you okay?" Lotta asked.

Suzanne and Helga seemed to care about his condition, too; he could tell by their new, similar, concerned looks. But Razz was not okay. He felt like a cornered animal.

Such a beautiful triumvirate would normally be considered a gift from God, but he sensed the Devil's work here instead. *Why would they want to kill me?* Even in a moment of egoism run amuck, Razz hardly felt he was that important, and he questioned his intuition once again. *God, I should take the night off, go home, and go to bed—alone.* Though he emphasized the "alone" part, even that seemingly safe decision didn't feel right. He had nowhere to go, so he decided to stay.

"Thanks, Lotta. Tell Louis I'll be right here running the restaurant, if he needs me. And, ladies, thank you. I wish you the best of luck in your business ventures. Have a wonderful evening."

He walked out from behind the bar, past the three man killers, and toward the front door, reasserting his authority as manager.

A group of four young surfers he recognized from early morning surf sessions sauntered in. Razz greeted them with a smile and a shaka, the universal surf dude sign, and he felt better. They exchanged greetings until the young men noticed the three beautiful women at the bar.

"Yo, check out the betties," bellowed one Spiccoli-like dude. Then he and two of his buddies laughed.

The best looking and most mature of the bunch walked over to Suzanne and offered his hand. "Please forgive my friends. May I buy you a drink? You're very beautiful and I'd like to get to know you."

Razz watched the young man, probably in his mid-twenties, model-handsome with short dark hair, gaze into her eyes. He wasn't intrusive; he was simply inviting her confidently. The man reminded him of himself in his younger days; he had used a similar technique many times. *Be yourself, but be clear about what you want.* Any woman had to respect that, especially if you looked like Adonis as this young man did. That's why both men were surprised when Suzanne walked outside with Helga, wordlessly dismissing him.

The young man shrugged off the rejection and, after some good-natured ribbing from his friends, the four found a table against the far wall and scanned the room for new prospects.

Razz couldn't shrug the episode off as easily. For a couple of women in town for one night looking for a good time, it didn't make any sense. They were very clear in their intentions for him. As much as he wanted to think he was the best catch in town, the spurned young stud was obviously a better one-night catch. And Suzanne had turned him down flat.

The whole scene bothered him and, when a black limousine picked up the two women out front, it bothered him more, because the limo reminded him of Louis' Mercedes.

No, it can't be. It's just another limo, probably a Town Car. They rented a car to travel in style, that's all. So what if Vista del Mar's only a hundred yards away, they wouldn't want to walk in the rain. Maybe they came from another engagement.

As thoughts tumbled around his brain searching for order, Razz pushed open the front door. He walked out into the rain, which was falling harder now, but all he could see were red tail lights as the vehicle made its way up the connecting bridge.

"Who were those women?"

He whirled and the mysterious women and their mode of travel were no longer a pressing concern. Standing in front of him, umbrella raised in an ineffectual attempt at staying dry, was his wife.

"Sarah." He hugged her without invitation. "I'm so glad to see you. You have no idea."

"No, I'm sure I don't," she said, wondering why he was so interested in a vehicle containing two beautiful women.

"Huh? Oh, I'm sorry, come in and dry off." Then he hugged her again, but, this time, she sensed his relief and began to feel some, too.

"Okay, okay," she said. "It's good to see you, too."

Still holding her, he noticed water cascading down his cheeks. He wasn't certain of the source until he felt a droplet caress the edge of his lips and he sensed the faint taste of salt.

"Razz."

He shuddered, but didn't let go. He was so tired from all that had happened in the past several weeks, he didn't ever want to let go of this moment or this woman.

"Razz, we've got to talk. I've found out some things."

His tears stopped flowing and his sense of security stopped with them. Resigned, he took his wife's hand and led her into the Surf's Up.

Within minutes, Razz had learned of the sordid saga of Natalie Wesson and more details about the equity purchase in the Gold Shore Hotel and Resort. Strategically seated far away from Sharky and Harvey Howells, his back to the wall with a clear view of the main restaurant and front door, Razz surveyed the room while Sarah confided in him. He eyed Lotta, unsure why she was still there. He sensed she was watching him, too, but he could never quite catch her in the act. Though he knew his paranoia was again flourishing, he was comfortable with the notion it was justified.

"Our lawyer thinks she was a hooker," Sarah said.

"What?"

"He thinks Natalie Wesson was hired to get my father to sign this deal. When he did, they killed her to shut her up."

Razz understood the meaning of each of her words separately, but the import of them all together had an almost unfathomable impact. He pictured the two gorgeous, classy women who had worked so hard to get a mostly-unsuccessful, mostly-broke, middle-aged stranger to go with them to their hotel for sex and he went ashen.

"What's the matter, Razz?"

He looked again at Lotta, and, this time, he saw her watching him back. She smiled reassuringly, but he was in a panic.

"So, so, you think Louis paid this woman to, you know ..."

"Yes."

"And then he had her killed?"

"There's no other good explanation."

"No, there isn't." He grabbed Sarah's hand and words flooded out. "Sarah, I'm sorry for everything. Please, forgive me. I've been selfish and neglectful, I've been disloyal—"

"Why are you telling me this?"

Her calm threw him. He expected her to argue, to storm out, to rid herself finally of this predicament of a husband, but she'd surprised him once again.

"Because you have to leave here and I wanted to make sure I admitted those things, in case I don't get another chance."

"Razz—"

"Sarah, take the kids and get out of here. Go somewhere, don't tell anyone where. Just go. Now."

"It can't be that bad."

"Those two women, the ones you saw. They wanted me to go with them, Sarah. Why me? Why now? Because they were going to kill me."

"Stop it."

"Lotta came in to give me the night off, so I'd go with them. Louis must know I've been snooping around."

"Razz, you're scaring me."

"Good. All those rumors I've been denying—he hires people to do his dirty work, Sarah. Those two tonight, that Wesson woman, maybe even Lotta, they're just his hired guns. When I didn't play along, he was going to get me out of the way. I know it. You've got to get away from here."

Sarah digested this flood of unsavory information, and then asked quietly, "So, why didn't you?

"Huh?"

"Why didn't you go with them?"

"Sarah—"

"Why?"

"We don't have time—"

"I need to know." She bit off each word sharply, while her gaze penetrated his soul, leaving him no room to evade her.

He hesitated, but not because he had to gather his thoughts or sensor his answer. No, her question was an easy one. He sensed an all-important truth weeks ago, but it had crystallized diamond-hard this evening during his confrontation with the two female predators.

"Because I kept thinking of you and the kids. And about how I wanted just one more chance to be the man you deserve, and to make everything up to you." He continued faster, more insistent, "But it doesn't matter now, I just need to know you're all safe. Sarah, please leave here."

She clasped his hands in hers, love and forgiveness filling her eyes. "You know I can't go now."

He struggled, almost overcome with emotion. "Jesus, Sarah!"

"Hey, we'll be okay."

This time, her composure helped calm him. He nodded, uncertain, but hopeful, she would be proven right.

"By the way, Merice wanted me and the kids to come over tonight," she continued.

"You can't go."

"I know, I know. I told her we couldn't, but she kept insisting. I think she wanted to keep an eye on us."

"Now you understand why you've got to go. They're watching us." As if to confirm his fears, he looked up and caught Lotta eyeing them.

This time, Sarah looked, too, but Lotta simply waved, as if seeing an old friend. "I never did trust that bitch," Sarah said, turning back. "Where could we go, Razz? We can't just disappear."

He tried to think of a safe spot and drifted back in memory to the happiest times in his marriage. He pictured their family's joy at San Margarita Hospital during the births of his two children, but they couldn't go to the hospital to escape danger. He pictured the Gold family mansion where they'd been married, but knew they wouldn't be safe anywhere near San Margarita. Then it came to him.

He leaned across the table and whispered, "Go to our honeymoon spot in the mountains. Don't tell anyone. Check in under another name. Pay cash."

"You'll join us tomorrow?"

"Can I get you anything before I go?"

They turned to see Lotta hovering over them.

"Hi, you may remember me, I'm Carlotta. I've worked with Razz for several years."

Sarah grasped her offered hand and squeezed—hard. "Hi, Carlotta. Sarah. It's nice to see you again."

Lotta's face contorted in pain until Sarah let go. "Yes, nice to see you, too," Lotta said with such fake sincerity that she left no doubt about their rivalry.

"Well, thanks for stopping by. If you'll excuse us, we have important family business to attend to." Sarah's emphasis of "family" was a warning to stay away from hers and raised the stakes, but Lotta saw her raise and went all in.

"Yes, of course." She smiled viciously. "So do I."

Sarah did not waver; her gaze was steady. That Razz felt weak-kneed convinced him which was the stronger sex.

Lotta turned to him, purring, "I'll check on you later to see if you need me for anything."

"No, nothing. Everything is fine. I'll just see you tomorrow."

"Oh, that's all right. I'll definitely see you later." She looked back at his wife. "Nice to see you again. Sarah, was it?"

Lotta felt her mission complete and walked toward the front door. Razz had never seen an ass move so much just from walking, but he wasn't impressed or interested, he just wanted to make sure she was leaving.

When she walked past the last window and out of sight, Razz turned back to his wife, took her hands and said, "I love you."

She squeezed his hands and said, "Be careful, Razz," then she grabbed her umbrella and coat and walked out.

Razz watched Petra deliver dinner to a table of four, Rick joke with regulars at the bar, and Chad reset silverware, and then he looked over at Sharky and Harvey Howells. Sharky was face down on the table, apparently passed out, and Howells was stuffing his face with salmon. Howells responded with a thumbs-up signal, content with the world.

If only I could feel so carefree, Razz thought, and then he cleared his table and went to the kitchen to check on his staff.

As the night passed, Razz wondered if every customer was a possible spy. Every attractive woman became a threat. Every man became a Louis ally with a concealed gun. For those reasons and one other, he spent as much time as possible behind the bar.

From there, he had a clear view of the street. He needed to know when Louis' car left the Pier. Once Louis was gone, he'd feel safer. Tomorrow he could join his wife and kids at their mountain hideaway, then call in his resignation and leave the restaurant business forever. Maybe they would take a long vacation, let tensions die down, and then figure out what to do and from where to do it. Maui sounded especially nice to him right now. He no longer cared about Louis' illicit dealings. He simply wanted to live a safe, quiet, long life with his family. He just hoped it wouldn't be too late.

At ten o'clock, with most of the remaining customers heading for home, Razz saw Harvey Howells waving frantically. He pretended not to notice, until guilt got the better of him. He had mostly avoided Sharky and Howells all evening, a task made easier by Sharky being passed out for much of it. Now he was sitting upright, and Howells was calling for reinforcements, so Razz relented and went over.

Before he even reached them, Howells blurted, "I think he's going to be sick."

After one quick look, it was impossible for him to argue. Sharky had surpassed looking like shit and was reaching death warmed-over territory.

"I don't feel so good," he said.

Razz grabbed him by his belt and collar and lifted him out of his chair. Fortunately, their target, the bathroom, was only fifteen feet away. After a momentary struggle with the door, they reached a stall with no time to spare.

As Sharky spewed brown liquid, his head engulfed by a toilet bowl, Razz questioned his choice of careers and friends. By the fourth round of heaving, Sharky had voided himself of poison and had begun to rejoin the living.

When he noticed his face was inside a toilet bowl, surrounded by stench, he responded quite naturally, "What the fuck?" And when he realized someone was holding him there, he flailed for freedom. "Hey, get off me. Get the fuck off me."

"Are you done? Are you okay?"

"Razz?"

"Yeah, you okay?"

"I'm not going to be if I've got to smell this shit much longer. Fuck you. I thought you were my friend."

Razz lifted his head from the toilet bowl. "That's better. That's the Sharky I know and love."

Sharky sat on his ass on the cold tile, getting his bearings. The room was spinning, his head was pounding, and the stench was as miserable as he was. He peaked into the bowl. "Oh, gross."

"You're telling me.

"I did all that?"

"Little ol' you."

"Fuck. Get me out of here."

Razz helped him stand on his own two wobbly feet. A hint of recognition in his glazed eyes, Sharky said, "Thanks."

"Let's get you some coffee."

After several splashes of cold tap water, Sharky felt better until he looked into the bathroom mirror. Then his memories came flooding back bringing with them more misery. His legs buckled and Razz caught him just in time.

"Come on, man, tell me all about it."

Between sobs, Sharky spoke about what was bothering him. He didn't even mind that Harvey Howells was there to listen. He told them how he and Terri had picked out house plants and that it was the first time he had owned a plant. He told them about his new chair, the first piece of furniture he'd owned that wasn't second-hand. He told them about how much he loved her, that it was the first time he'd ever truly been in love, and that now she was gone. Then he broke down and sobbed for several minutes.

Razz fretted whether Louis had left the Pier or not, but his friend needed him, so he stayed by his side. He couldn't tell him his suspicion, that the love of Sharky's life had been just another hooker hired for a job. A very beautiful and horny woman wins an average-looking man's confidence largely through sex, and then leaves without explanation. That it would happen to Richard Gold was plausible, especially to help facilitate a multimillion-dollar deal. That someone, namely Louis, would want to keep an eye on Razz because of his snooping around even made sense. *But why Sharky? What had he done to deserve such treatment? All he'd done lately is solve a murder involving a gay mayor.*

As Sharky sobbed and Howells wolfed down a second brownie fudge sundae, Razz wondered if Louis could have somehow been involved in the Wally Bumpers case, so he would need to keep an eye on the man most likely to solve it. He pictured Wally strung up directly under a restaurant now owned by Louis Marcayda.

Was that spot a coincidence or part of a larger plan? Did he do it to convince a stubborn restaurant owner to sell out? Or was he killing two birds with one clown by sending messages to both Ignacio Sol and Jaime Hidalgo? And why Wally?

Murdering a Pier clown seemed like a lot of trouble even to an imaginatively suspicious fellow like Razz. *If he wasn't involved in murder, why dig up a corpse that could implicate him?*

"That was great."

Howells held his distended belly, satiated and satisfied, undisturbed Sharky was sobbing or that Razz was tied in mental knots. All Harvey Howells understood right now was that he was a hero for helping to solve a murder. His obliviousness made Razz jealous.

"Glad you enjoyed it, Harvey. Hey, take care of our friend here, will you?"

He scowled. "Your friend."

With a look from Razz, he relented. "Yeah, sure. Of course, I will."

"Thanks, Harvey."

He squeezed the nape of Sharky's neck. "I've got to go back to work, but I'll make sure the coffee keeps coming."

Howells pushed the coffee toward him for encouragement. The kind gestures reassured Sharky enough that he managed to take a sip. For a moment, it looked like he might give the coffee back and more, but he succeeded in keeping everything down. Then he took a drink and held that down, too. He looked over at Howells and up at Razz and nodded his thanks, starting to feel better.

It appeared he would live, so Razz escaped to safety behind the bar. He looked out the window and saw the Pier blanketed in fog amidst driving rain. Metal support poles for the window awnings bent dangerously against the breeze, and he realized he had shirked one too many of his duties. If one of those poles snapped, an awning could crash through a window, and then he'd have to replace an awning and a window, not an inexpensive proposition.

"Razz, it's for you." Rick offered him the phone.

"I've got to get those awnings down."

"It's Lotta."

Lotta? The awnings would have to wait.

"Hey."

"Hey," she said. "Is everything all right?"

The awnings were beginning to slap violently against the side of the building. "Yeah, sure."

"Oh, okay. Well, I'm at the Sol a Sol. The place was dead, so I closed early. The staff is already gone."

The Surf's Up staff was twiddling thumbs waiting for patrons that were likely happily ensconced in their homes, right where they belonged on such a nasty evening. He hated to waste employees' time, but one question was more important than their time.

"Hey, is Louis still there?" Though he said it as nonchalantly as he could, he was nowhere near nonchalant.

"Why do you ask?"

"No reason."

"No, he left a long time ago."

His relief was overcome by annoyance that he had fretted Louis' false presence all evening. "Oh. Well, I guess I'll close up, too. Have a good evening."

"See you tomorrow."

Not if I can help it, he thought, as he hung up the phone. He looked back at his two remaining patrons, Sharky and Harvey Howells, then at his crew, Rick, Petra, Tom, Chad and Carlos, then at the awnings.

"Sorry, guys, you can take off now."

Carlos shrugged, Chad grumbled, and Petra said something in Russian with a tone that made Razz guess it wasn't "Have a good evening."

"Can I give you a hand with those?" Only Rick seemed to understand that taking down awnings in forty-mile-an-hour wind gusts was probably a two-person job.

"Yeah, thanks. The rest of you, go ahead."

Before anyone could leave, Petra's husband pushed open the front door. It only took a moment for everyone to realize he was drunk and less pleasant than usual.

"Give me beer," he said in heavily accented English.

"Sorry, we're closing, Vlad. Everyone's going home," Razz said.

Vlad glowered. "Food, too." That he had no intention of leaving was clear from his direct move toward the bar.

"Come on, baby. I'm tired. Let's go," said Petra.

Vlad scooped her into his strong right arm and swept her to the bar with him. He plunked her onto a stool and climbed onto the stool next to her. "I eat first."

When he pulled a gun from his waistband and placed it on the bar, the stakes were raised many-fold. Rick and Carlos looked to Razz for their next move, but he was looking at them for the same move. Tom and Chad backed away, very willing to let the others handle the situation.

"Put that away, you're embarrassing me in front of my friends," pleaded Petra.

"I'm your only friend here," said Vlad, ending the conversation.

She looked at Razz, but she could offer no help.

"How about a Heineken tonight?" said Razz, figuring acquiescence was a better choice than confrontation.

"I'll put a sandwich plate together," Carlos chimed in.

"We'll get the awnings," said Rick.

That Rick had included Chad in his offer gave Chad pause, but he reluctantly nodded his approval.

"No, no, you guys, go on. I'll take care of everything." The men were already in motion, and Razz was grateful beyond words. He didn't want his people at risk, but he knew their presence could help defuse the situation.

Unfortunately, Sharky's presence probably wouldn't. "Is everything all right?" He was unsteady in walk, speech, and mind, but his police instincts were taking over.

When Vlad put his hand on his gun, anticipating, Razz worried those instincts might get them all killed.

"Yes, yes, everything's fine. Vlad's a friend of the bar. Let me bring you some more coffee. Go sit down, please. I'll be right over."

Sharky stared at the back of Vlad's head, and then looked at Razz whose eyes pleaded for forbearance. He nodded and went back to his table without incident.

Razz breathed a sigh of relief when Vlad's hand left his revolver and went to his bottle of Heineken. Though his own hands were shaking, he poured a cup of coffee, excused himself, and went over to Sharky's table.

Sharky spoke before he could. "My gun's in my car up on Ocean. I can be back in two minutes."

"No."

"Gun? What's going on?" asked Howells, as if awakened from a pleasant dream only to find a nightmarish reality.

"Nothing, Harvey," said Razz. "There's nothing to worry about. Hey, I'll bring you another brownie sundae."

Howells refused emphatically. He'd had enough sugar and excitement for this evening.

Razz turned back to Sharky. "Do me a favor and just drink this. Everything's fine."

"Look, Razz, I'm drunk, but I'm not stupid." He took a drink of coffee and a look back at the Russian. "Just keep the coffee coming. I'm here if you need me."

Razz smiled, grateful.

"Uh, I should get going. It's late." Harvey Howells was standing and sweat beads dotted his face.

Once again, Razz was glad, for Howells' sake and that of every citizen of San Margarita, that he was stuck in a lab far away from the front lines of crime fighting. "Good idea, Harvey. Hey, come on back tomorrow."

Howells was making a beeline for the back door, which made Razz suspect he wouldn't be at the Pier again anytime soon.

"The awnings are tied down," said Rick.

"Thanks, guys. That's a huge help. You can take off now."

"Great, see you tomorrow," said Chad who didn't hesitate before scurrying out.

"You sure you're okay?"

Razz nodded. "Thanks."

Rick offered his hand. "I just wanted you to know, for what it's worth, it's been a pleasure working with you."

"What do you mean?"

"Any idiot can tell you're leaving."

Razz wondered how many others suspected his exit plans.

"I mean," Rick continued, "I don't know where you're going, but, if you ever find yourself needing a good bartender, I hope you'll give me a call."

"Oh. Sure, of course." He put his left hand on Rick's shoulder and clasped his right hand. "You're the first person I'll call."

"Take care of yourself."

"You, too." Razz watched him walk out and was comforted that one more person was safe.

"You've been hanging out with thugs and whores!"

Petra's angry voice made him wonder if his reinforcements hadn't left too early.

Sharky began to respond, but Razz stopped him. "Please, I'll handle it."

"We came here to get away from all that!" Petra jumped off her stool and headed toward the door, but Vlad caught her after only two steps.

"How else could I afford this?" he said calmly as he pulled out a black velvet box from his coat pocket. He opened the box to reveal a beautiful diamond ring.

"Oh."

Vlad slipped off her old ring, put it on the bar, and then replaced it with the new one. "It was time you had a real diamond."

"Oh." Overcome, Petra kissed him, clearly forgiving him for whatever had bothered her moments ago.

Razz was relieved, but couldn't help doubt the union's longevity. He noticed the handgun still on the bar and made the slightest of movements toward it. It was an unconscious reaction without malicious intent, but Vlad saw him.

The two men stared at each other, each was an equal distance from the gun, either could have reached it first, but Vlad was the one who moved. He casually walked over, took the pistol and tucked it into his waistband.

"Don't play with guns. They can be dangerous," he said, and then he put a twenty-dollar bill next to the old ring on the bar. He had finally left a tip.

With that, two giddy Russians danced out the front door into the fog and disappeared.

Razz ran over and locked the door. Sharky chugged the remains of his coffee, and Carlos headed for the back exit.

"Good-night," hollered Carlos, just before leaving.

"Thanks for the coffee," said Sharky, struggling to his feet. "You want a ride?"

"No, I've got my car. Let me get you a coffee and a cab to go." Razz would sooner crawl home than ride with Sharky, and he had no more time for baby-sitting.

"Just the coffee. Don't worry; I'll walk it off first."

Razz poured the remains of that night's coffee into a sixteen-ounce to-go cup. He looked at the black liquid uncertainly. "It won't win any taste contests, but it will help you feel better."

Sharky teared up.

"What's the matter?"

"Terri made really good coffee." Then he laughed. It was a laugh as empty as he felt. "He could come back. Maybe I should stay."

"Who?"

"The Russian."

Razz was relieved he was talking about a big Russian instead of a little Mexican. "I think Vlad will be busy with other things tonight."

Sharky thought about the young couple and again got teary.

"Hey, maybe it was a misunderstanding and she's home waiting for you right now." Razz could tell Sharky wasn't expectant, but his comment was enough to offer a flicker of hope.

"Yeah, maybe so. Hey, call me if you need me."

"I will." He gave him a hug, before pulling back. "You'll be okay, my friend."

Sharky was grateful for the manly affection. "You, too ... friend."

Razz followed him to the back, locked the door behind him, and watched him disappear into the night. Finally, mercifully, he was alone. Or was he? When he walked back into the restaurant, his long history at the Surf's Up flooded over him. Vintage surfboards adorning every wall seemed to speak at once, each board pleading for one more spin on the waves. Voices from his past spoke, too. A gruff male voice implored him for one more drink, a young woman's voice begged for time off to go to an audition, and voices from current and former patrons sent peals of laughter and argument reverberating through his brain. The voices brought back grand memories of the good times behind the bar, serving drinks, telling jokes, and gathering phone numbers, the frustrating times when he was learning how to manage a restaurant, and the recent difficult times when he was struggling with new ownership and his own conscience. Each voice vied for attention, growing louder in his brain, until they reached an almost unbearable crescendo. Then all the voices stopped at once and Razz knew it was over. He could not come back here. The Surf's Up was history, but he had one more thing to do before leaving the Pier for good.

He had unfinished business at the Sol a Sol.

34

He thought he would probably survive a dip into the water this close to shore, but he worried the waiting crowd would deride his ambitious attempt as folly. Just as his board began sinking, along with his hopes, a gust of wind, as if God, in his Infinite Pity, had blown him a kiss, straightened out the wave so it travelled almost parallel to shore. Instinctively, Robbie cut once again to his right toward the strongest part of the wave. After he easily dodged one last helpless piling, the conquered wave carried him tamely to shore.

Razz fingered the pistol in his coat pocket, checking and re-checking the safety lock. He'd never taken the gun from his Surf's Up office before, figuring it would be more dangerous for him than anyone else. But, tonight, he needed the companionship.

The Pier was eerily quiet as he walked toward the Sol a Sol, except for sounds of breaking waves. With the absence of restaurant and amusement park customers, the police station had closed early. Even the homeless had found more hospitable terrain. The park had closed, its workers sent home and its lights extinguished. The usually dancing colored lights of the Ferris wheel were inexplicably doused. Only two solar street lamps, already weakened from lack of sun that day, and exterior deck lights from the Sol a Sol lit his way.

The wind and rain had eased, but fog still hung heavy, shrouding the Ferris wheel so it looked like a huge metallic ghost. The roller coaster snaked its way through the mist, appearing and disappearing like a serpent winding through heavy brush as it searched for prey. Razz imagined malevolent spirits waiting in line to ride the now-motionless bumper cars, which made him wonder whether it would be a busy summer at the Pier. Then he tried to void his mind of all things but one—how to discover whether Louis Marcayda had been involved in the murder of Wally Bumpers.

If Louis had been, he, Sharky, and Harvey Howells would be responsible for the arrest of the wrong man for murder. That possibility was something he couldn't live with. Despite Hidalgo's DNA match, Razz knew Louis could have orchestrated everything—his ambitions and methods seemed boundless. It appeared he'd used Natalie Wesson to gather information, then had her killed when her job was complete. Sharky's supposed girlfriend, Terri, had disappeared. Razz knew he was lucky to be alive, if only because, this time, his guilt had been stronger than his desire. He would only know the truth, in his heart, by going back to the scene of the crime or, at least, the scene of Wally's discovery.

He played the facts over and over in his mind. Wally had been dead for several days before being tied to the pilings under the Sol a Sol where discovery would be certain and dramatic. He had been killed elsewhere and buried first, so he'd been exhumed before his corpse's Pier display. That it was a message sent clearly and profoundly was certain, Razz just didn't know by whom or to whom. That's why he had to go back. He had to know he'd done all he could to see justice served.

He wondered why he even cared about justice. It had never been a driving passion, and it wasn't going to bring Wally Bumpers back. If reincarnation could happen for Wally, it wouldn't have changed his life one iota, because he barely knew the man. Still, Razz cared about the truth. Perhaps, he wanted to assuage his guilt due to working for a possible killer, Louis Marcayda, and to make certain they hadn't indicted the wrong man. Maybe he had to do it to finally set a good example for his children. Maybe it was so he could regain his wife's respect and his parents' love. Maybe he just had to do it for himself, so he could believe he'd been worthy of that one glorious day in high school when he'd conquered the Pier, to feel his success hadn't been a fluke and that every one of his many failures since that extraordinary day during his limitlessly hopeful youth had been an anomaly.

He didn't want to run away this time; he didn't want to take the easy way out; he didn't want to succumb once again to his fears. He wanted to feel like a man. And to know he deserved to.

He shivered, partly due to the cold mist, but largely due to the fear he despised in himself, as he approached the Sol a Sol. He pulled his windbreaker closer around him alleviating only one of the causes of his shivering, then looked back down the Pier to be sure he was alone. When he did, he realized he was standing, illuminated, under a street lamp. He leapt back into the darkness, then tried unsuccessfully to comfort himself with the knowledge there was no one in the vicinity to notice.

Razz leaned against the Pier's protective metal railing and his pistol clinked against it. Cold, wet steel bit through layers of clothing into the skin of his back. He started moving again, making sure this time to remain out of the spotlight. There was no point in trying to deny his fears. He knew they would be his constant companion tonight.

He walked past the restaurant to check the area behind it. When the coast appeared clear, he muttered, "Shit," which reminded him he'd rather be almost anywhere else. After pausing to admire the stormy, white-capped waves of the Pacific, Razz entered the Sol a Sol through the back patio to avoid the glare of the floodlights in front.

The main room of the restaurant seemed smaller, the bar less inviting, and the color scheme less vibrant than he remembered, but he stopped before planning a full-scale renovation. It was no longer his problem.

He walked behind the bar, ignoring the squeak of old floorboards, and flipped on the viewing glass light before he could lose his nerve. Light from under the Pier flooded the room. He snapped the light off and the place fell dark. Looking through the front windows toward San Margarita, he could see only faintly the lights of Ocean Boulevard through the fog.

"Christ, what am I doing?" Before allowing himself an answer, he removed his windbreaker, draped it over the viewing glass, and again turned on the light.

This time, only the slightest overflow crept through his jacket's dark polyurethane. He ducked under the jacket and instinctively closed his eyes when they were bombarded by light. When he opened them, they were bombarded again, but this time, by the sight of something shocking, and also strangely comforting and familiar. A surfboard with a jagged chunk missing from its side, obviously a victim of some voracious, large-mouthed creature, bounced between pilings, its tether caught on metal rebar poking out from the side of one piling.

He recalled a similar scene from days earlier, and remembered exactly the almost-new, half-eaten Rip Curl board that had buffeted between pilings. Tonight's board was no Rip Curl. It appeared to be a cheap knock-off of a Corky Carroll, but all that mattered was that his friend, the swimming predator who had grazed his legs in greeting, or warning, was still out there, possibly nearby. For most people, that would have been a frightening thought, but it was oddly reassuring to him on this night. It felt good knowing something had found its life's purpose, which, in this case, was to eat everything in its path when hungry. Though the shark's work itself wasn't interesting, he envied the creature for its clarity. He hoped he'd be as lucky one day, but doubted his own purpose would ever be as simple or clear.

Looking down at the low-tidal waters, he noticed something that further stirred his imagination. A piece of bright red cloth floated into view. The cloth seemed to toy with a piling, approaching and then escaping its grasp, floating atop an oncoming wave then upon the receding tide, before it finally succumbed to the more powerful waves and draped itself around the piling.

Razz stared at the cloth. It was a garish red, like a color a clown might wear. *Could it have come from Wally Bumpers' clown suit?* He believed it was a clue, maybe the clue he needed to implicate, or clear, Louis Marcayda and, once and for all, be done with this part of his life. Then he wondered why the cloth would matter. *What evidence would it give? It can't tell who killed Wally or why. It probably wouldn't even have human DNA after days of washing in the surf.* After further inspection, he realized it was likely a woman's scarf, probably fumbled into the water by a tourist or blown off someone's neck by gusting winds. It was not from a clown's suit; it was not from Wally Bumpers. It was meaningless.

He withdrew from beneath his windbreaker and rubbed his eyes, his disloyal eyes that had encouraged his imagination to play tricks on him. He knew it wasn't a fair contest. His imagination always seemed to win over reason, usually to his detriment. A mangled surfboard and a woman's missing scarf were all he discovered so far. *Was that what I came back here for?*

Razz turned off the viewing glass light and searched the restaurant for anything suspicious. He checked behind the bar, in both bathrooms and in the kitchen, but found nothing unusual, no dogs named Scruffy, no renegade prep cooks, nothing that could implicate Louis Marcayda in anything other than owning a restaurant. He looked out the windows at the exterior porches, but knew he was only stalling, putting off the inevitable. He had to go back into Louis' office.

He walked upstairs, each creaky step reminding him of his noisy, unsubtle plan, because he would not be going through the ceiling into Louis' office this time. He would be going through the office door the quickest way possible. He planned to grab the mysterious ledger and the computer, drop them off at the City Hall police station with a detailed note, and then hightail it to the safety of the mountain retreat and his family. Then he would let the chips fall where they might. He knew those chips could fall hard right on top of him.

Razz pushed against the office door to test its resilience. It gave just enough to make him think he could knock it down, so he stepped back, and then surged forward. Making contact with his right shoulder sent shivers through the door, the door frame and his own torso, but neither gave in. Before he could doubt his plan, he backed up another step and again threw himself at the door.

This time, on contact, two things happened. The door frame gave in, as he'd hoped. Unfortunately, his body gave in, too. He heard a pop, and then blinding pain shot through his neck and shoulder before he crumpled to the hallway floor.

"Aaggh, fuck!"

He'd cracked and bent and nearly given up several times, but this seemed to be his last straw. Lying in agony on the dusty floor, he looked back at his life, something he'd done more in the past month than he'd done during the rest of his life's many months combined. Other than during his high school surfing feat, when great passion and purpose had overcome his natural diffidence and fear, he knew he'd floated on the wave of his life. He'd gone where it had taken him and he'd not bothered to steer, because it had been easier not to. Even the greatest accomplishments of his adult life, his marriage to Sarah and the births of his two kids, Caitlin and Ronnie, weren't by his own design. They were forced upon him by an unexpected pregnancy to a woman who had offered herself, but hadn't been chosen, only accepted. He realized he couldn't even take full credit for the people that made his life worth living today. The intense pain from that knowledge brought moisture to his eyes.

He struggled to sit himself upright and it seemed to give him better perspective. He envisioned his kids growing up fatherless. It didn't seem fair, especially after his good fortune with his own father, but he wasn't sure if it would be most unfair to them or to him. That Sarah could live without him was beyond doubt, but thinking of her made him smile and he knew he'd been lucky to have a life with her, however short. Now, salty water overflowed his eyes and he gulped in chunks of air between sobs.

If I ever get another chance with my family ...

Before he could finish his thought, he glimpsed Louis' office door through the distortion caused by his tears. The door was ajar. Only a thin golden chain kept him from his targets. He turned and reached high into a storage locker. Frustration mounted until he pulled out a long screwdriver. He placed the straight edge of the screwdriver into a chain link and pushed with his left hand. He needed more leverage, so he pushed with his chest against the handle, but only succeeded in hurting his chest.

Life is hard enough. Now I have to do things with one hand tied behind my back?

With the help of his good left arm, he lifted his right hand into place to limply hold the handle, and then slammed the handle's butt end with his left palm. Pain shot through his right arm again, but it didn't stop there. His left hand felt like it had been smashed by a hammer, but before he allowed that pain to stop him, he twisted his hips and drove his left hand into the handle butt once again. This time the chain link exploded open and the remnants of both chain ends clattered against the wood and the broken link tumbled end over end across the floor. The door was open.

Ignoring the stabbing pains, he dropped the screwdriver and strode inside to the desk. It was dark, but he knew exactly where everything was. He grabbed the accounting ledger. He unplugged the computer, maneuvered it onto the desk, and placed the ledger atop it. Cradling them both into his left arm, he ran out of the office and down the stairs. He rushed toward the back, but stopped when he reached the viewing glass. He'd forgotten that he left his jacket covering it. Razz hooked the jacket with his feeble right hand and felt the weight of his gun he'd left behind in his rush. Stunned by his incompetence, he bent over to hook his right index and middle fingers on his shirt pocket to support his arm.

At the door, he tried to maneuver the knob open with his right knee and forearm, awkwardly clasping it as best he could. The old brass slid against his sweaty arm, but the dry cotton of his trousers created enough friction for him to turn it. When he felt the release of the latch, he pushed the door open with his foot.

Outside, he took a breath of crisp, salty air and listened to the crash of waves against the Pier's pilings. Rain cascaded over him and gusting winds whipped against his face. He felt free.

But he wasn't done yet. He turned back to the door and reviewed his actions. He hadn't left anything other than fingerprints, and those were of little concern. He'd gotten what he came for.

There was only one more thing to do. To create an illusion of a break-in, if only for a temporary diversion to help him escape to his mountain hideaway, he smashed the door window with an edge of the computer and shattered a pane of glass.

As pointy shards sprinkled the planking around his feet, Razz allowed himself another moment of relief, but it only lasted until he realized he should have plundered the cash register. *That's what people do when they break in to businesses!* He pondered whether to go back in and kick open the register in order to propel his illusion forward, but something cold and steely pressed into his neck and he knew all of his illusions were over.

"You couldn't leave well enough alone, could you?" It was Louis.

Razz' impulse was to scream for help, but he figured that would only serve to get him shot in the head. Louis could claim ignorance when he found someone breaking into his restaurant and he'd acted to protect his property. It would all be written off as a terrible mistake.

"Put those in the trunk," commanded Louis, and a wiry, brown bodyguard took the computer and ledger.

"Take his coat."

Another wiry, brown guard obliged and quickly discovered the gun. He held it by its barrel with the coat's cloth to avoid fingerprints.

"I didn't think you had it in you, Razz," said Louis, oddly impressed. "Put that in the glove compartment, we may use it later. Let's go upstairs where it's private."

That Louis didn't seem surprised at finding him here made Razz realize again that he'd been in way over his head since the first time they'd met. He could never have outwitted Louis Marcayda, because Louis had too much practice at staying several steps ahead of everyone else, from cops who wanted his head to his competitors in the drug and prostitution trades who wanted it even more.

It made him wish he could go back in time and ride out his years on the safe, comfortable wave that had once been his life. Now he was sure the ride would be short. The wave would either crash spectacularly to smother him, or it would peter out and he would be dragged helplessly into a deadly undertow.

Pushed forward by the gun barrel, he hoped Louis' finger wouldn't slip accidently onto the trigger. He walked step after deliberate step upstairs to the office where he was sure he'd meet his fate. At the entrance, his fortitude faltered and he wanted to beg, plead, and whimper like a three-year-old, but he resisted. He went inside.

"Search him."

A guard took his wallet, keys, and cell phone, handling them carefully with a handkerchief, put them in a plastic bag, and set them on the desk.

"Tie him up."

He was sat in a wooden chair in the middle of the room facing what was left of the door. He saw three guards and Louis—four armed killers. Though he'd survived for long periods trapped under heavy surf, Razz felt claustrophobic when one of the guards taped his hands behind him to the chair back.

"You would have made a lot of money with me. I could have helped you."

"There's more to life than money," said Razz, mustering a note of defiance before focusing on his real goal. "Please don't hurt my family."

Louis sat on the couch and watched each of Razz' feet being taped to a chair leg. "You just couldn't leave it alone."

"What do you want with me?"

His eyes narrowing in anger, Louis spoke slowly, biting off each syllable as if to maim it. "Nothing now, absolutely nothing."

One of the guards smiled, but Louis wasn't joking around. "There's nothing on that ledger, you know. Nothing on the hard drive either. It's not even the same computer. Lotta didn't think you'd notice."

Razz closed his eyes, disgusted he'd come back to this place for nothing.

"You left tracks last night," Louis continued. "Lots of them." He nodded to one of the guards, and the man rolled off duct tape into an ever-growing sphere. "You're not as smart as you think."

"I don't think I'm smart," Razz said, speaking as honestly as he ever had in his life. "What's that for?"

The guard kept making the ball of tape larger.

"You don't need that. I promise I won't scream. Just leave my family alone. Do whatever you want with me, but leave them alone."

The man held up the balled tape. It looked to Razz the size of a small grapefruit.

"Don't, please."

Louis motioned the man forward.

"No, please! No! Help!"

The guard jammed the wadded tape into his face. Razz shifted, trying to dodge the ball of duct-taped terror. "No, help! Help!"

A second guard smashed the butt of his pistol into Razz' head and everything went black.

When Razz had regained most of his senses, he realized the tape wad, now lodged in his mouth, had cut off his ability to speak or breathe through his mouth. His eyes grew large with dread until two other realizations helped calm him. First, though the tape ball was incredibly uncomfortable because it almost continually set off his gag reflex, he could still breathe through his nose, so he knew he wouldn't die from it. Second, the intense pain from the back of his skull didn't seem to be killing him either, but it helped focus him away from the discomfort of gagging.

He could no longer plead for his family or try to appeal to whatever sense of fair play Louis Marcayda might possess in the deepest recesses of his soul. He felt impotent, worse than dead, but still his eyes darted, searching for anything that might help him survive.

Louis and his guards conferred in one corner, every now and again looking over to check on their captive.

Razz discerned nothing in the office that might help him escape, nothing he could use as a distraction or decoy. *If I did, where could I go?* His brain raced, trying to overcome the pain that derived from his body and his helplessness. He was so distracted that, at first, he didn't notice the ringing of his cell phone. Someone was calling him.

Louis went to the desk and looked at the phone's caller ID. "Your wife must be worried about you. Merice and I will console her after you disappear." Pondering the phone, he continued, "Did you know there's a chip in here that makes tracking this possible. I knew where you were all the time. Isn't technology amazing?"

Razz lowered his head, in shame and disbelief, once again having been outsmarted.

"When you escape to Mexico, the police will track you, and then you'll mysteriously disappear. You know, you really shouldn't embezzle from me, but thank you for all your fingerprints that will help prove it."

He powered down the phone. "Dump him in the Playa marsh. Bury this clown where we dug up the other one."

Razz' muffled protestations achieved nothing as the guards lifted him, chair and all, and began to carry him out. He squirmed like an unruly child refusing his medicine and mildly slowed their progress, until the butt of a pistol again sent him to the hazy edge of consciousness.

"Razz?"

Who's calling my name?

"Razz!"

He wondered if it was God calling him home, and then suspected he might not be that fortunate, given his many peccadilloes and shortcomings.

"Hey! Are you all right?"

The voice was more insistent and didn't sound like God or the Devil. It sounded suspiciously like Sharky.

Razz shook his head trying to clear the haze and opened his eyes enough to see two guards hurry past and out the door. Louis and the third guard were near the pier-side window peeking outside from behind the window shade. The guard's gun rested on the sill, trained on something, or someone, below.

"Razz, hey, I'm sorry about before, I guess I was a little drunk. Come talk to me, I don't want to go home yet."

Now he was sure it was Sharky, calling to him from the Pier. Razz could feel the pleading in his voice, pleading for forgiveness, pleading for a friend to help him forget his own pain. He considered rocking his chair to try to draw him to his rescue, but he didn't. The truth was that he was pleading, too, if only on the inside, pleading that Sharky would go home, or go somewhere, anywhere, other than the Pier. He knew their friendship might be the very thing that would get Sharky killed, even though it could possibly save him. Strapped helplessly to his chair, with a closing airway due to swelling from his chafed throat, all he wanted was to yell bloody curses to drive his one last hope away to safety.

He prayed for his friend's life. Though he was uncertain when he'd prayed last, he thought it likely when his son was born. Yes, he remembered he'd prayed that Ronnie would be a normal baby, with two hands, two feet, ten toes and ten fingers. He'd done the same thing when Caitlin was born and he hadn't felt the need to pray again until now. He hadn't felt hypocritical; he'd just wanted help, if he could get it. Now he wanted help again. He prayed Sharky would go away to somewhere safe and leave him to his own consequences.

"Help him be okay," Razz said internally and to Whoever might hear him. *"Please help him escape."*

He didn't feel deserving, but he didn't mind asking, especially for his friend. He pleaded audibly now, "Please, God, please." It was unintelligible, but loud enough to alert Louis.

"You got him?" he asked his cohort.

The bodyguard steadied his aim and slowly nodded yes.

Razz tried to scream, just as a muffled, airy blast from the gun's silencer coughed out a bullet. He saw a flash through the blind and, as it faded, so did his hopes.

"Got him," said the shooter, before pausing. "Oh, shit."

"You said you got him," said Louis.

"I did, but—"

"But what?" Louis pulled back the curtain. "Where the fuck is he?"

"I hit him solid, but he twisted … He fell through the railing."

Louis looked like he was going to erupt, but, fortunately for the shooter, he was interrupted by the clamoring of footsteps. The other two guards entered, winded.

"He fell before we could get him," said the more courageous of the men. "I mean, he's dead. He was hit good. I saw it."

The shooter looked grateful for the support, but Louis obliterated what little confidence any of them had.

"He'd better be ... for everyone's sake."

The three men knew precisely his meaning. If Sharky weren't dead, they would be.

"He couldn't survive the tides anyway, boss," continued the man.

Louis paused and this messenger squirmed like a schoolboy awaiting a paddle whipping from a cruel headmaster.

"Tell me, homeboy, what the hell do you know about the ocean?"

"Uh, um, I took an oceanography class at community college."

"Great, I've got a genius working for me. College boy, take your friend and go find the body. You may not have noticed, but there's a wharf below that railing. Those tides wouldn't help much if he were lying on it, would they, pendejo?"

The two men started to run out, but Louis stopped them. "Take this." He handed one a flashlight. "Check for blood on the railing," he said, before sending them on their way.

"It's tough to find good help, isn't it?" he directed to Razz, before getting back to business. "You're sure you hit him?"

"I hit him solid," said the shooter.

"Okay, now it's his turn," Louis said, referring to Razz. "Cut his legs free and take him to the car."

If deposited in Louis' car, Razz might as well be dead, because it wouldn't be long before he would be. He wanted to kick the guard, then whirl his chair into Louis and knock them both silly, but he knew trying a move he'd only seen accomplished in movies with ropes, wires, and slow-motion photography would be the real silliness. He wouldn't have gotten beyond the first kick before Louis would have splattered him. Then he realized his only advantage—they wouldn't want any remnants of him, including blood and brain bits, left in his office. Shooting him there would be a last resort.

His realization gave him little comfort. Although an office death would inconvenience Louis, he would still be unalterably dead. He couldn't let them get him downstairs into the car. He looked at the open, broken door and considered running for it, but it would only take him closer to the car and an inevitable death.

As the bodyguard cut away the remaining tape from the right chair leg, Razz saw his only hope—the window on the ocean side of the office. If he could maneuver over there before being shot, he might have a chance at hurling himself through to land in the water below. He'd have to hit the window just right, generating enough force to break through the glass panes and small frames holding them. If he missed, he'd go up against the thicker outside frame and would inevitably lose that battle. The drawn shade presented him a problem and an opportunity. Because he couldn't see the window behind the shade, it would make targeting more difficult, but the shade might help prevent the resulting glass shards from ripping into him and making his death slow and bloody.

He knew his plan was a long shot, but it was all he had. *How can I get close enough to try?* It seemed impossible, but when the guard dragged him from his chair, a siren blew. It rang out again, louder. Whether the siren was a coincidence or was God working in Mysterious Ways, it changed Razz' risk/reward calculations. If the police were on their way, he might be saved. If they flew past the Pier or if the siren belonged to an ambulance or fire truck, he might lose his best opportunity for escape. On the third siren ring, Louis stuck his head under the pier-side window shade to have a look. The bodyguard, more interested in his own safety than his duty, did the same.

Razz crept toward the ocean-side window only about twelve feet away, but, when he saw Louis notice his bodyguard next to him, he broke for the window. He was surprised he reached it before being shot.

But Louis had been surprised, too. He'd expected him to flee downstairs and, at first, he couldn't understand why he was scampering the wrong way. When he did realize what Razz was about to do, he didn't hesitate to fire.

The bullet reached Razz just as he leapt, chair and all, into the window, splintering the chair seat and entering his right buttock. His body's momentum, painfully aided by the bullet's force, helped him crash through the glass panes and their frames. The outer window casing groaned in disapproval, after years of benign neglect, but did not give way.

Though the pain in his backside was excruciating, Razz was thrilled to find his upper body hanging outside in heavy rain. The fog made it impossible to see the water, but he could smell it and his only chance for survival thirty feet away.

But he was caught on something. He squirmed, but all he accomplished was to dig a glass shard still hanging tight to its wooden frame deeper into his right thigh. A strangled cry stuck in his tattered throat. The pain was intense, but he realized two things that were worse. He no longer heard a siren, so whatever it was that had been approaching was no longer, and that very strong hands gripped tightly to each of his ankles.

"Oh, no, amigo, it will not be that easy. I've decided you need to suffer much more for the trouble you've caused me. You have not yet felt real pain."

Louis laughed like a man experienced in the pleasure of pain-giving. He twisted Razz' injured right leg to grind the glass further into it. The bodyguard enjoyed the show as he held tightly to the other leg.

His muffled scream hinted at unfathomable agony, but Razz was thinking of his wife and two beautiful children. By hurting them, Louis could hurt him even more. Fury overcame his fear, and he gathered himself for another escape attempt.

Louis violently twisted his ankle, grinding the glass shard deeper into his thigh. The pain was immense, but his anger was more so. Razz kicked out with a vengeance.

Its force surprised his captors and the bodyguard almost lost his grip. Though Razz' right leg was almost useless due to his injuries, his left was unusually strong from years of swimming and surfing and, on his second scissor kick, it broke free. Another quick, powerful kick with his free foot caught Louis squarely in the mouth, breaking his hold. He pushed off against the building and with one dolphin kick, the glass shard broke from its frame and both legs slid off the window ledge.

Amidst the driving rain, Razz was in free fall. At this moment, he wished he'd been a diver instead of a surfer, but body control gained from years of surfing would have to suffice him. Landing on his face might stun him into unconsciousness while falling backwards might break his back against unforgiving chair slats, so he curled and twisted just enough to—*smack!* The impact with the ocean's surface almost tore his arms from their sockets. His right temple and hanging thigh flesh pulsated from their collision with the water. The intensity of pain amidst the cold water heightened his awareness and he sensed bullets slashing past, but none seemed to hit him. Blood flowed from his body, turning the water slippery.

He continued his downward path, fighting against the buoyancy of the chair, and kicked deeper into the dark. He twisted again and moved toward what he hoped was open water. He sensed more bullets, but they no longer seemed as near, so he kept kicking the best he could. With each pump of his heart, more blood left him, but he felt like he could hold his breath forever. Pain was dissipating and he found himself at peace. The ocean always calmed him, but under these circumstances, the feeling startled him. To reassure himself he was still alive, he focused on his right thigh and felt the sting of sharp glass. He was indeed alive.

Forever came more quickly than usual, and Razz struggled for air. In the darkness, direction was relative; he had nothing from which to compare. He just knew it was time to breath. Although the chair had hindered him thus far, it began to aid him by floating him upward. He let it do much of the work and his exhaustion made him wonder how much blood he'd lost. He hoped he'd moved far away from the Pier into open water, but he knew if he didn't breathe soon, Louis and his guns wouldn't matter anyway. He imagined a huge rolling wave holding him under to aid him in holding his breath, but it didn't help this time. The tape ball gagged him, continually reminding him of his reality.

Razz no longer knew if the black surrounding him was due to the night water or looming unconsciousness, but he felt himself floating upward. Soon he heard a pitter-patter like thousands of fingers tapping. It was raining and he was approaching the surface.

With little time and oxygen to spare, he kicked, propelling himself upward. He could no longer feel his arms and the throbbing from his wounds had disappeared. He would have been convinced he was dead had it not been for a thunderous noise invading his brain.

The noise became deafening and he realized—he had surfaced! The storm was throwing rain to the earth in sheets and howling, swirling winds stirred waves bigger than he'd seen in years. He was tossed about like a rag doll, but he was in the water where he'd always felt the safest, and he was alive. Riding a wave up, he could just make out the horizon beyond until the wave passed and dropped him into a valley to wait for the next.

The rise and fall were comforting until he turned toward what he thought was shore. In the fog and dark, he saw something big looming in front of him. Worried it was Louis in a search boat, he started to submerge, but then he studied the object further. It grew upward to something even larger above it. His eyes widened as he realized the waves were about to smash him into a concrete piling.

The waves are forcing me back to the Pier!

35

Crouching in the cool water as he caught his breath, he urinated and never felt warmer in his life. Gathering his board and himself, he was accosted by slap-happy surfers.

"Way to go, brah."

"Awesome, dude."

"You gave 'em the old razzmatazz on that one. That old pier didn't even know what hit it," a grizzled beach bum chimed in.

Fortunately, Robbie hadn't hit it, at least not too hard, but that was how Robbie became Razzmatazz, or Razz for short, and it was a name that would stick to him, for better or worse, forever.

"Well, look again!"

Louis' men scurried around the wharf aiming flashlights though the driving rain and fog toward nothing in particular while Louis methodically searched, his gun cocked and ready to finish off anyone caught holding on for dear life.

"See anything?" he hollered through the cacophony of wind and water. When no one answered, he flashed his light in each man's face, one by one.

Only the third dared speak, "Boss, they're dead. The undercurrents will take them out to sea." It was the man who had studied oceanography. He averted his eyes, trying to avoid the flashlight's glare.

"We'll search until we find the bodies," Louis said, in warning as much as strategy. He inspected the wharf's northern perimeter as he moved toward the eastern edge closest to shore. When he arrived at the intersection, he looked up toward San Margarita and couldn't see any of it, not even the glow of street lights. For now, they would be safe. If he couldn't see the town, the town couldn't see him.

A big wave lifted the wharf then dropped it, almost knocking him overboard. A rapping noise from under the wharf caught his attention, but it stopped as quickly as it had sounded. Louis stared at the wharf's flooring as if he were seeing through it. Another smaller wave brought nothing, so he continued his search. Flashlight probing, he edged along, one foot forward to brace against the action of the waves until he saw what he was looking for—blood.

There it was, on the fire hose bumper which was nailed to the side of the wharf like a thousand inch worms to protect boats from damage. At first, he thought it might be paint rubbed off from a docked boat, but the floorboards revealed red-tinged water washing into the ocean. One of their quarries had been there. It just wasn't clear which one, where he might be now, or if he was still alive.

"Grab the boat!"

His men's faces revealed their doubt.

"And you row!" he directed to the supposed ocean expert.

After some fumbling, the men got the Coast Guard skiff turned over and into the water.

"Boss, there's only one oar," said the oceanographer.

"Grab it, let's go."

A second guard held back. "I can't swim."

"Neither can I," said the third.

"You'll be in a boat! How the hell did you guys get to America anyway?" Louis pointed to the second man. "You, stay here. Call if you see anything."

Palpably relieved, the man took out his gun, ready for his task of looking for clues in a fog bank. The oceanographer held the boat steady, but Louis stumbled when he stepped in. The other non-swimmer seemed paralyzed.

"Put this on," said the oceanographer, holding out an orange life jacket.

The man took it greedily, tossed it over his head, and clumsily climbed in. He landed with a thud, crawled to the back, and took a seat, clinging tightly to the boat rails.

The oceanographer threw two more life preservers into the boat well and got in. He pushed off from the wharf and the men were underway.

Razz braced his feet against a perimeter piling, struggling to keep from floating under the Pier where he might be dashed again and again into unforgiving concrete. Incoming waves forcefully pressed him into the piling, and then he was drawn away when they passed. Each time, he had to calculate the next wave, the incoming tide, the swirling winds, and try to hit the piling with his feet to cushion his blow. His right leg screamed in pain as the torn and punctured muscles fought to stretch in ways they no longer could. If he miscalculated and hit the concrete face-first, he'd likely be knocked unconscious and swept away to his death. Still strapped to the chair, hands taped behind him, he was losing blood and strength. He had to free himself from his wooden albatross. And he could think of only one way to do it—crash himself backwards into the piling and hope the collision would break the chair, but not him.

His maneuver would require the right wave. It had to be strong, but not overpowering. He remembered his first battle with the Pier and, suddenly, he was sitting on his surfboard on a November day during his carefree youth, waiting for The One, the wave that would carry him all the way under the Pier to shore and into history. The memory felt good, but he shook it off. He was nowhere near carefree youth now, and he needed all the focus he could muster.

He dunked his head to clear it and started timing his maneuver. As a wave passed, he pushed off toward the northwest, twisted one hundred and eighty degrees, and did two lopsided dolphin kicks before another wave caught him and forced him back toward shore. He ducked forward under the water. Anticipating, he tucked his legs in and floated with the wave until—*crack!* The right chair leg hit the piling first and the resulting torque sent his head hurtling toward concrete.

Crack! The wooden chair legs collapsed under the stress and tore away from the seat and back. His shoulders almost dislocated from the force and his head flew past the piling, missing by inches. Pieces of the chair floated away as Razz tried to right himself from his spin. Regaining his bearings, he saw he was headed straight for another piling. Hands still taped, he leaned back so he could hit it feet-first. He braced for impact, then—he missed the piling entirely. Blown off course by swirling winds, his body twisted sideways and he was hurtling faster toward another piling further under the Pier. At his current speed and path, he thought he would hit concrete torso-first and probably break most of the bones in his body. He kicked frantically with his left leg to steer himself, but he had little control—the wave, tide and winds were in charge. He braced for impact and prayed. *Please let me see my wife again.*

Miraculously, he struck the piling feet-first, but his legs collapsed under the pressure. His chest hit next, then the side of his face and head. Dazed, but alive, he clung to the piling, straddling it with his legs. He felt the granules of concrete tear into his cheek and the contact felt good. It felt solid and safe. The waves pressed him forward and pulled him back as they rolled over him, but he held tight. Images of Sarah, Caitlin, and Ronnie kept him going. He thought of his family playing in the water in their backyard. He thought of them at the dinner table, all together. He thought of them at Christmas at his parents' home.

My parents! They'll be sitting ducks for Louis' revenge! And it will be my fault! He'd sent his wife and kids away, but hadn't thought about his parents. He overcame his guilt and fear by remembering his only shot at helping them would come by escaping his predicament.

Floodlights erupted under the Pier, illuminating his fear and situation further. Someone had turned on the viewing glass lights! Razz was no longer cloaked in darkness and his urgency rocketed higher. He knew someone was coming for him.

He reviewed his meager options. Nothing looked good until he discerned a piece of rebar, a steel rod used to reinforce concrete, jutting from the piling. If he had hit the rebar, a remnant of shoddy construction, he likely would have been disemboweled, but it might help him rip the tape from his bound hands.

He edged to his left, holding on with his legs and balancing against the forces of wind and water, but, with his hands behind him, there was no way he could reach the rebar without being swept away in the attempt.

Ching! A bullet glanced off the concrete, spraying him with debris. Over his right shoulder, he saw his nightmare only ten feet away. It was Louis and his two cronies in the Harbor Patrol skiff. Louis took aim and Razz submerged just as another bullet hit the piling.

He scrunched into a ball and somersaulted forward to get his bound hands under his legs and in front of him. He wasn't as flexible as he once was and it took him several tries, but on his fourth attempt, he succeeded. But now he didn't know where he was in relation to his enemy and he had to come up for air. He sensed the flow of the water and swam with it, hoping he wouldn't crash into anything or anyone that might kill him. He bit into the duct tape wrapped several times around his wrists, but the tape was too strong. Finally, he had to surface.

Rain pelted the Pier's wooden boarding above him and winds swirled and howled, but Razz gulped breaths as quietly as he could. He saw nothing except a piling that was about to greet him head-on. Two kicks and a twist of his body helped him fend off a glancing blow with his forearms. But as he floated past, something tore into his right arm. He recoiled instinctively, but then thrust out his hands to grab on to a rusting piece of rebar. The steel stopped his momentum cold, again straining his abused arms and shoulders.

"Aaggh!"

"Over there!" It was Louis and he was close.

Razz tore at the tape, but the rebar only succeeded in drawing more blood. Three pistol shots in rapid succession cut through the air around him, before disappearing harmlessly into the water.

"Keep it steady, damn it!" Emerging from the fog, Louis and his makeshift navy were headed straight for the piling and for him. "Watch out!"

His oceanographer-turned-navigator paddled backwards, trying to lessen what appeared to be an inevitable impact. The third man, as ashen as any Mexican could ever be, heaved all over himself then collapsed into the bottom of the boat. Louis braced for the blow.

For Razz, the wooden craft loomed larger and it looked certain to crush him. At the last moment, he ducked underwater and heard the wooden side rail scrape into the piling. The V-shaped hull of the skiff struck him in the shoulder and pressed him tightly against the piling. The craft slowed and he realized he was trapped!

Above water, Louis picked himself up from the boat well and recovered his gun. "Be careful!"

His men had other worries. One was vomiting afresh and the navigator was trying to hold the craft steady to the piling.

"Boss," he said, "throw out the line!"

The boss didn't like taking orders from anyone other than his wife, but he grabbed the rope attached to the front of the skiff and raised his arm to throw.

"No! Throw it over here. The waves will take it and we'll grab it as it goes past. We'll secure the boat to this column."

Louis did as instructed, then went to the back and watched the rope bob its way toward the southeast. "I can't reach it."

The navigator strained to maneuver the skiff around the piling. "We'll float over. Just grab it as we go past."

"What if I can't?"

"You will. Here we go." He pushed off, grabbed the oar and paddled. "Get ready!"

Louis leaned over the rail and stretched out his right arm. "I can't reach!"

The navigator strained against the force of the waves. Losing the battle, he thrust the oar's paddle end out into the water in an effort to snag the line. Barely succeeding, he maneuvered the rope toward them until the tenuous hold gave way.

Louis saw they were being swept away. "Jump in!"

The navigator looked at him, surprised.

"Not you. Him."

He pointed his pistol at the third man, who was still safely curled up in his vomit, and pulled back the trigger. "Give me your gun, and go get the rope."

The navigator stopped rowing and grabbed the man's gun. They were floating further from their target each second. "Come on, you can do it."

The man didn't appear to believe him, even while he was flying into the water where the navigator had thrown him. The man thrashed frantically, despite his life jacket, and inadvertently captured the tow line. Greatly surprised and relieved, he held tightly to the lifeline, and almost cried from happiness. His body weight helped counterbalance the strength of the waves and slowed the skiff's momentum. Bobbing, coughing, and spitting out water, he held up the rope, proudly displaying his achievement. "I did it, boss. I did it."

"Good job," said his boss, reaching out. "Give me the rope."

The man looked into Louis' lifeless eyes. "No, no, I've got it."

"I meant give me your hand." Louis offered up his most convincingly-friendly smile to go with his hand.

The man wrapped the rope once around him and held to it tightly, before reaching out his left hand.

"Don't worry, I've got you." Louis pulled the man closer. "You said dead bodies will float out to sea from here, right?"

"Huh? Oh, yeah, the rip currents will take them out miles," answered the navigator, busy fighting to control the craft.

"So they won't be found?"

"It's highly unlikely."

"Good." Louis raised his pistol and what little blood left in the third man's face drained out. He pressed the barrel against his forehead and pulled the trigger. The blast rocked the man's head back, but Louis held on tight. Then he put the gun down on his seat, and grabbed the rope and the man's preserver.

"Hold this," he said, offering the rope to the shocked navigator. Louis struggled to remove the life vest as blood fled from the man's skull. Finally, he cut loose the corded vest belt, the vest slipped from the man's body, and his former bodyguard was released into the water.

Razz knew his end would be similar if he couldn't free his hands. The boat was now tethered and its tow line was beginning to move. They were pulling the boat closer! Razz worked his taped hands against the rebar, quickening his already frenetic pace, with the vision of Louis' cohort's splattered brain too vivid in his mind. Strands of duct tape frayed, but not as fast as his nerves. He poked his head out from behind the piling and saw the barrel of a gun pointed directly at him. Caught like a deer in headlights, he was sure he was done, but the boat rocked and sent Louis sprawling backwards and the gun's bullet surging upward. The bullet lodged into the Pier's underside just missing a cluster of gas pipes and electrical wires.

"God damn it!"

"I didn't do it."

Louis glared. "Just bring me in again."

The navigator pulled on the tow line as Razz struggled to rip off the tape. Torn halfway through, it was still too strong for him in his weakened state, but another image of his family kept him trying. He methodically cut at the tape strands bit by bit. He saw the edge of the skiff and strained to pull his hands apart as Louis came into view. First his shoulder, then his head, then, as the barrel of the gun entered Razz' sight, the tape gave way. He submerged just before Louis could get off a shot.

"¡Mierda!"

Razz breast-stroked with the current; his right leg was useless. The water was smooth, like silk, then he realized why—he was swimming through human blood! He felt like puking and tried to rise to the surface before he gagged. As he floated upward, something touched his foot and he imagined the dead man below grasping for him. The thought gave him the creeps.

Surfacing, he did a three-sixty, but couldn't see Louis. But he did see something else and it surprised him—a wooden boat oar was floating past. There was an abundance of flotsam due to the storm, but this oar was like manna from heaven. It would allow his body to rest.

He plopped his tired arms over the oar, ripped away the remaining tape, and fumbled to remove the tape ball from his aching jaws. After finally expelling it, he drew a deep breath, but his chafed, swollen throat rebelled and he coughed reflexively. Razz plunged his hand into his gaping thigh wound to search for any remaining glass, but if it were there, it would have to stay for now. He covered the hole with a flap of hanging flesh and pressed against it to slow any bleeding. Though he was weak, he thought he might be able to make it to shore without bleeding to death, dashing against multiple pilings or sinking into an undertow. He believed his prayers had been answered, until he saw the boat's bow slice again through the fog toward him.

The navigator switched his oar to the starboard side and paddled backwards causing the craft to turn sideways. Now, the port side and Louis faced directly toward him. Louis raised his gun and smiled.

Razz could try to submerge, but as soon as he twitched, Louis would kill him. Just when he needed a monster wave, the now lightly rolling waters betrayed him. After all the waves he'd ridden and all the time he'd spent in the water, in his time of need, the ocean failed him. But he'd had a good run. He'd enjoyed surfing, chasing surfer girls, and living the beach life. It was only when he attempted adult responsibility that he'd begun drowning.

He wondered how a bullet to the head would feel, but it wasn't a morbid fascination. He simply hoped it would strike him at a speed and place that it wouldn't register. Perhaps, floating free in the water would be his last sensation. It seemed the right way for him to go. He was so tired, he felt high. He rested his chin on the oar and smiled contentedly like a brownie-satiated stoner.

Louis didn't appreciate his nonchalance and his own smile faded. "What are you smiling about? You're about to die."

"I know," Razz said softly.

"With me, you could have had anything you wanted."

"But I already do."

Louis' index finger tightened on the gun's trigger, but Razz didn't flinch. Then the boat rocked and it was just enough to make Louis misfire.

"What the fuck?"

"I don't what happened," said the navigator, afraid he could become a target himself.

The rocking grew stronger. It was odd, because the boat was pitching front to back, but waves would have hit it broadside. Louis shot again and missed. He looked like he was about to blow a fuse.

Razz heard a grunt and his eyes veered toward the back of the craft. There, Sharky, barely alive, clung to a boat handle and gamely rocked the boat with one hand. Razz averted his eyes, but Louis had noticed and moved toward the back, his gun still trained on him.

Sharky was running out of steam, hardly able to hang on now, and Louis was only moments away from him. Razz had to make a decision: get shot and possibly save Sharky, or sacrifice his friend who appeared to be dying anyway in order to buy himself time.

"Sharky, watch out!" he croaked from his gnarled throat and sent the oar slicing through the water in his direction.

But Sharky didn't move, nor did the gun, and the oar curved off-course.

"Well, isn't that nice," said Louis. "Too bad it won't save either one of you."

"Sharky!"

Louis grabbed Sharky's wrist and drew him up toward him.

"Leave him alone!"

"You seem to be, how you say, up a creek without a paddle," he said, in answer.

Waves were beginning to kick up again, and Razz doubted he could fight them much longer, but he knew Sharky didn't have a chance, even if he escaped Louis' clutches.

"You should thank me, little man," Louis directed to his captive. "You never could get a woman like Terri on your own. That's right, I paid her to watch you."

Sharky's lips moved imperceptibly, but nothing came out.

"What?" Louis drew him nearer.

"She loved me," he whispered. Then his head fell back, the effort appearing to have taken his little remaining strength.

"She loved my money, but suit yourself."

"Boss, we need to go in," said the exhausted navigator.

Louis braced himself against the rolling waves. "Yeah, maybe you're right." He looked back at Sharky, disgusted. "I won't even waste the bullet." He let go of his wrist and watched him sink out of sight.

"Sharky." Razz tried to encourage him, but his mangled throat could no longer get his voice above the wind. Despite their love/hate relationship over the years, Sharky had lately become one of his only friends. He wanted to mourn his death, but was busy mourning his own.

"Let's go!"

Louis' voice brought Razz back to his present grim reality. The waves were pounding him and forcing him toward another piling.

Louis and his crony were making their way south and out from under the dangers of the Pier. Louis no longer cared about Razz, considering him as dead as Sharky, and was only concerned with his own safety. He gripped his seat, unhappily dependent on his navigator and the whims of ocean and weather.

Razz knew the waves and wind wouldn't stop them. The Harbor Patrol skiff was too strong and stable to succumb. That's why he was surprised when the craft rose in the water and then crashed down, nearly swamping itself.

"What the hell was that?" screamed Louis.

His skipper was picking himself up from the boat well and had no better idea than he did. Even Razz couldn't explain the type of wave that could have tossed the skiff in such a strange and chaotic way. He was only yards from a piling now and was moving way too fast to survive a head-on collision. He dove hoping to find calmer waters and breast-stroked toward the south. But he was too late to avoid a collision and the piling hit him directly on the side of his left thigh. The resultant charley horse sent shock waves up his spine and momentarily paralyzed him. The impact sent his upper body hurtling past the piling and twisting out of control. In mid-spin, he no longer could tell down from up, north from south, and his pain made caring impossible.

His velocity slowed and gravity took over and Razz felt himself sinking. The water became colder and calmer and so did he. His leg pain gave way to a numbing chill and he was grateful. Both of his legs were useless now and he was so tired. He felt like his consciousness was separating from his physical body.

This must be what dying feels like.

He had put up the good fight, he had shown a man's courage, and he was dying in a place he knew well and could call home. He recounted the major events of his life like he thought a dying man should, but it took great effort. And when he stopped sinking and realized he was ankle-deep in muck, he doubted his own death. He needed a breath badly and felt like he was about to gag on salt water. The pain from the cold and the abuse his body had experienced that evening came rushing back, and he felt very much alive. He tried to push off from the slimy, spongy bottom, but couldn't. He thrust his arms upward, but, before he could begin his first stroke, his fingertips caressed something he presumed was a passing fish. When that caress lasted for what he guessed was ten to fifteen feet worth of fish and then ended indignantly with a tail fin slap to his head, he realized it wasn't a fish at all, but was one of the scariest mammals on earth—after man.

He'd likely touched the smooth underbelly of a shark large enough that it could eat him. And that was definitely not the way he wanted to go out. He'd always surmised a shark bite would be one of the most painful of possible events and he had given Sharky lots of slack over the years because of his surviving such an experience. Razz was hopeful not to ever be able to compare notes. He thought back to his days-earlier leg brushes and thought how lucky he'd been over the years, but two personal incidents within two weeks made him wonder if Sharky's attack years ago had been such an anomaly after all.

He was rudely reminded his questions would have to wait when his gag reflex engaged and he ingested a mouth full of ocean. His body convulsed and he briefly lost control of his bodily functions.

Go up! Just go up! He tried to stroke, but couldn't tell if he was moving his arms. *Keep trying! Keep trying! Keep trying!*

When Razz reached the surface he was technically unconscious, but his body reacted, gasping and sputtering for air. The violence of alternately hacking up water and gulping bits of oxygen awakened him. Confused at first, when he saw Louis' boat being thrashed about by an angry shark, he remembered everything vividly.

Louis watched, mouth agape, as his cohort tried to ward off the shark. Surfers are told if a shark comes at you to punch it in the snout. The technique has been known to save a number of lives, but this particular shark didn't play by any known rules. Every time it was struck with the oar, it seemed to get angrier and attack harder. The shark rose from the water to reveal its tiger stripes and landed hard enough to almost swamp the craft. Then it got up a head of steam and rammed the craft's hull. The fiberglass and wood craft bent upon impact, but did not break.

Fifteen-foot tiger sharks weren't normally in waters so shallow and pocked with obstacles, and they'd usually moved to warmer climes by this time of year. But not much in Razz' life had made sense recently and he was just glad he wasn't its current target.

With a moment of relative calm, the shark seemed to have lost interest, but the navigator stayed vigilant, his oar cocked. Louis released his death grip on his seat and drew his pistol, ready for another attack.

"Get me out of here," he said quietly, as if the shark might overhear.

The man stroked the oar through the water and, when it wasn't snatched by an angry shark's jaws, he stroked again more forcefully.

"Faster. Come on," Louis said, his nerves frazzled.

They were progressing toward open water. Razz so wanted the shark to tear his enemies limb from limb, but it appeared they would escape harm-free. Worse, without them in the vicinity, he'd become the next prey. His arms were leaden, his legs were worse, and he needed a miracle to keep from drowning. Becoming shark food shouldn't have been a huge concern. He searched for the oar he'd sent toward Sharky in a futile attempt to save him and spied something several yards away bobbing in the water. He couldn't tell what it was, but if it was floating, it might help him float as well. He dog paddled toward it, but it might as well have been three miles away. At his rate of travel, he'd die long before he could reach it. But that didn't mean it couldn't reach him.

The object was inexplicably moving toward him. It was odd for it to travel diagonally against a wave, but when he recognized the orange blob, it seemed odder still. A life preserver was floating his way.

Razz noticed dark splotches juxtaposed against orange and he realized who had last worn the apparently-misnamed life preserver. It hadn't preserved Louis' guard-turned-corpse one bit. Then he thought he saw a bloody hand.

My God, the dead man is still holding on!

All manner of creepy thoughts came to him until he saw what was attached to the bloody hand. "Sharky! You're alive!"

Corpse-like, Sharky gamely kicked ahead, clutching the preserver with his one good arm. "You'll need this," he whispered before his hand slipped. Razz grabbed him and kept him afloat.

"Leave me."

"Sharky, we can make it."

Razz managed to get the preserver over Sharky's head, and then he went underwater to tie two straps around his waist. For a moment, he wondered if he'd rise again. Barely able to feel his hands, he finally got the straps tied. He gathered his strength to resurface, then felt something hard at his back. It was a piling.

He used one hand to climb up the piling while clutching Sharky with the other, but Razz knew he was only prolonging the inevitable. Surfacing, he searched for life-sustaining options, but they both seemed out. Louis was floating toward safety, and he felt the injustice flood over him like an oncoming wave.

The navigator paddled like his life depended on it as Louis shot into the water at an unseen foe. Razz ducked instinctively, but Louis wasn't even aware of him. He shot again on the opposite side of the boat, and waited.

"I think I got him," he said. "I got him! I killed him!"

He soon learned he hadn't killed anything, but may well have made it very angry. He and his navigator were both sent flying when their boat was rammed by an irate tiger shark. Louis hit his head on the middle seat and was knocked almost unconscious, but his cohort wasn't as lucky and landed in the water.

"Help! Help! Help me!"

It took several seconds for Louis to realize what had happened. But it took only the briefest of moments for him to understand he was in deep if he had to get back to shore by himself. He grabbed a life vest.

"Catch!" he yelled and hurled the vest overboard, slightly off-target.

The frightened flunky's relief was palpable when he finally corralled it. He wrapped a strap around his left arm twice, not even taking the time to secure the vest, and cautiously kicked back toward the boat.

Louis scanned the water. "Get the oar."

"We can float in from here."

Louis raised his pistol, making his appeal more clear. "We may need it."

The point was made and the man veered toward the floating oar several yards away.

Razz wished they would hurry up and get to safety, so he and Sharky would have a chance for the same. He didn't like their chances anyway, but he sure didn't want to float past an enemy with a pistol.

As if Louis were listening to his thoughts, he sent a bullet whistling past Razz into the piling. Razz looked back and saw him again take aim, but he also saw something else. The man with the life vest began bobbing up and down, a strange, wide-eyed look on his face. A sudden thrashing caught Louis' attention, and he turned just as the man disappeared underwater.

Several seconds passed, then several more. Suddenly, the vest popped to the surface dragging the remnants of the man's left arm caught in its straps. Momentum carried both into the air where they seemed to hover in warning, so survivors couldn't miss them. Other than his blood, which had begun permeating the waters, the arm was likely all that would ever be found of him.

Louis gawked at the now-floating, body-less arm and screamed, furiously firing into the water. He released four quick rounds before the gun clicked empty, then he grabbed the second gun and fired it wildly until empty.

Razz had seen the severed arm and expected the memory would haunt him, but nothing like it was now haunting Louis.

He continued pressing the gun's trigger, firing imaginary bullets on all sides of the boat, alternately screaming and laughing. "Fuck you, puta! Fuck you!"

He was out of his element against his new foe. This foe was as cunning and vicious as they came, attacking precisely and retreating as needed. The shark had already had its main course, and Louis didn't want to be dessert. When he finally realized the pistol was empty, he threw it with all his force, as if it, too, could kill the man-killer.

"Ha-ha! I killed you, shark! I am Louis! No one beats me!"

He seemed drunk with what he must have thought was power, yet was hysterical from fear. "Fuck you! Fuck you, puta! I killed you! Then, as sudden as his outburst, he quieted, before turning toward Razz. "And now it is your turn."

Because of the tides, wind, and waves, Louis couldn't reach them, certainly not by paddling with his hands, as he was doing now. But he was no longer concerned with reality. He imagined himself killing Razz and that vision was enjoyable enough to keep him fighting against too-powerful forces.

Then Razz saw the only thing that could help Louis achieve his new goal. One of the oars was floating toward the craft.

No! God, give us a break! We're likely dead anyway, but give us a chance. Please! Haven't we fought hard enough? Plead as he might, neither God nor Louis was done with them yet.

Following Razz' sight line alerted Louis to his discovery. "You'd be terrible at poker, my friend." He stretched out over the rail, ready. The oar was only a couple of yards away.

Razz' hand slipped from the piling and he went under. *Maybe this is for the best. If I surface, death will be much more painful. This is so peaceful ... so peaceful.* Then he remembered his helpless friend. *But I have to help Sharky!*

He barely raised his head from the water. He coughed out a mouthful and gasped for air, before noticing that Sharky was floating directly toward Louis—and so was the oar!

Razz had nothing left to offer. His friend's life was out of his hands. If Louis grabbed the oar, Sharky would be dead for certain, and it would be only moments before he reached Razz to finish him, too. He decided he'd drown before he let anyone beat him senseless, but Sharky didn't have that choice, floating toward his fate in the life preserver.

Louis reached further and further over the stern, but the oar remained stubbornly out of reach. "¡Mierda!"

He strained with his right hand, the tips of his left fingers clutching the gunwale, his right hip pressed against the stern, but still he couldn't reach. Suddenly, his fingers slipped and both arms plunged into the water as he tried to regain his balance. His arms thrashed against the water and his legs flailed as his mid-section teetered on the boat's gunwale. One foot caught the underside of the front seat, giving him some leverage. Just when it looked like he would regain control, a wave rocked the boat, his foot slipped from its hold and he toppled into the water!

Razz would have rejoiced had it been good news, but all it meant was that when Louis resurfaced, he did so with the oar in his hand. "Whew! Fuck, it's cold!"

Shivering, he dumped the oar into the boat and grabbed the gunwale. He struggled to lift himself over the rail, and after several tries, he fell safely inside. After a moment, he stood, breathing heavily, the oar in hand. Re-focused on Sharky now, he paddled.

"Sharky." Razz tried to yell, but Sharky wouldn't hear him anyway. He was unconscious.

Razz leaned his cheek into the piling, barely able to feel the rough concrete. He closed his eyes, but couldn't stop images of Louis beating his friend to a bloody pulp. When he looked again, he saw Louis, smiling viciously, holding the oar high, ready to bring it crashing down into Sharky's skull.

Louis' body tensed and his smile tightened, and Razz knew the moment of truth had arrived. But instead of drawing his weapon downward, a strange look came over Louis. He blinked in disbelief, and then looked at his left shoulder. A flow of crimson stained his wet clothes just below his collar bone.

Amidst the rain, crashing waves and swirling winds, neither man had heard a gunshot. Each looked for its source, but despite the dissipating fog, Razz saw nothing. Louis took a small step backwards as realization sank into his brain like the bullet had his flesh. He focused on something in the direction of the viewing glass light. Razz followed his sight line and could just make out a figure on the wharf.

This time, Razz heard the bullet whistle through the air. *Thump!* He knew by the sound and the look on Louis' face that it had hit its target.

The oar slipped from Louis' grasp and crashed into the boat well. He was rapidly losing the strength to ever again inflict harm on anyone as blood poured forth from two openings in his torso. Pain overtook disbelief and he staggered.

As the fog cleared further, someone came into view. Both men recognized him, but it wouldn't help Louis now. When a spurt of blood exited his mouth and dripped down his chin, anger welled up in him, but only for a moment. Then his face softened, all tension was gone, and he knew it was over. What muscle control he had left faltered, and he collapsed over the side and disappeared into the water.

Louis was gone.

Floating in and out of consciousness it seemed to Razz like hours, but it could only have been seconds before he saw a light. It was blinding, but because it was accompanied by the sound of an engine, he knew he would be safe. A rescue boat was coming.

Razz nodded faintly in the direction where he'd last seen Sharky, just before he passed out.

36

And that was how he had conquered the San Margarita Pier, part of which would only months later succumb to gravity and shoddy construction and crumple into the ocean. Its replacement five years later extended three times as far into the Pacific and was supported by four times as many pilings which insured Razz' courageous and idiotic feat was one that would stand forever.

Razz woke with a start as sirens blared, people hollered, and lights flashed around him. He felt like he was suffocating. He tried to focus his eyes, but couldn't. Vague shapes moved near him, but he couldn't move and he didn't know why.

"He's awake!"

The loud voice clanged inside his brain and he realized he had a terrible headache.

"This one's awake!"

Ow! Who's awake? And who gives a shit? Just stop yelling! Just thinking made his brain hurt.

Shapes were moving faster now and seemed to be gathering around him. A light was shone directly into his pupils, and he felt like his head would explode. He recoiled, closing his eyes.

"Good, good. Get him to an ambulance."

This new voice was more authoritative than the others. Had Razz not been so profoundly confused, he might have been reassured.

He felt himself moving, but he wondered how, because he couldn't feel his limbs. He re-opened his eyes and they began to focus. After a moment, he noticed he was bundled tightly in blankets and strapped to a stretcher, so some of his questions were answered. He heard the metal of hinges scrape annoyingly as he was carried up a gangplank. He began to recognize the images of the Pier, the Ferris wheel, the Sol a Sol, and pieces of his recent history came hurtling back.

The scraping metal reminded of weeks ago, the early morning when he'd used the wharf to enter the water before surfing. Surfing reminded him of the beauty and mystery of the ocean. The ocean reminded him of recent reports of shark attacks and the cool danger of sharks. And sharks reminded him of Louis, the ultimate shark. And then he remembered in gory detail the events of that evening, the terrible deaths, his ordeal to survive, and how his friend, Sharky, had tried to help him.

Sharky!

Waking amidst the cacophony, Razz had assumed he'd experienced a horribly bad dream, but it all felt too real now. He tried to speak, but words, even sounds, caught in his throat, which felt like coarse sandpaper. He squirmed to try and free himself from bondage.

"Easy, you'll be fine. We'll have you at the hospital in no time."

He looked up to see a young paramedic walking beside him, but he didn't recognize the man. Razz' eyes pleaded, but his vocal cords seemed stuck together.

"Here, take some of this. It'll help," said the paramedic.

Razz barely succeeded in drawing liquid through a straw held to his lips, but drops of wet coolness soothed his throat and began to free his vocal cords.

"My friend?" he croaked.

"We don't know yet."

The paramedic motioned toward an ambulance several feet away where Sharky, stretchered and cocooned like Razz, was about to be deposited. Only his ghostly white face was visible against which hideous, purple, bulging lips stood out. He looked deformed.

"Sharky." Razz coughed, and then tried again, louder. "Sharky! Hang in there, buddy. I'll be in to see you soon. Come on, Sharky! Please!"

"I doubt he can hear you."

Razz nodded, but kept his eyes trained on his friend, hoping. And, as Sharky was raised into the back of the ambulance, he thought he saw his lips quiver just before he disappeared out of sight. The movement was barely perceptible and Razz doubted anyone else noticed. Maybe it was an involuntary reflex, but, possibly, he had tried to form a word or smile in response, and that possibility was enough to give Razz hope that Sharky would survive. Then the doors were slammed shut and the ambulance sped off, its siren screaming.

It was only then that he noticed Johnnie Johnson. He was the man Razz had seen standing on the wharf. He was the man who had shot Louis Marcayda. Johnnie Johnson was the man who had saved his life.

"Johnnie! Thanks, Johnnie!"

Johnson, lost in troubling thoughts, looked over and nodded.

Razz' carriers lifted him toward the second ambulance's opening, but a woman's voice stopped them short.

"Razz! Razz!"

He craned his neck to view its familiar source. Cordoned behind yellow police tape, Sarah argued with a police officer.

"Sarah! Hey, that's my wife!" His volume wasn't strong enough to get the officer's attention. "Sarah!"

"Hold him here," said Johnson to the stretcher bearers, and then he raced over to mediate.

Soon, the officer lifted the tape and Razz' beloved wife was running his way.

"Honey! Oh God, are you all right?"

She was crying, but her love made Razz feel warm and safe for the first time in hours. "I'm fine now."

The paramedic motioned for people to give them privacy.

"What are you doing here?"

"Who do you think called the cops?" she said.

"Huh?"

"You didn't really think I was going to leave you alone, did you? Through 'better or worse'. Remember?"

He remembered all right. He just wished he had given her a lot more of the better.

"I called you, but you didn't call me back. I knew you would, if you could, so I came to find you. There was a man outside the restaurant, there were lights ... I got scared."

Razz owed her his life, but something nagged at him. "You were supposed to ... Where are the kids?"

"They're fine. They're on a little vacation in the mountains with your parents. They were only too happy to help out."

His parents were always there for him, just like Sarah, and Razz knew, once again, that he was a lucky, lucky man. But he had to get something off his very heavy chest.

He searched for the right words. "Honey, I'm … so ... flawed."

"I know," she said, without judgment.

"But I," he began, blinking back tears, "I cheated on you ... with Lotta."

She bowed her head and nodded, but didn't say anything.

Now he was overwhelmed and his tears were flowing. "I don't deserve you."

Sarah lifted her head and considered him deeply. After a moment, she leaned in and kissed him softly on the lips. "You will."

She smiled hopefully and, as tears washed down his face, Razz smiled, too. He knew he would try to deserve her from now on.

He would try very, very hard.

EPILOGUE

Reveling in his once-in-a-lifetime glory, Razz didn't even mind when, moments after he reached shore, he was arrested by the San Margarita police for reckless endangerment—to himself.

March 20, 2006

Though he was declared dead, Louis Marcayda's body was never found. Due to a list of felonies too long to mention, including the digging up of the already-deceased Wally Bumpers, the U.S. government confiscated several of his properties, including the Surf's Up and Sol a Sol. It is widely believed they only found the tip of the iceberg when it came to Louis' holdings.

Merice Marcayda escaped government prosecution by maintaining she knew nothing about her husband's illegal dealings and by being able to afford the best legal team, then she and her children escaped town. It is suspected they are living somewhere in Mexico.

Jaime Hidalgo was sentenced to ten years for involuntary manslaughter in the accidental killing of his lover, Wally Bumpers, during the heat of passion. Super-agent Grayson Lord has already sold the film rights to Hidalgo's story.

Phillip Wilson, former Chief of Police, was elected to replace Hidalgo as San Margarita's mayor in a special election. Johnnie Johnson took his place as Chief.

Shattered physically and emotionally, Sharky Sampson continues to recover slowly. Despite Sharky's crankiness, Razz has supported him every arduous step of the way.

In an unrelated case, Richard Gold was sentenced to three years in a minimum security facility for tax evasion and lying to IRS investigators. With good behavior, he could be out in a year and a half. His wife, Elizabeth, visits him every day.

While her father sits in jail, Sarah Gold McNeil manages what's left of his real estate empire and trust assets and she loves every minute of it. Razz hasn't said a peep about her working outside the home. Caitlin and Ronnie are growing up fast, but still love to fight over food and toys.

Razz bought the two restaurant leases at government auction. He wonders why whenever the bills are due. Without the patronage of Louis' hookers and gangbangers, business is down substantially. Lotta Gugliotta and long-time Surf's Up chef, Carlos, were fired and haven't been seen since. Much to Razz' chagrin, Harvey Howells continues to stop by the Surf's Up for the salmon special.

Razz works the day shift now, so he can spend more time in the evenings with his wife and kids.

THE END

Made in the USA
Middletown, DE
19 April 2022